DENNIS RILEY

FORTUNE'S SHADOW
MERCY'S LIGHT

FROM THE SECRET SCROLLS
OF THE IMPERARE

FORTUNE'S SHADOW, MERCY'S LIGHT

Written by Dennis Riley.

Darktalon Publishing, LLC

P.O. Box 7293

Amarillo, Texas

79114

ISBN 979-8-9885115-0-2

Cover art by MiblArt.

World map by BMR Williams.

City map by Melissa Nash.

www.authordennisriley.com

This is a work of fiction. Any similarity between the characters and events in this novel and those in the real world is just weird.

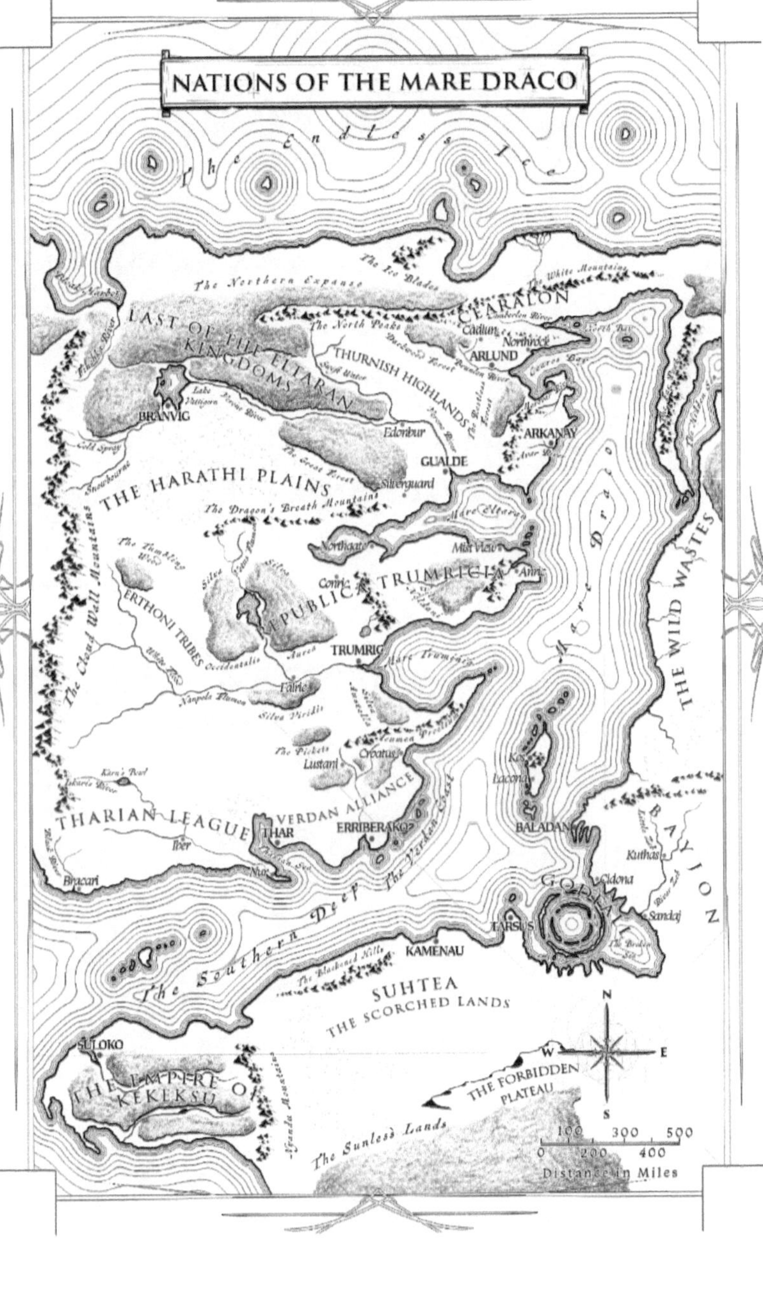

NATIONS OF THE MARE DRACO
The Endless Ice
The Northern Expanse
The Ice Blades
The White Mountains
CEARALON
The North Peaks
Cadun
Northrock
ARLUND
THURNISH HIGHLANDS
LAST OF THE ELTARAN KINGDOMS
Edonbur
ARKANAY
BRANVIG
GUALDE
Silverguard
THE HARATHI PLAINS
The Dragon's Breath Mountains
Mare Eltaran
Mist View
The Tumbling Wood
Northgate
REPUBLIC TRUMRIGIA
Anri
ERTHONI TRIBES
Conic
TRUMRIG
Mare Trumigia
The Cloud Wall Mountains
Falric
Lustani
Croatus
THE WILD WASTES
The Pickets
Kas
Iacona
THARIAN LEAGUE
VERDAN ALLIANCE
THAR
ERRIBERAKO
BALADAN
BAYION
Kuthas
Bracari
Nox
The Verdan Coast
GODE
Cidona
Sandaj
TARSUS
The Southern Deep
KAMENAU
The Broken Sea
ULOKO
SUHTEA
THE SCORCHED LANDS
THE EMPIRE OF KEKEKSU
THE FORBIDDEN PLATEAU
The Sunless Lands
N
W   E
S
100   300   500
0   200   400
Distance in Miles

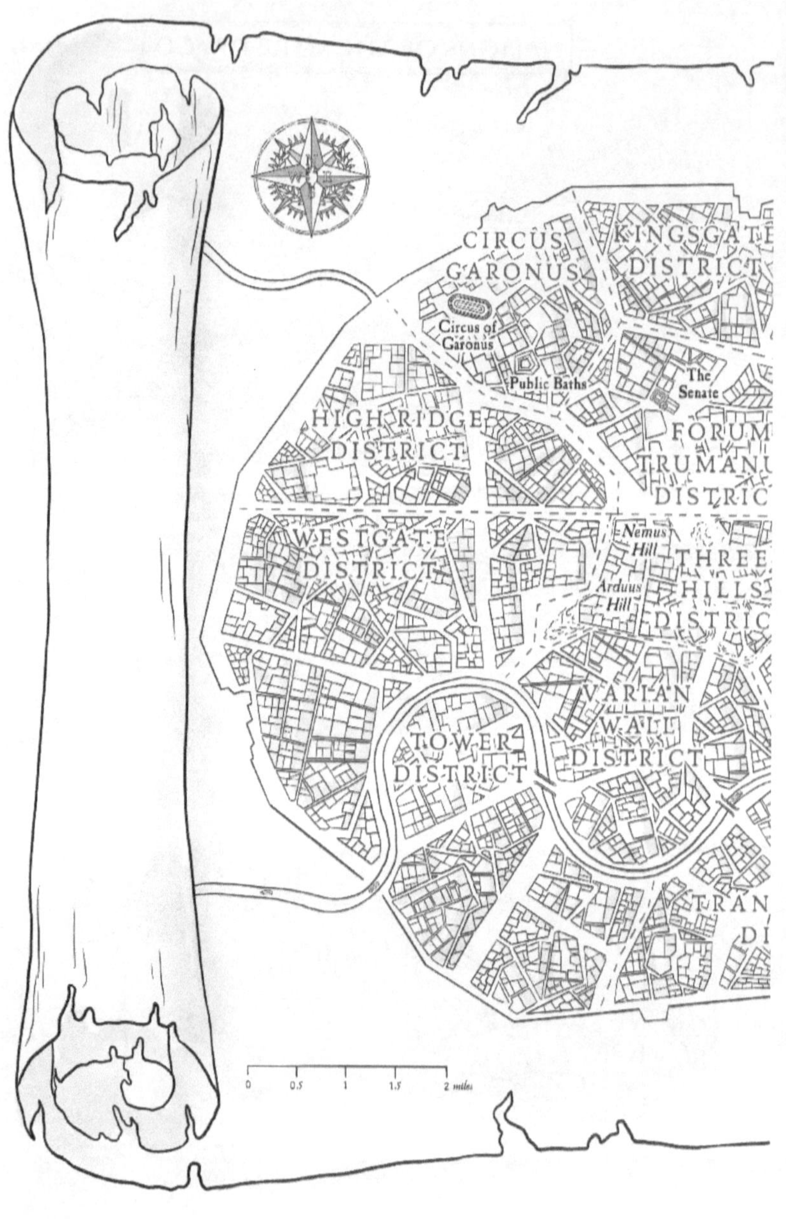

CIRCUS GARONUS
Circus of Garonus
Public Baths
KINGSGATE DISTRICT
The Senate
HIGH RIDGE DISTRICT
FORUM TRUMANUS DISTRICT
WESTGATE DISTRICT
Nemus Hill
Arduus Hill
THREE HILLS DISTRICT
VARIAN WALL DISTRICT
TOWER DISTRICT
TRAN DI
0   0.5   1   1.5   2 miles

The Amphitheater
of the Republic
The Nyssan
Theater
OLD HARBOR
DISTRICT
TEMPLE
DISTRICT
FOREIGN
DISTRICT
The Temple of Alakur
The Temple of Myrill
Sacris
Hill
The Collegium
Draconis Aurei
The
Quadrivium
Temple of Ulorin
FIRST
STONES
DISTRICT
PORTUM
MARE
DISTRICT
Portus
Towers
River
Docks
River
Market
The Old
Polyminia Theater
Calidius
Amphitheater
SNANPELA
STRICT

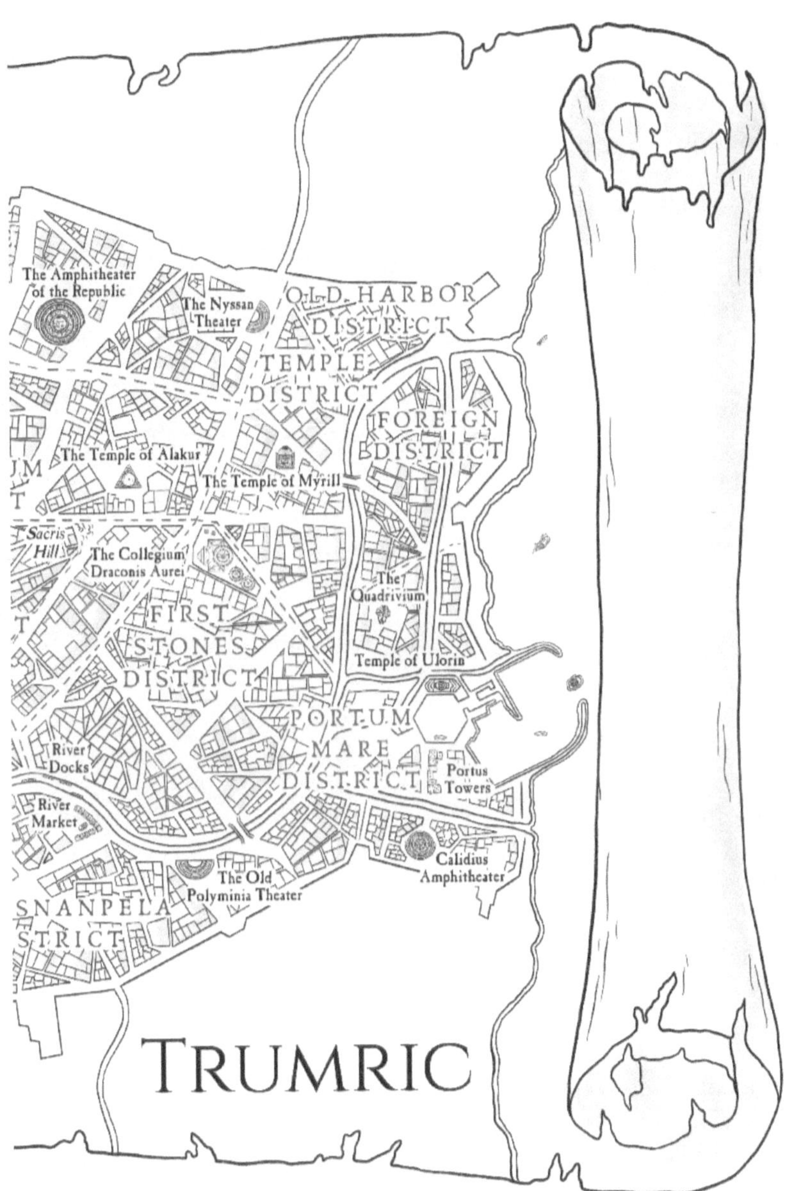

TRUMRIC

Table of Contents

A Neesis Throw!

Ulric dashed through an alley, dodging and leaping past the outstretched hands of begging strays, and burst into the stench of a fishmonger's yard. He deftly ran between the wooden stalls and workbenches piled high with fresh fish and viscera while ignoring the shouts and flashing knives of angry workers. Once across the yard, he vanished into a crowd flowing toward the heart of the River Market. When they turned onto Old Fluvius Road, he slipped away and leaned under the cool shade of a shop awning. Feeling a terrible ache in his contorted fingers, he slowly loosened his grip on the pouch he had been clutching. He had lifted it off a promising mark, for Marcus Octavius Ulric was a thief and a damned liar.

He quietly mouthed a prayer to Neesis, the goddess of luck, lust, and madness. Every thief needed a bit of luck, and even the most impious among them honored Her. She was an alluring yet capricious goddess, and the people of the Trumin Republic said it was impossible to distinguish Her blessing from Her curse. Trumins knew Her by three names: Neesis Fortuna, Neesis Amoris, and Neesis Insania. Thieves knew Her secret name, Neesis Umbra, their patron and protector.

He had counted on that protection thieving so close to the River Market, and he prayed the goddess had blessed him. He opened the pouch and looked inside: it held ten silver denarii, seventeen bronze sestertii, and a handful of brass and copper coins.

"A Neesis throw!" he said a little too loudly, attracting the curious looks of a few passersby.

A Neesis throw was the highest scoring combination a player could throw in the dice game, Spoils, and a popular expression of good luck. Spoils indeed! With such a sum, he could eat for days and still have coin. Ulric looked down at his threadbare blue tunic, frayed belt, and worn sandals. He smiled at the thought of a new belt; he had seen a beautiful leather one with bronze studs in the Night Market! Then his smile faded as he recalled the lessons of his childhood: once you have something worth taking, somebody will do their damndest to take it. Just as he had done.

He checked the street one last time and put the coins away. It wasn't an angry mark Ulric feared; it was his fellow criminals. He did not belong on the streets of the River Market, and the capital of the Trumin Republic was not his city. If the local gangs caught him stealing in their territory, the result would be disastrous, if not deadly. Ulric had to steal enough to survive but remain unnoticed.

I'm a criminal among criminals, Ulric thought. *Praise Neesis Insania, Goddess of Madness! For what other gods would have me?*

As he hid the pouch under his tunic, he recalled something the owner of the Polyminius theater had told him days earlier. The old fool had been trying to recruit him into his band of players when he had said, "Every villain thinks himself the hero of the play."

Am I the hero? I've played the villain for fat merchants and arrogant patricians, but I've also stolen from poor families and honest laborers whose only offense was having a little more than I did. True, I never killed anyone, but that's how Ghostwalker trained me. For him, it was more a point of professional pride than a fear of violence.

I can still see him in Bucco's taberna, one foot on the edge of a wine-stained table while he rocked back and forth on the rear legs of a rickety chair. With a cup in one hand, and the other resting on the smoky quartz pommel of his long spatha, a sword he never drew on a job, Ghostwalker would say, "Listen up, Darktalon—he always used my shadow name—'If you draw steel, then your skill is less than ideal.' Which means—you fucked up, boy."

Ulric's stomach grumbled, reminding him, hero or villain, a man must eat.

He followed Old Fluvius Road in search of something cheap. The road stretched along the southern banks of the great Nanpela River from the western fields, through the river docks, into the harbor, and then the sea. River and road bisected the city, separating the gently sloping plebeian lands to the south from the steep patrician hills and high ridges to the north. The River Market radiated south from the docks, part of the broader forum that straddled the river with a dizzying variety of shops and neglected public monuments.

Ulric pushed back several locks of night-black hair and looked up at the westering sun. The market was still busy, but the stalls and shops would begin closing soon.

For a few brass coins, he bought a bit of food from a street vendor: two pork skewers, a bit of flatbread, and a small wedge of cheese. *So many coins? Who is the thief here? How can anyone afford to live in this city?* Back in Mist View, where he grew up, everything was cheaper and, in a way, easier.

Ulric had long been the protégé of Mist View's legendary rogue, Arrius Ghostwalker. The association had provided a degree of protection, even prestige. Before Ghostwalker, Ulric ran with the Low Street Gang, a collection of orphans and castaways. A gang meant survival, no matter how meager or uncertain. There had never been a choice, really; lone wolves didn't last in the wilderness of Mist View's rough streets and back alleys. Except for Ghostwalker, he was an exception to that otherwise inescapable law. He walked alone.

Everyone had heard the tales: The Heist of the Noldani Vaults, Raiding the Temple of Ulorin, the Disgrace of Governor Livius, and surviving the labyrinth known as Xavarious' Playground. Those legendary deeds had earned Arrius Ghostwalker his reputation, and, eventually, his independence from the masters of all crime in Mist View—the Dark Assembly.

Lost in reminiscence, Ulric walked down unfamiliar streets without really seeing, all the while deftly juggling bites of bread, cheese, and pork. Traffic slowed to a crawl, and he found himself standing impatiently in front of a butcher's stall holding two long wooden skewers, now picked clean of meat. He subtly shifted the skewers in his palm and flicked his wrist in a lightning-fast side throw that shot the slender stakes deep into a goose hanging above the counter. A nearby matron gave a startled cry, attracting the butcher's attention.

A burly, thick-armed man in a greasy, bloodstained apron leaned forward, glancing at the goose, still gently swaying with two skewers protruding from its breast. Then he noticed Ulric's mischievous grin.

"Off with you, boy, before I shove a skewer up your ass!"

Ulric hated being called "boy." He had legally been a man at age fifteen and had grown much in the two years since. Was it his youthful face? No, likely his unfashionably long hair was to blame. Was it his fault coin for proper grooming was scarce? He glared at the butcher, noting his bulk and thick arms, and decided moving on was excellent advice.

He had barely turned his back to the butcher when the smirk left his face. *Showing off? So damn stupid!* Ghostwalker's voice echoed in his mind once again. *"Flamboyant moves are the mark of an amateur. Remember, economy of thought, economy of motion." By Neesis, I need Arrius here to knock some sense into me. But he can't. He's dead.* Ulric sliced through the crowd, his growing anger quickening his pace. *Betrayed by the Dark Assembly and crucified by the provincial governor as thief, murderer, and traitor of the Republic. Yet here I am, fled to the capital.* He laughed bitterly at the thought.

Ulric hadn't gone far before he was forcing his way through another thickening crowd. The people had gathered a respectful distance around a group of street performers: musicians, acrobats, dancers, and even a garishly dressed fabricator. The fabricator moved her hands in broad, theatrical motions, sending the long sleeves of her excessively orange robe swirling around her. Every movement added another detail to the vivid, kaleidoscopic images she created in the air above her.

Ulric backed away from the magical display, disappearing into the entranced crowd: laborers and matrons with their daughters and young sons, and slaves running errands for the wealthier households. It appeared a prosperous plebeian crowd with enough coin to spare but not so much wealth as to be filled with peacocking toga-wearing citizens and their ex-gladiator bodyguards. It was the perfect setting for a bit more pickpocketing, or 'tax collecting', as his fellow thieves jokingly called it. His fingers twitched at the mere thought, but Ulric knew not to push his luck. Neesis was a fickle goddess.

A proper bit of tax collecting took a crew of three: the collector, a decoy, and a lookout. Ulric pretended to watch the fabricator's magical display, stepping back and furtively scanning the cheering crowd. Nearby, a small boy at his mother's shoulder ignored the fabricator and stared at him. Ulric couldn't shake the feeling the child knew he was up to no good.

As suspected, a local gang had already targeted the show. The typical three-man crew was at work. On the lookout's wrist was a tattoo of a long, spotted fish with an exaggerated toothy maw. It was the mark of the Gutter-Fish, a gang that operated in the River Market and most of the Transnanpela District. They had the backing of the Imperaré, the masters of all crime in the city of Trumric.

Ulric couldn't afford to be noticed. If the Gutter-Fish discovered he was living rough on their streets, he'd become the target of harassment or, worse, recruitment. He'd have to move on or add a fish tattoo next to the Low Street standard. And after years of training under Ghostwalker, Ulric considered a gang like the Gutter-Fish beneath him.

He slipped out of the crowd and headed south. The day was growing long; the streets were emptying, and the shops were closing. Ulric had to decide if he would remain "camped" in the alley off Dyer's Street. Since arriving in Trumric, he had lived little better than a stray. He slept in alleys, under bridges, on the occasional rooftop, and for a few lucky nights, he squatted in an abandoned shop. Now, he worried, it was time to move on.

A quick, high-pitched scream pierced his thoughts.

Ulric skidded to a halt. All around him, merchants busily packed their wares, and matrons filled their basins at a public fountain noisily gurgling at the center of the square. He reached for the dagger hidden beneath his tunic and searched for the source of the cry. Then he heard a gruff voice from behind a tall rack of colorful fabrics.

"It's past the Kalends, and you've brought us fuck all for the month of Myrius!"

Ulric took a few steps forward, just enough to see past the wall of fabric. In a niche behind the rack, four men had surrounded a boy. They dressed in simple knee-length, short-sleeved tunics secured at the waist by fine leather belts. Each wore a garish assortment of copper, bronze, and silver jewelry, along with daggers. Their fish tattoos marked them as Gutter-Fish.

"Not my fault! Not really!" The young boy shrank against the wall, his voice breaking.

"Give the little turd another smack," demanded one man.

*The boy's too young for a gang. Must be an alley-worm. Walk on…
walk on.*

Alley-worms were street urchins pressed to scrounge, beg, or steal whatever they could. Gangs eventually recruited the ones that brought the most coin.

The circle closed in.

"Been too many warnings, little worm," said one man with a head of thick curly blonde hair and full lips. He was tall and athletic, like a statue of a Kreslan youth, and would have been just as handsome if not for his narrow and cruel eyes. He brandished a dagger and stepped toward the boy. "Others will think the Gutter-Fish have gone all soft if we don't bleed you."

"But I get coin. I do!" the boy protested. "Just… the bigger kids take it all."

The man leaned forward, bringing the blade close to the boy's trembling face. "Then hide it better, little worm." He carefully ran the dagger's edge across the boy's cheek. "Maybe some fresh scars will help with your begging?"

"Ha! If we don't get *our* cut, you get *yours*." The men laughed.

Four. Too many. I have to stay shadowed. Walk on… walk on.

Ulric walked on.

The young boy burst into tears and ran. The little worm was fast, but one of the Gutter-Fish was faster. He threw the boy back into the wall—hard. He hit with a loud thump and slumped against the stone, dazed. Ulric glanced over his shoulder and caught the boy's gaze. His tears blazed a white-hot path down a dirty face, and despite his helplessness, his eyes filled with a murderous rage.

At that moment, Ulric recalled another young boy whose eyes had held that same rage. A memory of years long passed, before Ghostwalker, before the Low Street Gang, even before begging on the streets. In the memory, he's crumpled against the wall of a Mist View brothel. *My head throbs. Everything's a blur. Did the man throw me across the room after I tried to stab him? I want to kill him; I have to kill him! But when I stand, the room spins. Tessa sits half-naked on the bed, staring in disbelief at her blood-stained hands. The man screams incoherent hate as he's dragged from the room. The smell of blood is thick in the air. More crimson gushes from deep wounds, and Tessa cries. The brothel owner is shouting something at the man about owing money for damaged goods. Tessa looks scared and begins calling out, quietly at first, then with increasing desperation, "I won't die, right? I can't die. You'll get a healer? I'll be alright! I don't want to die!"*

Ulric stopped. Turned.

Merchants were still packing, and matrons still tended their basins. Most didn't see the Gutter-Fish; others didn't care.

"Listen up, Darktalon, 'Where fist and steel would fail, a clever scheme might prevail.'" Expert advice, Arrius. A scheme? Yes. Clever? Not enough time for clever. Neesis Umbra, protect me!

Ulric needed a scheme—fast! Growing up, he had run dozens of simple cons, or schemes, with the Low Street Gang. Later, Arrius Ghostwalker had introduced him to the joys of the longer, more complex cons known humorously as honest schemes. Such schemes involved meticulous planning, elaborate set-ups, lies, misdirection, and even disguise and impersonation. More importantly, they demanded quick thinking and improvisation when things inevitably went wrong.

Ulric loved running schemes with Ghostwalker. His mentor had discovered early on he had a talent for deception. He had played many roles in his youth: a jeweler's treacherous apprentice, a moneylender's naïve clerk, a Kreslan boy gifted with prophecy, and even a nobleman's long-lost son. One of his proudest moments came when he and Ghostwalker celebrated a successful scheme to sell a fake Eltaran relic to a wealthy Bayjoni trader. Arrius had placed a cup of wine in his hands and said, "Darktalon, you're a damned liar." It was the highest compliment one could receive in the scheming trade.

In a flash, Ulric knew what role he had to play. He couldn't believe he would risk so much on a scheme that promised no coin. He ran back into the center of the square, looking over his shoulder and frantically shouting. "This way, Drusus! Yes, yes, gather Maro and the rest. I'm certain I saw young Gaius come this way!"

Ulric spun around, pretending to search the square, and headed straight for the Gutter-Fish.

"Is that you, young master Gaius?" He looked back into the square. "Over here, Drusus, I've found him!"

Ulric approached with shoulders hunched forward and his head slightly bowed. When he spoke, he tried to adopt that peculiar combination of obsequiousness and arrogance common among the puffed-up slaves of powerful patrician households.

"Young Gaius! What have these men done to you? If any of you have harmed him, my master will have you flogged and branded!"

He could see his performance left the Gutter-Fish equal parts confused, angry, and fearful. He was always better at improvisation.

Ulric reached out and hauled the boy to his feet.

"Who in Neesis' Shadow…" The blonde-haired man with the dagger lunged forward, grabbing Ulric by the tunic.

The little worm ran. The other Gutter-Fish closed in.

"Drusus! I am assaulted!" Ulric had to stop himself from cringing in embarrassment over his too-comical delivery.

He pulled the dagger-man off balance and sent him sprawling into another Gutter-Fish, creating a tangle of bodies and curses, and the little worm was gone.

Ulric backpedaled into the square, and the four Gutter-Fish followed.

"Now I have to find him again! Master Dives will be very upset." Looking about, Ulric put his hand on his hips and asked, "Where are Drusus and Maro?"

"You think you can get away with what you've done? Cause you're the slave of some rich cunt from across the river?" The Gutter-Fish led with his dagger, emphasizing each point with a stab of the air.

One man grabbed his shoulder. "Come on, Titus. No point to it now. The little turd isn't worth it."

"Too many eyes on us now," said another.

Ulric had maneuvered the four men into the square. Unable to ignore the Gutter-Fish, a few bystanders fled while others stayed to watch the confrontation.

The Gutter-Fish called Titus lowered his dagger. Ulric began to believe he would walk away; he could see it in the man's face. He almost couldn't believe his luck, but he reminded himself his goddess, Neesis, was Neesis Fortuna, the Goddess of Luck. Of course, it had all worked out!

A Gutter-Fish, who had previously said nothing, asked, "If he's a slave, why's he inked with the war-orphan sword and shield with Noldani eagles?"

Ulric's struggle with the Gutter-Fish had torn his tunic and exposed the Low Street standard on his chest. Throughout the Republic, street gangs founded by the orphans of its legionnaires used the gladius and scutum as their symbol's foundation.

"And where's your chain?" The man was referring to Titus' silver bracelet, which Ulric had palmed.

The dagger rose again, and the Gutter-Fish advanced. "Neesis' fuck'n tits! You trying to run a scheme on us? What are Noldani Eagles doing on our streets?"

Neesis, you fickle bitch! Forgive me, Goddess. It's not good deeds you love, but madness and bold action.

"You know, now that I think on it, the boy didn't look like young master Gaius at all!" Ulric produced Titus' silver chain and began spinning it on an extended finger. "I wouldn't waste an honest scheme on such small fry. I wanted a look at the competition. To my relief, all I found were amateurs and idiots who can't even run their alley-worms."

"Son of a whore!" said the two men in unison.

Titus screamed, "Gut 'em, boys!"

Ulric ran, and the Gutter-Fish were close behind. He snaked through the women gathered around the fountain, snatched a bucket out of a young mother's hands, spun, and threw it at his pursuers. Titus sidestepped, and the bucket struck the Gutter-Fish behind him with a loud thud and an explosion of water.

The man went down, bruised, soaked, and cursing.

Ulric fled onto a narrow, crooked street, sprinted a brief distance, then ducked into an even narrower alley between two tall buildings. Three Gutter-Fish were in close pursuit, with the fourth sloshing far behind. The three men ran into the alley in time to see Ulric leap at one wall, rebound high onto the other, then spring onto the opposite rooftop.

"He's a godsdamned filthy monkey!"

"Give me a hand up!"

"That's a waste of time! Circle around!"

"He's gotta come down somewhere!"

As Ulric vanished across the rooftops, Titus shouted after him. "We know your face! You hear me, you piece of shit! We know your face!"

The streets twisted and turned, gently rising the farther he traveled south. Finally, Ulric leaped upon the ruins of a crumbling wall and sat gazing over the winding Nanpela River and the sprawling city stretching from its banks. Within Trumric's stone walls and adamant gates, multistory tenement buildings of brick and wood mingled with the stone and marble homes of its wealthy citizens. Numerous buildings were painted or stained in faded Myrillian greens, Cathus reds, or Nyssan yellows, contrasting with the gleaming whites and golds of the city's fora, theaters, and temples. To Ulric, the city looked like a colorful stone mosaic whose pattern was beautiful and seductive but ultimately still a mystery.

He sat on the edge of the ruins for a long time, thinking.

I've been taught the Shadow Ways by the best. Tax collecting and lockcraft were skills I mastered long ago. I know the three principles of Ghostwalking, the Secrets of the Fade, the Thieves' Glimmer, and even the basics of Shadow Mind. I can read, write, and speak Trumin well enough to scheme any patrician, and I can recite the litanies of Neesis in the original Kreslan. Damn me through the Nine Gates before I go back to running the streets with a gang of amateurs and idiots!

Ulric was torched, caught in the light. He was exposed to the Gutter-Fish, and he had done it. He seethed with anger, but could he stay angry with himself? Should he have walked on and ignored the boy? Should he be angry with the Gutter-Fish? What had they done that the Low Street gang hadn't? What wouldn't he have done before Ghostwalker had found him?

Still, his foolishness had made the River Market more dangerous than ever. Opportunities for tax collecting coin would become rarer. He would have to move on or find other means to keep himself fed. Would he have to think of the unthinkable?

Embrace madness and learn a trade? Get a job? Days earlier, a chance encounter with an eccentric theater owner had led to an offer. At the time, Ulric had smiled a liar's smile and pretended to be interested. Now the idea didn't seem so absurd.

It couldn't be any madder than what he'd already done. He'd fled Mist View and risked everything to reach the capital of the Republic. There was no other city, no other arena, more dangerous or more rewarding. He came to the city of Trumric to steal a fortune and become a legend.

And if it was a crazy idea—why not? What better way to please the Goddess of Madness?

Something of Value

Luciano Porteles, criminal enforcer and assassin, ascended the gallery of the crowded taberna with a mission-driven stride. Tall and sinewy, he ignored the frightened looks patrons gave him as he passed, with most averting their gaze and others nodding in deference. A few even hurriedly descended the stairs back to the common room, leaving empty tables and half-filled cups. He walked like the alpha wolf among a herd of sheep, ambivalent to their stares, yet all the while scanning the upper floor for other predators. Four red scarves marked the Imperaré enforcers, one each at the ends of the gallery and two at the back near the bar. Then he spotted the obvious bodyguard: a Harathi with arms like the fabled Minotaur and no doubt the brains to match. And most importantly, he pinpointed his prey: a garishly dressed patrician fidgeting in his chair, eyes darting nervously from side to side.

Luciano eased casually into the chair across from the man and glared at him through strands of stringy, dirt-brown hair. He casually gripped the smoky quartz pommel of a sheathed spatha in one hand, his elbow resting on the arm of his chair, while the fingers of the other rapped repeatedly on the wooden table. He sat silent, staring at the man in front of him, who was now trying desperately to hide his nerves.

Quintus Marius Secundus was a thin and gangly man with receding blonde hair, opulently dressed and meticulously groomed down to his manicured nails. "Save your scowls—and your threats—you Verdan wretch," said Secundus. "We drink in the Quadrivium, so we both know you'll not start something here." The Quadrivium, by no means one of Trumric's finest tabernas, was undeniably one of its most famous. The establishment's location in the Portum Mare District guaranteed food, beverage, and a clientele from all corners of the Republic and beyond. And in service to that diverse crowd, the taberna had become known as a place to eat, drink, and discuss "business," devoid of the threat of violence lurking in every shadowed corner. Simply put, the Imperaré had declared the Quadrivium neutral ground.

The Verdan assassin chuckled and crossed his long, sinewy arms over his chest, knowing full well the man must have rehearsed that line all morning.

Secundus' eyes darted over the railing at the crowded room below: it was nearly dusk and all manner of liars, cutters, and thieves had filled the taberna to capacity. Luciano wondered if Secundus was considering fleeing the gallery. He must have thought better of it because he settled back into his chair with an air of weary resignation.

When Luciano finally spoke, his Verdan accent was thick, his speech slow and measured. "You have something of ours, yes?"

Luciano delivered the line not as a question but as an accusation. He had dealt with Secundus before and knew the patrician was easily intimidated. There was fear in his bulging eyes. Luciano's eyes remained sharp, hard, and unforgiving, like the edge of a knife. They were the perfect eyes for a killer.

"I… I'm not sure what you speak of," Secundus said, failing to mask the trepidation in his voice.

"You know, *Quintus*. You know." The name slipped slowly between Luciano's teeth.

Secundus bristled at the man's too-familiar tone.

"And you know who I work for, eh?"

Luciano had traveled to the Republic's capital as an emissary of Mist View's criminal interests. That city was the northernmost port in the Noldani province, a notorious region known for corruption, lawlessness, and rebellion. Secundus' ties to Mist View had made him a shipping fortune. His role as fixer and smuggler had made him even more.

Luciano's role had not made him a fortune, but it had made him infamous. Over time, he had become regarded as an effective enforcer and the Dark Assembly's most accomplished assassin, having earned the shadow name Hound of Nyx. This latest task, though, required more than just a kill. He was to give Secundus one opportunity to correct his error, as a show of faith, to one with such a long-standing relationship with the crime lords of Mist View. That would require some parley and not the back-alley sort he was used to. And it would mean he would need to converse in Trumin, a language that crept up his throat like bile.

A young barmaid approached the table. Secundus raised his empty goblet, but Luciano dismissed her with a wave. He shook the cup at the girl, but after meeting Luciano's gaze, she moved on to another table. Secundus, mouth agape, awkwardly followed the barmaid with his outstretched hand. He turned back to Luciano and glared.

"I don't care who you work for, Luciano."

"You should." Luciano bore a toothy grin, then continued. "Who I work for matters much, eh? You stole something in Mist View without Dark Assembly's sanction. Very valuable. Much trouble. Bad move." The assassin casually twirled a table knife through his fingers. "You give back, or you lose something very valuable, eh?"

Secundus straightened in his chair and delivered his next prepared line, matching Luciano's deliberate cadence. Luciano thought the arrogant patrician might be mocking him. Men had made this mistake before, and his response had always been swift and deadly. He knew his orders; he would have to stay his hand—for now.

"They don't have any reach here in Trumric. Besides, you wouldn't dare harm me. I have friends in the Imperaré. All I have to do is—"

Luciano slammed his fist on the table and leaned forward. "You lie! You no friend of Imperaré. I know you cut Imperaré out of your deal. Another bad move."

Secundus shot a side glance toward a nearby table.

Those killer eyes followed his gaze. "Heh, heh. You think I not see you hired sword, eh? Harathi. Beard. Furs. Axe. How much he cost you? Sixty denarii? Eighty? Heh, heh, heh. I gut him in one stroke."

Luciano leaned in closer, his snout a hair's breadth away from Secundus' now pallid face. "You test me, little Quintus. Hah! All you can do is what? Pee you pants? Cry on you whore-wife's bosom? I tell you last time, Quintus, you return what you stole, or we take something much more value from you." He spun the knife on the table, stopping it with his middle two fingertips when the blade pointed in Secundus' direction.

"Look… that… that item… I bought it fair and square! I didn't steal it! I paid honest denarii for it. I'm an art collector. Everyone knows it. I buy pieces all the time. I bought it, I tell you. I swear to you! I'm a collector!"

"Yes. I know. All Assembly knows. You brag much about your wealth. Your treasures. Your traps. Foolish."

Luciano settled back in his chair, glaring at the patrician but saying no more. Secundus stifled his fidgeting, but his fingertips unconsciously rapped a quick tempo upon the table. After a few moments of silence, he cleared his throat and spoke again.

"Well… perhaps my purchase did require some unfair dealings. But look, I swear, I didn't know it was yours! Or theirs! Or whatever! I didn't realize it belonged to"—he paused—"belonged to *them*. How could I know?"

"Thievery is dangerous business, eh? A man should always know who he steals from." The Verdan made the last statement with the gleeful satisfaction of a predator eyeing his cornered prey.

"I didn't steal it!" Secundus' voice was noticeably louder, and several nearby heads turned in his direction. He lowered his voice back down to a near whisper. "I didn't steal it. I bought it. Twenty thousand denarii. I admit the seller was a shady source, but I had no idea it was stolen! Certainly not stolen from *them*. Besides, it's gone now. I sold it myself to a business acquaintance. I don't have it anymore, and I don't know where it is."

"That is…" the Verdan searched for the right Trumin word. "Un-fortunate. That is unfortunate. For you. You have until new moon rises to return what you stole. Good night, Quintus Marius Secundus."

Luciano rose to his feet and turned his back on the doomed man. He knew what Secundus' admission meant and was looking forward to it. His thin lips stretched into an ugly grin, like the slit of a knife across his face. He walked past the Harathi bodyguard, spat in his drink, and descended the stairs of the Quadrivium, delicately caressing the hilt of his sword till he reached the street.

A Back Alley Parley

The amber hues of dusk melted quickly before the oncoming black of a conquered moon spreading over the city. Dreaded Nyx, Goddess Beyond, Goddess of Night, had once again seduced and corrupted Seranon, leaving the moon goddess unable to reflect her Father's divine light. Ulric smiled. He was always more at home at night, more at ease in the blackness. He longed for the deep pools of shadow gathering in the secluded alleys and alcoves of the city. They were mysterious, alluring, and often deadly.

Bah! Nothing in this city has been so bad as the Warrens of Mist View. I'm starting to think—

A fierce yank on Ulric's arm pulled him off the road and into a cramped alley. Before he could react, he was slammed against the rough bricks of a river dock warehouse. A cloaked and hooded figure stood before him. The man, easily a head taller than Ulric, was outfitted with expensive cloth and leather—this was no Gutter-fish. The man leaned his right forearm into Ulric's throat, pinning him against the wall. In his left hand was a stilius, a short needle-like blade, already piercing through the fabric of Ulric's tunic. He could feel the sharp tip of the cold steel pricking the skin of his belly. He glanced up and down the alley. No one else was around. The man could disembowel him in an instant, and there was nothing he could do about it. Was it a Back-Alley-Parley, a simple mugging? Or something worse?

"Boy should have ran more far away. Or hide better."

It was worse. The bottom dropped out of his stomach, and a chill ran through his veins. Ulric recognized the man's distinctive voice. He spoke broken Trumin, smothered heavily in a Verdan accent. Ulric pushed a single name past his constricted larynx.

"Luciano?"

"Boy flatter me. Remember me, eh?"

Ulric certainly remembered the olive-skinned Verdan, and Luciano Porteles, Hound of Nyx, was no friend. He and Ghostwalker had developed a professional rivalry and personal enmity for each other over the years, and their mutual hatred had erupted into shouting matches more than once. Ghostwalker found no honor in Luciano's role as an assassin, and Luciano had clearly been jealous of Ghostwalker's special status within the Dark Assembly. Ulric angrily recalled Luciano's snide grin the day Arrius was exiled.

Luciano held that same expression now. His eyes narrowed, and the corner of his mouth twitched into a feral grin. Ulric squirmed helplessly against the taller and stronger man's forearm, attempting to draw in a sliver of air. Luciano responded by pressing even harder into his neck.

"What's the matter, boy? Never remember boy being with no words before. Always big mouth. You have nothing to say to Luciano today, eh?"

Ulric, unable to inhale, let alone say anything, began to feel light-headed.

"Is different when not hiding behind you Ghostwalker's cloak, eh?" Luciano snickered. "The Ghost not here in big Trumric city." The grin vanished. "No, not here." He applied a little more pressure with the slender stilius. "Maybe Aguja feed tonight, eh?" he taunted.

Luciano didn't laugh as expected. He hadn't even sneered. Ulric searched the man's face, trying to discern some emotion. It certainly wasn't pity. Pity was not an emotion in Luciano's repertoire. Back in Mist View, he had been the Dark Assembly's number-one enforcer and assassin. Ruthlessly efficient. Brutally precise. Unequaled in his ability to carry out any job without mercy.

Ulric's face, which had turned bright red for a few moments, was now washing out to a pale blue. The world was spinning, and a cloud of blackness crept in from the edge of his vision.

"You feel it, boy? The dark taking over. You head feel so light, eh? You eyes heavy. You want to go to sleep now, eh, boy? Maybe you sleep forever, eh?"

Luciano's taunts sounded hollow and echoey, as if he were shouting them into the mouth of a cavern. Ulric's head drooped, but he snapped back up. Again, his head fell. The alley receded into darkness. His knees gave, though Luciano's own forearm kept him from sliding to the ground. Despite his struggles, his will broke, and his breath, vision, and strength all failed him at once.

Luciano took a step back, and Ulric fell to the ground like a discarded sack. He gasped, and each intake of air was a blaze of fire in and out of his lungs. He braced himself against the wall and felt his throat. The tenderness beneath his fingers told him it was badly bruised. Ulric stared at Luciano's Verdan leather boots while he tried to catch his breath.

After a few moments, Luciano spoke once more.

"You lucky, boy. I was not sent to kill you. No, no. Not kill. Sent to give you job. Give you new life, eh?"

The offer captured Ulric's attention, so he risked meeting the assassin's gaze, but stopped at the sight of a smoky quartz pommel protruding from underneath Luciano's cloak. He knew the sword, for there was no other like it; Ghostwalker's spatha!

How could Arrius' sword hang at the assassin's hip? Ghostwalker was gone, betrayed, his person and property seized, himself condemned by the magistrates of Mist View. Unless…

A terrible thought ignited, burning out all reason as it burst from his skull and raced through his limbs like liquid fire, leaving behind an ash of madness. Heedless of Luciano's reputation and the threat of his slender dagger, Ulric leaped to his feet and grabbed the hilt of Ghostwalker's sword.

"Arrius' sword! How? Were you the one?" he screamed, eyes wild with unspoken accusations. "Did you betray him?"

Luciano stepped back, momentarily surprised by his sudden strength, but before Ulric could pull Arrius' spatha from its scabbard, the assassin twisted his hand off the hilt and raised the stilius, spinning the slender dagger in a blur of steel to strike its pommel into his temple.

A flash of light. Pain. Darkness.

"Bad move, boy." Luciano's words drifted slowly to the alley floor, where Ulric rubbed the growing knot at the side of his head. "You know nothing. Foolish to act when you don't know truth.

Ghostwalker not teach you this? Worse, act on truth you hope to be."

"How then? Arrius' sword? Are you saying you didn't steal it? By right, it should be mine," he shouted with increasing defiance. "You two hated each other. I was his protégé! I carry his legacy!"

Luciano calmly placed a boot on Ulric's chest and slowly pressed him back into the dirt. "Then, boy, you have no problem with job. Easy thing for young thief carrying Ghostwalker's legacy." Luciano expelled a hyena-like cackle.

Ulric said nothing.

"I see, yes. I see. No laughing today, eh? Just get down to business, as the Trumins say. Forget sword. We get down to business, boy."

At that moment, Ulric wanted nothing more than to remove the dagger from under his tunic and launch it at the arrogant Verdan's face. But he didn't have the strength. He had the will but not the strength. Luciano had beat it out of him. Instead, Ulric stared at him, listening, but he pictured his lifeless body sprawled out in the alley, a dagger in his eye socket, river flies buzzing in and out of his mouth.

"Here is job. You do this, boy, and you good with Assembly. Do this, and we see what you learned from Ghostwalker, eh."

Ulric gritted his teeth and glared at the Verdan. Luciano grabbed him under his armpit and lifted him. Ulric's birthing defiance must have been obvious, for once again the assassin maneuvered his dagger onto Ulric's belly.

"You got no manners, boy. You need to listen. Show respect when you better is speaking."

Ulric shadowed his hate and met Luciano's gaze with a blank stare.

"Better, better boy. So. There is man. Very rich man. Name is Secundus. Quintus Marius Secundus. Has big manor in hilltops of Trumric. He collect art like rich men do. You boy, you steal one piece and bring back, no harm, no break, you back in good with Assembly." Luciano loosened his grip on Ulric's arm, allowing him to slide down the wall. Luciano took a half-step backward, dagger still in hand.

Sitting awkwardly on the ground, Ulric stretched his neck from side to side, mouth open, still drinking in the much-needed air. He could taste the mixture of mucus, spit, and blood that had collected at the back of his throat. He was tempted to spit the mess on Luciano's boots, but at the last second, he turned his head and spat on the gravel. Speaking would be painful, but he couldn't hold his tongue any longer.

"Art? You want me to steal…" Each syllable brought with it a knife-strike of pain in his throat. "… to steal art? I'm to trade… trade my life… for a painting?"

Luciano paused before answering, an unsettling twinkle in his eye.

"No, no, boy. No painting. Statue. Ancient statue from Suhtea. Body of lion, wings of eagle, face of man. Solid gold and big as a cabbage. You steal gold Suhtean statue."

Ulric, still light-headed and dizzy, gently patted the back of his head, wincing when he found a growing bump where his skull had struck the brick wall.

Meeting Luciano's gaze again, he sarcastically asked, "May I stand up now?"

"*Claro! Claro!* Of course, boy."

Ulric braced himself, one arm against the wall and the other on his knee. He was weak and should have let out a groan of pain as he rose, but he had no intention of giving Luciano the satisfaction. When he had steadied himself, he looked Luciano straight in the eye, saying nothing with his lips but volumes with his gaze.

"So. You steal gold Suhtean statue from Secundus. Bring back to me at Quadrivium, eh? All straight with Assembly. Any questions, boy?" The Verdan spoke the last three words slowly and then offered Ulric a toothy smile.

Ulric had several, but before he could ask the first, Luciano thrust his fist into his gut. Ulric hit the ground hard; the breath knocked out of him. Facedown in the dirt, his cheeks stung with embedded gravel. His lungs once again grasped at the air for relief, and stars of pain overtook his vision. He no longer heard the nearby river. He didn't even hear Luciano's footsteps as he departed. There was only the sound of Luciano's hyena-like laughter fading into the distance.

A Divine Visit

The young healer knelt over the wicker cradle, her dark curls dangling over the crying baby like strands of black ivy. Though a green linen palla hid her face, the tenderness with which she pressed the back of her hand against the infant's forehead suggested soft features hidden beneath. The child's face was ablaze with fever and looked an alarming mustard yellow, its dark hair sweat-soaked and matted. It took in labored breaths in between weak cries. The girl pulled her palla down, revealing sun-kissed caramel skin and large, warm eyes. She stroked the infant's yellow cheek with one hand as she pressed a finger to her lips.

"Shhhhh." The whisper sounded like gentle ocean surf. "Shhhhh."

The babe stopped crying and looked up at Julia with wide eyes, but now each breath had become a struggle as if it were facing a great wind.

With mounting dread, the baby's parents watched their child struggle for its life. Julia pulled a clay vial from the folds of her tunic. She removed the stopper, then raised the vial into the air with both hands as if offering it to the gods. The infant drew in an uncomfortably large breath, startling the mother. Julia shot her a reassuring gaze, and the mother placed her own trembling hands around the vial. Julia silently mouthed a quick prayer and lowered the slender vial, then she dipped a single finger inside and withdrew it. It glistened wetly in the candlelight.

The father fidgeted uncomfortably as Julia squeezed the baby's cheeks, forcing open its mouth. His wife placed a hand on his knee, settling him with a look. When Julia placed her finger in the infant's mouth, it suckled immediately. Relief and hope washed over the parents' faces, and when the babe had sucked the last of the liquid from her finger, its cries returned.

Julia stoppered the vial, handed it to the mother, and then spoke over the wailing infant. "Do as I have done twice daily. Once at dawn, then again as the sun retires in the west."

The parents nodded in unison.

"Eat plenty of cabbage and peas," Julia said. "Meats if you can afford them. If not, then fish sauces like garum and allec. Avoid bread and porridge. Feed the babe generously. Three to four times daily."

The mother nodded.

Julia's gaze moved to the father. "Tomorrow morning, go to the market and buy a dove. Bring it home and build a fire. Use green leaves and grass, wet tree limbs. Myrill delights in the smoke; it honors her. Then, in the light of the new day, make a sacrifice of the animal."

The father nodded.

After clasping the couple's hands, she said, "Say this prayer of healing three times a day. Myrill rejoices in your prayers and shall reward your child with mercy. I will teach you the prayer. You must recite it three times."

Suddenly, the child stopped breathing.

"Quickly now… close your eyes!"

The young couple complied, gripping each other's hands tightly as they did so.

"Listen closely and repeat after me." Julia took a deep breath and recited the prayer as quickly as she dared. "Thou art the queen of divinities, O Myrill. Thee, divine one, I adore and thy power I invoke: graciously vouchsafe me this which I ask of thee: and with due fealty, Myrill, I will repay thee thanks. Entrust to me now this healing virtue of thine: let healing come with thy power: whate'er I do in consonance therewith, let it have favorable issue. Finally, now, O Myrill, let thy majesty vouchsafe to me what I ask of thee in prayer."

Upon the first recitation, a cool breeze drifted past the three. Like feathers brushing across her skin, Julia felt a gentle tickle on her arms and neck. Julia's heart raced. Could it be? How?

Mother Myrill? But… I am unworthy, Goddess. I am cast out. I no longer wear the robe. I… am… pariah.

After repeating the chorus, a mixture of aromas wafted through the room: rosemary, cinnamon, lavender, and something else—something unfamiliar—yet sweeter than honeysuckle. At times, the scents greeted their nostrils singularly, yet at others, they melded into new and intoxicating combinations.

You… you are here! I feel your presence. Yes! Are you here to save the child? Please! She's called Amara.

When they had completed the third and final recitation, the delicate string plucks of an unseen lyre echoed in the insula, a quiet melody of celestial notes. Then silence.

Who am I, Mother Myrill? I am no one. But this no one thanks you. Thank you for your mercy and love so this child may be healed, reborn with your divine touch.

"Open. Your. Eyes."

A sudden wail pierced the silence, and Amara's parents rushed to their daughter's side.

Julia slowly opened her eyes, and while her smile spoke of contentment and peace, her brow betrayed darker feelings hidden beneath the surface. A laurel of leaves tickled her head, its white berries sparkling in the soft light of dawn, casting luminescent ripples upon the walls as pearls lustering in the sea.

The couple looked at one another and silently communicated their astonishment, then embraced. When they returned their attention to Julia, the laurel was gone.

And with it, so too were the infant's cries.

When the parents leaned over the cradle, their astonishment returned seeing their child's head encircled in the leafy laurel. When the baby smiled at them and cooed, the mother broke out in tears while the father, trembling and speechless, turned gratefully to Julia.

Both mother and father watched with astonishment as the baby's eyes cleared and the mucus caked in their corners dried up. The sickly saffron tinge faded from its face as the child continued cooing at its parents and the strange young woman. The mother embraced her, pulling her close as the father gripped his wife's shoulder tightly.

"Gods... Gods be praised... Julia," the mother stammered.

"How?" was all the father said.

A long pause filled the room.

"If… if you've been… if you can call upon…"

"By the Gods, girl, why are you not at the temple?"

Julia averted her gaze.

"He's right, Julia."

She fidgeted with her own palla, pulling it from her shoulder and draping it over her face to conceal her blushing cheeks.

"We've never seen… You have the gifts, girl. You should be at the temple. I'm sorry, child. I meant no disrespect. We just—"

Julia lowered her head and watched the couple through curls of dark hair. They furrowed their brows at each other as Julia gathered herself up, preparing to leave.

"Wait. What's wrong? What have we said to upset you?"

The aromas faded, and Julia could no longer hear the lyre's melodies. Donning her palla to conceal her frustration and tears, Julia snatched up her healer's bag and pushed through the door of the dilapidated apartment without another word.

The streets had lightened in the last hour, and the sun's first rays filtered through the morning clouds as she made her way through the neighborhood. She quickened her pace as she walked east down the narrow street until it intersected another; there, she paused, taking a moment to get her bearings.

"Lost, are we?"

The voice, a familiar gravel-filled throat that spat its words onto the street, came from behind her.

Julia turned to see the blonde-headed Titus, flanked on both sides by a Gutter-Fish thug, approaching with one hand resting on the hilt of a dagger tucked into his belt. The two thugs, acting in unison, slapped their leather cudgels into the palms of their hands as they sneered and leered. Titus stopped and towered over her, adopting an impatient look while fondling the dagger at his side.

"I thought we had made it clear to you, girl. Twice already, in fact. Stop tending to the sick in our district."

Julia gathered her courage around her like a soldier's armor, lifting her chin high as she replied, "Titus, I believe. You are Titus, are you not?"

In response, the Gutter-Fish gang leader sucked in his tongue and tilted his head toward her. "You think this is a game, girl? You've crossed the Gutter-Fish, and that means you've crossed others as well."

"As I recall, Titus, you eagerly accepted my help when you sprained your wrist some days back. What changed? Is someone paying you to harass me?"

"We don't reveal client names, stupid girl."

"Oh, so someone has hired you to harass me!"

Titus pulled the dagger from his belt. "You stupid bi—"

"What a surprise!" A feminine voice rang out. "Running into the two of you at the same time in the same place, and both so far from home. Julia, dear, have you been out all night again? A girl needs her beauty sleep, you know."

The girl had mousy brown curls that turned under just above her shoulders. Her eyes conveyed kindness, but her devilish smile said otherwise, and though she walked with the grace of a patrician, the men's toga she wore betrayed her true station.

"Ide? It's… it's so good to see you. But—"

"Look here, whore." Titus whipped around and pointed the end of his dagger at Ide. "Just 'cause I take your sister for the occasional tumble don't mean you can stick your tits in Gutter-Fish business!"

"Titus…" The voice was sultry but carried a girlish lilt. "You cut me with your words. I would never nose into Gutter-Fish business, and certainly not yours, darling." Ide took a half-step closer and ran a finger through her tangled hair. "Truth is, I'm jealous of Murena. I'm just a girl waiting for her turn, you see." She winked at Titus, then turned about, ignoring the glares of the two heavies.

Titus licked his lips in response.

Glancing back at Titus, Ide said, "If you've got the coin, that is."

Titus clenched his jaw, then released a half-hearted laugh through his teeth. "Tell your sister I'll see her soon. And maybe, just maybe, I'll bed you after. If you're lucky." He turned his attention back to Julia. "As for you, girl… no more healing in Gutter-Fish territory. Or next time"—he thrust the dagger toward Julia—"there'll be blood."

Ide slipped past Titus and grabbed Julia's hand, but before she could drag her away from her three assailants, Titus seized Julia under her arm and jerked her toward him. His face was so close she could smell the fish sauce and olives on his breath.

"Next time, girl. Blood."

Ide yanked her free from Titus's grasp, whisking her down the street, and the two of them blended into the early morning throng of people.

Julia and Ide hurriedly made their way through the crowds until they felt a safe distance from Titus' threats.

"Here's Dyer's Street, Ide. The clothier I work for is just a few blocks away. If I hurry, I still might be able—"

"Wait!" Ide tugged on Julia's palla and pointed down an alleyway just beyond the intersection. "Isn't that the one you've been going on about?"

In the long shadows of the early morning, a young man with unfashionably long night-black hair sat on a crate at the end of the alley, his back to the two girls. Julia felt Ide's stare, and though she tried her best not to, she revealed a coy smile.

"It is. I knew it." Ide bumped Julia with her shoulder. "Not every day you see a man in this city with that hair."

The young man removed his boots, shaking them out and setting them on the ground one at a time. The stranger finished nibbling the last bits of roasted meat from a wooden skewer, then flung it upwards, impaling it into a tattered cloth canopy. He winced, then reached across his chest and lifted his tunic, revealing a bruised muscular back.

Julia, her pulse racing, stared at the boy as he massaged his ribs.

"Meat for breakfast." Ide glanced at her flustered friend. "Is that what you're craving, Julia?"

Julia continued staring.

Ide's eyes drifted from Julia to the stranger, then back to Julia again. Shaking her head and giggling, she said, "I bet it's tasty." She jolted Julia back to reality with another bump.

Julia looked at her friend with glassy eyes. "Huh… What?"

"And he's been in a scrap."

"Poor thing. He's hurt."

"Know any good healers that could tend to him?"

"Now you're just making fun."

"Maybe. But only because you're so fun to make fun of. Here's a real question for you, though. Why exactly haven't you talked to him yet? Didn't you say you spy—oh, excuse me, spot—him almost every day?"

"Yes, he often walks down Dyer's Street and Via Lucretius where the theater is, sometimes directly under the theater loft where I sleep."

"Sounds like *he's* the one spying on *you*."

"Don't be silly, Ide. Why would a man like that be spying on me?"

Ide raised her eyebrows and pursed her lips. "First of all, he's barely more than a boy, from what I see." She raised her eyebrows at Julia. "And I'd like to see more, I might add…"

"Ide!"

Another shoulder bump and wink. "And second, he wants what all boys—all men—want. C'mon, Julia. You're a beautiful girl, and those dark eyes and curly locks attract interest."

"I'm not like you and Murena. I can't just... well... you know."

"I'm not suggesting you be his whore. Quite the opposite. You could use a dangerous-looking man like him—for protection. Today won't be the last time you'll have to deal with that idiot Titus and his even more idiotic lackeys. Use your charm and those dark eyes to pull him in. Then once you've snared him, use him for protection... and other things." She accompanied the last words with a knowing wink.

"You never stop, do you?"

"I can't. What else would I do?"

Julia embraced her friend tightly, then held her shoulders at arm's length. "I'm on a different path, Ide. Blessed Myrill will protect me. I don't need a street rat. Not for protection. Not for anything. Can't a girl just have a distant crush?"

"You silly girl. You're a season older than me but still so naïve."

"I know. But Mother Myrill guides me."

Ide lifted her eyes and shook her head.

"I have to get to work. I'll be late as it is. Thank you for coming to my rescue, Ide. See what I'm saying? I don't need some handsome stranger. I have you."

Ide giggled again. "You just called him handsome."

The Gray Outcast

"The Gray Outcast was alone." Ulric spoke the words from a corner of the theater, and under his breath, he added, "Lucky fool, then. A man's only really free when he's alone."

"Oh, don't say that." Startled, Ulric turned toward the voice. A young woman stood at his shoulder and leaned in, brushing against him. "Those lines are for the chorus." Dark, expressive eyes seized Ulric through a bob of curly black hair. "You'll be auditioning with the Outcast's monologue"—she reached across his chest and pointed a slender caramel finger—"further down the scroll."

Ulric tried to escape, but his own eyes lingered too long, lost in the curves of the girl's long, pale yellow tunic. Embarrassed, he cast his gaze back toward the scroll. "Uh… chorus, monologue. I see now."

"You, boy! Stand at the center," called a voice from the orchestra. It was the theater's owner and manager, his voice sounding impatient, with a hint of a northern accent.

After his run with the Gutter-Fish the previous day, Ulric sought the theater owner he had met in the River Market. As luck had it, instead of picking the old man's pocket that day, he had ended up debating philosophy for the better part of an afternoon. And today, in his hour of need, he found the Polyminius Theater holding open auditions. Clearly, such luck was a sign from Neesis.

Ulric hurried to the center of the stage, his eyes following the dark-haired girl as she retrieved a pair of cymbals. She turned, and their eyes met again; she smiled and gave a subtle nod of encouragement. He looked forward, unfurled the scroll, and held it at the ready.

Again, the manager called from the orchestra. "Piso, provide us with the chorus if you please."

A tall man, aging but still handsome, stepped forward. Ulric watched everyone's eyes abandon him to look toward Piso. Standing next to the veteran actor, he could feel himself fading from the stage. Piso's voice filled the old theater with practiced ease.

"The Gray Outcast was alone. His enemies abroad had plotted his downfall, ensuring his implication in the highest treason. His enemies at home in Trumric had made sure swift and ignoble exile followed. His previous life as a wealthy patrician, an honored veteran, and esteemed warrior-priest of Cathus was gone.

"Only the Outcast remained, alone on an island no bigger than his former estate. Far from home, outcast of city and temple, he was exposed to evil. The legend says the dark God of the Sea was so eager to claim the Outcast's spirit he rose from the Abyss to inundate the island in filth and slime and every horror of the ocean's depths!"

Another call from the orchestra. "A storm sets the mood!"

The dark-haired girl released a crash of thunder, and Ulric imagined the sea roiling below. The time had come for the Outcast to declare his defiance to the storm-wracked sky.

Ulric took a step forward and read from the scroll. "I stand before you, under the gaze of Alakur, Brightest and Greatest, and

Cathus, his Hand of War, no base exile! If alone and outcast, I am to face all the horrors of Hell; then I do so not as dutiful Trumin but as a constant son of Cathus! Why should I look to Trumric any more? What ally should I invoke when, by honor, I have earned the name of dishonorable?"

"Continue," directed the theater manager. "Don't break the rhythm. Louder! With confidence!"

"Nay, then, if these things are pleasing to the gods, when I have suffered my doom, I shall come to know my sin; but if the sin is with my judges, I could wish them no fuller measure of evil than they, on their part, mete wrongfully to me!"

"Enough!" the manager shouted, ending the audition. "I think I have your measure, young man."

The speech from the final scene of *The Gray Outcast* left Ulric feeling like an intruder upon the stage. A few of the actors still lingering in the auditorium gave some half-hearted applause, but the sweat creeping down his brow betrayed him. Above the rows of stone benches, tattered awnings hung limply in the still, warm air, doing little to cool the theater. He lied to himself, blaming the heat for his sudden discomfort.

He looked around, searching for a consensus on the faces of the actors. The troupe's leading man, Piso, wore a mask of boredom, loosely and arrogantly. At his side stood a shapely woman whose fair hair fell scandalously long and flowing over an ample bosom. Ulric silently thanked the shade of consul Trumerus Garonus for insisting women be allowed to perform in the theater. Raising his gaze, he found her expression intense, seductive even, but unhelpful. Hovering close by, two of Piso's young protégés played their roles of two unimpressed actors perfectly. The girl with curly black hair and dark eyes looked disappointed. Her two cymbals hung limply at her sides in a decidedly un-thunderous epitaph to his audition.

He even snuck a furtive glance toward the front of the theater house at the back of the stage. The two-story building presented an imposing edifice of marble columns and ornate niches occupied by the statues of gods and goddesses, past consuls, and forgotten patrons. Although their paint had long since faded and had even begun peeling away in some places, the statuary still watched over the theater with authority. Their stony faces betrayed nothing.

Ulric glanced down into the orchestra and looked at the owner and manager of the Polyminius Theater. The man was Leufroy, an odd-sounding Gualdean name to Ulric's Trumin ears. The old man's narrow face, stony and pompous as the theater's statues, animated with excitement as he bounded up the brief stone steps and joined everyone on stage.

"Brave heart, young Ulric! The Gray Outcast is no role for a novice. I always like to throw our recruits to the lions, so to speak. Then I can see if they possess the flame. Only a select few have the fiery passion needed for the stage." He placed a hand on Piso's shoulder and looked at Ulric. "I told you I could spot talent, young man. Well, Piso, what do you think?"

"Cool. Chilly, perhaps?" Piso looked him over like a sculptor studying a block of substandard marble. "Still, there may be a spark."

Leufroy nodded several times. "Yes, yes, with the right kindling, we may fan that spark into a flame. Who knows, maybe one day, an inferno?"

Ulric tried to hide his surprise, fearing to appear overeager; it was a poor performance. "I'd be honored to join the Polyminius! In whatever capacity you'll have me."

"We do need someone to launder our costumes and sweep the aisles," said one of Piso's lackeys. Another snickered, and the girl with the cymbals glared at them. Ulric was used to responding to insults with fists, but he kept his mask of the aspiring actor in place.

The fair-haired woman came forward and stood close to Ulric. Dangerously too close. So close he could feel her heat; her perfume smelled of violets. "Now, now, we should make our newest member feel welcome. Don't you agree, Piso?" She took a step back, and with a flourish, extended her hand. "I, Claudia Severa Major, humbly welcome you to our modest theater." Severa ended with a slight bow and a healthy display of cleavage.

Ulric lightly grasped her hand, returning her bow. "And I, Marcus Octavius Ulric, am honored to be received by such a beautiful and gracious woman. I am honored to be welcome in the company of such a fine troupe of actors." Inspiration inflamed Ulric's performance as a gracious courtier; Severa's beauty was all the spark he needed.

Her flirtatious display had loosened Piso's mask of boredom, and one of annoyance took its place. "If you want to learn an actor's craft, young man, follow my lead." Piso deftly took Severa's hand and guided her a few steps back. "But only on the stage, if you please." Severa's face remained placid, but several other actors couldn't resist a few snide comments.

"My first lesson," Piso continued, "touches upon an actor's most important weapon: his voice. It must be distinct, razor-sharp, and powerful. Sometimes used sparingly, but when it strikes, it must strike precisely and with maximum force. You must hone your voice, Ulric, like one hones a blade."

"Yes, you need a robust voice, one filled with confidence," Leufroy proclaimed. "Were you raised in one of those stern households where children received a quick thrashing if they were noticed or grew too loud?"

"It's true, master Leufroy; I was raised to never be seen nor heard." Ulric grinned, barely suppressing a laugh.

"We'll train those bad habits out of you, my boy! But not today." Leufroy turned to the theater and seized everyone's attention. "Ahem! We're nearing the eleventh hour, so auditions are over." The Republic divided each day and night into twelve hours, so the day was nearly done. "This evening, I have landlords, creditors—and, mercifully—patrons to attend to. We'll meet again the day after tomorrow, at the eighth hour."

Everyone scattered, shouting their excuses and goodbyes. For one awkward moment, Ulric was once again alone upon the stage. He took two quick steps and launched himself into the air, gracefully landing near the center of the orchestra. The theater was a sad affair of worn benches, cracked columns, and crumbling plaster, but he didn't care. Today it was a grand palace full of promise. He ran toward the main exit, ready to see what possibilities the evening would bring.

Suddenly, the immediate possibility was crashing into the helpful young woman with curly black hair. Ulric slid to a stop and performed a pirouette around her at the last instant, gracefully avoiding a collision. He stood there a moment too long, unsure what to say.

"The girl with the thunderbolts!"

She unleashed a torrent of words with scarcely a breath between them. "Oh, what a fright! I thought we'd both hit the floor. Maybe you should be a dancer? I'm Julia, by the way, Persius Julia. I thought your audition wasn't so bad. And never mind Cordus and Ebbo; they're fine once you get to know them. You can learn a lot from Piso. And what would we all do without Leufroy?" She finally took a breath, looked away, and asked, "What did you think of Severa?"

"I see you took Piso's advice."

"Huh?"

"Speak sparingly, but when you do, strike with maximum force!"

Julia blushed and tried to pull one of her curls straight. It defiantly sprung back into a coil. "Sorry."

Stop trying to be clever, Ulric, you ass.

"No, no. No need to be sorry. I'm glad we ran into each other. Or nearly ran into each other. I have to go, but maybe you can help with my voice training at our next rehearsal?"

Julia's eyes smiled. "Of course, I'd be happy to help."

"Until then, Persius Julia." Ulric gave a slight nod and moved toward the exit.

"I know what it's like not to have a home!" Ulric froze. "I've been sleeping in the theater loft. Leufroy knows, but he's never said anything. I'm sure he's all right with it… I think."

Ulric's body tensed. He slowly turned and said, "Seems an odd confession, given we just met. Why tell me this?"

Julia began nervously playing with something hanging around her neck, concealed under her tunic. "I… I've seen you sleeping in the alley off Dyer's Street. So, I thought…"

Ulric stepped forward. His pale blue eyes were as hard as ice, and his voice was razor sharp and precise, like a dagger. "Spying on me?"

Julia took an abrupt step back. "Oh, no… I would never. I work for a nearby clothier. I need to be there very early, so I couldn't help but notice—completely by accident, of course!"

Stop being paranoid, Ulric thought. *You're a fool. What connection could she have with Luciano or the Dark Assembly? Unless…*

"Please forgive me, Julia." Ulric's voice was warm and soft again. "It's all rather embarrassing. Sleeping amongst old props and costumes has to be better than any alley."

"It is; I should know." Julia covered her head with a green palla and gracefully draped the rest of the garment over her left arm and shoulder. She took a step toward the exit and looked back. "There's a high window at the back of the theater. An easy climb, thanks to an old stone pine. I—"

A beautiful young woman admits she's been spying on me, then invites me to a secluded rendezvous? No, thank you! I wasn't raised to play the fool.

"If I slip in, I'll be quiet," Ulric lied. "It may be late, and I wouldn't want to wake you. Now, I really have to get going. Goodbye, Julia."

Ulric bounded through the city, making a game of dodging the thinning traffic. For the moment, he tried to forget Luciano and the Dark Assembly. Instead, his thoughts turned to the theater.

The old Polyminius Theater promised a few honest coins and the opportunity to perfect his craft. Wasn't acting a congenial breed of deception? Thieving required a myriad of skills, but deception was crucial. And despite the uncertain audition, he already considered himself something of an amateur actor. He hadn't practiced in a crumbling theater standing in an unfashionable district of the capital but on the streets and back alleys of another faraway city. What had seemed madness a few short days ago was now the perfect complement for his craft.

His thoughts inexorably returned to Julia. Her kind if manic manner had been as disarming as her slender curves and dark eyes had been distracting. Julia was an enticing mystery, possibly dangerous.

Who is she, really? Where is she from? Why is she so interested in me? Is she running a scheme?

The mystery of Julia would have to wait. It was going to be a busy night. He had an unwelcome heist to plan.

The Wrong Job, Gone Wrong

Ulric prowled the dark streets east of the River Market in quiet fury. In his anger, he dropped all masks. There was no Ulric the homeless stray, no foolish slave, no aspiring actor. There was only Marcus Octavius Ulric, known in the shadows of Mist View as the thief called Darktalon. And like all thieves, he wanted to stay out of sight. He was still in the Transnanpela District, which was Gutter-Fish territory, so he picked his route carefully, all while trying to make sense of Luciano's unexpected ultimatum.

How did I let Luciano get the drop on me? How did he get Arrius' sword? Did he torch Ghostwalker? Betray him to the magistrates? And how did the Dark Assembly find me so quickly? Why make such an unusual offer? Who is Quintus Marius Secundus, and why must I steal his golden sphinx statuette by tomorrow evening?

It's nearly an impossible task! I have a day to plan and execute the lift of a patrician's priceless treasure. I have to prepare with scant gear and even less coin. And do it in an unfamiliar city while dodging the local gangs and the Imperaré.

Right, the job's just plain impossible.

He stepped from the comforting darkness of a narrow alley onto an unfamiliar road heading east toward the sea. It was a direct, open route, but it would save much-needed time, so he risked it. Ulric Darktalon swaggered onward. A man trudging toward him slowed, hesitated, then hurriedly made for the far side of the street. The thief smiled and returned to his dark thoughts.

The worst part of it all was that he didn't give a fig for the Dark Assembly's goodwill. They had revoked their protection from his mentor, leaving Arrius Ghostwalker at the mercy of the Trumin courts.

Two couriers and a praetor were dead, and the dozens of scrolls they carried, official documents and letters bound for the senate, were missing. Ulric knew Ghostwalker could lift the papers off a couple of senatorial couriers as silent and unseen as a midnight breeze, and, besides, spilling blood had never been his way. For such a job to have gone so spectacularly wrong, the couriers must have been forewarned, or some unknown third party had interfered. Now, Ulric wondered, given the uncharacteristic violence, if a certain Verdan assassin hadn't been involved. At the time, he had received no answers, only a terse note the morning after.

It had simply read: Wrong job, gone wrong.

It was the signal to fade into deep shadow and wait for the search fires to dim. It meant living rough on the streets or in prearranged hideouts, never staying in one place too long. So, Ulric disappeared as soldiers marched into the poorer quarters of Mist View like an invading army: searching, terrorizing, and killing when resisted.

Long, dangerous days passed. Ulric fled through a thickening fog of fear and despair, practicing the secrets of the fade as Arrius had taught him: avoiding routine, changing disguises, street encampments, and hideouts seemingly at random. Each night, whether sleeping with strays in a filthy alley in the Warrens, in dank tunnels beneath the Tiers District, or in the comfort of a borrowed bed, he slept fitfully, worried Arrius had been captured or worse, slain in a desperate battle with a dozen soldiers. What if Arrius had fled the city and left him behind? How would he ever know? Then, after several days, he realized the soldiers didn't know where to look or who they were looking for. It was all just a desperate show of force! The provincial governor had to report to the senate he had done something; the death of a praetor couldn't be ignored, after all. Either a scapegoat would be found or, after enough time had passed to impress the Senate with his diligence, the governor would recall the soldiers. Like a slender green shoot breaking through hard stone, hope broke through Ulric's despair. How could he have doubted Neesis' love for a thief as legendary as Ghostwalker?

But Arrius himself had warned Ulric that Neesis Fortuna was a fickle goddess, and on the third day before the Kalends of November, the whisper crept through the streets like a freezing mist to whither all hope: the murderer of the couriers had been found—a thief called Ghostwalker.

Arrius was imprisoned to await a swift trial and certain execution if found guilty, which was almost a certainty given the governor's need for a scapegoat. Ulric never really doubted his mentor had stolen the senatorial scrolls—which were never recovered—but he refused to believe he had murdered anyone. Still, Ulric's slender blade of hope remained, tenaciously clinging against the hard stone of truth. The Dark Assembly would make things right, he told himself. It was their purpose, after all. Were they not the masters of manipulation, intimidation, and bribery? Would they not provide Arrius with the best orator and lawyer in Mist View? Or, in his hour of greatest need, organize a daring escape?

In the end, it was easier to let Ghostwalker become a scapegoat for the Trumin administration rather than risk the shadow government that ran the streets of Mist View.

Once the Dark Assembly had exiled Ghostwalker, their impenetrable tangle of laws and customs demanded the same fate befall Ulric. Even so, it would have been easy for him to regain their favor. By Ghostwalker's design, the affair hadn't implicated him. He could have remained in Mist View if he had petitioned one of the criminal collegia for patronage or, if things got desperate, joined a sanctioned street gang.

I can remember everything so vividly, except for Arrius. He's indistinct, like a nightmare, only becoming clear at the very end. Mist View is an inky silhouette against a gray sky churning with the first winter storms. The crowd is noisy and excited, despite the freezing wind. The thrill of watching condemned men die warms them. Arrius' body is slack upon the cross; he no longer has the strength to hold himself up. Streams of blood along his naked body have frozen into black crusts. He shivers violently with what little strength he has left. The cold will be a mercy, I think.

He spots me in the crowd, I'm sure of it. At that moment, his image becomes clear. I can recall every detail of his face. He looks right at me as if he wants to tell me something: one last lesson or maybe a warning. He hasn't the strength to push words past his shivering lips. Instead, he winks and struggles to smile.

I turn and run.

And I haven't stopped running.

To the Nine Gates with the Dark Assembly! To the Wyrm with Luciano!

Ulric slipped off the road into deep shadow and wiped the tears from his eyes. He had foolishly let the final mask fall.

This is what dwelling on the past gets you. Womanly tears when I need to be hard as iron.

He continued making his way east, following the Nanpela River toward the Portum Mare District and the sea. While he tried to make sense of the job, he rubbed the still-tender bruises on his neck. The Dark Assembly didn't want him dead. Why would they? The Dark Assembly and the Imperaré had several treaties that forbade them from operating in each other's territory. Sometimes they ignored these agreements, but if caught, the consequences were severe. Why had they given him this peculiar job? The Dark Assembly had leverage over him, and he was expendable. Was it that simple?

Fine! If the Dark Assembly needs a job done in Trumric, why not ask for the best?

If the cost of leaving Mist View and the Dark Assembly behind were one last job, then he'd gladly pay the price. Even if part of the cost was coming face-to-face with the Imperaré.

***

Ulric was looking for a shop in a particularly dangerous neighborhood of the Portum Mare District. The roads were unlit, tight, and twisting, and every alley and alcove was potentially a black maw filled with dagger teeth. He passed by hard-eyed men openly negotiating knife and shroud work before crumbling walls covered in crude graffiti of genitalia and fornication alongside the musings of long-forgotten Kreslan philosophers. Prostitutes and shadow-dust dealers populated every street corner instead of the laborers and bargemen more common to the Transnanpela District. These streets were owned by criminals and run by criminals. They were more home to Ulric than any market square or theater could ever be.

The Portum Mare district, Ulric thought, *isn't all that different from the warrens of Mist View. There must be streets like these in all the great cities.* He recalled part of a list from one of Ghostwalker's many lessons. *Places like silver-rich Conric immured in the mountains; scarred and demon-haunted Anric; upstart and proud Gualdé; fabulously wealthy Kos with its strange temples; remote Baladan shrouded in secrecy; even Arkanay, whose borders—so it is rumored—welcome all evil.*

The shop resembled a refuse pile in both its organization and variety. The mess filled an unknown number of small rooms on the first floor of a dilapidated insula, a five-story tenement building that stood near the sea. On the doorframe, there were two glyphs: two interlocking circles intersected by a key and the number XVII. The circles represented two coins and meant a fence operated here. The key represented the tools of the thieving trade and, together with the coins, meant those tools were available for sale.

The number XVII was an ill omen. It was an anagram of VIXI, which means "I lived" in Trumin. Another way of saying, "I am dead." The Imperaré was not without a sense of humor. They had adopted the number seventeen as a mark of their sanction and a warning of their protection. It was an Imperaré shop and the last place Ulric wanted to be.

"It's late! If you insist on bothering me, you better have coin." The voice was low and menacing, like waves crashing onto a rocky shore.

An older man appeared from behind a shelf filled with metallic bits and bobs. He was tall and lean, and his once-black hair had begun to fill with flecks of gray. He reminded Ulric of a thin strip of iron that had been beaten once too often.

"I have coin. And cause to spend it."

The man's pale blue eyes softened. "In that case, welcome. I'm Silo. What are you looking for at this late hour?" He cast his arms wide and spoke warmly. "I have furs from Cearalon in the distant north. From the mysterious east, I have silks and spices from Bayjon and Kanchea. From the southern deserts of Suhtea, I have relics from ages long forgotten. I even have Eltaran jewelry." Silo cast his eyes over the chaotic piles of junk and gave a wide smile. "Just good luck finding it."

Ulric returned the smile. "Furs and silks, I do not doubt. Save the Eltaran trinkets for the gullible. My name is Ulric, and I've never seen an Elt."

Silo burst out in genuine laughter. "Well, boy, if you haven't seen them, how could they be?"

Ulric knew there were no Eltarans, and anyone peddling their wares was running a scheme. Still, there was something about Silo's laughter that made him feel foolish. He wanted to ask why he was so certain, but there was the pressing matter of the impossible heist.

There was no one else in the shop, so Ulric took a step closer and said, "Forgive me, Silo, but I'm pressed for time. I need a coil of light rope and a three-pronged grapnel, preferably with a Whisper enchantment. Oh, I also need a new 'snake' lockpick; mine bent on the last job."

Silo's eyes hardened; the strip of iron had returned. "I don't know you. If I don't know you, you shouldn't be here." Silo stepped away and loudly proclaimed, "I'm closing early tonight. Out!"

Ulric expected this and had his lies ready. "Wait, Silo! I admit, I'm new to the city, and I'm not sanctioned yet." He put on his most humble and apologetic mask. "I'm not trying to scheme you. I need to make a big impression before I petition the Imperaré. I have a job in mind that should do the trick. One that won't stir up any trouble."

Silo looked straight at Ulric. "Ha! A likely tale."

He knew he was moments away from being physically thrown out of the shop.

"Wait! Do this, and I'll owe you!" It was the next part that hurt the most. "And I'll pay double the usual price!"

A Stray Problem

After handing over all his coin to Silo—even Titus' silver chain—Ulric's mood had become as black as Nyx's icy heart. He was broke—again! Worse, the thought that Luciano had played some part in Ghostwalker's fate was growing like a tumor, threatening to consume all reason with thoughts of vengeance, with a need to claim Arrius' sword from the assassin's bloodstained hands.

Not yet. Focus on the sphinx job first. Then I'll send the assassin to the Underworld!

He slowed as he neared a familiar alley off Dyer's Street. Like all alleys, it was narrow, neglected, and dirty. Unlike other alleys, it held something of value. He stopped and peered into the darkness, where his eyes, long ago grown accustomed to the night, saw shapes, silhouettes, and reflections of light where others would have only seen blackness. Two men were in the alley, one curled up, sleeping in the dirt, the other sitting, leaning against a crumbling wall. The faintest glint revealed a knife in the hand of the sitting man.

"Gods Above, Gods Below!" He swore under his breath. He needed something hidden in the alley, and he wanted to retrieve it unseen. Luciano's demands didn't allow time for fear or hesitation. He stepped toward the alley, and the smell of urine and stale wine hit his nose like a rancid fist.

From the darkness, the sitting man said, "Keep walking, boy. This here's our camp."

He didn't need trouble from a couple of drunken beggars—or strays, as they were known in the larger cities of the Republic. The Strays were a loosely organized collection of beggars and scavengers, the lowest of the low. He knew from experience the deformities they displayed for sympathetic coin were often a scheme; a stray was rarely as helpless as they appeared.

Ulric tried to talk his way past the two men. Ill-prepared, he blurted out something close to the truth. "I camped here before. I need to grab something I left behind. Then I'll be gone."

The man drunkenly rose from the wall. "Oh, you left something nice here? Maybe we take a look?"

He roused his companion with a quick succession of kicks. "Up, Musca! We have a visitor. Bearing gifts." He gave Ulric a mocking, near-toothless smile.

Neesis, please damn these fools and me along with them. Never tell the truth when a good lie will do!

"What? Leave me be, Ruga!" Musca emitted an unhealthy-sounding belch and, with much difficulty, pulled himself out of the dirt. He leaned drunkenly against the wall. "Huh? Who's that?"

The one called Ruga didn't take his eyes off Ulric. "The little shit says he's left something valuable in our camp." His eyes narrowed as he pointed the knife at Ulric. "He's going to find it for us."

"No, you'll move on to stink up some other alley, you toothless baboon."

"There's two of us, you little shit!" He lashed out with the knife. "We'll cut you!"

Ulric's insult had inspired the reaction he wanted. Unlike earlier with Luciano, there were no distractions, no surprise; there was only Ruga's lunging knife. Instead of recoiling, he stepped into the attack, entrapping Ruga's arm while simultaneously striking him hard on the neck. Ruga grunted and dropped the knife.

The man's stench nearly caused Ulric to lose his rhythm. He grabbed a handful of greasy hair and yanked Ruga's head down while twisting his body. The stray was on his back in an instant. He dropped his right knee on Ruga's neck and had his steel dagger out before Musca had pushed himself off the wall. He couldn't resist a certain satisfaction listening to Ruga squirm and struggle for air.

Ulric stared at Musca and grinned. "Are you and your friend going to move on, or should I bleed him first?"

Musca staggered back a step and spread his hands wide. "I never flashed steel. To the Nine Gates with it! We'll move on if you let him go."

Ulric watched the two men stumble away down Dyer's Street; then, he disappeared down the alley. He had to work quickly, fearing they would return with other strays or, worse, Gutter-Fish. Several paces beyond the stray's camp, he knelt in the center of the passage and began furiously pushing refuse aside until he exposed a small iron grate. The sound of draining water rose from the sewer below. He grasped the grate, pulled and set it aside. He lay flat on the ground and reached inside the narrow shaft. When he stood up, he held a dark bundle the length of his forearm.

He replaced the grate, hurriedly covered it with trash, then ran to the opposite end of the alley, toward the river. The bundle held all he had brought from Mist View: a long dagger, three throwing knives, an expensive black cotton tunic, charcoal gray woolen pants, black leather gloves, a dark leather belt and pouch, soft black leather boots, his prized lock picks, lucky coins, and a unique piece of clear quartz. All this was wrapped in a woolen cloak and hood with a mottled black and gray pattern.

He checked for any sign of strays, and seeing none, he relaxed. Where to next? Find a new place to camp near the River Market? Or far from the Gutter-Fish?

Delicate fingers tugged at a dark curl, and eyes the color of a warm night demanded attention. At the theater, those eyes had seized his own and caused the rest of the world to fade. Everything about Julia fascinated him.

And that's why he couldn't trust her.

Am I being paranoid? Still, if this is a trap, best to find out now. Otherwise, rehearsals are going to be awkward.

His destination was the theater loft—and the mystery of Julia.

A Tearstained Tragedy

Ulric rose unseen along the old stone pine tree like a wisp of dark smoke. The tree's rugged trunk blossomed into a wide umbrella canopy to brush against the back of the Polyminius Theater, just as Julia had said. A faint light emitted from an open window on the second story. Crouching on one broad branch, he crept toward the opening and peered inside.

A small lamp illuminated the room. It was bigger than Ulric expected, filled with stacks of crates, chests, and piles of costumes and props; so many potential hiding places made him nervous. At one end, a narrow flight of steep stairs led to the backstage area. At the center of the far wall, Julia stood in front of a polished bronze mirror draped in a long-sleeved robe of deep blue with an exotic headdress. With her black hair, dark brown eyes, and light caramel skin, Ulric thought she was the very image of a Bayjoni princess.

He hopped down from the window and into the room. Julia snatched the headdress from her head and spun around. "Ulric! I wasn't sure you'd come. You really shouldn't sneak around. You nearly gave me a fright!"

"Uh… I'm here." He placed the dark bundle he had been carrying on the floor, then stood there embarrassed, saying nothing.

Julia tossed the headdress aside onto a pile of colorful costumes and stepped closer. Her eyes focused on his bruised neck. "Are you—"

"Is that costume for a particular play?" He asked quickly, cutting her off. He stepped forward and cast his eyes around the loft, half expecting another ambush.

Julia took the hint and ignored the unsightly bruises. "Have you ever seen The Jinn's Last Wish? Or A Princess of Bayjon?"

"No, I haven't. We should perform them one day. You could take the lead."

Julia rolled her eyes. "Can you imagine Severa letting anyone else take the lead?"

Ulric donned a shocked look. "Claudia Severa Major renounces the lead? Take a minor role, like a common pleb? Alakur forbid!"

She released a full-throated laugh. "We'll have to make do with the minor roles."

"Stick me in the chorus. I don't mind. But why not Julia in the lead? How long have you been with the theater?"

Julia turned away and began rummaging through the props while she considered the question. "If you're trying to ask politely how long I've been sneaking into the loft, it hasn't been long. Since the Ides of Trestilis."

She pulled a comically fake breastplate from a nearby pile and pressed it against Ulric's chest. "Before that, I shared a room with two other girls. The rent was cheap—very cheap. Then I found out why." Ulric held the prop as she stepped back and looked over the room. "The girls had an arrangement with the owner of the property. To stay, I had to... become part of the deal." She chewed the corner of her lip as she searched, finally handing him a prop sword. "And that's how I know what it's like to sleep in alleys."

Ulric had witnessed countless such deals play out over his brief life. He tightened his grip on the wooden sword and imagined thrusting the real thing into Julia's former landlord. "Horrible! Who was this old goat? Where?"

"Oh, it doesn't matter now. There!" Julia stepped back and appraised her costume choices. "The very image of Silent Legionnaire #2. You'll stand stoically in the background as all the women in the audience swoon." She blushed, spun around, and began nervously searching through another pile of costumes.

Ulric looked down at the sword, pretending to be unfamiliar with the weapon. "I don't imagine a soldier's life is right for me." He had to remind himself he was supposed to be interrogating her. He set the props aside and prepared his next question.

"So, your family…" He watched as Julia stretched over a pile of costumes to reach a high shelf, the curves of her body straining against the fabric of her robe. "Hmm…?"

Julia grabbed two masks off the shelf and tossed one to Ulric. "What was that?"

"Uh, nothing." He looked down at the dour and exaggerated features of a Kreslan theater mask.

Julia's mask was just as elaborate, but the expression was one of mirth and mischief. She held the mask over her face and, in a deep sonorous voice, said, "Hear now the tearstained tragedy of Julia and Ulric, who never got a lead role!"

Ulric couldn't help but smile. "Now don't be so sure." He grabbed a dragon-headed rod from the corner and placed it in Julia's hand. Her touch was warm and soft. "One day, you could play a famous magus like Servilia Penna of the Collegium Draconis Aurei."

Julia lowered her mask and stared into the eyes of the dragon. "Ugh. Magic seems like such hard work. I prefer the carefree life of a poor actress." She tossed the prop aside. "Besides, I knew someone who was accepted into the Aureum Draconis, and she was both tedious and insufferable."

Ulric spotted a familiar-looking dark green robe with brown trim, neatly folded at the end of a long pile of blankets and cloaks. He reached down and with one motion, unfurled the robe. "If not a magus, how about the role of a beautiful young priestess of Myrill, queen of the gods?"

"Give it back!" Julia was not smiling.

Confused, Ulric handed her the robe. She carefully folded it and placed it back where he had found it.

"I'm sorry, Julia. What—"

"Nevermind that… costume. Let's find another."

Julia flitted about the loft, occasionally stopping to comment on a costume or make a funny face at a prop. As Ulric watched, his earlier suspicions slunk away in embarrassment.

When Julia returned, she held a golden laurel leaf crown with two pointed ears carved at its sides and a jewel-encrusted scepter.

In reality, they were cheap gold-painted wood and glass props. She placed the laurel crown upon his tangle of dark hair and pressed the scepter to her lips while she considered his new look.

"There! If not a soldier, maybe the role of an Eltaran prince?" Julia stepped closer. "I suspect you're an impulsive troublemaker like all Eltarans."

Ulric feigned hurt. "Impulsive? Me? How would you even know? We only met earlier today."

Julia took another step. "Aren't you forgetting? I've been spying on you, remember? Following you on the streets, watching you in alleys." She looked up at Ulric with dark, inviting eyes. "You are impulsive, aren't you?"

Ulric imagined the intoxicating touch of Julia's perfect lips, the heat of her body, the crush of her breasts against his chest, and it began to drive him mad. It was the madness of Neesis Amoris, goddess of lust. He leaned forward, ready to take her into his arms.

Julia slipped out of his grasp and burst into laughter, forcing Ulric back with a thrust of the bejeweled scepter. "You are impulsive!" Ulric's face reddened. "Ooh! Are you blushing?

"No! I just thought..." *Oh, shit. I sound like a fool. Neesis Amoris, guide me!*

"That I wanted you to kiss me? Maybe I did," Julia replied slyly, "but I'm not as impulsive as some people I know."

"Good. Those people must make terrible fools of themselves."

"And to think this is only our first night sharing the loft," Julia said with a wicked glint in her eyes.

"So? If I can avoid making a fool of myself again, I won't get kicked back into the alley? Is that the deal?"

"There's no 'deal'." Julia's eyes narrowed dangerously. "Stay here. Or leave," she said with an edge in her voice. "If you meant what you said—"

Ulric spread his hands in surrender. "I'm sorry. It was a poor joke. I am impulsive, as you discovered. And I meant what I said."

"It's fine." Julia's smile returned. "Enough of that. Let's talk about anything else."

Ulric took the Eltaran crown from his head and held it before him. "I have an odd question."

"You've had a lot tonight. It will be my turn soon. Ask your odd question."

"Do you believe in Elts?"

Julia squinted her eyes and pursed her lips at Ulric. "Believe?"

"Do they exist, silly?"

"Elts? Oh, Eltarans! The Children of Eltaruo, the God of Magic? Of course, they exist," Julia said in a tone that could have been discussing the likelihood of tomorrow's sunrise.

"Have you ever seen any? I haven't!" Ulric asked in increasing exasperation. "But some people in this city act like they expect to run into one around every corner. So, have you ever seen one?"

"Yes. I... think."

Ulric lowered his head and stared at Julia from under his brow. "You think?"

"There was a delegation of Eltarans in the city for General Macula's triumph. Yes, I distinctly remember they marched in his triumphal parade."

"My history's a bit foggy, but wasn't Macula's victory over the Harathi nearly a decade ago?"

"That sounds right."

"So you were, how old?"

Julia stared at Ulric in mock anger. "Fine. I was five. I had to sit on my father's shoulders to watch the parade, but I know what I saw."

"Any recent sightings?" Ulric pressed.

"No, but everyone in Trumric knows an Eltaran delegation visits the Senate every spring. Ambassadors from the last Eltaran kingdoms."

Ulric crossed his arms. "I'll just pop over to the senate-house, then." He let out a sigh. "Everyone's so certain about Eltarans, but nobody can produce one."

Julia stuck out her tongue. "You'll just have to trust me. Now I have a question."

"Fair enough."

"You weren't born in the city, were you? I think I hear a slight provincial tone. Noldani?"

"Damn, I've been trying to get rid of my accent."

"And what tearstained tragedy of love and betrayal drove you to Trumric?" Julia asked in a playful tone.

Ulric sat on a crate. "Oh, it's a common enough tale. My father had retired from the IX Legion and was granted land in northern Angrus. He married a local girl, my mother, and together they made poor farmers. Debts mounted, the land was sold, and we moved into the great city of Anric. My family opened a metalwork: blacksmithing, tools, hinges, locks, that sort of thing. Not a year later, when I was fifteen, a pox swept through the city and took my mother. My father took to drinking and drunken brawling, which eventually took his life. His debts took the shop, so I had next to nothing. I was on the streets. I took what little I had left and sailed to the capital. You know the rest." Ulric always had several lies at the ready.

Julia sat next to Ulric and put her arm around his shoulder. "It may be a common story, but it still sounds horrible."

He felt suddenly ill. He felt like the damned liar he was. "Julia, what I told you—"

Julia looked away. "I wonder what's worse? To lose parents through death?" And for the first time, Ulric heard her voice turn hard and bitter. "Or losing family because they have cast you out? 'Swift and ignoble exile'? Wasn't that a line in your monologue this morning? And there was another line." Julia turned back to Ulric, and tears filled her eyes. "'But if the sin is with my judges?' If the sin is with my judges, what then, Ulric?"

He opened his mouth to answer, but she cut him off. "Enough questions for tonight. I'm tired." She hurriedly wiped her eyes. "You can sleep over there." The hint of a wicked smile crept across her face. "Close, but not too close. Make a pallet out of a pile of old costumes. So much more comfortable than an alley. Goodnight."

"Goodnight, Julia"

He began gathering blankets and cloaks to create a makeshift pallet, setting questions about Julia's family aside for another time.

Once they were both settled in, Julia blew out the lamp, plunging the loft into darkness. He tried to put her out of his mind, but despite his best efforts, all he could think about was her arresting eyes, teasing lips, and delightful laughter. He smiled in the dark, remembering the funny faces and silly comments she made about the costumes and props. All except the robe!

The robe was made of expertly woven thick cotton. It was no cheap costume but an actual temple robe. It had to be hers. He must have upset her when he treated it as just another prop. How did an acolyte of Myrill come to be living in a theater loft?

"Julia?"

"Yes?"

"Is it true a priest on pilgrimage can demand aid from any citizen? Do they honor that in Trumric, like they do in the provinces?"

"More odd questions? If by aid you mean food, water, and sometimes a place to sleep, then yes. Of course, it's honored in the capital. Now I'm very sleepy, and I have to be at the clothier's by dawn. Goodnight."

"Thank you, Julia, goodnight."

Soon, Ulric would have to hand over the golden sphinx to Luciano. Between retrieving his kit and visiting Silo's shop, he had the tools he needed for the job. What he lacked was information. What he needed was a good look inside the home of Marius

Secundus. And with Julia's unwitting help, they would invite him inside.

Bitter Herbs

Julia tottered at the entrance to Fimbria's Dyers and Clothiers, unsure of what she had just heard. The foreman repeated himself, this time loud enough for everyone to hear.

"I said, dismissed! Go home, girl! You're no longer needed!"

The words struck her like a lash, stunning her on the spot. She stood in the entryway, speechless; the heat rising in her chest and face, reddening her cheeks as the other workers gawked. She stared at the foreman, a lean towheaded Kreslan, for far too long as embarrassment gave way to anger. She imagined charging forward, questions and accusations flying, driving him back until he tripped into the vat of yellow dye behind him. Then the rest of him might match his absurd hair! But Myrill is merciful, and the foreman had always been fair, so when she finally spoke, her words were as meek as they were expected.

"Why? What have I done?"

The foreman cited her tardiness of the previous morning, but there was a tinge of shame in his voice, an evasiveness in his eyes.

Julia had her answer.

Without another word, she turned and stepped onto Dyer's Street and began the journey back to the theater loft with steady, measured steps that grew quicker and more erratic with each footfall. She lurched to a halt, took a deep breath, and turned to face the dawn.

"O Myrill's mercy renewed each dawning light; I seek to be merciful, kind, and spirit bright," she whispered, repeating the prayer several times until she let out a long, slow breath, expelling the last of her rage.

Oblivious to the morning traffic, she walked on, dabbing at the sudden tears blurring her vision with the edge of her green palla.

Anger? Now, tears? Equally useless, she thought as she finished drying her eyes. *Why are Titus and his Gutter-Fish—such a stupid name!—trying to ruin me? My life is already ruined. I saw to that without the aid of any lowborn plebs. Now all I have left is helping, healing others, and they're trying to take that. Who would want to drive a healer from the Transnanpela District? There's precious few of us south of the river, and the Temple of Myrill can only tend to so many. It makes no sense. I only know crying about it or throwing a fit won't help.*

Julia turned onto Old Fluvius Road and followed the course of the great river until she reached the Polyminius Theater, where she found the main gate open and the building swarming with tradesmen and scribes. They appeared to be inspecting and measuring everything: the orchestra, the seating, the stage, every column, niche, and statue. Leufroy was nowhere in sight, so she headed straight to the theater house and the loft, grateful to avoid another undignified climb up the stone pine. Most of the workers ignored her, others gave a polite morning greeting, but one gangly and ugly stonemason made an offer based on two assumptions: she was an actress, and all actresses were whores. Julia had learned to deal with such men and had no mercy for them.

"Find me a man, and I might!" she shouted as she walked past.

Behind her, as she ascended the stage, everyone burst into raucous laughter and jeering. *If I'm to be no more than a lowborn actress now, I'll play the part*, she thought. Spinning around at the top of the steps, she gave the now red-faced stonemason a rude gesture. He mumbled an ineffectual insult and dismissively waved her away with one oddly crooked arm.

Broken, she guessed. *Years ago. Ill tended and the bone poorly set. Particularly unfortunate for a stonemason, I'd think.*

Was that it? Had she unknowingly botched a job? Harmed when she should have healed? Had someone she failed hired the Gutter-Fish?

Julia tried to remember all the people she had helped since arriving south of the Nanpela River. She had provided poultices and medicines for a variety of minor ailments from the river to the southern ruins, from the theater to the last eastern bridge. She had tended accidental scrapes, cuts, sprains, and even the fractured leg of an unfortunate drover. His leg had set well. He had been so pleased he had sent his wife bearing food, salt, and a handful of denarii. And, thanks to her friends Ide and Murena, she had tended to Titus and his thugs, usually after a brawl with the gangs from the harbor.

No, she concluded as she climbed the steep stairs to the theater loft. *There's no one. So who, then? Someone's paying the Gutter-Fish. Who have I offended?*

Exasperated, Julia charged into the loft with an audible cry.

"That sort of day, is it?" Ulric called from across the loft. "And to think, the first hour is barely over."

Julia started at the sound of his voice, having expected to find the loft empty. She had assumed Ulric would be out in the city doing… Ulric things, whatever they were. Instead, he knelt on the floor, hurriedly rolling up the dark bundle he had brought with him the night before. It seemed to contain his only possessions, and she wondered what secrets he hid within the black cloth. Perhaps she'd take a peek if she got the chance. He tied off the ends of the bundle, looked up through a curtain of night-black hair, and smiled. Oh, she'd have to be careful of that smile, she warned herself. After all, what did she really know about him?

Ulric stood, pushing his hair out of his eyes. "Aren't you supposed to be at a clothier or something?"

Julia went rigid, hardening to mute stone. She didn't want to discuss her dismissal, but she had to say something. *What should I say? That I'm nothing but trouble? That it feels like the entire city has turned against me?* When she finally spoke, her words and lies shattered the awkward silence in a breathless explosion. "Oh, I was: Fimbria's Dyers and Clothiers. But they sent me home. Not just me; some of the other girls, too! It's just that business has been so slow lately, but I'm sure things will pick up." *Myrill, forgive me!* "If I seemed upset coming up the stairs just now, it's because of all those tradesmen infesting the theater. One made a rather vulgar remark. A stonemason, I think. Very ugly. Very rude."

Ulric's smile vanished, tossed aside like one of the theater masks lying about the loft. "Shall I sort the bastard out?" His tone was as hard as ice and sharp as a razor, the same tone that had frightened her the previous day. He marched for the stairs.

"No need." She threw up her hands to stop him. "I, uh, *sorted* him already."

"Really?"

"Oh, yes. I left him red-faced and speechless."

"Ha! Arrius always said, 'An unkind word from a beautiful woman cuts deeper than any blade.'"

"Who?"

"Arrius?" Ulric looked surprised at the question. "An old tutor from Anric."

"Oh." She looked back toward the stairs, where the sound of workmen echoed from below. "Sorted or not, I think I'd rather be anywhere than here today. Walk with me! We can pass the time in the River Market."

"The River Market?"

Did she hear hesitation? A faint note of trepidation? "Problem?"

"No, of course not. It's just… I don't swim."

He looked serious, but she laughed anyway. "Now you're being silly."

"No, I'm not," Ulric protested. "It makes perfect sense: *river*… market. Very dangerous. But I'd wager you're worth the risk." He flashed another captivating smile and ran at the back of the loft, leaping and running several paces up the wall before springing for the rafters. He hung swinging from a beam by one well-muscled arm, grinning.

"Myrill, have mercy! What are you doing?"

Ulric extended his free hand. "That black bundle there. Toss it up."

Julia picked up the bundle. It was surprisingly heavy, and she again wondered what secret treasures it concealed. She threw it, and Ulric swiftly hid his secrets in the shadows of the rafters.

"There! In case there are any thieves among the laborers. Anything you want to stash up here? Any valuables?"

Julia's hand wandered toward her breast, reflexively moving to protect her own secret treasure hanging concealed beneath her tunic. She snatched her hand away. "No, nothing. I'm just a poor actress."

They strolled along the river docks, meandering through the morning crowds from street stall to taberna, from busy shop to pier. Ulric began the walk by asking Julia about her past and her family: two subjects she tried to never think about. So she deflected his questions and, instead, tried to learn more about him. Who is he, really? The unfortunate son of a failed metalworker from Anric? The overly eager, aspiring actor she had met yesterday? No, there was something else; something hidden, something dangerous.

After a short time, it was clear Ulric was no more willing to discuss his past than Julia was hers. He had a way of leading the conversation into loops and knots, never really revealing anything. She gave up, and their conversation drifted to the one topic of mutual interest: theater gossip. She shared tales of Piso's young protégés, Cordus and Ebbo, and all the mischief they fell into; of Leufroy and his never-ending struggles with patrons and creditors; and of Severa's scandalous affairs and Piso's rages.

"Praise the goddess Nyssa, to whom all theaters are dedicated! And most of all, praise her dark sister, Neesis Insania! This theater sounds like a mad place!" Ulric leaped upon a pier post and hopped—no, not hopped, practically danced—from atop one wooden post to another. "I think I'm going to love it."

"Careful!" Julia ran along the pier, pushing her way through the crowd, desperate to keep pace. "What if you fall? You can't swim, remember?"

He stopped and stood on one leg, throwing his hands wide and wobbling back and forth in a pantomime of falling. "Oh no, I forgot! If I fell, would you try to save me?"

She looked into the swiftly moving waters of the Nanpela: she hated boats and had never learned to swim. "Yes. Then we'd both drown because I can't swim either."

"Then we best get off this pier." He tumbled forward and somehow flipped onto the pier, nearly knocking over a passerby. He apologized profusely to the man, then hurried her off the docks. "Come on! I suddenly feel like we can afford a late breakfast."

He took her straight to a nearby popina, a street side bar selling wine and cheap food, and bought them both a cool drink and a bit of bread and dried fruit to share.

Julia sat down on a bench, popped a sweet slice of dried apple into her mouth, and snuck a glance at Ulric. She caught him staring at her, and he awkwardly looked away, then turned back and smiled. She returned his smile and repressed a giggle. Was he trying to impress her with all the acrobatics and now the meal? Of course, he was. And it felt wonderful; she had to admit. Men had rarely tried to impress her in the past: that privilege was reserved for her older sister, Julia Major. As the eldest daughter, she was destined to marry whomever their father chose, his only concern being the size of the dowry and who would best strengthen his political influence. Still, interested families saw an advantage in gaining the bride's favor, so a parade of some of the most prominent young men in the city had done their best to woo her sister.

Julia's destiny had followed another path, having been promised to the Temple of Myrill since before her birth. There had been no advantage in gaining her favor. So, what did Ulric hope to gain? Was it as simple as what her friend Ide had said? Did he want what all men wanted? And what if she wanted it too? What use was propriety to a woman bereft of family and cast out to live homeless among lowborn plebs? Now she was nothing more than an actress, which came with a certain reputation. Actresses were wild and free-spirited; thought of as little better than prostitutes. They could do as they wanted. Take whoever they wanted.

And they would not obey! It shamed Julia to think she had considered abandoning the sick and injured because of a few idle threats from the likes of Titus. She would follow her heart and do as she willed, and that meant doing Myrill's will, whether or not she was at the temple.

And what of the handsome stranger sitting next to her? She hadn't seen the true Ulric yet; of that, she was certain. There was menace and violence hidden in the way he moved. She had seen and heard a glimpse of it when his pale blue eyes turned to ice, and his tone sharpened to a cutting edge. There was a hint in his lies, for no failing metalworker could afford a tutor for his children, and a warning in his praise, for Neesis was a goddess of the Underworld, seductive but treacherous. He hid part of himself from her, something dangerous, maybe even something wicked. She could only see Ulric's shadow, its dark contours shaped to his will. And like the shadows on the wall of the philosopher's cave, it was an illusion distorting the truth.

Ide had suggested she use Ulric as a bodyguard, a shield against men like Titus. Pit one dangerous man against another? Would that be wrong? This wasn't a day at the arena where her family watched professional gladiators fight and condemned men die.

Yet, the very day after Ide suggested it, Ulric showed up at the theater. That's too great a coincidence. It must be Myrill's will! Or... Neesis? Then which aspect of the goddess: fortune, lust, or madness? I feel like my life's become twisted up with all three!

What to do? Julia, the actress, wouldn't hesitate.

"Ulric!" she called, nearly leaping off the bench. "I just remembered an errand we must do today."

The day warmed up fast as Alakur's light burnt off the early morning clouds. Julia led Ulric out of the heat of the market and into the welcoming shade between two towering insulae. The first floor of each tenement building was dedicated to commerce, and several busy shops lined the narrow street. The space, while cool, was cramped and filthy, still littered and stinking with the remains of the previous night's refuse. As they walked down the street, they carefully picked their route while keeping one watchful eye on the balconies and windows above.

Julia stopped in front of a counter filled with fresh vegetables and herbs, where a flustered young boy rushed to fill a matron's order. Once he handed over a small bag of lentils, the impatient woman hurried off in a huff while the boy glared and silently mouthed a string of vulgar insults. His rage exhausted, he finally noticed his other customers.

"Julia!" He nearly jumped out of his skin with surprise and embarrassment. "Don't tell my father! If I'm caught being rude again, he'll beat me for sure. Please!"

The boy made himself look so pitiful she laughed. "Don't worry; your secret is safe with us. Not a word." She looked at Ulric. "Right?"

"That's right. I'm no snitch or squeaker."

"Is Gracchus here today?"

"Yes. Father and mother are both in the back. And your herbs are ready!"

Julia stepped through a curtained doorway near the counter and entered the rear of the shop. The room was small, dark, and cool and smelled of old wood and the sharp, earthy fragrances of vegetables and rare herbs. Two tall shelves ran down the center of the shop, leading toward a counter at the back where Gracchus and his wife, Corda, worked.

As Julia approached, Corda smiled and offered a greeting, but Gracchus stiffened and frowned. He said nothing.

Something was wrong. Gracchus had always been excessively friendly, even to the point of playfully flirting with her in front of his wife. She looked back at Ulric, perusing the middle shelves, and he returned a quizzical look as if to ask, 'what now?'.

Before she took another step, Gracchus said, "Forgive me, but your order isn't ready. The fennel and yarrow root, uh, went bad. And my supplier of sunblossom didn't turn up. No telling when I'll get any again. Best try again after the Ides… maybe the Kalends."

"But Cassius said my order was ready."

"That scatter-brain?" Gracchus laughed, nervously glancing toward the curtained threshold as his wife looked on with increasing confusion. "My son doesn't know his head from a hole in the ground."

He was lying. It was obvious. Titus and his Gutter-Fish were behind it, no doubt. The Julia of the past, Julia Minor, the dutiful daughter, would have accepted defeat and meekly walked away. But not Persius Julia, the wild actress!

"Shame upon you, Gracchus! Your lies and your cowardice are an affront to Alakur and Cathus. Titus told you not to sell to me. Admit it!"

Gracchus said nothing. He only stared nervously at the entryway, struck dumb with guilt.

His wife, Corda, spoke up. "Husband? Why not just—"

"Quiet, woman." Shaken from his stupor, he shoved his guilt aside for feigned indignation. "You insult me in my own shop? How dare you! Get out!"

Ulric peered around the corner of a shelf and asked, "Are you trying to run a scheme, Gracchus? You're not very good at it, you know?"

"Yes! No more scheming. Hand over my herbs or return my money."

"Fine, girl! I will. Another day. But now, you need to leave. It's not safe—" Gracchus became suddenly silent and jerked back from the counter, his mouth slack and his eyes widening with fear. He frantically waved his wife toward the back door, hissing under his breath, "Away with you, woman. Quick!" Corda retreated through the door and was gone.

Julia turned. A dark silhouette blocked the threshold, one hand holding aside the curtain while the other toyed with a dagger.

Behind her, Gracchus shouted, "I'd not sold her anything!" He continued in a broken and stammering voice. "Just like you said. Tell Evander that. Tell him I did as told. Tell him, Titus!"

Titus ignored him and leaned on the threshold with a mocking casualness. An ugly smile scarred his face as he addressed Julia. "What did I say about 'next time', Julia?"

Julia tried to reply, but her words jammed in her throat as a numbing wave of fear washed over her body, drowning her earlier resolve.

Titus swaggered into the shop, another Gutter-Fish close behind. He held his dagger before him, twisting the blade to catch the dim light. "Blood, right? Something about blood?"

"Not in the shop!" Gracchus protested. "Anywhere but here!"

"Shut your fucking mouth," Titus growled while locking eyes with Julia. He stalked forward, leaving the other Gutter-Fish near the entrance. "What did I say?" he asked in a low, rumbling voice.

Julia stepped back and felt the hard counter against her back. Titus' cruel smile returned as he slid the flat of his blade across her cheek. She recoiled from the cool metal, bending farther against the counter.

"I want to hear it from your filthy whore mouth."

Where was Ulric? She glanced past Titus and saw only his friend, now eagerly brandishing a large knife of his own. *Gone? I should have known; for all his bravado, he's nothing but a coward!*

"I—"

"Say it!"

Julia shrunk from his hate-filled scream, flinching as spittle struck her face. *If I'm to remain alone, so be it. Mother Myrill protects me.*

Let the Underworld take Titus and his damned thugs! She straightened and met Titus' gaze with her own defiant stare.

"You said there would be blood if"—she paused to glower at Titus—"you caught me healing anyone. Surely, someone as dull as you can see I'm only shopping!"

Titus was momentarily taken aback. He even appeared embarrassed for a moment, as if Julia had caught him breaking his word.

"Word games, bitch!" said the other thug.

"Right. Just word games," repeated Titus with renewed confidence. He grabbed her arm and jerked her toward him. "Let's go play a different game. Play it as good as your friend Murena, and if Neesis Fortuna smiles upon you…" He slid the point of his dagger down her neck and over the swell of her breasts. "I'll let you go with another warning. Just a little cut on your whore face."

A cold nausea seized her, and the room seemed to pitch and sway as if it was only a tiny raft on a storm wracked sea. Could Myrill let such a thing happen? But she knew it happened, and far too often in the rougher districts of the city. Why had she thought she was different? Had she thought herself better than those other unfortunate women? Was this to be Myrill's punishment for her hubris?

She summoned her remaining courage. "Don't you dare. The gods would curse you!"

The other Gutter-Fish leered hungrily at Julia. "I know just the place, Titus. Not far from—"

A sudden crash silenced the thug. Titus spun about, painfully twisting Julia's arm but clearing her view of the room. The man fell at Ulric's feet in a shower of broken pottery and a cloud of finely crumbled yellow-green leaves that filled the shop with an earthy, woodsy scent.

Gracchus groaned, seemingly more concerned for his herbs than either Julia or the Gutter-Fish.

Ulric kicked the thug's fallen knife and sent it spinning across the floor to disappear under a far shelf. "Sorry I didn't do that sooner, Julia, but I had to find the right herb to overpower the stench of these Gutter-Filth."

Titus peered at Ulric with cruel, narrow eyes—eyes that widened with recognition and hate. "You! Sweet Neesis' Shadow! The thief from Weaver's Square? I want my silver chain back. And I want blood!"

"You?" Ulric repeated in a ridiculously mocking tone. "Thank you! I've always wanted to be greeted with a surprised shout of 'You'! It's a sure sign of success." Then he flashed what Julia thought was a most charming smile.

Titus screamed in frustration and yanked Julia to his chest, one steel grip crushing her arm against her bosom and the other pointing his dagger toward her throat. "More word games? You're just like this stupid bitch! Maybe I should shut up the both of you for good? I'll start with her." He raised the dagger and pressed the point against her neck.

She froze at the touch of the sharp steel against her throat, her eyes locked on the dagger. "Ulric...."

Ulric threw out his hands in surrender. "Easy! Easy, Titus. If it's silver and blood you want, they're right here." He thumped his chest. "Let Julia walk away, and I'll go with you wherever you like."

Titus tightened his grip. "Not a chance."

Ulric said nothing. Julia watched with growing hopelessness as, one after the other, expressions of searching, desperation, and panic played across his face.

Titus stepped forward, dragging Julia with him. "Out of my way… Ulric. Now I know your name," he added with a look that promised he'd find him again. "Praise Neesis."

Ulric backed up but still blocked the path to the street.

The thug on the floor stirred.

Titus took another step. "Stand aside. And don't follow me. These streets belong to the Gutter-Fish."

Julia felt a rising panic. Could Ulric do nothing? Would no one help her? Could she escape on her own before Titus—No! She couldn't think of it. *Mother Myrill! Gods! Protect me!*

"Wait! Wait!" Ulric sounded desperate, but he stopped backing up. "Not a chance, you said, right, Titus?" A thin, knowing smile crept across his face.

"That's right. Now, out of my way."

Ulric took a step forward and pressed a sandaled foot onto the neck of the prostrate thug. "Leaving now would be a dangerously impious act for a follower of Neesis Fortuna. Wouldn't you agree?"

Titus stopped and pressed the edge of his dagger against Julia's neck. "What are you talking about? More word games?"

"No. A game of chance." Ulric reached into the small pouch on his belt and produced a denarius. He held up the bronze coin, flipping it from one side stamped with the helmeted head of Cathus, the God of War, to the other side displaying triumphal chariots. "Such games are sacred to the Goddess, as I'm sure you know. Let's decide our fates on the flip of a coin."

Titus' posture shifted nervously against Julia's body. The absurd idea tempted him. She could feel it! Hope blossomed in her heart once more. The gods *were* merciful.

"I'd have to be a fool," he said. "Mad, to risk such a thing."

"And Neesis adores madness. Do you fear Her judgment?" Ulric accused more than asked the question.

"No. I—"

"Do you fear I have Her favor? Because you should. You're unworthy of the goddess!"

"Shut up."

"You're unworthy of Her divine luck! You pervert the lust She inspires! Her divine madness is to be embraced!"

"I said, shut up!"

"And we both know Her secret aspect, Her dark shadow that hides all thieves. How could you have Her favor when it is I who has stolen from you?"

"You bastard! I'm Titus! Leader of the Gutter-Fish and a soldier of the Transnanpela Collegium. Neesis Fortuna has always smiled upon me. Who in the Nine Hells do you think you are?"

"Me? I'm just a humble actor playing the role of a thief, so you have nothing to fear. Now, under the auspices of Neesis

Fortuna, I make this bet: I'll flip the coin three times, and if it doesn't land chariots up each time, I'll stand aside. But if I win, both Julia and I walk out of here, and you won't harass her again."

Titus considered. "No. The stakes aren't balanced. If I win, I take Julia, and you surrender to the Gutter-Fish."

Ulric was silent for a long moment. "Agreed."

"And," Titus quickly added, "I want chariots; you take helmets."

"But I already called chariots."

"And I don't want helmets!"

"But… a coin toss is sacred," Ulric protested. "There's a procedure."

Julia couldn't believe such a ridiculous method would decide her fate. The whole thing was absurd! And now they were arguing like children.

"Toss the infernal coin!" she cried.

Both Ulric and Titus were stunned into silence.

"Fine! I call helmets. And now for the first toss."

Both men mumbled a quick prayer to Neesis, then Ulric made a flourish with the coin and tossed it into the air. He caught it, flipped it onto the back of his hand, held his fist toward Titus, then revealed the coin.

The War God's stern features gazed out from beneath his helmet.

Titus cursed. "Your luck won't hold."

Ulric merely smiled. "Let's find out."

He retrieved the coin and repeated the toss. The denarius flew high and wide, and Ulric had to stretch to catch it.

Again, it landed helmet side up.

"Yes!" Ulric cried. "Neesis loves me."

"No! Wait! Is this some horseshit trick? Show me the coin again."

"No tricks." He held up the coin, showing Titus one side, then the other. Helmets and chariots flashed in the dim light. "And now we'll see who has the Goddess' favor." He prepared to make the final toss.

Julia felt the sudden cold, sharp sting of the dagger's point. She released a high-pitched yelp, more from surprise than pain. Merciful Myrill! Had Titus decided to kill her, anyway? "Wait, wait, wait!"

Ulric froze, the coin still held in his fist.

Titus said, "I'll make the final toss." Julia knew from his cold voice and dead stare that there would be no argument.

"If you try that," Ulric replied, "your grip could loosen. Maybe Julia escapes on her own. Our bet doesn't cover that. Then, as they say, all bets would be off."

"I'll take my chances. Give it here." Titus held out the palm of his free hand as best he could while maintaining pressure on Julia.

The thug under Ulric's foot stirred again. He tried to rise, but Ulric stamped his foot down, driving his face into the floorboards with a smack. "Stay down. Don't move. A coin toss is sacred." He stepped forward and reluctantly dropped the coin in Titus' open palm.

Titus held the coin between his thumb and forefinger and checked each side. Helmets and chariots, as expected. He made a loose fist and deftly slid the coin over his thumb, ready to flip it into the air. "It's going to the floor."

Ulric, uncharacteristically quiet, merely nodded.

Titus flipped the denarius into the air, and every pair of eyes followed the fateful coin. It hit the wooden floor with a crack that seemed like thunder and bounced back into the air, ringing like Ukorus' anvil. It hit the floor again, spinning wildly. Everyone edged forward, waiting in terrible anticipation for the coin to fall.

With a final, resounding thud, the coin fell helmet side up.

Ulric looked to the heavens and shouted, "Sweet Neesis!" while Titus simply stared at the coin. Julia released a heavy sigh and tried to drag herself away from her captor.

"Take the bitch!" he screamed.

Titus pushed Julia away with such force she crashed into a shelf and would have fallen to the floor if not for Ulric. She collapsed into his arms, a great relief and strange joy overtaking her. He pulled her tight, and she relished the warmth and strength of his embrace. She was safe.

"I won't harass the girl again," Titus said, his eyes down and locked on the unfortunate coin.

Julia felt a warm wetness trickling down her neck like a bead of sweat.

"Others will. I can't stop that," he added in a flat, defeated monotone.

Julia pressed her body against Ulric's and wiped the sweat away.

"You can walk out of here, but… when I see you on the street, Ulric…" He finally looked up and stared daggers into his eyes.

Julia looked down at her fingers. They were smeared red.

"We know," she said. "Blood."

Julia watched Ulric weave through the thickening crowds, never slowing, never stumbling, not even jostling another passerby. He dragged her along in his wake, but it was all she could do to keep pace and stay on her feet! *I'm getting hot, tired, and pummeled by a rude mob*, she thought. *Surely, we've run far enough?*

"Ulric, stop!"

He skidded to a halt and jogged a few paces back to her side. "What? Signs of pursuit?"

Julia vigorously fanned her heat-flushed face with the loose fabric of her palla. "No. Signs of exhaustion. Surely, we're far enough from Gracchus' shop by now?" She smiled that certain way and looked up at Ulric from beneath dark lashes, a technique long perfected with an impressive record of success. "Can't we simply *walk* back to the theater?" she said, with extra emphasis on 'walk'.

Ulric glanced at the surrounding crowd. "You're right." He held out his hand and asked in a sonorous voice fit for the stage.

"I was going to summon a litter to convey you back to the theater, my lady, but as I'm broke, will you walk by my side instead?"

Julia stared at his hand and hesitated. Why? Did she think him presumptuous? No. That wasn't fair at all, not after the way she had flirted. So, why did part of her try to push him away? She liked him. She wanted him. Why play games now? He had even saved her life.

But that was it; her guilt made her hesitate. She had lied. She had manipulated. She had originally dismissed Ide's advice because she thought it dishonest. Immoral. Then when fate brought her and Ulric together, she took Ide's advice anyway and told herself men were a shield and Ulric's arrival was the gods' will.

No! Hesitation. Guilt. All things for Julia Minor, not Julia the wild actress!

She grabbed his hand. "I'd be delighted." Then she hooked her arm in his and led him through the crowd at a leisurely pace. "This is much nicer. Now we can talk. And I have to ask: how do you know Titus?"

"I had a run-in with the idiot yesterday. I caught him and his gang bullying orphaned children. Such a fierce bunch," Ulric added sarcastically.

"Yes. Simple-minded but fierce."

"Hmm? Oh, no. I meant the orphans."

Julia stared at Ulric and couldn't tell if he was joking. Ide had warned her not to underestimate street urchins and strays, after all.

"And how long have you known Titus?" he asked.

"What?"

"He said he had warned you before," Ulric said.

"That's part of what makes this all so maddening! I'd met Titus months ago through two of my friends, Ide and Murena. Back then, he never said an unkind word. If he spoke to me at all, he was either crudely flirting or asking for help. I even set his wrist after a nasty brawl. Then suddenly, it's been nothing but threats."

"Someone's hired the Gutter-Fish."

"That's what I thought too. Obvious, I suppose. Still, I should thank you."

"Oh, you're welcome." Then, after a moment of silence, Ulric asked, "What for, exactly?"

"For dealing with those two idiots, of course."

"You're welcome. And thank Neesis Fortuna! I knew you'd be safe because the goddess loves me."

Julia pursed her lips. "Careful, Ulric. That sounds like what my tutors would have called hubris. But, yes, praise Neesis. To think our fates depended on a coin toss! Three helmets in a row!"

Ulric pulled Julia close and nuzzled her ear, sending shivers down her spine. He asked in a conspiratorial whisper, "Would you like me to tell you a secret?"

She leaned into him and replied, "I love secrets."

"I cheated."

"What?"

"Now, Neesis does adore me, but She is a fickle lover." He stepped back and suddenly held between his thumb and forefinger a familiar-looking denarius imprinted with the helmeted head of

Cathus, the God of War. He flipped the coin around to reveal an identical image on the opposite side.

Julia gasped. "But you said a coin toss was sacred to Neesis."

"Not more than your virtue."

Julia considered that an excellent point, but then she remembered something that made no sense. "Wait. You first called chariots. How did you know Titus would call helmets?"

"When you're running a coin toss scheme, you can never really know what your mark will call. Best to be prepared." Suddenly, the coin in his hand displayed a parade of triumphal chariots—on both sides.

Julia's eyes went wide. Was this a clue to Ulric's past? "Is this a sort of magic? Are you a fabricator?"

He laughed. "Sorry to disappoint you, but it's not magic. It is a sort of fabrication, though." He extended his hand toward her, the chariot coin held between his thumb and forefinger, then he uncurled his fingers to reveal the helmet coin couched deep within his palm alongside an ordinary denarius. "Centuries-old tricks perfected before Eltarus took pity on men and gave our ancestors magic." He then showed her how he could effortlessly switch the coins, slipping them between and around his fingers lightning quick while her sight was distracted or momentarily blocked by his other hand. Even after his demonstration, she still couldn't follow the coins, no matter how hard she tried.

"But Titus made the last coin toss himself. How did you manage that?"

"The final toss was pure luck. Praise Neesis!" Ulric looked to the heavens and smiled, then tucked his coins away.

When Julia and Ulric stood under the broad stone pine at the back of the Polyminius Theater, Ulric asked, "What I told you earlier, about the 'sort of fabrication'; that's part of the Shadow Ways. Normally, sharing that with an outsider would get me killed if I was still an… insider. But I'm not. Not anymore. I guess none of this is making any sense. What I'm trying to say is I've shared a secret, so… why are Gutter-Fish thugs trying to stop you from helping people?"

"I don't know!" she said, nearly shouting as she struggled to contain her frustration.

"No idea? Really?"

The hint of skepticism in his voice set her frustration-free.

"Yes! Really! Why would these imbecilic, lowborn thugs not want their neighbors healed? Who rejects the wisdom and ministration of a healer?"

Ulric stepped back and held up his hands in surrender. "You're right. It makes no sense."

"Thank you! It doesn't."

"Did you offend someone powerful? A patrician family, perhaps?"

"I don't see how."

"It would make the most sense. The pampered, privileged rich think nothing of stepping on *lowborn* plebs like us. A cowardly patrician hiring a gang like the Gutter-Fish to do their knife work is typical. We're little better than slaves to people like them, right?"

"Yes… of course." *Fine, maybe I shouldn't have said 'lowborn' in front of him. How much has he guessed about my past?* "Still, I don't recall offending anyone."

"Yet someone's offended. So that leaves three possibilities: either you offended without knowing, offended but forgot, or we're missing something entirely."

Julia deflated and exhaled a great puff of air, sending a flurry of dark curls flying. "I don't see how that helps at all!"

Preparation and Prayers

Ulric crossed the river and wandered through the Three Hills District until he found the home of Quintus Marius Secundus. The residence was like the home of many other wealthy patricians: an expansive rectangular building of stone, brick, wood, and clay-tiled roofs. Its narrow side faced the street, where a brief set of steps led up to two impressively ornate and heavy-looking doors.

The front doors are no way in for a thief, he thought. *There's always some unfortunate slave charged with sleeping across the threshold.*

He retreated across the street, taking refuge from any prying eyes in the narrow path between two similar homes, flattening himself in a sliver of noonday shade as he considered what lay beyond the front doors. They would no doubt open to an entrance hall, which would lead to a larger central hall: the atrium. The atrium would have an open roof directly over a small pool used to collect rainwater.

I could climb over the roof and drop into the atrium. No, too near the bedrooms, and with my recent luck, I'd end up face-first in the pool.

Leading off the atrium, there would be bedrooms, a dining room, and, most importantly, an office or study called a tablinum.

If Secundus is like every other self-important patrician, he'll use the tablinum to show off his wealth to guests and business partners. I bet I'll find the sphinx there.

One or more short halls would lead from the atrium to the peristylium: a decorative garden with an open roof surrounded by a columned passage. Bathrooms, a kitchen, the summer dining room, and the tablinum could all be accessed from the garden. Next to the kitchen, there would be a small entrance, most often used by slaves and tradesmen. Behind the peristylium, there may be a large walled vegetable and herb garden, a luxury for the wealthy. The best way inside could be through the open roof of the peristylium.

So, I know the layout of the typical patrician home. Damn lot of good that will do me if this Marius Secundus isn't typical. What about this job is typical? Nothing, that's what. I need to get inside and see for myself.

Ulric squinted against the midday sun, peering down the narrow side street running along the length of the building. His eyes focused on the slave's entrance, a narrow but stout-looking wooden door. It was past the sixth hour, and the last of Secundus' clients and petitioners had left. A short time later, a tall man with a head of thin, receding blonde hair emerged. He was dressed in an immaculately white toga and followed by a small entourage of slaves in colorful tunics.

Even his slaves are well-dressed! Secundus must do very well for himself. Maybe I'll pick up a few extra trinkets tonight.

Ulric pulled the hood of Julia's temple robe over his head and hurried across the road. The front doors were no way in for a thief, but they would be perfect for a young follower of the goddess Myrill.

Not long after he and Julia returned to the loft, she had descended into the theater to speak with Leufroy, whose commands and decrees were echoing around the auditorium and likely irritating the workmen. It was the perfect opportunity to grab Julia's robe from beneath the pile of costumes that made her makeshift bed and slip out of the loft.

Midway across the street, Ulric felt his stomach churn and his chest bound in thick, tightening ropes, making breathing difficult. It was a terrible, unfamiliar feeling. It felt like—guilt.

To hell with that! he thought. *I'm only borrowing the robe. I'd have asked, and she'd have said yes, but it would have taken too long to explain. No, this is what they call… stage fright? Yes, that's it. Stop worrying! This should be a simple role for the Polyminius Theater's newest member.*

When he reached the doors, he paused, took a deep breath, adjusted his posture, and put on an unassuming face. He knocked loudly.

One of the heavy doors swung open, revealing a towering brute in a simple white tunic. His strong build and bored expression marked him as the archetypal guard. Before Ulric could utter a word, the slave spoke in Kreslan-accented Trumin.

"My master Marius Secundus is done doing business today." The bored expression did not change in the slightest.

Ulric added a blend of apology to his humble character. "I am Calidius Lurco from the town of Aqua Fusca. I am an acolyte of the goddess Myrill come to Trumric on a pilgrimage to Her grand temple." Ulric looked to the slave for some reaction and concluded he may have been a species of statue. "I'm afraid I am a little lost. I humbly request some water, a modest bit of food, and, if possible, directions."

"The mistress of the house has given me a club"—the slave reached behind the door and produced an effective-looking cudgel—"and commanded me to beat any beggars."

"Would you deny the priesthood its ancient rights?" Ulric stood tall and gave the slave an accusatory stare. "Is your master aware of how you dishonor him?"

Talk of rights and his master's honor left the slave looking confused and fearful. "Uh, you are a priest?"

"I am a humble acolyte of Mother Myrill," Ulric said, straightening to his full height and raising his voice. "May She have mercy on idiots everywhere! If you do not—"

A second slave, smaller and much older, appeared. Despite his size and age, he exuded authority. With one withering look, he sent the hulking doorman shrinking into a corner of the hall.

"Forgive us, young pilgrim. He"—the old man gave a dismissive nod toward the corner—"is a recent acquisition and is still learning the Trumin way. I am called Glycon. If you need food and water, I can escort you to the kitchens."

Ulric stood straighter and tried to look dignified. "I am heartened to see they still honor the proper religious traditions in the city. Convey my gratitude to your master."

He followed Glycon into the atrium while the guard shut the doors and returned to the boredom of his post. The pair crossed the richly appointed room and headed toward a short hall. Ulric's eyes were drawn to the pool at the center of the atrium; paintings of dolphins and naked sea sprites frolicked in the clear water. In the middle of the pool, a painted bust of Marius Secundus topped a marble pedestal. Ulric noted the sculpted head of luxurious blonde hair and suppressed a laugh. Then he saw the door, and neither naked sprites nor a patrician's vanity could compete for his interest.

In most wealthy homes, the tablinum was an open chamber at the center of the building, allowing an unobstructed view from the entrance hall to the peristylium at the rear of the building. Secundus' office was walled off with a single door visible from the atrium. The door was one of intricately carved walnut with bronze fixtures and what Ulric recognized as a very expensive lock. Behind that door, he would certainly find the sphinx, along with the rest of Secundus' treasures.

Ulric and Glycon passed through a hall leading to the peristylium, then headed into the nearby kitchens. The tablinum had another door opening into the courtyard. It was otherwise identical to the extraordinary door in the atrium.

Once in the kitchen, they served Ulric a plate of cold lamb, bread, a handful of dates, and a cup of cool water. While he ate, Glycon described the route to Myrill's temple, but all he could think about was the lamb.

Sweet Neesis! I wish I could steal this man's cook. A pity I have to return the robe before Julia notices it's gone. I should try this scheme again.

The food and directions were consumed, and he sensed Glycon was eager for him to leave. A slave took his empty plate, and Glycon approached. "Forgive me, but it would be best if you were gone before the mistress of the house returns."

Ulric stood. "Yes, I must be off to the temple. If you don't mind, I'll leave by the side door so as not to disturb anyone further."

"Of course, of course. But before you depart, we have one humble request."

Several slaves had gathered near the kitchen, all looking expectantly toward Ulric. The attention made him nervous.

"Really, I must—"

"Will you lead us in a quick prayer?" Glycon asked. "The Goddess holds the unfortunate and those in bondage close to her heart."

Ulric panicked. "Uh…"

"Please, help us express our gratitude and devotion to Myrill so we may receive her blessing." The old man was nearly begging.

"Yes. Yes! We shall pray to the Goddess!" Ulric said with false enthusiasm. "Let's move into the courtyard." They entered the peristylium surrounded by half a dozen or more slaves. He had desperately wanted to remain a background player, but his character was an unexpected hit with the audience. He positioned himself near the narrow hall that led to the side exit and faced the small crowd.

Hands raised into the air, he called to the heavens. "Myrill, merciful goddess of rebirth and healing, look into the hearts of these wretched and miserable slaves. Grant them your blessing, however ill-timed and inconvenient their sudden piety might appear." Ulric was eager to stop there, but he thought it would be a terribly brief prayer. After an uncomfortable pause, he said, "O' great goddess, forgive the wretched weakness that condemned them to bondage. May their master continue to care for them and not beat or abuse them… unless they deserve it!"

A few slaves exchanged confused glances but were clearly afraid to say anything.

Myrill, if you're listening, please forgive me.

Ulric backed away toward the exit. "May Myrill bestow her blessings upon you all." Another uncomfortable pause, then he announced, "I must go. I must give out the auspices and collect the sacrifices." He turned and bolted for the exit.

Once a safe distance away, Ulric pulled off Julia's robe, carefully folded it, and tucked it under one arm. He headed south toward the theater, hoping to get some rest before returning to steal the sphinx later that night. He had everything he needed: his old thieving tools plus a few recent additions purchased at Silo's shop and now a look inside the Secundus home.

He smiled with the memory of another of Ghostwalker's lessons: 'Listen up, Darktalon. We sweat and bleed during training and preparation, so the job stays cool, bloodless, and free of aggravation.'

Well, Arrius, here's looking forward to an aggravation-free evening.

A Damned Liar

Ulric crossed the Nanpela and returned to the Gutter-Fish-infested streets south of the river. He needed to slip Julia's robe beneath her sleeping pallet before she had a chance to notice it was missing, and he had no idea if she was still at the Polyminius Theater or on some errand of her own. Hopefully, she stayed inside the theater: the streets were simply unsafe until they could sort out the Gutter-Fish. Or, what if she had returned to the clothier? He didn't know what arrangements she had with her employer, but most laborers worked until noon; some unfortunate few worked as long as there was sunlight, with a short break in the afternoon to escape the worst heat of the day.

Beautiful Neesis! I'll take night-black streets and cool alleys over hot fields and sweltering shops. Fools! How I pity these honest laborers; summer's not yet here, and it's damned hot already.

Julia was not a simple laborer; he knew that much. The more he tried to predict what she would do, the more he realized how little he knew about her.

For the second time in as many days, Ulric walked down unfamiliar streets without really seeing. The previous day, in the River Market, Neesis had been watching, and his luck had held. Now, the fickle goddess of fortune must have been looking elsewhere because his luck ran out. On a busy street between two insulae, the crowd parted to reveal Titus standing before him.

"Sweet Neesis!"

"Don't bother calling for Neesis Umbra, you wormy little shit!" Titus' challenge sent people scurrying off the street. "I told you there'd be blood if I saw you again. Now we'll see who has Her favor."

Ulric's instinct was to run, but he couldn't stand to let Titus win a competition for Neesis' blessing. "If you had the Goddess' favor, you wouldn't have found me on your own. No gang to protect you now."

Ulric still had Julia's robe awkwardly tucked under his left arm. He didn't dare toss it aside, so he let it drop into his left hand.

"Pfft! Pity your whore isn't here to see this." He lunged toward Ulric.

Ulric took his momentum and redirected Titus into the nearest building. He grinned as his face made a loud, satisfying smack on impact. The Gutter-Fish spun around; his cheek scraped and bloody from the rough stone.

"Don't you dare pull that Kanch shit on me!" Titus referred to the peculiar fighting styles of the Kanchean people.

Titus came fast with several swings and jabs. Ulric backpedaled furiously, evading what blows he could, blocking others. He captured one clumsily thrown punch, twisted and locked the elbow, then spun Titus halfway around before tripping him onto the street.

A few people who had been watching from the safety of their apartments leaned out of their windows and cheered.

Ulric couldn't resist taking a moment to gloat. "Neesis favors the man standing in the street, not lying in the street. Oh, and it's not Kanchean 'shit'. It's part of the Shadow Ways. It's wrestling from the Kreslan Isles and mind tricks from Bayjon as much as Kanchean fighting. But what would a Gutter-Fish bereft of Neesis know about that?"

Titus pushed himself up to his hands and knees, then drew a dagger from his belt. "You whoreson piece of shit! Blood! I'm going to cut your fucking tongue out!" He rose to one knee. "I'll cut out all those fancy words. Take back my silver. Then I'll make sure one of my boys gets his hands on Julia!"

Ulric's eyes focused on the dagger. "Threaten Julia again, and by Neesis, you'll end up more gutted-fish than Gutter-Fish."

Titus released a hate-filled scream and rushed forward. Ulric leaped back, barely avoiding a series of well-delivered slashes and stabs. Instinctively, he blocked one cut with the bundle in his left hand, realizing an instant too late what he had done.

Julia's robe!

"God's damn you!" The attack had partially unfurled the bundle, revealing several long slashes. As he stared at the damage, he couldn't imagine the lie that would make it right. He could only curse Titus again. "Arakru take you! Damn you through the Nine Gates!" Few curses were worse than invoking Arakru, Alakur's brother and King of the Underworld and of all the Gods Below.

"What's that? I cut up your pretty stola?" Titus asked with glee. "Were you off to play the catamite for some wealthy old man?"

The crowd watching from the nearby buildings jeered.

Ulric's mind churned. Could he say nothing about the robe? Hope Julia didn't notice. Fake the theft of other props to cover its disappearance? Tell the truth?

"Or was that a gift for Julia? Ah, did I ruin it?" Titus laughed.

Worse, such a sudden turn of events caused him to doubt Neesis' favor. The only way to win back the Goddess's blessing was through madness and bold action! He cast the robe to the ground. "You won't get back your silver 'cause I never return what I collect from feeble marks. Besides, I already sold it to Silo."

"Silo?" Titus repeated.

The Gutter-Fish tensed when he heard the name. The flash of fear in his eyes told Ulric the name had power on the streets, more power than a simple fence should wield. Silo was a mystery for later. Right now, he wanted to hurt Titus.

He glanced down at Julia's robe and said, "It's your funeral shroud, Titus. You've got the dagger. I've got nothing." Ulric made an inviting motion with both hands. "Come on, let's see who truly has Her favor."

"Yes, enough play. I'll cut you up like your pretty dress, then leave you bleeding in the street." Titus charged, dagger in hand.

The pair crashed together, and Ulric meant to send him tumbling into the street once more. Titus couldn't keep his footing, but this time he took Ulric down with him. The two fell in a jumble of limbs, each hoping to avoid accidental impalement.

The spectators cheered louder than ever. They were eager for blood.

Ulric's maneuver had gone all wrong; the fight had gone to ground—as most fights did. There were no more taunts or insults. Each fighter spent all their strength toward gaining the dominant position. A dagger gave Titus the advantage, and Ulric soon found himself pinned, desperate to keep the blade from his throat.

The dagger descended.

Responding to the panic in Ulric's eyes, Titus said, "That's right... you never had Her favor!"

Ulric struggled to hold the dagger back. Titus slammed his other hand on the pommel and leaned into the attack. The blade drew closer.

Ulric's muscles burned, his arms weakened; he had to get rid of the dagger—and fast. But how? He no longer had the strength to halt the dagger's descent.

The steel point cut skin.

Then he remembered what Julia had said earlier: "I even set Titus' wrist after a nasty brawl."

He quickly lifted one hand up, enveloped the fist wielding the dagger, and pulled and twisted it toward the forearm—hard. There was a grunt—an odd popping, snapping sound—then a scream.

The dagger fell, landing next to Ulric's ear. Before his foe could escape, he flipped him onto his back and slid his right arm under his head. Titus tried to throw him off, jamming his forearm up into his neck. Ulric's already bruised throat throbbed painfully, but he pushed hard on Titus' elbow and shoved the side of his head down and against the arm, pinning the limb across Titus' own throat. Ulric reached out with his right hand and clasped his left bicep, completing a vise around Titus' neck.

The Gutter-Fish tried to say something, but it came out as only incoherent gasps and sputters. Ulric slid his body to the side, repositioned his legs wide, leaned into the hold, and tightened the vise. Titus thrashed and kicked while delivering a few ineffectual blows with his free hand.

A few moments later, he lay still.

Ulric released the hold, grabbed the nearby dagger, and sprang to his feet. All around him, the crowd cheered. It felt good, but they would have just as gladly cheered Titus. To the crowd, it had all been like any other gladiatorial match. Now it was time for the mob to dispense judgment. They shouted down their verdict from the safety of their apartments, and the majority wanted death.

Terrible advice. Killing Titus in broad daylight won't intimidate the Gutter-Fish. It would only make things worse. If I walk away now and run into his gang, I'll take a beating, maybe get knifed, maybe even killed, but it could be a clean death. If I shroud Titus, then the Gutter-Fish would make it nasty. I'd take a long time to die.

Ulric had seen what torture could reduce a man to before the end. It was one of the few things he truly feared. Dagger in hand, he leaned over Titus and pressed the blade against his chest. In one swift motion, he cut the tunic open and took a small coin pouch. He stood and cast the dagger aside.

The crowd erupted into a round of half-hearted boos.

He retrieved the robe and ran for the theater. Behind him, several strays swarmed from every nook and alley and descended on Titus. Ulric looked back one last time to see Titus being stripped naked in the street to the sound of jeers and laughter. Neesis Fortuna, the Goddess of Luck, had made her choice.

The easy part was over. Now he had to face Julia.

The gates of the Polyminius Theater were open. After Ulric's dash across the city and the fight with Titus, he didn't relish the climb up to the theater loft, so he slipped inside the main entrance. The theater owner, Leufroy, his leading actor Piso, and a small band of stonemasons, sculptors, and painters were all gathered on the stage. They were having a vigorous debate on the price of renovations, and the sound of their haggling filled the theater as well as any drama.

Ulric stayed out of sight, made his way to the stage building, quietly ascended the narrow stairs, and entered the loft. There was no sign of Julia. He looked down at the ruined robe in his hands and tried to think.

If the robe disappeared, Julia would naturally suspect Ulric and never trust him again. He could fake the theft of other costumes and props to cover up the missing robe, but there would be the same problem. If he told her the truth, she'd know the story he told about his life was a lie. Julia would learn he was a thief and a damned liar, beholden to the Dark Assembly and men like Luciano Porteles.

Ulric looked down at his hands, where he had wrenched and twisted the robe into a tight cord.

He let out a terrible scream of frustration and shame. He fell to his knees and slammed the robe to the floor. "Gods damn me! Damn me a fool! Why did I hope anything could be different?" Ulric's face twisted with anger and regret as he slammed the robe into the floor again.

He had torched himself with the Gutter-Fish, making the streets around the theater more dangerous than ever. His stupidity would drive Julia away just as they were drawing closer.

Sandaled feet rapidly ascended the narrow stairs. It could only be Julia. He stood up, straightened his tunic, slid the robe behind his back, and turned to face her.

"Ulric!" What followed was the usual breathless torrent of words. "Where did you go? What do you do most days? I came up here to cool down. You should hear what Leufroy is planning for the theater! It's all very exciting. And very expensive sounding. The statuary alone…"

"Hello, Julia. I… well, I…" He didn't hide the worry on his face.

"Is there something wrong?" She noted the fresh scrapes and bruises on his arms and legs. "Oh no, did you get into some fresh trouble?"

"I'm afraid I did! I was walking through the streets west of the River Market when some thug attacked me."

"Myrill have Mercy! In broad daylight? Why? What did he want?"

"It was a robbery, but a rather ridiculous one. I have little, but I wasn't about to hand it over." Ulric stood taller, defiant. "So, we fought. And I was doing well, but then he pulled a dagger!"

Julia gasped, and her dark eyes went wide. "What did you do?"

"I ran!" Ulric stated matter of factly

"What could you do? He had a dagger."

"But that's not the worst of it. I did something stupid, something I regret." Ulric let a mask of shame descend over his face; it required little acting. "I think Leufroy may be furious if he finds out."

"What? What did you do?"

"I took a costume, uh, no, I borrowed a costume. I was bringing it back when the man attacked me." Ulric produced the robe from behind his back and let it unfurl. "When he came at me with the dagger, it was in my hand, and it got cut up."

Julia stared at the robe, saying nothing.

"Do you think Leufroy would even notice?"

No response. She stared at the robe in silence.

"Or I could pay him back somehow?"

Julia stepped forward and snatched the robe from Ulric's hands with a ferocity that set him back on his heels.

"Merciful Gods Ulric! Of all the costumes, why take this one? It's not a costume at all: it's my temple robe." She looked at the slashed fabric and fumed. "Or it was!" She shot him an accusatory stare.

"I'm so sorry, Julia. I didn't know," Ulric lied.

"You didn't? Really? Is that why you were asking about the rights of priests?"

Ulric took a defensive tone. "I asked because I'm from the provinces, and you were born in the city, nothing more."

"And to what profane purpose did you put my robe?"

"You're right! It was a stupid idea," Ulric conceded. "I thought I could use it in a scheme to beg for food or maybe a small—tiny—donation."

"Ulric! Has madness taken you? The punishment for impersonating a priest is a public flogging at best, and often death." Despite her anger, there was worry in her voice. "Tell me you didn't do it."

"No, I didn't," he lied again. "It was a stupid idea. The more I thought about it, the more foolish it seemed. I was coming back to the theater to return it when I was attacked."

Julia eyed her robe and Ulric feared she was considering his lies and excuses. She began nervously fidgeting with something hanging around her neck, concealed beneath her tunic.

"Oh, it's ruined! The robe was one of the few things I had kept from the temple."

"I'm so sorry, Julia!" And it was the truth. "I'll get you another. Somehow, some way. I'll do it!"

"It's not that simple. Oh, I don't know what to believe." She looked to the heavens in exasperation. "Has everything you said been lies?"

"Julia, I—"

"No! Right now, I'm too angry to talk." She tossed the robe aside and ran for the stairs, then looked back at Ulric. "When we meet again, you tell me everything. No more lies."

No more lies. The thought echoed in Ulric's mind as Julia descended the stairs. He dreaded the idea. Lies were a weapon, a cloak, and a mask, three tools essential for any thief. Not that Julia didn't deserve the truth: she did. The problem was he doubted they could survive the truth. And what good was the truth if it lost him, Julia?

Once again, she was distracting him from the sphinx heist. He could almost hear Ghostwalker readying another lecture. It promised to be a challenging night, and he needed to rest. He laid down on his makeshift pallet and tried to force her from his thoughts. He closed his eyes and tried to clear his mind.

But it was no use, and an hour later, he admitted there was no rest to be had. He gathered his pack and exited the loft through the window. He wandered the back alleys near the river, trying to review his preparations for the upcoming theft, but he heard an echo of Julia's demand for the truth in every footfall.

He needed a distraction. What better distraction than the greatest city in the world? He crossed the river and headed northwest for the High Ridge District. His first stop was the public baths. Long ago, Ghostwalker had taught him a combination of common oils and perfumes that conspired together to give a man no scent. It was something often overlooked by amateurs, as many an errant thief was sniffed out. After the baths, he visited several busy popinas, drinking a little while listening jealously to the carefree crowds. Eventually, he found himself in a brothel, where he flirted with the girls until they realized he wasn't spending any coin and tossed him onto the street.

It was the day before the Nones of the month of Quartilis, and the hour was late and the night black. Now was the perfect time to steal a patrician's priceless treasure.

Little Jinn

Julia stormed out of the theater, the tempest swirling in her dark eyes, scattering any workmen who crossed her path. She rode the winds of her rage on careless wings, flying down the Via Lucretius heedless of Gutter-Fish or destination.

"A thief! That's what he is!"

Several passersby gave her outburst a sidelong glance before walking on, and, embarrassed, she bowed her head and draped her palla over her like a deep hood. She quickened her pace and returned to her angry thoughts.

Of course, he's a thief. Really, Julia? What did you expect? It's obvious. He walks the streets like a thief. He speaks like a thief. Talks about secrets and shadowy ways. And, he consorts with thieves: he already knew Titus! Oh, and don't forget, he steals like a thief. From me!

For too long, Julia had been aware of nothing but her anger and the paving stones beneath her feet, but now the memory of Titus was a needling reminder of the dangers that still lurked in every alley and hidden alcove. How far had she run? Where was she? She raised her eyes and cast off her palla. A fountain of stained slate blue stone towered above her at the center of a broad basin. Some long-forgotten artisan had sculpted it to resemble a hidden grotto where Julia thought she could almost see the god of deep waters and dark secrets peering out from behind a wall of stalagmites.

Somehow, even the fountains south of the river seem sinister.

Without thinking, she had followed the well-worn path of habit and walked to Fontus Square and the public fountain nearest the theater. She made her way through the noisome crowd to the edge of the basin, where surrounded by a gaggle of playfully splashing children, she filled her cupped hands from the spitting mouth of an eyeless fish. As she drank, her gaze wandered back to the image cleverly hidden at the center of the sculpture: Fontus, God Below, God of Deep Waters, and Dark Secrets.

Hmm, why haven't I noticed you before? Do you only reveal yourself to a mortal tormented by secrets? I have a few. Who is Ulric, really? Who hired the Gutter-Fish? Why, after all that I've done, has Myrill chosen me?

Julia dropped to her knees and offered a silent prayer.

O' Fontus, God Below, Keeper of the Eternal Spring and Guardian of the Hidden, hear my secret desire! Reveal my tormentors, and I will sacrifice a shameful secret.

"There she is!"

It was a man's voice. Myrill, Have Mercy! More Gutter-Fish? Julia shot to her feet and turned to see the father of the infant she had healed days previously fast approaching with another man in tow.

"And praying, too. What did I tell you, huh? Pious as the river is long. Blessed, I say." He turned to Julia. "Salve, Persius Julia. May I introduce my friend, Rasmus Calussa?"

"An honor to meet you," Rasmus said, sounding far too honored for Julia's liking.

She hid her discomfort behind her widest smile. "Lucius, how is your daughter?"

"We did just as you said, and little Amara is perfect. Praise Mother Myrill. And you too, of course."

Julia noticed the nearby crowd had taken an interest in their conversation, which only made her feel like a fraud. It was Myrill who had saved the infant Amara, not her, not the disowned daughter, not the temple outcast.

"Uh, good. Good! Thank you, Lucius."

Perhaps sensing her discomfort, Lucius made ready to leave, but Rasmus turned back and blurted out, "Julia, could you visit my sister?" As he continued, it was obvious it pained him to speak of her illness. "Her name's Liana. She's had strange pains in her chest for some time. Won't ever talk to me about it; Alakur knows I've tried. Won't go to the temple. I'm thinking… maybe you'll bring Myrill to her!"

Yes, she thought, *if I can bring Myrill to Liana, I will! I've vowed to do Myrill's will, and it can't be helped if some mistakenly praise me too. As long as I always remember it is Myrill I honor, Her power I channel, Her wisdom I strive for, then I need not feel ashamed.*

Julia looked into the crowd where a man with a tattoo of a toothy pike fish leaping across his face waited for her answer. After what Ulric had done to Titus, she knew any further defiance of the Gutter-Fish would only invite death.

"Mother Myrill is merciful! I will visit Liana and do all that I can!"

Julia learned all she could of Liana, then hurried out of Fontus Square before she and Rasmus could make more of a scene than they already had. Once back on the Via Lucretius, she did her best not to break into a run despite the pursuing fish-faced thug and his two previously unseen companions.

Where was Ulric? She needed him now, but she had stormed off and left him at the theater. And for what? A robe that belonged to a younger, innocent Julia? An expensive piece of cloth, now bereft of meaning? No. She left because of his lies.

What will he do when he discovers mine?

As she passed a wide alley, an old woman called her name in a Bayjoni accent, the Trumin thick and heavy in her mouth with each final syllable oddly stressed.

"Trumera Julia Minor! This way, little jinn."

It was the voice of Nahi, her mother's most trusted slave, and steward of her private affairs. The woman had raised her mother in the fabulous palaces of the Mittani royalty back in Bayjon and had, in turn, helped raise Julia in her father's grand estates in Trumric. She had called Julia 'little jinn' for as long as she could remember, naming her after the mischievous spirits that roamed the Bayjoni wastelands.

Julia ran to her without hesitation. "Nahi!" Her troubles couldn't keep a wide grin off her face as she hugged the ancient woman.

The old slave squirmed out of Julia's grip and straightened her black palla. "Careful! These old bones are brittle."

"What are you doing here?" Remembering the threat of the Gutter-Fish, she quickly added, "Nahi, listen, there are three men following me. Dangerous men. We have to go."

"What I'm doing here, little jinn, is waiting for you. I'm going to take you to your mother, who is nearby. As for these 'dangerous men'? Bah! We'll find no such thing here for the daughter of Mittani kings and the bride of a Trumin conqueror." With that pronouncement, she turned and walked deeper into the alley. "Please, your mother is waiting."

Her mother? Here, south of the river? Stunned by Nahi's revelation, she hurried to catch up, following the old woman into the alley where two men stood guard before the entrance to a small, neglected yard, bordered and well hidden by the surrounding buildings. The men were giants, easily a head and a half taller than Julia and frighteningly ugly with their wild hair and long, thick mustaches. They were slaves taken from a land in the far north, favored by the wealthy as bodyguards and gladiators due to their size and ferocity. Nahi brushed them aside with a wave of her hand.

A litter sat at the center of the yard. Its elegant design, smooth golden wood, and heavy white curtains looked out of place in what recently must have been a stray encampment. A group of litter bearers rested in one corner while two other Northmen stood nearby.

Nahi walked to the litter and whispered something through a narrow gap in the curtains.

Julia watched her old nursemaid, torn by a mixture of hope and dread. Her mother had come to take her home, surely? What other reason could she have to risk such poor and dangerous streets? So, after long months of exile, her father had forgiven her, but Gnaeus Trumerus Julius, the Ravager of Gualdé, the

Conqueror of the East and twice consul of Trumric, would expect something in return for his great magnanimity. Her dear father would want contrition, at least, if not outright servile abasement.

She again recalled the line from *The Gray Outcast*, 'If the sin is with my judges, I could wish them no fuller measure of evil than they, on their part, mete wrongfully to me!' What of her father's sins? Yes, she had done wrong. She had brought shame down upon her father's famous name. But, in his wrath, had he not swung Cathus's bloody sword of vengeance too wide? Cut down both guilty and innocent alike? What if she was not ready to forgive him?

Nahi beckoned her to approach the litter, then held back the curtains and waited. Julia took a deep breath and one last look at the old woman. Her expression was flat, stony, unreadable: the way she always looked when there was hard work to be done.

Karânî, a princess of Bayjon and the daughter of the King of Kings of the Mittani Empire, reclined within the litter draped in cloth and silks of dazzling red and gold. Neither her ink-black hair nor her caramel skin kept her from looking like the very image of a wealthy and powerful Trumin matron.

Julia sat across from her mother and sunk awkwardly into the luxurious cushions. Hardly the dignified beginning she wanted. She needed her anger, so she remembered her father and straightened her back, holding herself rigid despite the soft cushions. Then she donned a mask of pride and righteous anger.

Karânî leaned forward, her dark eyes glistening. "Julia—"

"Why have you come, mother?" she asked in a tone that sounded like an accusation, one reserved for an uninvited guest.

"Now, after months of exile, father forgives me? Has he even considered that I may not want to come home?"

Every word was a struggle, needing the pressure of her rage to push them past her lips. It was Julia's hardest performance yet, but she could not let it appear as if she was running back to her father like a whipped and cowed dog called to heel.

"Oh, my poor little Julia!" Karânî's eyes filled with tears as she threw her arms wide. "Embrace your mother."

The sight of Karânî's tears smashed her proud demeanor like a cheap theater mask. Julia fell sobbing into her mother's arms; finally, her shame, loneliness, and despair were allowed a voice. Julia closed her eyes and thought of nothing but her mother's warmth and her familiar scent of smoky juniper berries and honey. She thought of going home.

Then a parade of unexpected thoughts marched through her head. *What of Ide? Could we still be friends? It would be goodbye to everyone at the theater. Could I remain a healer? Or would it be marriage to some rich old man? And Alakur and Myrill save us if I ever look at Ulric again!* Julia settled back into the cushions and wiped away the last of her tears.

Karânî gave her daughter an appraising look as she composed herself with Nahi's help, who, unbidden, had swept in with a silken cloth and everything needed to touch up the kohl around her eyes.

"How have you been? I worry about you, living south of the Nanpela. Do you still have your old tutor's gift?"

Julia's hand instinctively drifted toward her neck. "Yes, mother. And I'm fine."

"Good. And don't waste it on some stray peasant: they're all thieves and liars. Are you well?" she asked. "You seem terribly skinny. Are you eating enough?" Her mother continued before she could reply. "Nahi, give Julia some money: twenty denarii at least."

"Yes, domina. With joy." The old woman began collecting silver coins from a purse hidden beneath her palla.

"Mother, I'm fine! I eat… often enough," she protested. "I don't need money." *But why*, she wondered, *do I need money if I'm going home?*

Julia leaped out of the litter, shoving Nahi's outstretched hands aside. Silver coins scattered everywhere, clattering on the ground and thumping across Karânî and into the cushions.

Nahi fell to her knees, collecting coins and tsk-tsking her disappointment. "Ah, little jinn. Wicked jinn. Forgive me, domina."

"Forgiven, Nahi." Karânî pulled a denari from the crimson folds of her stola. "Julia, don't be foolish. Everyone needs money."

More foolish than I've already been, you mean? "Why have you come, mother?"

"I've come because I love you, Julia. Regardless of your father's… position on the matter, I always will. I'm here to warn you. You're in danger."

"Danger?" Julia said the word simply, betraying nothing, but she saw Nahi glance up with a sly look. Did she tell her mother about the 'dangerous men' following her?

"Yes. And not the sort I imagine you endure every day living among these peasants. Your renown as a healer has grown, and it's not escaped the attention of the Temple of Myrill and their new high priestess."

"New high priestess? Octavia—"

"Dead. The temple is trying to keep it quiet. Pompilius Gemella is the new high priestess. Her ascendancy will be announced to the public after Octavia's official funeral during the upcoming Myrillia festival."

"What does this have to do with me, mother?"

"Quite a lot, unfortunately."

"How?" Julia asked. The little courtyard grew smaller, and the warm air turned thick and stifling. It was all becoming overwhelming.

"Politics, of course. Now, imagine, just as Pompilius Gemella begins her reign as high priestess, the mob discovers the reason a gifted healer isn't at the temple where she belongs is because her beloved predecessor, Octavia, accepted a bribe from a wealthy senator, eschewing Myrill's Mercy for greed and casting a blessed young woman into the streets.

"What would the mob think if they knew Octavia died not two months later of a wasting disease that no temple physic or prayer could cure? How would that knowledge taint Octavia's hand-picked successor Gemella?"

"The temple?" Julia didn't want to believe it. "The priestesses?" She couldn't believe it. "How could Myrill allow it?"

"Oh, Julia. You studied at the temple. You must have noticed mortal women and men walking the halls. Not gods."

"But Myrill—"

"A god's concerns are wider than the heavens and deeper than the seas," said Nahi.

Karânî gave her a faint smile. "Yes, listen to old Nahi. Your goddess will do as she wills in her own time. Octavia's fate says Myrill still keeps an eye on Her temple."

After Julia's disgrace, her father had disinherited her. Had she not been legally bound to the temple, he would have been within his rights to have sold her into slavery or even put to death if he was willing to risk further scandal. Still not satisfied, he donated tens of thousands of denarii to the temple and promised Octavia the dedication of a dozen shrines across the Kreslan Isles—all to see his daughter cast out and thrown into the streets.

And now Octavia was dead.

The temple taught every acolyte the limits of Myrill's mercy. Her mercy had to be rooted in the truth. It could grow beyond justice, beyond what one was simply due—for mercy was always a gift, not a good to be bartered at the market. However, mercy must never violate justice. To pervert justice is to pervert mercy, to make it false.

"Yes. I believe Myrill will set things right."

"Until then, Pompilius Gemella has paid someone called Cornelius Brocchus to put an end to your fame. Brocchus is a local warlord who runs all the gangs along the river. Has anyone threatened you?"

"No. No… no one."

"Thank the gods!" Karânî had been leaning forward, growing tenser with every word of her warning. Now, she fell back into her litter. "Be sensible, daughter: no more healing!"

"No."

"What?" Her mother seemed sure she misheard.

"Should the sick and injured suffer because of politics?" Julia asked.

"Don't be naïve. I'm told this Brocchus is very dangerous."

"I'm not naïve, mother. I know."

"At least wait until after the Myrillia."

"I'll not be ordered about like a slave to protect Gemella's secrets!"

"What of our secrets! Our family name!" Karânî screamed.

Julia stepped back, stunned. "Is that the real reason you came?"

Her mother leaned out of the litter, her hands reaching for her daughter. "No. No, no, no!"

Julia recoiled.

"He doesn't know I'm here. It's just Nahi and me. Your old tutor, Joveta, warned me. I came as soon as I could."

"It's true, child. Your father isn't behind this," Nahi said.

"Tell me, mother," Julia said, suddenly as cold and treacherous as thin ice, "have you heard anything of Antonius?"

Karânî tensed like an animal pacing the edge of a deceptively frozen lake. Then she sighed and leaped forward. "I'm sorry, no. And I don't expect I will."

"No, I suppose not," Julia replied. "A man condemned to slavery in the silver mines of the Crag Mountains doesn't live for long."

"Julia—"

"Very convenient for father. Perhaps getting myself knifed and thrown in the river would be the *political* thing to do?"

"Julia! Don't say such things!"

"Don't worry, mother." Julia smiled her wicked little jinn smile. "I'm going to do the least political thing I can. I'm going to the temple. And Myrill have Mercy on Pompilius Gemella!"

THE SPHINX

The victorious moon hung like a disc of blackness in a star-filled sky, with only the thinnest crescent of light at the edge hinting at Seranon's coming victory against Nyx, the Goddess Beyond Night. Ulric crossed into the Three Hills District near the end of the third watch and paused, drawing an invisible "∞", called a lemnis, in the air with his left hand. He hadn't recalled doing that since he was a boy, wishing Tessa luck before the doors of the brothel were cast open.

Tessa sits in a bloodstained bed, dying. She stares in disbelief at her red, dripping hands.

Ulric convulses, tossing his head to the side, trying to cast out the memory of his adoptive mother. Tonight, he doesn't need the distractions of the past. He needs the blessing of the Mother of all Thieves.

Neesis! Look to the shadows! Another one of your unruly brood of unfathered children is about to risk it all. A single throw in the dark will determine my fate. Tonight, bestow upon me your blessing, your divine luck!

He approached the patrician neighborhood of Marius Secundus from the west, traveling along the fountain-lined street known as Via Fontum. The road was broad, dark, and empty, with only the faintest sigh of a sea breeze to compete with the endless gurgle of its many and varied fountains. In the distance, four red stars glowered over the eastern horizon: the eyes of the gargantuan draconic towers of the Collegium Draconis Aurei. The Collegium was miles away, but he still felt the gaze of the dragon towers bearing down upon him. Their eyes were always lit with mystical flame—day and night—never to be extinguished. Were there other eyes behind the flames? Had they already spotted the trespassing thief? He was exposed on the wide avenue, and so quickened his pace.

Ahead, from a narrow cross street intersecting the Via Fontum, booted-footsteps approached. Instinctively, Ulric hid behind the nearest fountain. In stark contrast to the other fountains, this statue took the form of a malevolent woman with a bulbous nose and fork-tongued, snakes dancing around her head and water gushing noisily from a mouth full of fangs. Though its silhouette was not much wider than Ulric's own, it was better than no cover at all.

Four men entered the intersection. They carried short swords strapped at their sides or cudgels either in hand or tucked in their belts. *Not good.* They wore matching green tunics; like a uniform. That made no sense, but then he remembered patricians hired mercenaries to patrol the streets near their homes. *Bad.* Such men would give no quarter in pursuit of their coin, and magistrates would turn a blind eye to any "justice" dispensed by guards the wealthy hired to protect their own neighborhood. And there was something else: the lead man held a torch in one hand and in the other he held the leash of a great mastiff, its snout sniffing the night air in between labored pants. *Much worse.*

The boots stopped, but the sniffs continued.

Ulric took slow, deep breaths and froze. He knew better than to hold his breath; holding meant eventually exhaling, and not quietly. He could hear the men muttering to each other. What were they saying? He couldn't make out any actual words over the sound of splashing water and hoped the noise cloaked him as well. It was then he noticed the deep shadow cast by the fountain opposite him. Though the moon was a sliver in the sky, it seemed to beam brighter than Seranon's full glory. Was it the moon? Or was it the dragons' eyes? Either way, Ulric felt vulnerable.

One man said something unintelligible. Then Ulric heard booted feet and heavy paws treading toward him. With each of the man's steps, Ulric took a mirrored step, keeping the fountain between himself and the curious mercenary and his hound. Ulric peered at him from the corner of his eye. He was a broad-shouldered brute with a long scar along his jaw that shone sickly white in the starlight. The mastiff at his side was a massive gray-black beast of pure muscle and teeth. The man gripped the hound's collar and waited while the beast sniffed the air.

Ulric's ears pulsed with blood, and his breath quickened. He waited as well.

"Nothing down here, Vinic," the man muttered. He returned to the others, and they continued south on the unnamed street. When he could no longer hear their footfalls, Ulric took in a deep breath and exhaled it like a satisfying puff of smoke.

His earlier visit to the public baths had paid off. *Thank Neesis for Ghostwalker's concoction.*

Still, Ulric couldn't shake the feeling of being watched. He exited north onto the cross street, where the light of the dragons' eyes, if not Seranon's, was fainter. The encounter with the patrol had convinced him it was time to take to the rooftops. He ducked into an alleyway and unfurled his pack. With a series of swift, fluid motions, he tore off his blue tunic, turned it inside out, and slipped into one of night black. He stepped into a pair of dark woolen pants and traded his sandals for a pair of black leather boots. Next, he tightened a leather belt around his waist, pulled on a pair of black leather gloves, and secured his pouch and weapons. Then he inspected his lock picks, quartz, rope, and enchanted grapnel. Finally, the empty pack became a hooded cloak of mottled black and deep grays.

He leaped deftly onto a window ledge, grabbed the lip of the roof with both hands, and pulled himself up. He moved swiftly along the peak of the roof: cowl up over his head, back hunched, shoulders up, knees bent, weight shifted onto the balls of his feet, and arms spread at his sides for balance. With his cowl and cloak on a near moonless night, he moved like a black phantom dancing across the city.

Ghostwalker called it 'the dance of the rooftops'.

And Ulric was a gifted dancer.

A short time later, Ulric had cut a more or less direct path across the lavish homes of Nemus Hill. His route across the rooftops had helped him avoid the gaze of watchful slaves and hired mercenaries. Now the streets were empty and the homes silent except for the few slaves beginning the fourth vigil of the night. He stopped a stone's throw from Secundus' home and listened. The lingering sensation of being watched kept tugging at his mind.

It's those damn dragon towers! Who are they trying to impress? Everyone, I guess. A curse upon all magi!

He dropped into an alley pungent with spices from the discarded remains of some patrician's evening meal. Ulric ignored his hunger and crouched at the edge of the building, peering across the road. He could see the narrow path running the length of Secundus' home. The slave's entrance was a faint outline in the darkness. Beyond were the kitchens, the peristylium, and the ornate garden where he had led the household slaves in prayer.

Ulric took a deep breath of night air, drinking in the shadows until he felt a familiar surge of overwhelming sensation. Arrius had called it "thieves' glimmer." His pulse raced, his breath quickened, and his eyes narrowed until a hint of a smile overtook the corner of his lips. Slowly, the darkness retreated, revealing distinct shapes where there had only been faint shadows, and the midnight silence was drowned out by a cacophony of sounds. The glimmer was an essential tool of the Shadow Ways: it sharpened senses and heightened awareness.

Thank you, Neesis.

Ulric peered carefully down one side of the street, then the other, his heart ready to burst from his chest. Not a soul to be seen. Not a footstep nor a voice, nor even a breath—save his own—to be heard.

Now.

Like a cat with its prey in sight, he darted across the road and flattened his back against the stucco wall of the estate. All was darkness and silence. He crept further down the path until he was opposite the garden. He reached into the cloth bag at his side and pulled out the enchanted grapnel attached to its rope. Fixing his gaze on the shingled rooftop before him, he flung the grapnel, which disappeared over the peak of the roof without a sound. Tugging on the rope, it tightened instantly. He gave the rope another yank.

Ha! First attempt. A Neesis throw!

Ulric gripped the rope with both hands and, with one last yank, climbed the stucco wall. In no time, he was on the upper roof. The grapnel had lodged at the edge; below it, the lower roof angled into the open air, circling the peristylium. Ulric retrieved the dangling end of the rope and coiled it onto the shingles.

He eased forward and peered apprehensively into the courtyard, still feeling eyes bearing down on him.

It was a beautiful garden of little paths and stone benches surrounding a small fountain topped by frolicking sea sprites. The domus was silent except for the sound of trickling water. The fragrances of lilies, jasmine, and other night-blooming flowers rose from the peristylium to compete with the herbs from the vegetable garden at the rear of the home.

Ulric carefully descended and stepped onto the ceramic shingles of the lower roof. The soles of his soft leather boots made virtually no sound as he crept toward the edge. Ulric was as invisible as a teardrop in a rain shower, yet the feeling of being watched kept gnawing at him.

The Eyes of the Dragons? Even behind these walls?

He pushed the notion aside and refocused his mind on the task at hand. There was no sign of Secundus or his wife. Their bedroom was nestled near the atrium, toward the front of the home. No slaves. No guards. No mastiffs. He was amassing a sum of good fortune tonight. One of the large iron braziers anchoring the corners of the garden was lit, casting a faint red light between the columns.

Odd. It's a warm evening. Gah! Quit letting your mind wander, Darktalon!

He lowered himself over the edge of the roof, his feet dangling above the garden lawn. He released his grip, landing on the soft damp grass. Ulric dashed between two columns and straight for the inside of the wall he had just scaled, flattening himself against its surface. He heard the voice of his surrogate father:

'Walls, corners, ceilings, and rooftops. These are the pathways of ghostwalking.'

He made his way quickly around the tiled floor, which encircled the peristylium garden and extended itself, becoming a sidewalk connecting the front of each room. He glided toward the ornate walnut and bronze door of Secundus' office, silent as winter snow. As he passed the third room…

Footsteps!

Ulric froze, hugging the inside of the nearest column. He did not look around; instead, he focused on the footsteps. The rush of thieves' glimmer still heightened his senses.

Two bare, calloused feet. Marble floor. Nervous cadence. Twenty, maybe thirty feet away. Getting nearer.

In a flash, he scaled the marble column, the soft material of his gear dark and silent. At the top, he wrapped his arms and legs around the column, clinging with all his strength. The intricate patterns of his cloak melted into the shadows where the column met the ceiling. He froze. Only his eyes moved as they narrowed and looked toward the sound of the footsteps.

A young slave dressed in a simple tunic walked cautiously down the hall. His eyes darted left and right as he nervously rolled a yellow weed-flower between his thumb and forefinger. The slave came nearer, and the muscles in Ulric's arms and legs burned. Sweat beaded on his forehead. The slave stopped directly underneath Ulric. He lifted the flower to his nose and sniffed, casting a furtive look across the garden. Ulric's legs were trembling, and the grip in his arms weakened.

At the other end of the peristylium, a delicate hand opened a curtain, revealing the warm glow of candlelight from within. A second hand emerged, beckoning the man with the curling and uncurling of a slender finger. Only when the giggling woman pulled the young slave through the curtain did Ulric finally exhale and release his embrace of the column.

He again made for Secundus' tablinum at the center of the southern wall. Ulric was gambling the sphinx statuette was within. Surely the only locked doors secured Secundus' most valued treasures. Flattening himself next to the door, he tried the handle; locked, of course. Ulric drew in a deep breath. He praised Neesis for his luck, but she was a fickle goddess, and there was no telling how long it would last. He snatched his lock picks from his belt, knelt in front of the door, and went to work.

First, he went through his brief collection of skeleton keys, more out of procedural habit than hope. No luck. There were strange runes etched into the bronze plate surrounding the lock. He silently prayed to Neesis that they weren't magical. On the other side of the peristylium, the two mischievous slaves had begun their lovemaking in earnest. They tried to be quiet, but with Ulric's glimmer-enhanced focus, the garden sounded like a brothel. He inserted the tension wrench into the lock, gently twisted, and began probing with his new snake-pick. It wasn't working: the lock was more intricate than any he had encountered before. He needed to hurry and finish before the slaves. He abandoned the snake-pick and inserted both a barb and dragon's tail. While working the two picks in unison and keeping pressure on the tension wrench, there was finally the gentle click-clack sound of the tumblers falling in place.

Moments later, Ulric pulled on the handle, and this time the door opened. The two slaves were reaching a crescendo, and he feared they would rouse someone. He slipped inside the tablinum and pulled the door nearly shut. He listened: water splashing in the fountain, a gentle breeze rustling the garden flowers, and the sighs and grunts of two idiot slaves that sounded like lightning bolts to his ears. Neesis be praised. There was nothing else. The household was oblivious to his presence.

Then why do I still feel like I'm being watched? Is there something you should tell me, O' glorious and beautiful Goddess? Huh?

Receiving no answer, he shut the door and peered into the darkness. He could see vague shadows of a desk and chair, maybe a bench, but not much else. The room's only source of illumination was what little the stars and the sliver of moon offered. The faintest light shone through narrow slit windows bordering each door. Ulric reached into his pouch and pulled out the piece of clear quartz he had brought from Mist View. Holding it between his thumb and forefinger, he brought it close to his lips and whispered Kreslan words into it.

"Κλέψτε όλο το φως, δώστε μου θέα."

The quartz snatched streaks of light from the air as if stealing them from the moon. A simple enough trick for anyone who knew the enchanted stone's command phrase. After a short time, the stone glowed like a small candle. Ulric held the moonstone out at arm's length, surveying the room. Colorful frescoes covered the walls, and an ornate desk and chair sat at one end. Behind the desk, shelves lined the wall, bursting with piles of scrolls and rows of books. Centered on the shelf above the chair, the glint of gold caught Ulric's eye.

A gold Suhtean sphinx.

Ulric heard the faintest of whispers. He closed his fist around the glowing quartz, plunging the office back into darkness. There was the rustling of a curtain and the sound of bare feet on marble tile hurrying toward the atrium. Satisfied, the reckless slave was returning to his post.

Ulric made quick but careful work of the theft, checking for any traps or alarms before moving the sphinx. He secured the statuette inside a sack, tied it to his belt, and made for the exit. On his way out, he paused by a marble bust of a stoic-looking man sitting atop a cherry wood pedestal. Draped around its neck was a white gold amulet inset with a decent-sized amethyst. Ulric winked at the bust, slipped the chain off its neck, and dropped it into his pouch with a smile.

This should cover the cost of the gear I had to purchase and then some! Besides, what does a philosopher need with a gold necklace, anyway?

He slipped out of the tablinum, securing the door behind him. There was a sudden tug at his side and the sound of tearing cloth. He looked at his waist; the sack was in shreds, dangling from his belt.

Ulric searched the ground for the statuette. Nothing. He stood and locked eyes with the sphinx. A shocked gasp escaped his lips as he stumbled back into the tablinum door. The sphinx hovered in the air before him, languidly flapping wings of solid gold. Its broad, man-like face regarded him with disdainful curiosity.

Secundus had the statuette trapped! Ghostwalker had warned him of such things: it was called a Guardian Transfiguration. It was a rare and expensive spell. It could make a man's own treasures his best defense against thievery.

Ulric slowly slid to his left, hoping to escape. The sphinx floated along with him in a mockery of natural flight.

Ulric jolted forward, ready to run.

The statuette opened its mouth and released an unsettling, human-sounding scream as a cloud of blue mist spewed from its gaping maw. A sweet, floral smell filled his nostrils: Suhtean blue lotus. The peristylium spun, and Ulric Darktalon fell into darkness.

Aguja's Sting

Earlier that evening, from ink-black alleyways and shrouded rooftops, Luciano Porteles watched Ulric skillfully blunder into his trap.

Norbait hurbiltzen da! What egingo duzu? The assassin's dark thoughts formed swiftly in his native Verdan. *Zergatik climb tximino bat bezalako column bat the garden hainbeste offers so many opportunities? Showing off? You have skills, boy. It looks like that bastard Ghostwalker taught you something, after all. A shame he taught you arrogance instead of service and humility; he never taught you your place in this miserable world. If he had, you would know the Dark Assembly has forgotten you. Ah, but Luciano does not forget.*

Ulric dropped from his hiding place at the top of a column and headed for the tablinum door. The master assassin turned toward the front of Secundus' home and descended into the darkness of the atrium.

Luciano's soft boots were silent as he crossed the marble tile, circling the atrium pool and exiting into a small hallway. Candles burned in an alcove within, illuminating the lalarium, the household shrine. Paintings of nude men and women covered the walls, some dancing, some fornicating. In the alcove, a pair of tallow candles illuminated a statue upon a wide pedestal: a wreath-crowned male poised as if in mid-dance. In one hand, he raised a chalice in celebration, and in the outstretched palm of the other, he presented a balance, one side heavy with the weight of many coins. Luciano gave a slow nod to the statue.

He continued down the hall and stopped before a door. He pressed his ear against the rich wood and listened.

He's snoring. Good. I need to begin before the screaming starts.

Luciano knew Secundus and his wife slept in separate rooms, but there was always the possibility of a late-night carnal visit from one of his slaves. The master of the house was sleeping soundly and, hopefully, alone.

He slipped inside and pulled the door closed without a sound. The interior of the bedroom was typical of a wealthy Trumin: large, opulent, and garishly decorated. On the far wall, a fresco of a naked woman greeted him. She was on her knees; arms outstretched invitingly, a seductive smile on her painted lips. Luciano saw something familiar in her sharp, bird-like feature, her long, flowing auburn hair. It was his wife, Aquila! He would have burst into laughter if he dared to make a sound. He wondered if the painting revealed the true Aquila. Or was it simply the fantasy of a man trapped in a marriage that had grown stale? What did it matter? She would be a widow soon.

Quintus Marius Secundus lay sleeping in a cotton tunic upon an enormous bed surrounded by many pillows. He was snoring loudly. Alone.

So it's your volcanic snoring, not just your dull manner, that drives out your fortunate wife. Such a pity if the lovely Aquila had been here, eh?

Luciano advanced, pulling his slender stilius from its scabbard. He brought it close to his lips and whispered, "Ah, Aguja, my little Needle, we play tonight." He stood over the man and pressed the tip of the dagger at the base of Secundus' neck while covering his mouth with his off-hand. Secundus woke, squirming and screaming into Luciano's gloved hand.

"No struggle. Bad move. You die. Aguja never miss her mark."

Secundus stopped flailing. He bargained for his life, but the assassin only heard a smothered drivel. Luciano put pressure on the dagger, pricking the skin. The muffled pleas ceased.

"Good. Good. Good," he said slowly, softly, as if calming a skittish horse. "We talk now, eh? No run. No scream. Just talk. Talk or Aguja, she drain you."

Eyes still wide, Secundus nodded his head.

"Good." He withdrew his hand from the man's mouth, though he maintained the dagger's pressure. "No more lies. The Quadrivium was place for lies. Here? With just you, me, and Aguja? Here is place for truth."

Secundus whimpered under Aguja's sharp pressure but did not speak.

"The Dark Assembly know what you did. You bought nothing. You hired Arrius Ghostwalker to steal Eltaran scroll from Senate couriers. Men of high rank. Now dead men. Big trouble for Assembly."

Secundus tried to sink further into his bed. "It wasn't my fault. The man I hired had come with the highest recommendations." As he continued, his voice trailed off to a mere whisper. "There was to be no bloodshed. You must believe me."

"Oh, I believe you. I believe. Ghostwalker would never kill so foolishly."

"What? Then who?"

"Eltarans, of course. How you be so stupid?" Luciano watched Secundus' face drain to an even paler shade of white, something he didn't think possible without Aguja's aid. "Yes," he said, drawing out the syllable, "scroll cause everyone much trouble. Must return to Eltarans."

Secundus stiffened and stared at Luciano in unblinking fear.

"Now. You tell Luciano. Who you sell scroll to? Who you buyer?"

Secundus hesitated. Luciano did not. He backhanded the man in the face. "Who you buyer, Quintus?"

"I… I… I don't know! I swear!"

"Oh, Quintus. Why you no tell truth? Make worse. Much worse." He paused, melodramatically looking about the room, then returned his gaze to the patrician once more. "Tell me, Secundus. Where you Harathi man, now? You trade Harathi for more men? Soldiers? They not here, eh? They watch over you valuables? You really thought Assembly take trinkets as payment for betrayal? For all the trouble you caused? Not good for you. Not good when you lie."

He grabbed Secundus' ear between thumb and forefinger, pinching and twisting it at the same time. As he was about to cry out in pain, Luciano shook his head in disapproval.

"All right. It's just… complicated."

"Pain is simple." Luciano twisted the ear until it emitted an unsettling popping sound.

"Please, stop! I'll tell you. Just stop. The original commission was for a magus. Magus Modius Nero. But… I sold it to another magus instead."

"Why?" Luciano asked. "Sound like bad business."

Secundus' eyes darted to the fresco of his kneeling and seductive wife, then back to the assassin. "My reasons are my own."

Luciano nearly burst out in a peal of hyena-like laughter but only smirked instead. "Who is other magus? Who has scroll?"

"I don't know exactly who she is! I'm telling you, I don't know!"

"She?" Luciano asked.

"She sent someone to handle the transaction for her. Some half-breed brute. Couldn't even speak Trumin. I don't know his name. Or hers!"

"Couldn't even speak Trumin." You arrogant bastards think the entire world needs to learn your pointlessly convoluted language. Bah! Every man knows the language of pain and fear!

As quick as snapping jaws, Luciano moved the stiletto blade from Secundus' neck to his face, slicing a long sliver of flesh just under the cheekbone. Everyone would have heard his cry of pain had Luciano not stifled it with his gloved hand.

"No. Lies. Quintus. Aguja's sting is—"

The master assassin searched for a Trumin word.

"Persuasion."

A trickle of blood rolled down Secundus' cheek and fell onto his pillow, mirrored by a single tear descending from the corner of the terrified man's eye. He was trembling now. Shaking from head to toe. Luciano had seen fear like this before. He feasted on it. It invigorated him.

"Name? Tell me name, Quintus. And maybe Aguja spare you pain." Luciano pulled his hand away, waiting for a response.

Secundus' chest heaved as he gasped for air, desperately trying to form coherent sounds through a fog of panic and fear. In between labored breaths, he offered three words:

"Magus... Vipsania... Tertia."

Damned Magi. In the Republic's capital, that could only mean the Collegium Draconis Aurei, and that meant trouble. Political trouble. Luciano's mission had been to punish Marius Secundus and retrieve the scroll, if possible. To penetrate the Collegium and steal from a magus would require supreme artistry and daring. He never doubted his own capabilities, nor did he fear magi, for he had been born and trained in Verdith, where an elite of squabbling sorcerers plotted and ruled. No, the move was too bold for the Dark Assembly. The Archon would never approve. He would have to return to Mist View for new orders. It was time to finish the job.

"Good. Good. Aguja helped you remember. Maybe she help more, eh? Better now, before Eltarans find you."

Secundus' eyes filled with dread, then settled into a look of childlike pleading. Luciano met his gaze with an odd mixture of warm reassurance and cold ambivalence. From outside came a commotion: a strange scream, then a man's voice yelling, giving orders. It was the perfectly timed distraction he had been waiting for. Luciano's eyes darted from Secundus to the door, then back. The two men locked eyes as Luciano plunged Aguja into his prey's throat and backed away. Secundus, gargling in his blood, convulsed and reached out, though the Verdan was already at the door.

Luciano Porteles, master assassin, emissary of The Dark Assembly, had once again completed his job and left Domus Secundus as unnoticed as he had arrived.

Aquila Secunda

The sphinx swooped down on huge outspread wings and pinned Ulric to the ground with cruel talons. He tried to push the leering beast away, but his arms would not move. He screamed, and the sphinx evaporated into a blue fog, surrounding and suffocating him. Somewhere beyond the thick haze, a woman laughed.

A nightmare! How long was I out? The blue mist was real enough. What did it do to me? Head spinning. Feel so sick. Can't move. Arms and shoulders on fire. Wrists bound. I'm hanging? Not good.

With effort, he dragged his feet into position and struggled to stand. Keeping his eyes shut, he reached out with his other senses. The warm night air, garden smells, and cool marble underfoot meant he was still in the peristylium. Nearby, he heard more laughter: rough men. Not the voices of household slaves but something worse. The air shifted, and the scent of an expensive perfume overpowered him.

For a long moment, he kept his eyes stubbornly closed, fearing to see how dire his situation was, but how could he hope to escape while blind? So he opened his eyes.

It wouldn't matter. Escape was an impossibility.

Whatever the sphinx exhaled has left me barely able to stand. They've stripped me of everything but my pants and hung me between two columns. Secundus has brought in four armed men; they carry themselves like soldiers. And they've added two iron pokers to the brazier. Could it get any worse?

A woman's voice, cold and patrician, emanated from the edge of the garden. "Glycon, do keep the coals hot. The wretched dog is awake."

With short, quick strides, the speaker came into view. The woman was tall with sharp, angular features that gave her a cold, predatory beauty. An expensive blue silk stola trimmed with a yellow meander pattern and pinned with gold fibulae adorned her slim body. Her auburn hair was pinned up in the customary style of a married woman. She stopped behind the brazier and watched Ulric with a dangerous intensity. The slave called Glycon stoked the coals to a red glow, then retreated to the edge of the peristylium. There was no sign of recognition on the old man's face, only an indistinct nervousness, an uncertain fear. Ulric met the woman's gaze and suppressed a shudder. She stood tall and imperious, bathed in the coal's harsh red light, her image twisting and distorting through the rising heat. She reminded Ulric of an avenging goddess.

With several abrupt motions, she looked over the courtyard and called out, "Glycon, where is Quintus? I instructed you to rouse him."

The old slave stepped forward out of the shadows; his head bowed low. "Forgive me, domina. I knocked. I called out. He did not reply."

"And your efforts ended there, no doubt." She cast an exasperated glance toward the mercenaries. "Sometimes, I don't know why we pay to feed all these slaves. Useless, the lot of them."

Sounding bored, the tallest mercenaries said, "As you say, Aquila Secunda."

Looking back to the chastised slave, she commanded, "Come along, Glycon! My husband wouldn't want us to start without him."

"Yes, domina. Please forgive me, domina!" The slave hurried after her as she exited toward the atrium.

The armed men relaxed as Secundus' wife disappeared from view. One of them, a man as broad as he was bald—and he was very bald—said, "By Cathus' crooked cock! This is shaping up to be a long night." Two of his companions nodded their agreement.

Ulric guessed the long hours lying in wait for a thief that might have never arrived had taken their toll on the men's mood. The fourth man, the tallest of the group, disagreed. He looked at the night sky and said, "It'll be the tenth hour soon. We'll be in our beds before sunrise."

"You're always the cheerful one, Helva," said a man with a pockmarked face. "It's why we let you talk us into taking these damned fool jobs."

The mercenary they called Helva strode over to Ulric and roughly grabbed a fistful of black hair. He bent Ulric's head back and gazed down menacingly. His breath smelled of garlic and onions.

"You've stayed quiet so far—smart. Now the smart thing is to start talking. Marius Secundus will have questions, and you had damn well better answer as if your miserable life depends on it because it will. If you keep my men and me here past—"

An anguished scream from the atrium cut off Helva's threat. In an instant, he was halfway across the courtyard. "Pavos, Myros—with me, Wultgar"—he pointed at Ulric—"watch him!"

The bald man and the pockmarked man ran after Helva, leaving Ulric alone with a longhaired blonde mercenary with a deep scar along his neck. The man grunted, folded his arms, and glowered at Ulric.

Left alone with one guard, Ulric sought desperately for an opportunity, but there was none. They had expertly secured his arms, and his mind was still woozy from the strange blue gas.

What in the Nine Gates is going on here! Think! They knew I would steal the sphinx tonight. How did they know? Did I let something slip earlier today? And that scream?

Before he could speculate further, Aquila ran into the peristylium with Helva close behind. Rage contorted her formerly austere face, her hair was loose and wild, and her red-rimmed eyes were wet with tears. In one talon-like hand, she clutched a bronze statuette of a Suhtean sun god, uplifting a solar disc in the form of an expensive glass mirror. Aquila charged straight at Ulric, raising the mirror as she closed in.

"You murderous little filth!"

"I murdered no one!" Ulric protested.

He was about to add it was a point of professional pride when the mirror descended. He wrenched his head out of the way, but the heavy bronze frame connected painfully with his right shoulder. The second blow struck the side of his head, opening up a short, bloody gash. For an instant, he imagined kicking Aquila into the brazier, but he still had enough sense to recognize a bad idea. He dodged another blow aimed at his head; it bruised his arm instead. The fourth blow slammed flat across his cheek, shattering the mirror and showering his face with sharp chunks of glass. The fifth blow sent the world spinning, and Ulric's feet fell out from underneath him.

Helva's powerful voice interrupted her next swing. "Aquila Secunda, you had questions?"

Aquila stayed her hand and turned to glare at Helva. "What?"

"Kill him now if you wish. I only interrupt to offer a respectful reminder."

Pavos and Myros marched into the courtyard, their military discipline on display. "We've searched the home. There is no sign of any other intruder," Pavos reported.

"Orders?" Myros asked. Helva looked back at Aquila.

Calm descended over Aquila like an early frost. Her grip on the bronze mirror went slack, and she casually cast it aside. "Glycon, you wretched worm!" The old slave appeared and dropped to his knees, prostrating himself before his mistress.

"Yes, domina!" There was fear in his voice.

"That's right, grovel, you wretched fool. I'm still deciding whether to burn you on your master's funeral pyre. Now, gather the rest of the household and bring them here."

As they questioned the household slaves, Ulric tried to ignore the throbbing pain in his head and piece together what happened.

Luciano! One of the Dark Assembly's best assassins arrives in Trumric, and a wealthy patrician is dead the next evening. It's no coincidence, but maybe our meeting was? The job never made sense! I'm too unimportant to have been in the Assembly's plans. How could I have been so stupid to believe they would have reduced a killer like Luciano to the role of errand boy?

No, I was deceiving myself. Getting spotted by Luciano was plain bad luck. He must have seen an opportunity to make his job a little easier and continue his feud with Ghostwalker.

Ulric stiffened and tested the strength of his ropes. His aching muscles strained and the ropes bit deep into his wrists. It was no use.

Somewhere in the shadowed colonnade of the peristylium he thought he heard the echo of Luciano's mocking laughter.

Pride and Vengeance

Aquila dismissed the bulk of the slaves and had lamps hung, filling the courtyard with their soft golden light. Glycon placed an ornate chair behind Aquila, where she perched herself on the edge of the seat while the old slave stood a respectful distance beside her. The men gathered around, and Helva tended to the brazier of coals. He nodded at the bald man, Pavos, who removed his tunic, exposing a broad, muscled chest.

Aquila spoke first. "Who sent you to kill my husband?"

"I killed no one!" It was the truth, but he knew the truth wouldn't help. Pavos' fist smashed into his side, sending a shock of pain through his ribs.

"So you had a companion? He was to murder my husband while you merely stole our property? What's your name, filth? The name of your accomplice? Your master? Speak, damn you!"

Silence.

A sudden blow to the stomach knocked Ulric's breath away. Two more quick blows to his chest and ribs left him slack and swinging from the ropes.

"Listen up, Darktalon. 'Rats go squeak, squeak, but from men, nary a peep.' Which means—we never betray our own or share secrets with outsiders." I remember, Arrius. You never gave up a single name. The vicars of the Dark Assembly praised you for your loyalty as they left you to face torture and crucifixion. But what do I owe Luciano?

More blows and more questions.

"Who are you?"

Silence.

"Who wanted my husband dead?"

Silence.

"Why steal the sphinx?"

Silence.

"Name your accomplice!"

Silence.

Every question, every silence, was punctuated by another blow. Ulric remained stubbornly quiet, responding to each blow with a grunt or a gasp but never an answer.

The blows stopped. Pavos paused to stretch his arms and massage his knuckles. It was a warm spring night, and his exertions had left a sheen of sweat on his bald head and chest. He exhaled and gave Helva a sidelong glance. "Bed by sunrise, huh?"

Ulric's head throbbed, his shoulders were in agony, and his ribs ached. He had received several beatings in his short life and even given a few. Beatings he could endure, but it wouldn't end there. The glowing brazier of coals remained close at hand, a constant promise of unimaginable pain to come. Throughout the questioning, Helva had patiently tended the coals while watching Pavos work. He extracted one poker and inspected its white-hot point.

Ulric had one last chance to speak. "You look tired, Pavos. How about we let the lovely Aquila have a go? I've known men to give good coin to be beaten by a long-legged she-wolf like her."

Wultgar's scarred throat emitted a sound something like laughter. Pavos' anger was palpable, but Helva looked at Ulric with an expression somewhere between admiration and pity. Disappointingly, Aquila's face remained neutral except for a slight twitch at the corner of her thin lips.

She gave a subtle nod to Glycon. "I would love some wine, and I'm sure these hardworking soldiers could use some cool water." The slave bowed low and scurried away.

Soon, Aquila held a silver goblet of wine, and the men had taken their fill of water. Helva returned to the brazier and extracted a poker, its tip glowing like a baleful star. He slowly walked toward Ulric. "I tried to warn you, boy."

Ulric could feel the heat from the iron before Helva's final step.

"Who sent you to murder my husband?" Aquila demanded.

"To the Nine Gates with the lot of you!"

Helva brought the iron close. Ulric tried to twist away, tear his arms free, but the ropes holding him allowed no escape. Blazing iron traced a line across his chest, leaving a trail of raw, blistered, burning flesh. The pain was beyond anything he had endured, anything he could have imagined. The smell of burning flesh filled his nostrils, and his screams filled the peristylium.

"The name of your accomplice?" Aquila asked.

"I… murdered… no one," was all Ulric would say between halting breaths.

Helva slapped the red-hot iron on the inside of Ulric's thigh. The poker burned through the thin material of his pants in an instant. He frantically tried to escape the heat, kicking and swaying on the ropes like a mad puppet. Unexpectedly amused, Aquila exploded in scornful laughter.

She leaned forward in her chair. "Oh, he's quite a sight now, isn't he?" she said with relish. "I do hope my poor husband is looking down on your just torment and enjoying it as much as I am. Now, torch his legs, roast his feet, and make the wretch dance for me. If I don't get answers, I'll at least have entertainment!"

Aquila asked the same questions again and again. Helva applied the iron again and again. The pain never ended; as one poker cooled, he brought the other forth from the fire. Ghostwalker had taught Ulric how to overcome and ignore pain, but those disciplines were no match against the burning hell of the irons. Ulric's pride demanded silence. He tried to expel his agony through clenched teeth, but it was of no use. Every tooth in his head would shatter first. Better to scream, he told himself. And he did.

Ulric screamed, cursed, and muttered in a haze of agony, but he gave no answers. The memory of two men gave him rare strength: Arrius Ghostwalker and the assassin Luciano Porteles. Ulric wanted nothing more in life than to live up to the legend that was Arrius Ghostwalker. He never knew his real father, but it didn't matter because Arrius had become his true father. As for Luciano, when, in a moment of weakness, Ulric thought of saying something, anything, to stop the pain, he imagined the burning iron on Luciano's flesh. Love and hatred, pride and vengeance: these gave Ulric the strength to endure the unendurable. For a time, at least.

A splash of cool water struck Ulric's face. He had passed out, and for an instant, he thought he had awakened from a nightmare, but it was all too real. The questions and the pain began again. In his delirium of torment, Ulric imagined his captors had made a critical error.

My arms are bound, but not my legs! At the right moment, I could kick Helva into the coals. Then the coals would set his clothes on fire, spill onto that damned harpy Aquila, and turn her ridiculously expensive stola into a torch. Fire everywhere! The house would burn! My ropes would burn, and I'd be free!

Helva retrieved a fresh iron from the fire. Ulric lashed out with a kick that connected powerfully with the man's gut. He groaned and stumbled back toward the glowing brazier, regaining his balance at the last moment. Helva glared at Ulric, and the look on his face told him the mercenary knew what he had planned.

"You whoreson piece of shit!" Helva swung the fresh poker hard into Ulric's ribs, holding it there as he shrieked and the flesh blackened. "Pavos, Wultgar, hold the bastard's legs."

Pavos and Wultgar rushed forward, and both roughly grabbed a leg. Now, Helva brought the hot iron down on the fresh, untouched flesh of his back, buttocks, and thighs. Aquila held her questions while Helva sated his anger.

Ulric's world was reduced to agony and the anticipation of agony. He felt merciful darkness descending again, and he began praying to Neesis: not an oath, not a curse, not an insincere litany, but a true prayer.

O' Neesis, fickle and alluring goddess of Luck, Lust, and Madness, hear me! Your priests say you favor the bold, the fools, and the thieves. I've been all three! They say sometimes you give your blessing to those who risk it all on a single throw in the dark. What was coming to the capital to make my fortune, if not that?! All I ask is a chance. Give me a chance, and I'll escape from here, claim Ghostwalker's sword, and send Luciano to your ample bosom. Give me a chance, and I'll tell Julia the truth! If you do that, I'll steal a fine lamb to sacrifice at your altar. Or, if there are no lambs about, three pure white doves. Oh, and if doves… are scarce… I promise…

"By Alakur's Light! He's out again. Bring more water! We'll bring him around."

Aquila stood up. "Wait!" Speaking to no one in particular, she said, "I'm surrounded by all these powerful, strapping men and… useless. Just useless. Oh, don't give me that look, Helva. You'll be paid as promised. Glycon! Fetch a tablet; I have a message to write. Oh, and bring the young Gualdean slave, the one with the funny name."

"Faro, domina?" asked Glycon.

"Yes. Now hurry." She dismissed him with an impatient wave.

"May I ask what we are to do now, Aquila?" asked Helva.

"You may because you already have. I'm growing impatient for answers, and as enjoyable as all this is, it's not working. I must turn to more reliable but far more expensive methods. Don't worry; I'll still need you and your men a while longer."

Glycon returned carrying a small, rectangular wooden box and a long, thin stylus. An athletic-looking young slave, whom

Ulric recognized as the sly lover from earlier, sheepishly followed. Glycon handed Aquila the tablet and stylus. She opened it and began writing on the wax within. Once finished, she handed the tablet back to Glycon, who handed it to the young slave.

"Listen closely," said Aquila. "You are to run to the Collegium Draconis Aurei and present this message to Magus Modius Nero at the Tower of Storms. Wait for his reply. Return with the magus or news of his coming."

"Yes, domina. I remember the way. I know where to find magus! Run all the way!" The young slave gave a nervous bow and ran out of the courtyard.

"Glycon, clean up this awful mess. As for our filthy little thief, I want him out of my sight and out of my home until Nero arrives."

"And where should we keep him?" Helva inquired.

"Take the wretch out back and toss him into the icehouse. There's only one way in, and it has a sturdy door. You can guard him there until the magus arrives. His magic will make quick work of his stubborn silence."

Ulric hung slack and motionless from his ropes, listening to Aquila's plans. They had put the irons away, at least for now. Even though his body was a mass of burns, cuts, and bruises, and the slightest movement was agony, he praised Neesis. This reprieve from torture was Her blessing and his only chance: the Goddess of Luck never guaranteed success. He would lose all if he didn't escape before Magus Modius Nero arrived. While he had learned the basic trances of Shadow Mind from Ghostwalker, he had never had the chance to study its ultimate secrets. Without mastery of that esoteric discipline, there was no resisting magical compulsion. Once he told the magus and Aquila everything, Ulric knew he was as good as dead.

A Wild Plan

Julia looked down at her ruined acolyte's robe and frowned. She swept her hands across the bundle, but its fine cloth remained soiled with street filth. She pressed and smoothed the rents in the fabric with firm strokes, but the cuts would not heal.

It was nearing the eleventh hour of the night and almost as many hours since she had begun her vigil. She adjusted her aching knees on the unforgiving marble steps and once more looked to the Temple of Myrill for a sign. The sacrificial altar remained unattended on its high podium, looking forlorn and somehow ominous under the shadowed forest of towering, painted columns. Above, the temple dome loomed black against the starry sky. She listened. Silence. The temple remained shut against her, distant and indifferent to prayer.

A faint wind passed through the columns of the temple portico, fluttered the few remaining torches along the steps, and plucked at her dark curls—barely making a sound above her labored breathing and the muttered prayers of her followers. The night air was warm and faintly scented with spices and incense from the surrounding gardens and shrines of the Temple District. Since midnight she had heard the occasional call of some unseen nightbird or the steady marching of passing guardsmen, but otherwise, Julia marveled at the silence. After her exile to the poorer districts of the city, there had hardly been a night unbroken by shouts or screams.

On the steps below, her companions, over two score men and women from south of the river, noted her silence, and, one by one, their prayers ceased.

"Julia?" It was Lucius. She recognized his voice; heard his doubt.

"The doors will open!" she said as if her words alone could knock the heavy bronze aside. "I will speak with the high priestess. We will have our blessing."

Julia twisted her hands into the ruined fabric of her robe and began slowly rocking back and forth, chanting, singing, and praying. Behind her, a chorus of voices joined her with renewed vigor.

What if the doors remain shut? What if Julia, the outcast healer, blessed of Myrill, is revealed to be a fraud?

Her history lessons had been rife with those who had tried to manipulate the mob and failed. They had all met a bad end. A violent end.

No, she wouldn't let guilt distract her. She banished the thought as unworthy of either Julia, the outcast healer, or Julia, the wild actress. Besides, a thief and follower of Neesis may have inspired her plan, but she believed it had the blessing of Myrill.

After her mother's warning, she had run to the theater to retrieve her acolyte's robe, delighted by the idea of throwing it into Pompilius Gemella's face but unsure what she would say to Ulric so soon after their argument. She found the robe where she had left it, but he was gone and, despite her anger, she wondered where to. She even wished Ulric had been there to share his thoughts on her wild plan, for despite her anger, she feared they wouldn't let her on the temple grounds, let alone grant her an audience with the high priestess.

Julia folded the robe, trying but failing to ignore the unsightly cuts made by Titus's rage and Ulric's madness. Then she knew what he would tell her! Ulric would say the wilder, the better! Her plan must be as mad and unpredictable as the thief! He had saved her from Titus by striking at his devotion—his obsession—with Neesis Fortuna's favor. So Julia would use Gemella's obsession with politics against her. Did she fear the mob? Julia would unleash the mob upon her!

Well, as big a mob as she could gather.

Julia raced out of the theater and back to Fontus Square, where she began her search for Lucius and his friend. She found the pair drinking at a nearby popina alongside several of their coworkers from the river docks. This time, when Lucius praised her piety, she accepted it without embarrassment, even encouraging him to share the tale of his daughter's miraculous recovery. Soon she had the attention of the entire popina. As she cast her gaze over the rapt crowd, she thought, *So, Severa, is this what a lead role feels like?* She knew such perfect moments were as brief as the flash of a thunderbolt and had to be seized with alacrity and skill. Julia didn't feel ready to stand alone on the stage, but everything hinged on this single performance. Recalling Severa's training, she prepared to speak, slowing her breathing, perfecting her posture, and, most importantly, controlling her fear.

"It is true! I have been visited by Mother Myrill! When I've come to the aid of my friends, my neighbors, the faithful people of this city, She has shown mercy and gifted us with Her divine presence. I asked… why? Why would Myrill Regina, consort of Alakur and Queen of the Gods, listen to me?

"I was born to a family of no consequence. I was no one. I thought myself unworthy. But it is the gods who determine our worth. Now that I doubt Her no longer, Myrill has revealed Her will to me."

Julia paused and watched the question she had sown take root within the crowd: what did the goddess desire? So far, her plan was working, but she feared she had gone too far, claiming to speak for the goddess.

"I must lead a delegation of the faithful to Her temple before sundown today. We will pray upon the temple steps while I await an audience with the high priestess." Then, as if someone had inexplicably switched the lines of a play, she said in a voice not quite her own, "If I am a worthy messenger, the faithful will receive Myrill's blessing. When sudden rains quench night's flames, you will know Her mercy."

She had meant to ask simply for help to gather citizens for a prayer vigil, but Myrill must have sent her unexpected words of augury. It could only mean her plan pleased the goddess, no matter its wild insanity.

Near the end of the day, Julia arrived with her followers, over forty women and men led by Lucius and his wife—her sister watched over their infant daughter. Julia arranged everyone upon the temple steps, and approached the altar, where a small group gathered to prepare for the evening invocation. The coming night would see the first sliver of a victorious moon, so the priestesses would ask Myrill to forgive her daughter Seranon, the Moon Goddess, and grant her the strength to cast Nyx back into the Beyond.

A mousy-looking acolyte in a well-kept robe stepped forward. "Come no closer to Myrill's sacred altar!" She glanced at the crowd spreading across the temple steps and pointed past Julia with one nervous finger, adding, "You must wait with the others. Prayers begin at sundown."

"But we have not come to pray for Seranon," Julia said.

"I don't understand," said the acolyte, snatching her hand back as if Julia was Nyx herself. The young girl retreated and turned to the priestesses for help.

Her companions finally looked up from their preparations, noticing the crowd with some alarm. Not surprising, Julia thought, since the evening invocation was a quotidian affair, rarely attended by more than a handful of people.

The young acolyte returned with the lead priestess in tow, a tall woman with the honey-colored hair, pale skin, and the finely chiseled features that Trumin men prized. Thanks to her poise and slender figure, she wore the plain green and brown linen of her robe as if they were the latest Kanchean silks. Julia tried not to hate her.

"I am Metella, priestess of Myrill. And you are?"

"I'm called Julia."

"Why have you come, Julia, if not for the evening invocation?"

"I must speak to the high priestess."

The woman shook her head. "Very unlikely. Speak to her about—"

"Julia! Trumera Julia Minor!" cried a second priestess. Julia recognized the unpleasant screech. It belonged to Damia, a woman who never ceased offering unwanted snark and dull commentary during their time together at the temple. For some unfathomable reason, she had kept her red hair styled short, like an acolyte. Julia thought it looked like she had hacked at it with a dull kitchen knife.

"You know her?" asked Metella.

"Julia *Minor*," she said, ignoring Metalla and emphasizing the Minor with disdain. "I thought you would have fled the city. I'd never imagined you'd show up on the temple steps leading a rabble."

"A rabble!" Julia's dark eyes flashed with anger. "This is no rabble but a gathering of the faithful. How do you see a rabble? Is it the sight of poor clothes or worn sandals? Or do calloused hands and bent backs offend you? Does not Myrill's Mercy extend to everyone? Is not the greater portion of Her mercy reserved for the less fortunate?"

"Of course it is." Metella gave Damia an embarrassed sidelong glance down her perfect nose.

"Careful, Metella. There's things you don't know. She's trouble."

Julia ignored her and asked Metella. "You want to know what I would discuss with the high priestess? For one, I'd ask what wickedness makes a priestess confuse Myrill's faithful with a troubling rabble."

Damia's face became as red and uneven as her hair. "How dare—"

Metella quieted her with a look. To Julia, she said, "I'd remind you that all who serve Myrill deserve your respect. I'll pass on your request, but Octavia has seen no one for many days."

Julia stepped back onto the temple steps. "Who said I wanted to speak to Octavia?"

Metella's eyes narrowed with confusion, but Damia's face betrayed resentment and guile. Julia knew then that Pompilius Gemella had kept Octavia's fate secret from many, if not most, of Myrill's priestesses.

While leading her third Hymn of Myrill Sanatio that night, Julia looked to the west. The moon had finally slid under the High Ridge skyline; the eleventh hour had begun. And still, the temple doors remained shut. She considered stomping across the portico and pounding on the doors, but that would only reveal her growing desperation. *But I am desperate*, she thought. Julia stood, stretched her aching legs, and took one hesitant step.

The sudden crack and metallic groan of heavy bronze doors cut the hymn short. Everyone looked to the temple, where orange torchlight flickered through the portico, and then looked expectantly at Julia. She gave a reassuring smile and ran up the steps straight into Damia, torch in hand, leading several temple guards.

"Normally," Damia began, sounding particularly pleased with herself, "first-year acolytes sweep the steps clear of trash to prepare for dawn prayers, but I begged the high priestess for the privilege."

Julia looked the guards over: eunuchs, one and all, slaves chosen for their size and fanatical devotion to the goddess. Each wore a simple belted green tunic and carried knotted leather cudgels. There was no doubt they would follow Damia's commands.

"Is this the will of Pompilius Gemella?"

Damia snarled and motioned toward Julia with her torch. The two nearest guards rushed forward and seized her by the arms. "Still your tongue! What you think you may know doesn't matter." Stepping closer, she whispered, "Seems those rough river-men couldn't teach you the value of silence. We should reclaim our silver."

Julia struggled against the guards, but their merciless grip only tightened. On the steps below, the unexpected violence spread panic through her followers. A wild plan was ridden with loose reins, but hers was about to slip from her grasp.

"I know everything, Damia. I know of Myrill's judgment and Octavia's fate. As an outcast, I know wickedness and temptation, so I bear a warning from the goddess. I must see Gemella, lest she repeat Octavia's mistakes."

"You claim to speak for Myrill?" Damia sounded incredulous, but there was fear in her eyes.

"You knew the rumors about me. You know why I've been harassed. Why doubt it?"

There was a long silence and then a glance and a nod from Damia, and the two guards released her. She spun on her heels and headed into the temple.

"Come."

Julia obeyed, and the two guards followed close behind, leaving the rest assembled near the altar. Damia dropped her torch into a soot-stained sconce while the two eunuchs pulled the massive doors shut. They continued through high-ceilinged marble halls filled with the scents of soil and leaf lit by the golden light of Eltaran lanterns. She had forgotten the warm glow of the magical orbs; their light was like the air moments before a perfect dawn. Memories of walking the temple's serene halls flooded her mind, and a terrible longing threatened to drown her, but she looked at the bundle of cloth in her hand and knew there was no going back.

A Spell for Vanishing

Helva and his men hauled Ulric to the icehouse: a compact stone building sunk into the ground of the vegetable and herb garden at the rear of the home. They cast the door open and dragged him into a cold, dark chamber at the bottom of a brief flight of worn stone stairs. The lamp Myros was carrying revealed a rectangular room, over half of which was filled with tightly packed stacks of ice blocks surrounded by an insulation of hay. Nearer the entrance, shelves stuffed with clay pots stood over a short row of amphorae, two-handled jars with tall, narrow necks.

Helva cast a critical eye across the icehouse and gathered a collection of ice picks, hammers, and sharp tongs. "All right, this place will do," he said. Myros sat his lamp on a shelf, and Pavos and Wultgar let Ulric drop to the stone floor.

Pavos looked at the others. "We're gone once the magus arrives, right?" There was a hint of fear in his voice.

"Ooh, the big soldier's scared of a little magic? You gonna run home and suck your mama's tits?"

Pavos grabbed his crotch. "How about you suck this! Don't pretend those dragon magi don't put you on edge like they do the rest of us!"

"Quiet, the two of you!" The men ended their bickering and waited for orders.

Helva rubbed his hands together. "Damn, this place is chilly. A man could freeze his balls off in here."

Pavos blurted out, "Well, it *is* an icehouse, isn't it?"

Helva's eyes narrowed in annoyance. "Myros, Wultgar! Let's see if Aquila needs consoling. Pavos, stay here and guard the thief."

Pavos threw up his hands. "Hells! Why me?"

"Because those are my orders!"

Helva left with a laughing Myros in tow. Wultgar lingered, flashed a ragged smile and a rude gesture toward Pavos, and then caught up with the others.

Ulric had been silent, trying his best to remain unnoticed. A hard kick in the gut from Pavos proved he was not forgotten. Ulric groaned and folded into a ball, shivering on the icy floor.

"That's right, cry while you can, you little bastard." Pavos began pacing across the small chamber, rubbing his bare arms against the chill. He muttered curses against Ulric and Helva, but most especially, the cold. When he had finally had enough, he stopped and turned toward Ulric.

"Why the fuck am I standing in this godsdamned icehouse! Huh? Answer me that, you little turd. I'll be outside, right by the door. You lie there and don't even think about starting any shit, you hear me?" Pavos took down the lamp, headed up the stairs, and slammed the wooden door behind him with a loud thud. "I'll be right here, you little bastard." His voice sounded distant and muffled through the door.

Ulric was alone, unobserved, and kept by one reluctant guard. Praise Neesis! This was Her blessing, and he had to prove worthy of it. He slowly, painfully, picked himself off the cold floor and surveyed his makeshift prison. The faint light streaming from under the door was more than enough for a thief versed in the Shadow Ways.

Helva had taken all the tools that could have easily been turned into a weapon. This left numerous clay pots, jars, and pitchers holding water, wine, honey, and various other foodstuffs. And ice. Lots of ice. Other than awkwardly turning a small pot or chunk of ice into a bludgeoning or stabbing weapon, there wasn't much to work with. Nothing he found inspired any clever escape plan, and his search grew more desperate.

There had to be a way. He stopped searching and took a deep breath to calm himself. Without a task to keep his mind distracted, the pain returned and nearly overwhelmed him. He hobbled toward the narrow stairwell and lowered himself to sit at the edge of the steps.

Even if I escape from the icehouse, he thought, *what would I do? My head's throbbing, my whole body aches, and these burns fill every movement with misery. I'm useless if I can't control the pain. If I'm to have a chance, I need to go within; I need to build a wall around the pain. I need Shadow Mind.*

Ulric closed his eyes and forced the light of his waking mind to fade. He drifted deep into the shadows of his own thoughts. It was part of a discipline Ghostwalker had called Shadow Mind; it took his mind to a place where necessity could forge thoughts into commands. Ulric focused on each terrible wound, one by one. The pain made it nearly unbearable at first, but slowly, deliberately, he locked each ache, cut, bruise, and burn behind iron walls of will. Each wound screamed and raged against its new prison, but their voices became dim and distant as he rose back into the light of waking awareness.

While he had remained within the shadows of his thoughts, Ulric had sat motionless on the stairs, his eyes closed and his breath shallow. When he seized control of his body, he came to with a sudden jolt and slid off the edge of one smooth step, down hard onto another. And like that, Ulric had a plan.

It was time to escape the icehouse.

He leaped up with newfound energy. He grabbed a pitcher of cool water from one shelf and poured its contents over the worn stone stairs. Kneeling in front of the stacked ice blocks at the rear of the stone chamber, he gathered a handful of small ice chunks and shavings found at the base of the stacks. Returning to the stairs, he spread the handful of ice over the last step, then gathered more ice. He covered the next step with ice and repeated the task until bits and chunks of ice covered half the stairs. With luck, anyone coming down would slip and fall hard onto the stone steps. Now it was time to lure Pavos into the trap.

Although Helva had scoured the icehouse of anything dangerous, he had left Ulric with his greatest weapon: his voice. After an evening dominated by silence, it was time to speak. He would take Piso's advice: speak precisely and strike with maximum force. He thought to shout a few choice insults at Pavos, but he remembered how the man dreaded the arrival of Magus Modius Nero. A more elaborate performance would do the trick. What he needed was a spell for vanishing.

Ulric moved to the center of the icehouse and cleared his throat. He prepared to fill his voice with a confidence and arrogance he did not feel.

"Pavos, you fool! You've left me unguarded, my hands unbound and free to cast any spell I please!"

"Spells… what are you going on about?" There was a nervous edge in his voice.

"I shall vanish from this place, and then I shall have my revenge!"

"Shut up, or you'll get my revenge up your scrawny ass!"

"I'll see you again, Pavos! Oh, yes! I'll see you, but I'll be the last thing you never see before the end!"

"Quiet, damn you!" he blustered.

"ΣΠΑΣΤΕ ΤΑ ΤΕΙΧΗ ΑΥΤΟΥ ΤΟΥ ΧΩΡΟΥ, ΠΕΡΑΣΤΕ ΠΕΡΑ ΑΠΟ ΑΥΤΟ ΤΟ ΜΕΡΟΣ. ΣΠΑΣΤΕ ΤΑ ΤΕΙΧΗ ΑΥΤΟΥ ΤΟΥ ΧΩΡΟΥ, ΠΕΡΑΣΤΕ ΠΕΡΑ ΑΠΟ ΑΥΤΟ ΤΟ ΜΕΡΟΣ!"

Ulric reached a crescendo and then silence. He quietly moved to a corner nearest the stairs, retrieving the now-empty water pitcher as he did so. His 'spell' had been a nonsense rhyme spoken in Kreslan. He doubted Pavos knew the language but couldn't be sure. He prayed to Neesis his admittedly ridiculous plan would work.

"Ha! Like you have any magic, boy." Pavos waited in silence for a reply, but none came. He called again, "No more tricks, you hear!" No response. "Answer me!" Pavos picked up the lamp sitting nearby and threw the door open. There was a long moment of silence.

"The beating I'm about to give you will be nothing like before! That was a bit of lovemaking compared to what's coming up." He began his descent. "When I find—"

His threat was suddenly cut off as his feet flew out from under him, and he landed hard on the stone stairs. His bald head made a loud and satisfying crack, and his limp body slid down the last few steps. The lamp hit the floor, sputtered, and went out.

Ulric didn't wait to see if Pavos was dead or merely stunned. He sprang out from the corner and brought the empty pitcher down on his forehead with all the force he could muster. It shattered, leaving a deep gash on Pavos' rapidly swelling face. The mercenary lay motionless on the stairs but still breathed. Ulric began searching the body for anything of value when he heard someone enter the garden.

No time. He had to escape now!

Ulric crept up the stairs. Mryos, lamp in hand, approached, trampling over a row of rosemary shrubs. He called into the darkness, "What's with all the shouting? Helva's about had it with you."

Ulric exited the icehouse and moved unseen to the far side, out of Myros' line of sight. He needed to get out of the garden and onto the streets. The walls surrounding the garden were very high, unbroken by gate or door. It would be a hard leap in his current condition. The icehouse roof would be an easier climb because the building was partially sunk into the soil. A leap from its roof to the garden wall would be much easier. Myros drew closer. Ulric pulled himself onto the roof, but he was too eager for the safety of the streets and jumped from the icehouse a moment too soon.

Myros saw the open icehouse door and picked up his pace. "Pavos, you filthy whoreson, if you're having a bit of fun down there... I'll..." His shouts trailed off in disbelief as he watched Ulric disappear over the garden wall. An instant later, he was raising the alarm. "Helva! Wultgar! Prisoner's loose! Over the east wall! Come quick!"

Ulric dropped into the street, all the while cursing himself for his amateur mistake. He didn't need another homily from Ghostwalker to know an impatient thief was a dead thief. Other voices joined Myros in the garden. Ulric didn't hesitate and ran down the street as soon as he regained his footing. As the clamor faded behind him, Aquila's scream of anguish and frustration rose into the night. Ulric smiled.

THE DANCE OF THE ROOFTOPS

The perfect hush of predawn covered the sleeping city. All decent citizens were still abed, and the most ardent tradesmen had yet stirred. Only a few unfortunate slaves, standing the fourth vigil of the night, had their peace disturbed by the sound of hard boots on paving stones and the rough hue and cry of mercenary soldiers. Fewer still saw the men's elusive quarry: a burnt and broken young man, barefoot and nearly naked.

Ulric fled through unknown streets, and his three pursuers drew ever closer. He had not run far before the road had curved eastward, leading deeper into the Three Hills district: very much the wrong direction. He caught his breath and tried to get his bearings. It was the eleventh hour, still dark, but the stars were already fading in the eastern sky. He wanted to be across the Nanpela River before sunrise.

Three men carrying torches appeared at the far end of the street and began running toward him; they were Helva, Myros, and Wultgar, of course.

Ulric silently cursed their efficiency. *To the Nine Gates with this lot! I'd thought I'd leave them scrambling and confused. No, it's over the wall, torches in hand. No time to lose! Bastards!*

The chase continued. He told himself he would have lost his pursuers long ago if he had only had the time to learn these unfamiliar streets. Of course, being tortured hadn't helped. Helva and his men had no such disadvantage, and it was becoming clear they knew the district well. Helva had displayed an uncanny ability to predict what route he would take. They were close. He knew it.

Ulric had been making his way steadily south and downhill. The homes of wealthy patricians had slowly given way to more modest dwellings, shops, and well-kept insulae. He stopped before a narrow cross street dominated by a three-story building filled with apartments above several closed shops. A tradesman loaded a bundle of sacks onto a cart hitched to a single sleepy-looking donkey. The man tossed another sack onto the pile, straightened his back, and gazed past Ulric quizzically.

Wultgar and Myros had stepped into view, each emerging from a side street, one to the east, the other to the west. As one, they began moving toward him. Ulric spun around to run back up the street, only to see the way blocked by Helva. The mercenary drew his sword and smiled grimly.

"That's right, thief. Nowhere left to run."

Ulric took one last glance around as the mercenaries drew closer. He shot Helva a derisive sneer.

"Nowhere you can follow!"

He turned and sprinted toward the tradesman's cart. Leaping upon its side and vaulting in reach of a second-story balcony, he swung over the railing and onto the deck before the man's yelp of astonishment was complete. He had run the length of the balcony and jumped onto the roof of an adjacent shop before Helva had sputtered out an order for Wultgar to follow.

Helva's shouts faded in the distance as Ulric raced southward. The roof suddenly ended at a narrow alley, which gaped like a black abyss in the predawn darkness. He picked up speed and soared over the gap, landing lightly on the roof of the next building. He paused, seeking a route to keep him off the streets for as long as possible. His goal was the Pons Polyminia, an ancient bridge spanning the Nanpela River. He saw a promising path just as Wultgar's heavy steps crashed onto the rooftop behind him.

Ulric cursed. His pursuers had surprised him again. He took off, looking over his shoulder to see Wultgar clear the alleyway as easily as he had. It was the dance of the rooftops again, but now he had a partner. Ulric would take the lead, but the penalty for any misstep would be death.

The two dancers cut a path south toward the river. Wultgar followed Ulric's lead, drawing ever closer. Ulric would change the rhythm with erratic steps and sudden moves, but Wultgar would not slow. He would lead the dance through treacherous terrain demanding complicated steps, but Wultgar would not falter. Ulric danced to the music of his bare feet slapping on roof tiles, the wind rushing past his ears, and the pounding of his heart. All else was silence. There were never any shouted insults or loud boasts from Wultgar, just insistent, silent pursuit.

Sweat covered Ulric's body, and his breath came in ragged gasps. He was growing tired, and he hoped Wultgar was, too. So far, the mute Northman had matched Ulric step for step, proving his agility, strength, and stamina to be equal to or more than his own. One last test would make the difference between escape or capture. He saw the perfect opportunity and adjusted his path; it was time for a test of balance.

Ulric leaped down onto the flat roof of an insula, disturbing several families who had been sleeping there to escape the heat. Before they could shout an objection, Wultgar landed with a heavy crash. With a frustrated grunt, he shoved one man aside and continued the chase.

Ulric made for a neighboring building with a tall, narrow peaked roof, the length of which ran perpendicular to the southern edge of the insula. He leaped and landed on the narrow summit and ran down the length of the roof. The narrow peak provided little more space than a tightrope. He stopped and turned to watch Wultgar. The mercenary hit the tiles with a heavy thud, paused to regain his balance, then took a few hesitant steps forward. Ulric turned and ran for the far end of the roof, hoping to goad Wultgar into picking up the pace. He stopped when he heard the expected crash and skitter of loose tiles.

Wultgar's feet had flown out from underneath him, sending several tiles sliding down the steep roof to disappear over the edge. Wultgar tried to find a foothold and regain the summit, but every movement dislodged more tiles. He fell flat and slid down the roof, picking up speed as he frantically tried to save himself. As he reached the edge, he looked at Ulric and uttered a strange grunting cry, which Ulric guessed was a curse. Wultgar disappeared over the edge, and a moment later, a sickening, cracking, crunching sound made Ulric wince.

The rooftop dance had ended in death.

Myrill's Favor

Myrill's shrine rested beneath the boughs of an ancient fig tree. A sparse wood grew around it, dark and wild under a high dome of intricately carved stone. The Goddess looked resplendent in gilded wood, marble, and ivory. Myrill sat upon a modest throne, yet the statue was twice as high as any man. Flames crackled and hissed within three bronze bowls set at her feet, and starlight from the dome's oculus rained down cool shadows upon her crown. So lifelike was its painted facade, Julia imagined it would rise and begin passing out judgments. She had forgotten the name of the master who had sculpted it, but they said he had wept upon its completion and thereafter abandoned his craft.

She and Damia made for the shrine, and the two guards followed at a respectful distance. They crossed the springy damp grass, and Julia breathed in the earthy scent, missing her once frequent trips into the countryside.

A dark silhouette resolved against the fire's blinding glare: a robed figure wearing the broad headdress of the high priestess knelt in fervent prayer. Other women stood nearby, the ever-faithful attendants of Myrill's Enduring Flame.

Julia and Damia knelt before the shrine and mouthed their own brief prayers. Pompilius Gemella was already standing when they rose, summoning Damia with a disappointed frown. The young woman blanched, then, with a snarl, thrust a finger toward the ground, telling Julia to stay put. Damia rushed to Gemella's side, and the two conferred in hushed tones for some time.

Julia obeyed and studied Pompilius Gemella from afar. She looked young for a high priestess, with only a few gray hairs visible among her brunette locks. Maybe she was thrice as old as Julia? Maybe a head taller? Her gilt wood and ivory headdress made her look taller still. And she had a round, pleasant face. *Unfortunate*, she thought, *as it's so much easier to hate someone if they're ugly or too beautiful.*

The high priestess approached with a slow, precise gait, her hands clasped tightly before her. "Octavia the Elder was a pious and noble woman. I loved her. As did we all." There were words of affirmation from Damia and the others. "When she fell ill, we did all we could, but no skill we possessed or physic we brewed could save her. Our prayers went unanswered. So, I comforted her as fever consumed her mind and pain wracked her body. I tended the lesions and boils that erupted over her skin. I bathed her after she vomited and shat out the last of her insides." Gemella kept stalking forward, forcing Julia to take two hurried steps back. "I held her hands—such small weak things—and we prayed for Myrill's mercy."

Gemella finally halted her advance, standing before Julia, rigid but for a barely perceptible tremble, the high priestess' eyes boring into hers.

"I'm sorry," Julia said. "I'd not wish such a fate upon anyone."

"Octavia's fate was to linger. On and on, she suffered. In the end, there was only Gemella's mercy."

Julia stood in stunned silence, unsure how to reply to her strange confession. The high priestess let the silence deepen, then turned and walked back toward the shrine, motioning for Julia to follow.

"When Octavia took your father's coin, she thought only of the good it could do, but if the people knew what she'd done, they'd fear Myrill's will was too easily swayed by men's silver. They would be wrong, Julia. Octavia always meant to expel you."

Julia had told herself she would have remained at the temple if not for her father's bribery, but the instant Gemella denied it, she knew it for the lie it was. Just another fiction in the life of Trumera Julia Minor.

"Even so, I would have prayed for mercy and forgiveness, but I only learned of Octavia's passing yesterday."

"Curious." Gemella extended an arm, and a priestess rushed to place a metal rod in her hand. "Only a few within the temple know, yet…" She let the question hang in the heat-distorted air, idly stoking the sacred flames in the central bowl, sending crackling sparks rising into the darkness.

"I *am* the former daughter of a consul of Trumric." Julia hoped that made her sound resourceful and formidable.

"Hmm." She handed the glowing rod back to the attendant. "Your mother, Karânî, no doubt."

Something in Gemella's tone pricked at Julia, but she said nothing.

Gemella gazed into Myrill's sculpted visage. "I've prayed for mercy. Silence. I've prayed for guidance. Again, silence. Always silence." She gave a rueful little laugh and turned to Julia. "Now I'm told you come bearing a warning from the Goddess Herself."

"I do."

"Let's hear it."

Despite having hastily practiced half a dozen possible speeches, she wasn't sure what to say. Then the shrine and surrounding wood took on the aspect of a dream, remote and unreal, yet somehow distinct and present. Behind Gemella, Myrill reclined on her throne, sending a shower of unripe figs thumping to the ground. The Goddess spoke, and trance-like, Julia repeated her words. "The stench of past sins cannot be masked by the perfume of fresh transgressions. Do not let Octavia's offense stain you further. Persecute my faithful no more."

The waking dream ended. The trees were a sparse wood, and Myrill was only a mute statue, although many eyes had cast a curious glance toward the ancient fig tree.

"A rather self-interested warning."

"I am the one being persecuted."

"Persecuted?" Gemella said incredulously. "Why? Because we asked you to stop treating the sick? You're not properly trained, child."

"No one from the temple ever asked." Julia twisted the remnants of her acolyte's robe into an even tighter bundle. "Instead, I was harassed! Threatened! Assaulted! I was commanded to ignore sickness and suffering by base killers and thieves!"

Damia stepped forward, eyes downcast. "Forgive me, high priestess, but I used the Transnanpela Collegium as intermediaries. I fear, in hindsight, they were ill-suited for the task."

"I would say so!" Gemella said. She turned to Julia. "Their Senatorial mandate is to maintain order, you understand. And it's so dangerous south of the river; they know only the heavy hand. Could you forgive us, Julia?"

Could Gemella be telling the truth? Had she been too eager to cast her as the villain? Nothing seemed to play out quite as she had planned.

"Of course, I could forgive, but… my training?" Julia unleashed a breathless torrent of words in her defense. "What better training than this temple? I nearly completed my acolyte studies. And I was an advanced student. Often praised for my work. Ask Drusa or Joveta. I never reach beyond the limits of my skill. I don't flail about blindly. Too risky. If I can't help someone, I recommend an apothecary or direct them to this very temple. I'd say I'm better trained than half the so-called healers in this city!"

"Take a breath and consider what you're saying, child. Nearly completed is incomplete. You're dangerous. And you're no healer. You're a temple outcast with a following who believe you're Myrill blessed."

"They see what you will not." Julia sighed. When she continued, she tried to sound a bit less manic. "They see what I long denied. Though outcast, the Goddess speaks to me. Or through me. Why I've been chosen, I have no idea. Myrill will not have me abandon the sick and the injured."

"Every year, young girls are paraded before the temple: daughters of smiths, drovers, and magistrates, all of them—and none of them—the next chosen ikon of Myrill. These are not the old days of heroes and kings and divine ikons. Whatever doom took the Eltarans caused the gods to grow subtle and remote. I refuse to believe the Goddess speaks to the likes of you and not her high priestess!"

"Myrill spoke to you mere moments ago, but you were not listening."

"You're referring to your 'warning'? Usually, there's more wide-eyed ecstasy and hair-pulling. I suppose, as an actress, you know the value of a restrained performance."

"Yes, I'm only Persius Julia, a poor actress, and a gifted healer. And that's all I intend to be—if you call off your collegium thugs." Julia no longer doubted Gemella was behind her harassment, not Damia.

"Then you must cease tending the sick," replied Gemella, "and cede any authority over your followers to the temple."

Julia stood tall and took a long stride forward. "I will not." Then she hastily added, "And I don't have authority over anyone."

"You think you can defy the temple without consequence?" Gemella approached and faced Julia, her air of bemused condescension replaced by a withering scowl. "You've claimed to speak for Myrill in front of multiple witnesses. I could have you before a magistrate. The censors, even."

Julia knew she would do no such thing. A public trial would expose the very secrets she desperately guarded. And while Persius

Julia could not afford a worthy advocate, Gemella no doubt feared the mother of Trumera Julia Minor would pay for the best.

"Yes, call the magistrates," Julia said with exaggerated enthusiasm. "Oh, but they won't be taking new cases until the sixteenth day before the Kalends. Or you could heed Myrill's warning and leave me be. All you've done so far is guarantee people will ask unwanted questions."

"I grow tired of being lectured to, child."

"There'd never have been a possibility of scandal if—."

"Enough! You dare speak to me about scandal? You? The common actress? The temple outcast? The disinherited daughter?"

Julia flinched at the last as the hot flush of shame flared on her damp skin. What could she say in her defense when Myrill's own words had been ignored? Her plan had given her the audience she had desired, but it was Gemella who had dominated the meeting from the beginning.

"Tell me, Julia, *ikon of Mercy*, how many lives have you destroyed?"

Julia shrank away, once again feeling small and unworthy. Gemella pressed forward.

"My past—"

With eyes held fast on Julia, Gemella asked, "Do you know the details, Damia?"

"No, high priestess," Damia replied, sounding reluctant to be brought into the conflict. "Only the rumors."

"Our little Julia, our paragon of righteousness, was only a second-year acolyte when she began sneaking away to the Nyssan

Theater to meet with an actor, Lutatius Antonius. Antonius was young, dashing, and unscrupulous. Bad enough, but he and his friends were also members of the Flavian faction: the sort that rabble-rouse for plebeian causes. The sort that does far, far worse. Isn't that right, child?"

"How could I have known?" Julia said meekly.

"If you hadn't been a whore, your father would never have been in danger. That's why there are rules. But I digress. Of course, the Flavian faction hates the Trumeran faction, led by her father. I suppose it was the whole point of sleeping with Antonius."

Julia wanted to scream it wasn't true, but she wouldn't lie before Myrill's shrine.

Damia reluctantly asked, "What happened?"

"Julia helped Antonius and an associate, Quintus Barba, sneak into their family estate, ostensibly to steal her father's speeches against Flavian land reforms. But that's not what they wanted, was it, Julia?"

"Antonius was innocent. We had no idea." Julia's protest could barely be heard above the hiss of the sacred fire.

"No idea of what? Will you not say it? You deign to lecture me while unable to face your own sins?"

Julia had shoved the thought, the memory, into a black well of nothing for so long that she had believed she was wholly innocent. "But if the sin is with my judges" had been a comforting line in a play she had recited often, but she could no longer deny her own past misdeeds.

"I led an assassin into my father's home," she said in a voice free of all doubt, "and for that, I was justly exiled. The would-be assassin paid with his life. Antonius and his family were harshly punished, beyond the bounds of justice and without regard to Myrill's mercy. But… if I had respected the rules of the temple and the gods, Antonius and his family would be alive and free today."

Gemella stood silent, surprised by Julia's honesty. She took a moment to compose herself, then said, "Now you understand why this nonsense must end. We can't let the people think someone like *you* speaks for the Goddess."

"Gemella, Myrill speaks to me because I listen. I can face my past because tonight, I learned that past sins cannot be forgotten or rectified by fresh transgressions. You heard the Goddess but denied her. You ignore her warning at your peril."

"You foolish, deluded child! Now you threaten me? While holding on to the fiction Myrill has chosen you: a near patricide!" Gemella pressed forward, shaking with rage, but Julia stood unyielding. "Absurd. Why would the Goddess speak to one so unworthy when Pompilius Gemella was her loyal priestess? The Pompili are as ancient and noble a name as the Trumeri, with former consuls and generals in my line of fathers. I've never debased myself. My Trumin blood runs pure. Perhaps it is the taint of Bayjoni blood that breeds treachery and wickedness? But it's not your father's fault. He didn't have a choice since Karânî was a war bride, pimped out by the Mittani Empire to secure peace with Baladan. I guess one whore begets another—"

Julia cut off Gemella's insult with a jarring slap, the resounding whip-crack sound evoking gasps from the nearby priestesses.

"My mother is the daughter of kings!" *Oh, Goddess, forgive me!*

The guards who had escorted Julia into the shrine rushed toward her.

"Foolish child! You've struck a sanctified religious officer of Trumric. We won't have to bother with magistrates. I can have you scourged. Or even put to death."

It was true; she had broken a sacred law of the city and was now at Gemella's mercy. The thought churned her stomach with dread and sent her stumbling back, her knees nearly buckling.

Merciful Myrill! How could I have been so naïve? What was I doing coming here with so much anger? Now I've failed everyone. As the guards drew near, she tried to think of a way out. *What would Ulric do? What wild plan? A lie, no doubt. I could claim my followers would spread the truth of Octavia's death across the city if I didn't return to them by sunrise! And if she believed me, I would put innocent people in danger. I'd prove myself as foolish as Gemella by trying to cover one sin with another.*

"Or," Gemella continued, her voice now calm, "you disavow your rapport with the Goddess and swear before Her shrine to heal no more. Then you can leave. Unharmed. Decide quickly. Dawn approaches, and you grow ever tiresome."

"After everything I've said, you think I would renounce the Goddess and abandon the sick?"

The guards closed in, and before they seized her, Julia threw her acolyte's robe at Gemella's feet.

"What?"

"Once proud garment, now useless costume. I see now it was ever the mere trappings of piety; no better than your own soiled cloth!"

"Bravo! Did some sodden poet write those lines for you? Nevermind. Damia! Bring me a branch: strong but supple. I'll begin her scourging myself."

The two guards flanked Julia and, at a nod from the high priestess, each seized an arm. Damia began to speak but seemed to think the better of it and hastily retreated toward the wood in search of a branch.

Gemella stepped closer and began unwrapping Julia's palla from her shoulders. "I take no pleasure in this, child. It's all very distasteful, but you've forced my hand. I simply must punish you. Such arrogance, such defiance against temple and state cannot stand."

Julia wasn't even sure if she was being insincere, so she ignored her and watched Damia instead. The flame-haired woman stood under a holly oak and pulled a small pruning knife from somewhere within her robes. She stretched high overhead and sought a branch that would please Gemella.

"Scourging is quite terrible," Gemella continued as she tossed Julia's palla aside. "You'll cry out. It's unavoidable. Beg for mercy, even. But like my poor dear Octavia, there will be only Gemella's mercy."

"Now, who dares to speak for the Goddess?"

Damia reached for one branch after another, but they seemed to twist and bend out of her grasp. Each attempt became more frantic, and when Gemella shouted her name, Damia nearly jumped out of her skin and grabbed the nearest fallen branch.

"Here, high priestess," Damia said. She took a moment to catch her breath and handed over a slender oak branch.

Gemella looked at it disapprovingly, then swung it through the air in several long arcs, making a sound like a swarm of angry bees. "It will do."

The two guards flanking Julia spun her around, grabbed her wrists, pulled her arms out taut, and took a step back. They lifted her into the air, leaving her feet barely brushing the grass. She stifled a scream. It felt like her arms would pop out of their sockets.

A tremor passed through the wood, and the flames guttered in an unfelt wind, sending the three attendants rushing to the great bronze braziers.

Gemella grasped the back of Julia's tunic and addressed the two guards, saying, "You are not to look upon her nakedness. Look to the heavens instead."

Once the two eunuchs were dutifully staring up at the dome's oculus, Gemella tore down Julia's tunic, exposing her back and a small crystal vial of bright blue liquid dangling from a silver chain.

"What's this?" Gemella yanked on the vial for a closer look. "A physic? Myrill's Tears! Stolen before your expulsion?"

"No!" Julia protested, struggling to speak against the chain pressing against her throat. "A gift from my old tutor, Joveta. Ask her if you doubt me."

Gemella pulled the chain free and handed the vial to Damia. Then she raised the oak branch high overhead, and the sound of it cutting through the air filled Julia with dreadful anticipation.

"You must be punished."

Forgive me, Myrill. I've been a poor servant. As blind to my own failings as Pompilius Gemella.

Gemella screamed: a sudden cry of surprise or shock rather than pain. Julia strained to look behind her, but she could only see the alarmed faces of her guards. Then the surrounding wood shook, and the trees bent in a phantom gale as the sacred fires erupted in great swooshes of flame.

Damia cried, "Myrill, forgive us!" The guards released Julia, and fell prostrate, mumbling prayers of repentance.

Julia tumbled to her knees and turned to see Gemella struggling against the oak branch, which had once again become a living thing, entwining itself around her arm and shooting new roots into the soil. The holly oak sapling had trapped Myrill's high priestess in its rapidly growing embrace, pinning her arm high above her. She grabbed the still slender trunk with her free hand and tried to pull herself free, but wicked thorns burst from the bark, piercing her flesh.

"Damia! Help me. Guards, hack it down! Free me!"

The guards looked up but dared not move. Damia took Gemella's bloodied hand. "Gemella, the Goddess speaks. Listen."

Julia stood and gathered up her tunic. "Myrill is merciful, and I pray She will forgive all of us for our foolishness this night."

Gemella stopped struggling against the oak. "Yes. Mother Myrill is merciful." At her words, the branch-turned-sapling released her and took the shape of a mundane young holly oak. The high priestess took a moment to compose herself, and all eyes were upon her. "You may go." Then she turned to face Myrill's shrine and said in a halting voice, heavy with shame, "Go with the temple's blessings. Now I must pray, for there is much to consider."

Not knowing how to respond, Julia simply said, "Thank you, high priestess."

And she again thanked Myrill for showing mercy to such an unworthy servant as herself. *I do fervently hope I won't make a habit of needing to be saved. I must have been a terrible nuisance these past few days!*

As she struggled to get dressed, thanks to her aching shoulders, Damia came to her side and helped pin her tunic back in place and wrap her in her palla. "I apologize for my earlier cruelty; I'm not deserving of forgiveness, but please consider Gemella. Octavia was like a mother to her, and her passing embittered her greatly."

Julia smiled. "All is forgiven, Damia."

Damia grinned broadly, which had ever been an uncommon sight even during their acolyte days. "Myrill spoke to me! For the first time since I was a little girl." She returned Julia's silver chain with its gently glowing vial. "You carry Her mercy in your heart, Julia. She told me one of Her wayward daughter's unfathered children needs you. You must return to where it all began before sunrise, or he is lost."

Julia gasped.

"Myrill's 'wayward daughter'? 'Unfathered children'?" Damia asked. "What sort of trouble are you in?"

"Oh no!" Julia exclaimed. "It's nearly the twelfth hour, and I have to run across the city!"

Why Endure So Much?

Dawn was approaching, and Ulric had returned to the streets to take refuge in the places blackness still lingered. He crept through back alleys and narrow side streets. He was patient. He joined with the fading shadows and waited. The Polyminia Bridge was close. He was confident he would soon be across the river and within the relative safety of the Transnanpela District. He had left Pavos dazed at the icehouse, bested Wultgar in the test of balance, and had not seen nor heard any sign of Myros and Helva since he took to the rooftops.

All around him, the city roused itself from slumber. He could hear families moving about their homes, smell the spices of their morning meals, but he ignored his hunger and kept his eyes on the bridge from the cover of a shadow-drenched alley. A handful of tradesmen and laborers had trickled onto the streets. The great bridge, spanning the breadth of the river over twenty-two stone arches, was wide enough to allow three wagons to cross, but only a small group of drowsy-looking men trudged across it. They were heading north toward Ulric.

He needed to cross while traffic on the bridge was still sparse, and now was his chance. With one last glance along the street, he left the safety of the alley and jogged toward the bridge, unable to outrun the numbing exhaustion that was overtaking him. The pain of his wounds would inevitably break out of its prison, and soon. As he stepped onto the bridge, all he could think of was the sanctuary of the theater loft, where he would put Julia's healing skills to the test.

Ulric crossed paths with the laborers. Most of the men ignored him, assuming he was a stray or some other homeless wretch. A couple of them summoned enough interest to hurl a few insults, but he kept his head down and walked on. Then the bridge vibrated faintly with a familiar yet dreadful rhythm. The impact of hard boots on paving stones grew louder, like approaching thunder. Helva had found him!

There was no escape but forward, across the bridge. Ulric ran with what little strength he had left, but he feared it wouldn't be enough.

Despite the ample space, the laborers threw themselves against the nearest railing to make way for the charging mercenary; then, they ran to the north side of the river. Helva was closing the distance fast, and Ulric had to face him head-on rather than risk being tackled at a dead run. He came to a stumbling stop near the center of the bridge and nearly fell but reached out at the last moment to prevent a crash onto the paving stones.

Helva stopped twenty paces away, breathing hard with the exertion of the chase. Ulric stood, bent over, hands on knees, gasping for air. They both eyed each other warily while they caught their breath.

"How are you standing, let alone running, little thief?" Helva asked. "You're a canny one; I'll give you that."

"And you and your men"—Ulric stood and exhaled—"are damned persistent."

"Wultgar?"

Ulric shook his head. "He took a tumble."

"May Cathus honor him, and Alakur bless him." The conviction in Helva's voice surprised Ulric.

"Myros?"

"The fool's probably lost. I'm sure he'll be joining us before long." He slowly, deliberately, drew his sword. It was a gladius, a short sword favored by the Trumin infantry; a broad steel blade ending in a triangular point. "Feel like answering any questions now?"

Ulric shifted his weight. "No."

"Fair enough."

Still, something appeared to gnaw at him. "Marius Secundus expected to be robbed, but he didn't expect an assassin. You were set up, and I'd bet good coin you knew it."

Ulric was silent for a long moment. Finally, he said, "You're right. I was set up. I knew as soon as I woke in Aquila's little torture chamber."

"Why the bullheaded stubbornness!" Helva asked. "Why endure so much to protect the people who betrayed you?"

"Sorry, you get the one answer. I was granting the last request of a dying man."

Helva laughed bitterly. "You've got balls on you, boy, no doubt!" He moved toward Ulric, sword at the ready. "You've cost me too much in time and reputation to let this end any other way. I'll try to make it quick, but no guarantees if you insist on jumping around."

"Fair enough."

Helva readied his wide-bladed sword and quickened his pace, but a whip-crack sound brought him to a staggering halt. The right side of his face swelled as a cascade of hot blood obscured his vision. He hadn't even seen the throw that sent a sharp bit of paving stone slamming into his face above his right eye.

Ulric had been concealing the stone from Helva since he had pretended to stumble and fall at the end of their chase. Now the mercenary was surprised and off-balance. Ulric had to make the most of it. Ghostwalker had taught him much about fighting, but always with an eye toward evasion and escape. He had seen Arrius use the Shadow Ways to move and fight with a grace and speed that was unnatural, nearly magical, but he withheld training in those deeper arts with vague excuses that the time wasn't right.

Silently cursing his mentor's timing, Ulric sprang forward, closing the distance in an instant, coming at Helva on his blind side. He dodged a wild thrust and intercepted Helva's sword arm, using his momentum to pull him off balance. Ulric slammed a heel into the side of his left knee, sending the bigger man down.

Ulric had been ready to die. When he turned to face Helva on the bridge, there could have been no other outcome. The mercenary had experience, height, and sixty pounds over him, not to mention the only weapon. Neesis had given him a chance, he reminded himself, and he was duty-bound to put in a good showing. He lied to himself, of course. Somewhere in the back of his mind, he still hoped for life. He still longed for the impossible, the wild luck that could lead to escape. Or… why not hope for victory?

Ulric watched Helva go down and moved in to disarm him. Instead of landing hard and flat, Helva rolled and sprung up with surprising speed, sending a thrust toward Ulric's belly. He tried to arrest his forward momentum, but it was too late. The steel point slid deep into his left side; the wide blade was cold, violating agony. He screamed and threw himself backward off the gladius before Helva could twist the blade. It exited with a nauseating squelch and a gush of blood. Ulric clutched his side and stumbled back several steps until he fell against the bridge's western railing.

Helva stood, towering over Ulric like the bloody cyclops of legend. "I warned you about jumping around, thief." He stepped forward to deliver the killing blow.

With his last bit of strength, Ulric threw himself over the railing and into the dark waters of the Nanpela River.

Black river and sky tumbled around him; then he hit the water flat and hard. He sank deep, and the current swept him under the Polyminia Bridge. He surfaced in the darkness beneath one of the bridge's great stone arches, surprised to be alive. Sputtering, he struggled to keep his head above water. With more frantic splashing than swimming, he covered the short distance to the nearest arch wall, only to become entangled in a mass of detritus stuck under the bridge. Ironically, the floating debris was now the only thing keeping him from drowning. In the black beneath the bridge, Ulric recoiled to see a dead body floating alongside him. He calmed himself and forced his eyes to see where others could not: the 'body' turned out to be only a bit of driftwood and trash.

Ulric was alive, but he would soon bleed out if he didn't get help. His thoughts turned again to the theater loft and Julia. First, he had to escape Helva. The mercenary was still on the bridge, peering into the darkness and searching the river. Thanks to Neesis, Ulric could give him what he was looking for. He took a moment to untangle the suspicious-looking driftwood and pushed it into the middle of the water underneath the arch. The current caught it and took it downriver. He waited and listened. There were shouts from somewhere above. Myros had finally joined Helva. When he heard them running toward the northern bank of the Nanpela, he knew the ruse had worked, thanks to the remaining dark and a bit of luck. He silently thanked the Goddess.

Ulric made the slow and painful swim from one arch abutment to the next until he reached the southern bank. He dragged himself onto a stretch of mud and flipped over onto his back, gazing up at the sky. All the stars had faded as the black of night retreated, leaving a pale amethyst cloak overhead. Soon, there would be no shadows left to protect him. The night was nearly over; the time of thieves was done.

The agony of every crushing blow, bloody cut, and hellish burn shattered their mental prison gates. They ran rioted across his body, sending a convulsive shudder through his aching muscles.

Get up, you worthless whoreson! You're alive! You've done it! Now you can lie here and die alone and friendless, or you can get up and live to see that

Verdan bastard eat steel. Arrius would love to see that! Besides, you promised Neesis you would if only She gave you a chance. And She gave you plenty!

Ulric pulled himself out of the muck, and the pain made him scream out in defiance. He stood and took one halting step forward.

"I'm not friendless…" he mumbled to himself.

Julia's my friend. He remembered their night flirting in the loft and their confrontation with Titus and his Gutter-Fish. *Maybe more than a friend, but I'll never know if I die here.*

He looked down at his side to see his wound oozing blood through the thick mud covering his body.

"She should be handy with a needle and thread, at least."

Myrill's Mercy

Ulric made his way through alleys and side streets, trying to avoid the increasing traffic on the roads as dawn drew near. He marched inexorably toward the Polyminius Theater, his wounds making the effort ever more difficult. The thought of Julia was the one thing driving him on, guiding him. It didn't matter anymore if she could help or not. He didn't want to die alone.

Near Dyer's Street, a group of women walked down the road, busily chatting. They carried a variety of jugs and basins, no doubt heading for the nearby public fountains. Fearing his bloody appearance would elicit more screams than help, he desperately sought a hiding place. He ducked down the nearest exit: a broad alley running due east. Unexpectedly, he exchanged one group of gawkers for another.

He had stumbled into an encampment of several strays. He thought, given his condition, he'd fit right in. The idea made him laugh out loud, causing his gut to wrench in pain. His croaking laughter sent an alley cat darting out of his path, attracting the attention of the closest strays.

The men turned and watched as Ulric staggered closer. He avoided their gaze and plodded down the center of the alley. All he wanted was to reach the far end and be gone. An old man with an unkempt beard and a head of wispy white hair under a tattered blue cloak stood up.

"Myrill's Mercy!" he cried, his voice cracked, weak. "What has this city done to you, boy? Best stop your wandering and take a rest here." The blue-cloaked man reached out and put a trembling hand on Ulric's shoulder. "You'll be safe here."

"Got to keep moving. Julia." Ulric kept his eyes fixed on the far end of the alley.

A younger man, dressed in little more than rags, approached and looked at Ulric's wounds. "Who did this, brother?" When he received no answer, he said, "Rest. We've even stashed a bit of food we could share."

"No! Thank you, but no. I can't." Ulric stumbled down the alleyway. "Thank you, but... I have to go."

A few steps later, he found the way blocked by a stray with a familiar-looking, near-toothless smile. It was Ruga, the stray he'd fought with two nights before.

"Hear me, brothers! This is no fellow stray!" Ruga jabbed an accusing finger toward Ulric. "This here little shit is a thief and knife man that nearly bled Musca and me the other night."

Musca sprang from the shadows. "It's him, alright! He came at us with boot and knife, demanding what little we had."

More strays stood and shouted their support.

The blue-cloaked man tried to calm the encampment. "Whatever disagreements the other night, this morning, he's joined the lowest of the low. We should welcome the boy and help where we can."

Ulric had little faith that the debate would end in his favor. He lunged forward and pushed Ruga aside with a feeble move that left the stray more surprised than off-balance. Ruga and Musca watched Ulric run for the eastern end of the alley at a pitiable pace. They laughed, and several other strays joined in.

"Bring him down, brothers!" Ruga and Musca ran after Ulric and a few other strays followed, despite the protests of the blue-cloaked man and his followers.

With a vengeful mob behind him, the only way out was forward. Ulric ran toward the end of the alley. High, dark walls perfectly framed the eastern sky and freedom. The fierce glow of impending dawn filled the sky. Against that backdrop of promised salvation, a woman appeared on the street, her dark curves silhouetted in fire. He marveled at seeing such an ugly moment filled with unexpected beauty.

Unseen hands shoved Ulric to the ground. The vision of salvation was gone. Ruga, Musca, and the strays closed in. With curses and spittle, they began kicking away what little life he had left.

After everything, to be killed by strays! How embarrassing.

The woman on the street screamed and ran into the alley. "Stop! Leave him alone!"

The strays ignored her. "For Myrill's sake, mercy!" No one heeded her call. In desperation, she tried to pull the nearest man away from Ulric. "Please, stop. I beg you!"

"Away with you, girl!" Ruga spat. When she wouldn't let go, he struck her down into the filth of the alley. "Be gone, girl, or I play nasty with you after we've stomped this rat!"

Ruga tried to turn away but stood dumbstruck instead.

The woman slowly rose as if lifted by an unseen hand. As she stood, the sun dawned behind her, filling the alley with a fierce golden light. A nimbus of holy fire framed her dark hair, and her eyes shone with righteous anger.

Julia had come to save him.

She spoke with the voice of the Goddess. "The dark rage within your spirits shall be calmed! Let the dawning light fill your hearts with Myrill's mercy!"

Each man stopped and stood entranced. They gazed into her blinding beauty, and it reflected the ugliness of their own souls at them. They heard the Goddess' words and recoiled in horror at the memory of their murderous fury. The weight of their guilt drove many to their knees; others wept and fled from the light, hoping to hide their shame in the shadows.

Trembling on his knees, Ruga tried to look into the morning light but could not. With bowed head and clasped hands, in a weak voice filled with shame and sorrow, he said, "Mercy. Mercy, Goddess. Revered priestess, forgive me… I did not know."

Julia looked down with pity. In her own voice, a voice filled with kindness, she said, "Myrill forgives you. Carry Her mercy in your heart; you honor the Goddess when you share it with others."

"Thank you, priestess!" Ruga rose to his feet. He kept his head bowed and repeated, "Thank you. Thank you!" He turned and ran out of the alley.

Now alone, Myrill's divine light faded, and Julia fell to her knees next to Ulric. Seeing the extent of his wounds for the first time, she feared he was dying. Tears welled up in her eyes, and she looked to the heavens. "Merciful Gods, what am I to do?"

A Thief's Gratitude

Deep in the recesses of his mind, Ulric heard something—an echoed voice—gentle yet purposeful. He strained to open his eyes, but his lids were as heavy as lead coins.

"Ulric. Open your eyes and… Look. At. Me."

The voice was familiar in all the best ways: calming, reassuring, beckoning. Once more, Ulric tried to open his eyes. His eyelids cracked the dried blood cementing them shut, and the dawn sun blinded him. Slowly, a woman came into focus. The overpowering sunlight obscured her face but gave her silhouette a divine halo. He peered up into her gently smiling face, her dark hair blending into the fiery dawn sky.

Red curls…

"Tessa? Mother?" he whispered, almost imperceptibly.

So… I'm… dead? And Tessa is here to greet me?

Ulric squeezed his eyes shut and fought to order his thoughts. He slowly reopened his eyes and saw the woman's hair was a bob of black curls.

Dark curls… like a Bayjoni princess…

"Julia?"

She said nothing. Instead, she reached into the front of her tunic and pulled forth a silver chain. A small crystal vial no longer than the end of her thumb dangled from the end, holding a liquid the color of a cloudless sky. Nestling the vial on her bosom, Julia reached behind her neck and carefully unclasped the chain.

"Julia!" he rasped through blood-caked lips. "So that's what you were hiding under your tunic? Thank Neesis. The best of fortunes, I ran into you."

Julia tilted her head, and her gentle smile widened. "Shhhh."

Such a beautiful face.

She released the vial from its silvery bond and twisted off the stopper. Ulric watched as she held it between the fingertips of both hands and reverently lifted it to the sky. She closed her eyes and mouthed a silent prayer. He studied her lips, trying to make out the words, but to no avail.

What beautiful lips.

Julia finished her prayer and lowered her gaze from the heavens. She held open Ulric's lips and dribbled the cyan liquid into his mouth drop by drop.

There was a strange tingling. It started on his tongue, then spread through his neck and shoulders. Soon it made its way into his chest and abdomen, down his arms and legs, and finally to his fingers and toes. He watched in awe as the bruises on his arms disappeared. The gash in his side closed up, and the nasty burn on his ribs shrunk and vanished. He watched as the many cuts, abrasions, and burns covering his body healed. The wounds were gone, leaving behind only the filth and blood from the night's tribulations.

Julia brushed a tangled lock of hair from his forehead. He said nothing, only listened. He listened to her eyes; they spoke volumes.

Such beautiful eyes.

They were the last thing Ulric saw before succumbing to blackness once again.

Ulric opened his eyes and squinted at the sunlight, wondering how much time had passed.

Moments? Hours? How long?

Julia asked, "What happened to you?"

She cradled him in her arms and leaned forward, covering his face in soothing shadow. He opened his eyes wide and looked up into her dark eyes, still wet and raw with tears. The morning sun hung low in the sky behind her, illuminating the green palla she had draped over her shoulders. The same buildings lined the alleyway as before.

Praise Neesis! There's still time!

He prepared to rise, expecting a painful struggle but sprang to his feet in one powerful motion. The pain, his constant companion since awakening in Aquila's courtyard, was gone. A divine energy and ecstatic joy filled his body and spirit. He spun around, looking at his arms and torso in astonishment. Underneath the dried blood and caked mud, the burns, bruises, and cuts were gone. Even the terrible wound from Helva's sword thrust had vanished.

Uric looked down at Julia. "How?"

Julia rose to her feet, her face beaming, and held up the empty vial. "A physic, brewed in the Temple of Myrill and blessed by the Goddess."

"It must have cost a small fortune! I don't know how I could ever repay you. I'm not sure what to say, but… thank you. Thank you, Julia!"

She took a step forward and extended her hand to Ulric. "We can walk along the Via Delubrarum and give prayers of thanks before Myrill's shrine. On the way, you can tell me what happened. And I'll tell you about last night. I discovered who was behind the Gutter-fish, and I put an end to it! With Myrill's guidance, of course."

Ulric took a step back and looked away as if he'd barely heard a word she'd said. "Yes, praise Myrill. Tell me all about it. Later." Then his voice hardened. "Now I've got a man to kill."

"Myrill's Mercy! You want to kill a man?"

"You asked what happened to me. You wanted the truth when we next met? Then I'll tell you what happened."

Ulric's jaw and fists clenched at the memory of betrayal, humiliation, and torture.

"Luciano Porteles happened to me. And now"—his eyes blazed with hate as he forced his next words through gritted teeth—"I'm going to happen to him."

"Ulric, I don't know who this Luciano is. I don't know if he deserves death or not. I know Alakur's divine will and Myrill's mercy healed you. You don't have to repay me, but you can repay the Goddess by forgiving this Luciano."

Ulric erupted in a short, bitter laugh. "Mercy for Luciano! Madness worthy of a disciple of Neesis Insania!" With a wry smile, he asked, "Are you sure you're honoring the right goddess?"

Julia's eyes narrowed to dark slits as she crossed her arms. "Only fools mock the gods, Marcus Octavius Ulric."

Ulric crossed his own arms. "Lucky for me, Neesis has a sense of humor, Persius Julia."

The two stood glaring at each other for a long moment. Julia's posture and expression shouted: 'Say something stupid again, please.' Ulric's face replied: 'I'll think of something!'

But Ulric couldn't think of anything to say, so he threw up his hands. "I don't have time for this. Luciano may have already left the city. We can argue theology later."

He turned and hurried out of the alley onto Dyer's Street. Julia let slip an aggravated cry and caught up with Ulric, matching his pace.

"Do not be so dismissive of mercy and forgiveness, Ulric. It is through Myrill's mercy that I was here to save you. 'Alakur, Father, and Guardian of all mankind, to You is given care of my fate. May You watch over me, Your humble servant; and Myrill, Mother and Healer of all Alakur's children, to Your mercy do I appeal, may You strengthen my bones and heal my wounds.' So say the divine teachings." She made the last statement as if it would end all future debates.

"Now you're quoting the priests' texts to me?" He rolled his eyes, but Julia didn't notice.

"'Let us then, as servants of Myrill, therefore march boldly to Her throne, that we may thank Her for granting us help in our time of need. For no man ever made it far without Her mercy.'"

"Shall I recite the litanies of Neesis while we're at it? Besides, forgiveness is fine for family and friends, but Luciano is neither. And mercy? Mercy is earned. The only thing Luciano has earned is swift retribution."

"Are you saying 'Nee-sis'? Myrill's wayward daughter? Nyssa's dark sister? One should be careful when dealing with the Gods Below. A proper Trumin doesn't honor an Underworld power so ardently. One of my tutors called it 'fashionable Kreslan dissidence.'"

Ulric stopped and turned to Julia, disrupting the early morning traffic and causing several nearby collisions.

"Julia, I'm not even sure I know what that means!"

People continued moving past the squabbling pair, muttering and scowling as they went.

"It means, Ulric, show your gratitude by giving up any ideas of vengeance. Last night I was nearly undone by my anger, and only Myrill's mercy saved me. Saved you." She extended her hand once again. "Come with me before running off and doing something foolish."

"Myrill will have to do with a thief's gratitude, as it's not mercy I need," Ulric said with increasing frustration. "It's the blessing of Neesis! When I face Luciano, I'll need all the luck I can get. I vowed I'd send him to the Underworld. I have to do it."

Julia's hand dropped, and her eyes welled with tears. "Please, don't go. I won't be there to save you a second time."

"You're afraid I'll be killed? Is that what this is all about?" Ulric spoke as if the past argument was a misunderstanding of no consequence. "No need to worry, Julia! Neesis is with me. It's Luciano who'll die today, not me!"

Resigned, Julia slowly shook her head. "Oh, you're such a fool."

She threw her arms around Ulric's neck and kissed him. Surprised, he hesitated but then pulled her close, reveling in the touch of her soft lips and the curves of her perfect body. After a night of endless cruelty, her tenderness was shocking.

When she stepped back, he asked, "What was that for?"

"Luck!"

He broke into a wide grin. "I knew you were goddess sent."

Ulric ran down the street, eager to begin the hunt for Luciano. He drew in a long breath. It was refreshing. It was the first one in a long while that didn't taste like blood and desperation. Instead, it tasted like revenge.

Madness and Bold Action

There you are, you Verdan devil. I see you.

It hadn't been difficult to track Luciano down to a particular merchant ship bound for Mist View. The combination of his tall, lean frame and heavy Verdan accent had made the job all too easy. First, Ulric had to run through the Transnanpela and Portum Mare districts, picking what pockets he could. By the time he reached the docks, he had collected enough to buy a second-hand tunic, frayed leather belt and pouch, two double-bladed throwing knives, and a well-worn gladius.

He watched as Luciano finished an animated discussion with the ship's captain. Whatever the man had told him, it had not set well. It was only the third hour of the day; had Luciano tried convincing him to push off before high tide? Regardless, it was obvious he and his passenger were not seeing eye-to-eye. When the captain turned his back to him and walked away, Luciano spat on the deck. The captain, either oblivious or unconcerned, entered the ship's castle.

Luciano turned toward the side of the ship and wrapped his hands tightly around the rail, his teeth grinding. He scanned the docks, then released a growl of frustration and marched to an open hatch and stomped into the lower decks.

Ulric came out from behind several barrels of crabs and dashed for the side of the ship. As he shimmied up a mooring line, he caught sight of the ship's name engraved and painted in black on the hull: "Neesis Insania."

He grinned from ear to ear.

Taking a moment to check that no one could see him, Ulric leaped over the railing and landed on the deck, his bare feet hardly making a sound. He crouched low, made for the trapdoor, then descended enough steps to nullify his profile on the ship's deck. Pausing, he summoned the heightened awareness that was the thieves' glimmer. He heard only the drone of the bustling docks, busy sailors, the creaking ship, and the rats scrabbling in the hold. Confident he had boarded undetected, he pulled the two throwing knives from his belt and went below.

His glimmer-enhanced eyes cut through the gloom, scanning the hold—larger than he would have guessed—over twenty paces wide and well over double that in length. The space was dimly lit by two lanterns hanging overhead. Numerous vertical wooden beams dotted the hold, spread apart every five or six paces. Close by, several hammocks hung between the beams. Deeper within, stacks of crates, barrels, and amphorae lined the hull. The whole place smelled of old timbers, bilge water, and unwashed crewmen. At the far end, Ulric spotted the silhouette of his mark, crouching under the low overhead.

"Change you mind, Captain? Set sail now, eh?"

"It's me, you lying piece of shit."

Luciano spun around, unsheathing his sword in a single, fluid motion. He held Ghostwalker's long-bladed cavalry sword, and the strange etchings on the blade flared in the faint lamplight. His eyes narrowed, then widened with surprise.

"Boy?"

Without saying a word, Ulric slung the pair of throwing knives. Impossibly fast, Luciano swept his spatha through the air, batting away one blade with a metallic ring as the other knife narrowly missed the assassin to impale itself in a nearby beam.

"Why you here? Is boy crazy? You want to die?" He mockingly tapped the blade of his spatha on his palm.

Ulric snatched the gladius from his belt and brandished it at the assassin. "You set me up, you Verdan bastard!"

"You not like Luciano's little joke, eh? You good... distraction while Aguja bleed fool Secundus. I thought student of great Ghostwalker could steal a statue."

"The sphinx was trapped! Don't lie and say you didn't know." Ulric marched toward Luciano, vengeance in his eyes.

Luciano cackled and took a confident step forward. "Yes, yes, trapped. Screaming statue, very clever. I no lie. Only the fearful lie. Why should I fear a boy?" Luciano's hyena-like laughter filled the cabin.

"And the gas! The blue lotus gas! I never had a chance!"

"Gas?"

Ulric lunged, his gladius flashing like lightning but never connecting. Luciano countered, swinging his blade quickly but awkwardly from a cramped, crouched position. Ulric retreated. The assassin instinctively straightened up for a downward thrust but struck the crown of his skull on the low overhead. Massaging the growing bump with his free hand, he stepped back, putting some distance between himself and his foe.

"The widow had me strung up! Tortured with hot irons! Imprisoned!"

Ulric pressed forward, matching Luciano's retreat and thrusting his gladius with each step. Luciano blocked each attack until his spatha thwacked heavily against a beam, sending pulses of pain into his wrist. He flipped the weapon to his offhand and went on point; his sword extended before him. He clenched and unclenched his free hand over and over, trying to shake off the numbness.

"Hot irons? I see no marks. Now, who lies?"

Ulric charged in again, but this time Luciano fell back and swung around a beam, using the momentum to position himself behind him. Ulric expected such a move and rolled behind his own beam, assuming a high guard stance.

"You escaped. Good! So Ghostwalker training not useless? Now boy track me down: bad move." He pointed his spatha toward the stairs leading to the main deck. "Go."

Ulric hesitated. Despite the advantage his smaller stature and shorter blade gave him in the cramped hold, he hadn't come close to landing a blow. "I can't. I only survived by Ghostwalker's teachings and pure luck. So I made a vow to Neesis Fortuna to reclaim Arrius' sword and take revenge!"

"Stupid boy! We keep fighting here, Imperaré take us!"

To Ulric's surprise, the assassin dashed toward the stairs. Luciano must have had enough of fighting below decks, where Ulric had the advantage.

Ulric raced along the inner hull and leaped between two hammocks, imposing himself between Luciano and the exit. The Verdan sneered and readied another assault. Ulric reached into the pouch at his belt, grabbed a handful of fine sand, and flung it at the assassin's head. Luciano tried to shield his face, but not before the sand grains found their mark. He retreated into the interior of the hold, blinking and squinting his stinging and watering eyes.

"Gah! Street rat tricks!"

Luciano moved behind a row of barrels and rubbed the sand from his eyes. "I knew you not a man. You a tricky street rat, just a squirmy gutter fish. Like Ghostwalker."

Ulric said nothing.

Through squinting eyes, Luciano peered into the dimly lit hold, but Ulric remained motionless in the deep shadows of the cargo hold. With mounting frustration, the Verdan screamed, "I kill you now, boy. Is that what you want? But you anger Luciano! Now… I make you suffer first."

Ulric said nothing. He watched Luciano draw closer, his spatha a deadly point of steel extended before him.

A faint sound drifted through the creaking hold. Movement in the dark. Luciano turned, tightened the grip on his sword, and brought it closer to his chest.

Ulric sprang out from the shadows and charged at Luciano's back. The assassin spun around with a backswing on target to take

Ulric's head off, but at the last moment, he dropped to his knees and slid under the slicing blade. As he passed, he slashed at his legs, but only cut through the hard leather of his Verdan boots. Ulric silently cursed his luck.

When Luciano turned around, Ulric was already on his feet in a defensive stance. Both combatants eyed one another, each waiting for the other to make a move.

Luciano struck first. Ulric backpedaled and tried to block the attack, but the assassin's long blade caught his shoulder, piercing through cloth and flesh alike.

Ulric screamed and landed clumsily on the floor, the impact knocking the gladius out of his hand. It took an unfaithful bounce across the deck toward Luciano. He grabbed his throbbing shoulder, and crimson squirted from between his fingers. His eyes darted from his sword, lying just out of reach on the deck, to Luciano's bloodied spatha. He frantically looked around the hold, then began scooting backward toward one particular beam.

Neesis rewards madness and bold action!

Luciano grinned, took an unopposed step forward, and with a defiant glare, he picked up Ulric's gladius. He turned it over in his hand for a moment, then tossed it aside.

"Now I make you suffer, boy."

A feral, mocking smile stretched across his face as he advanced toward his defenseless prey. Still gripping his bleeding shoulder, Ulric picked himself up off the floor, using the nearby beam to steady himself. As Luciano sidestepped around a pair of amphorae, Ulric shuffled his feet to keep facing his opponent. He winced as he slowly swiveled around the beam and straightened his back.

Luciano paused.

Do it, you Verdan filth.

Ulric fluttered his eyes closed, then back open, then closed again. He loosened his neck and drooped his head, matching the movement of his eyelids. His hand fell from his shoulder, wet with blood. He looked up at Luciano with the face of a defeated man.

"No, no, boy. You not die easy I think, eh?"

Luciano closed in, sword at the ready.

One chance!

Ulric's eyes flashed open. With surprising speed, he knocked Luciano's blade aside, grabbed his forearm, and yanked him forward. He sidestepped, kicked the Verdan's feet out from under him, and sent him lunging toward the beam… and the waiting point of Ulric's double-bladed throwing dagger.

Die, you bastard!

But Luciano saw the throwing knife; one bladed end embedded in the oak beam, the other end waiting to take his life. He twisted his torso, and the blade tore through his leather jerkin but drew no blood. The assassin spun himself behind the beam and, with an effortless swing of his spatha, knocked the would-be murder weapon to the floor.

Ulric's heart sank.

One chance…

Luciano made his way to the stairs and said over his shoulder, "We end this, boy. Come on deck. Die in light."

Ulric pressed his hand against his wounded shoulder and winced. He dropped to his knees and cast his head down, smashing his fist upon the deck. Defeat was no longer an actor's deception; now, it was as real as if the knife had plunged into his own chest. He knelt on the deck for a long moment, beaten. Then a wild thought crept into his mind.

To fight Luciano topside in broad daylight—and wounded—is madness.

Ulric gathered his strength, retrieved his gladius, and ascended the stairs, ready to face Luciano Porteles once more.

Luciano rested against the mast, casually holding Ghostwalker's spatha in one hand and a Verdan stilius in the other. Ulric knew the slender needle-like dagger to be Luciano's weapon of choice, designed to deliver the killing blow to a wounded opponent. He drew in a slow breath and took a few unsure steps toward the assassin.

"You street rat or you bilge rat now? Crew know they such big rats below?"

Madness.

Again, Ulric advanced, more boldly this time. His mind wandered.

The ship's name: Neesis Insania. That can't be a coincidence!

Luciano, the hyena, cackled, boiling Ulric's blood. He tightened the grip on his sword, and his face flushed with rage. This bold madness, he knew, would culminate shortly.

The assassin spoke through gritted teeth. "I make you suffer now, boy. Only after will *Aguja* pierce you gut. You not die quickly, tricky little rat. I promise you. Only after you suffer. Only after."

If death came, could he face the end with the dignity Ghostwalker had shown? Or would he shame himself? He'd seen so many die poorly in the gutters of Mist View.

Ulric slid his rear leg back and assumed a high guard, bracing for Luciano's first attack. It came swiftly.

The Verdan charged, now unhindered by the cramped hold, driving Ulric back across the deck, the sheer ferocity of the attack battering down his defense.

The duel had caught the attention of the ship's crew. They gathered on deck, astonished looks on their faces. Ulric narrowly avoided a blinding strike—and paid the crew no more heed. He fled behind a stack of water barrels and took a moment to catch his breath.

Ulric overheard the captain barking orders to a crewman. Something about "the Portus Collegium," followed by quick footsteps descending the ship's ramp.

Luciano leaped at the barrels, bringing his spatha down toward his head. Ulric rolled aside, and the blade lodged deep into the top of a barrel. Ulric lunged with his gladius. It was a weak thrust and barely pierced through the Verdan's leather jerkin. The assassin let loose a cry of frustration more than pain, and Ulric escaped just as he freed his blade.

My grand revenge: a few drops of blood!

Ulric fell back, wary eyes locked on his opponent.

"Do I frighten you, eh, little street rat? You know you end is coming." Luciano cackled as if he had made some grand joke.

Before Ulric could reply, the assassin was upon him, his blade nothing more than a blur of steel as he unleashed a barrage of swings and thrusts. There was no parrying this time; Luciano's attacks were swift and precise. Razor sharp steel slid along Ulric's thigh, and he screamed. Then the broadside of the assassin's blade struck his wrist. The pain was unbearable; his gladius flew from his hand. Before the sword had clattered to the deck, Luciano's boot heel slammed into his wounded shoulder, sending him sprawling onto the deck. The pain in his thigh, wrist, and shoulder was excruciating. He struggled for breath while the sky spun about the mast of the ship in a nauseating dance of defeat.

Luciano came into view, towering over him with spatha and Aguja in hand.

"You had chance to walk away, boy."

Ulric tried to scoot away, but Luciano stomped a boot down hard on his bleeding thigh. He screamed. He longed for the calm, the comforting distance given by Shadow Mind, but there was only the overwhelming fear of the waking world. Luciano stood over him, gleeful hatred in his eyes, the needle-like dagger ready to strike. What would it feel like as it pierced his skin? His ribs? His heart?

Ulric liked to think he didn't fear death. No honest Trumin should. Upon death, the spirit became a part of Alakur's court in the Empyrean realm or that of his brother Arakru's in the Underworld. For Ulric death had always meant Neesis' welcoming embrace into the Underworld. Or it did? Now death meant a vow unfulfilled. Would the Goddess forgive him? Or would he suffer the fate of all who offend the gods? Cast out through the Nine Gates: nine hellish realms of suffering leading to the Wyrm, the thing that coils and gnaws within the chaos at the center of creation.

He waited for Aguja's plunge.

Luciano sheathed his dagger and lodged his spatha in the nearby mast. He dropped his full weight on Ulric, pinning his arms against the deck with his knees.

"I going to enjoy this, boy."

The first punch was pure pain. The second struck with a loud crack of bone, though he was unsure whether it was Luciano's knuckles or his own nose. He was only vaguely aware of the storm of blows that followed.

He had gambled, as always, but his luck had run out. Fortune's well had run dry.

Luciano, his chest heaving, unsheathed Aguja. Licking the sweat from his lips, the Verdan stared into Ulric's eyes as he raised the dagger.

Dazed, he closed his eyes and waited for the end, but still, there was no Aguja. No needle-like blade punctured his chest. The dreadful anticipation was maddening. He found himself thinking not of damnation, but of regret. Of Julia.

I told her not to worry. And now I'm dead. I hope she doesn't think her kiss wasn't good enough? I'm sure it was a lucky kiss. I failed. I failed everyone. Arrius… sorry.

"Julia… sorry… Julia."

The deck vibrated with a sudden stampede of heavy boots. He opened his eyes. A group of tattooed thugs brandishing a variety of street steel had surrounded them. Luciano furiously plunged his precious Aguja into the deck. Moving his gaze back to Ulric, the Verdan spat out, "We play again soon, boy."

A giant of a man loomed over Luciano, his presence making it clear neither of them had any chance of escape. Two other heavies carrying short swords and punching daggers flanked the brute. Ulric guessed they were "Harbor Men," judging from their telltale ink. Behind them stood four other men, all sporting red scarves on their arms and wielding vicious spiked clubs. Another man stepped into view, tall and lean, wearing a crimson scarf around his bald head. These last five men must have been from the Portus Collegium, the official port authority. Though not as wild and dangerous-looking as the Harbor Men, Ulric feared these men the most, for they had the sanction of the Imperaré and were authorized by the Republic to maintain order on the docks of Trumric.

The bald man gave a subtle nod to the brute, who then grunted an order at the two Harbor Men. They yanked Ulric to his feet.

Ulric said nothing. He made no attempt to resist. He had thrown the dice, and it was a losing throw, what gamblers called a "canine cast"—the dreaded double ones. The game was over.

The Imperarê

"Get those two off the street!"

The man was a towering Northman, red-haired and bearded, dressed in the strange, checkered tunic and pants of the tribes beyond Gualdé. He angrily stalked across the road, sending people scurrying out of his way. When he thudded to a halt in front of the Imperaré and Harbor-Men who held Ulric and Luciano, he said, "The Chief wants this kept in the shadows, you idiots."

The bald Imperaré man with a red scarf tied around his forehead shoved his way past the Harbor-Men. "Too late, Gwynedd," he said. He nodded toward the canal bridge where a curious rabble had gathered. Turning back to the newcomer, he smirked. "We're torched."

"The Chief wants what he wants," Gwynedd said matter-of-factly. He took several steps forward, forcing the smirking man to retreat. He leaned down and placed his fire-scarred face a hair's breadth from the frightened man's nose. "We get off the street—now!"

The smirk surrendered. "Of course, Gwynedd! Where to?"

He scanned the street, suddenly looking bored. "It'll have to do. Now march!"

Gwynedd led the troop a short distance down North Canal Street and forced their way past a small crowd gathered outside a butcher's shop.

He threw the doors open and pushed Ulric and Luciano through. His men poured inside over the protests of the butcher, a plump Kreslan with a pinched and mottled face like an overripe pear.

"Out! Epicydes' shop is closed," Gwynedd said.

"What is this? What is this!" The butcher threw up his hands and started running back and forth along the length of his counter. "Oh, no! No one has to leave! You can't do this, Gwynedd! The Festival of Mantius is nearly here!" He looked like he was performing some wild temple dance that only grew more frantic as his customers fled. "I'll lose a small fortune!"

Gwynedd ignored the absurd display. "Take those two in the back and keep a close eye on them." As everyone filed past, he pulled one of the younger men aside. "Not you, Nepos. You run and tell the Chief we're here. He's probably already heading for the harbormaster."

Finally, he turned to Epicydes. The man's outburst had exhausted him, and he leaned on the counter, looking red-faced and indignant. Now he had Gwynedd's attention, and the butcher's eyes lit up with anticipation. Before he could utter a word of protest, he erupted in a girlish shriek and threw himself away from the counter. To the butcher's eyes, Gwynedd's axe appeared as if by magic. It hit the counter with a loud thwack, messily bisecting a goose he had been preparing for a now absent customer.

"One word, butcher—one word—and you'll be hanging in the back with the rest of the rotting meat."

The man struggled to catch his breath but said nothing.

"Good. Now, let's wait quietly for the Chief."

Ulric had heard it all. He had been listening, watching; he needed to learn all he could about his captors. They were both Harbor-Men gang thugs and Portus Collegium enforcers, yet they took orders from a Northman named Gwynedd, who received his orders from the 'Chief'. Whoever the chief was, he was Imperaré, and that meant power.

They slammed Ulric into a corner of the back room and tossed Luciano into the other. He sat up, feeling the ropes biting into his wrists. Leaning back, he tried not to grimace when the pain shot through his shoulder. The men had taken positions around the room and now stood vigilant, their hands on their weapons. The dripping carcasses of a hog, two goats, and countless fowl hung from the ceiling, and rows of fresh fish lined the shelves. Everywhere he looked, there were hooks, knives, and cleavers. The floor was stained and filthy with slaughter, and flies buzzed. The place smelled of fresh meat, rancid fat, and blood.

If it is to be interrogation, torture, and murder, then you couldn't have picked a better stage, Gwynedd.

Ulric kept his eyes down, avoiding the hard gaze of his captors, but it was really Luciano whom he didn't want to see. The Verdan assassin, like Ulric, hadn't said a word since the Harbor-Men dragged them off the Neesis Insania. During their forced march from the docks, Luciano had stared at him with contempt-filled eyes and a predatory smile. The assassin had dared him to meet his gaze. He had felt the gloating triumph in those eyes, felt Luciano's hate burning him. When he turned to face him, he knew the assassin saw the defeat in his eyes. Luciano's outburst of hyena-like laughter had unnerved even their captors.

Ulric tried to take some slight satisfaction in the thought that whatever the Imperaré had planned, Luciano would get the worst of it. His own transgressions were minor compared to a Dark Assembly assassin caught performing shroud work in Imperaré territory. He hoped they would execute Luciano in a gruesome and creative manner. He planned to watch.

Ulric closed his eyes and took those pleasant thoughts with him into Shadow Mind. Whatever was to come, he didn't need the distraction of his wounded shoulder and thigh. The butcher shop faded, and he focused on ending the bleeding and subduing the pain. Two minor wounds were a simple Shadow Mind exercise, and he quickly confined the pain behind high walls of will. He intended to remain in the trance but sensed a change in the room. He emerged from the depths of his mind to see men standing taller, adjusting their weapons, and looking more alert. The Chief had arrived.

Ulric heard a voice, a voice that sounded unexpectedly familiar. "I know that look, Epicydes. You'll be compensated if you keep your mouth shut and smiling."

The Chief strode in, with Gwynedd close behind. The man was tall with familiar looking gray-flecked hair the color of iron and a lean body that must have known a lifetime of soldiering. Ulric had seen through the friendly shopkeeper mask the moment he had stepped foot inside Silo's shop in the Porte Mare district. When Titus blanched at the mere mention of his name, he knew he was more than a simple fence, but he would have never guessed Silo was an Imperaré boss.

Silo spoke with an unnerving cheerfulness. "What have we here? Two drunken brawlers disturbing my peaceful harbor?" He pantomimed leaning in for a closer look, then stood and smiled. "Why no, it's our old friend Luciano Porteles, the so-called Hound of Nyx, and the boy who wanted to make a big impression without stirring up too much trouble."

Silo paused for a response, but neither spoke. He walked over and knelt close to Luciano.

"Say, Luciano, you wouldn't have come to the capital to murder Quintus Marius Secundus by chance? Seems somebody bled him good and proper last night. *Quite the coincidence, eh?*" He emphasized the last with an exaggerated Verdan accent.

Luciano said nothing, just glared at Silo. Ulric saw the fires of an old hatred being rekindled in those eyes.

"Then again"—Silo gave a sidelong glance toward Ulric—"the widow thinks a young dark-haired thief may be to blame. Though she's reported he's likely dead."

Silo stood up and returned to the center of the room. "And now we catch you two dueling on board a ship bound for Mist View. Another coincidence? Oh, Neesis, you must be having a bit of fun with these two!"

He looked at his men and asked, "What do you think, boys? A disagreement over spoils? A lover's quarrel?"

The men chuckled and tightened their grips on their weapons.

"The Imperaré demands justice for the murder of Marius Secundus. If one of you doesn't give me something to work with and fast, things will go very, very bad for the both of you." Silo strode back to Luciano. "Listen, you Verdan bastard, I don't like you, but I wouldn't wish what they'll do to you on anyone!"

Luciano remained stubbornly silent.

Silo turned away in disgust and approached Ulric. "And you. Ulric, right? You came into my shop and lied to me like I was some simple mark. I ought to gut you and throw you in the river!"

"Well, Silo, that's how my morning began, so you'll have to fucking do better than that!"

The sound of his own scream shocked him. He hadn't wanted to say anything, yet his frustration and despair had spoken for him. Rather than the expected blow, it was the sound of Luciano's hyena-like laughter that jolted him. Silo returned to the bound assassin.

"This all a laugh to you, Luciano?" His tone was suddenly flat, somehow more menacing.

"If boy"—he struggled to contain his laughter—"not scared, what you think"—he burst into more laughter—"you get out… of me, eh?"

"Scared? Get out of you?" The jovial tone returned, but Ulric couldn't say which was more frightening. "You make this sound like an interrogation. This is just some old friends having a chat."

With the word "chat," Silo kicked Luciano square in the teeth, and the laughter stopped. His head snapped back into the wall with a loud crack. Stunned, he toppled into the corner.

"Welcome back to Trumric!" Silo launched another kick into Luciano's gut, and the Verdan folded over with a grunt.

"I wanted to catch up on old times, and you laugh in my face." He stomped hard on Luciano's knee. He groaned and spat a curse through gritted teeth.

"Why would you insult an old friend like that?" He asked with feigned sorrow. He placed a foot on his neck and pressed.

Luciano did his best to spit blood on Silo's boot. "Nothing! Nothing for you, Silo!"

Silo grinned and leaned forward. "You stupid Verdan swine. Nothing for me, *eh*? So you admit you have something to bargain with! You want to hold it from me out of spite?" Silo's grin turned ugly, and he stomped hard on Luciano's neck. The helpless assassin began kicking and squirming but to no avail.

"You insult me, Luciano. Maybe I'll lose my temper, like the old days? Maybe I won't tolerate insults from foreign swine and break your neck here and now? Maybe the truth behind Marius Secundus' assassination is worth nothing compared to the satisfaction of hearing your neck go crack-fucking-crack!"

Ulric had remained quiet, hoping not to catch Silo's ire. He watched Luciano's beating with growing anticipation. It may not have been the creative execution he had been hoping for, but he silently cheered on Silo's threat of murder, anyway.

Crack-crack! Let's hear it! Come on, Silo, what are you waiting for? Break that Verdan bastard's godsdamned neck!

Silo pulled his boot from Luciano's throat and stepped back.

What? No!

Ulric could only guess Silo saw some sign of acquiescence in the man's eyes.

"Talk," was all Silo said.

Painful coughing wracked Luciano's body as he struggled to gulp in air. He pulled himself up, leaned back in the corner, and nodded toward Silo.

"Dark Assembly, send me, yes," Luciano began in a hoarse, damaged voice. "Last winter, Secundus make deal. Something big. Too big for Assembly. Too big for Imperaré. Cuts everyone out. Hires Ghostwalker. Things go right. Things go wrong. Secundus get prize, but powerful offended. They make Ghostwalker no more. Boy here, Ghostwalker's... don't know Trumin word."

"Discipulus. protégé?" Silo prompted.

"Yes. Boy thinks he special. He blame Secundus. Boy traitor to Dark Assembly. He run from Mist View to capital. Want to avenge Ghostwalker."

"What! Lies! Don't believe—"

Silo casually pointed at Ulric. "Shut it."

Ulric caught the hint of a sly smile on Luciano's split and bloody lips. He continued his lies. "Assembly send me. I tell him boy in city, looking for revenge. I tell Secundus he return what he took. Have till next Kalends. If no, I come with more than words. I leave to report. Stupid boy, attack me. After avenging

Ghostwalker, he no want life no more?" He turned to look at Ulric. "Boy's stupidity get us both killed now, eh?"

Silo turned to his men with a look of exaggerated frustration. "God's Below! That was painful to listen to! You've lived in the Noldani province for how long now? And you still speak Trumin like an idiot child."

Silo's men laughed while Luciano quietly seethed.

"Gwynedd," Silo said.

The scarred Northman stepped forward. "Yes, Chief?"

"What does the philosopher say about truth?"

Gwynedd straightened and looked ahead as if reciting a lesson. "So near is falsehood to truth that a wise man would do well not to trust himself on the narrow edge."

"Did you hear that? Perfect Trumin! And where he comes from, they practically run naked through the forests and sacrifice their enemies to strange gods."

Silo and his men laughed again. Gwynedd laughed, too, but kept his eyes fixed on Luciano.

"Well, young Ulric? Seems we're on the precipice between truth and lies. Care to take us over the edge? What do you have to say for yourself?"

Ulric's mind was reeling, trying to make sense of Luciano's story. Was any of it true? Ulric knew the best lies wore the trappings of truth, just as Luciano's absurd story had. Where did the truth end and the lies begin? The Dark Assembly had wanted Marius Secundus dead for a reason; that much was clear. Could Arrius' last job have been for him? The job that led to his betrayal, capture, and execution? Or had Luciano woven Ghostwalker into his lies to confuse him? What was stolen? And from whom?

There's no time to sort through it all! Gods Above! If this philosopher—Which one? Doesn't matter—isn't right. Lies can't save me here. Time to leap back from the edge.

"Silo, we're all damned liars here. I was taught lies are a weapon, a cloak, and a mask, an essential tool for any thief. But, unlike some Verdan fools, I know lies can't save me now. So, I'll take the philosopher's advice and step back from the narrow edge and speak only the truth. I was Arrius Ghostwalker's protégé. When the Dark Assembly exiled Arrius, by their laws, I was out, too. So, when I left, I betrayed nothing. I arrived in Trumric after the Ides of Eltarius, having never heard the name Marius Secundus. Hoping to operate on my own, I kept shadowed. I admit I begged, tax collected, and ran a few minor schemes to stay fed."

Ulric paused, searching Silo's face for any sign or reaction. The Imperaré boss grinned and began clapping his hands together. "Do you hear that, men? Such a talent for horseshit! We need to get this boy north of the river running honest schemes by nightfall, or barring that, at least in the Senate."

Another round of laughter, this time at Ulric's expense. As usual, the truth appeared to gain him nothing.

Of course, the truth only brings mockery! Sweet Neesis, why did I think this was a good idea, again? Well, I've thrown the dice; no choice but to play out this round.

Ulric hid his disappointment and forged ahead. "Luciano ambushed me in the Transnanpela River Market on the third day before the Nones. He said the Dark Assembly wanted me to steal a golden sphinx statuette from Secundus. It was to be the price of my freedom. He made it clear I had no choice. I know it makes little sense that a man of Luciano's skill and reputation would play the role of messenger. Why did I believe it? I was caught off guard and too desperate to see it for the obvious lie it was. Now Luciano wants you to believe that same lie, Silo."

Ulric took a deep breath. "I prepped as best I could, given my limited time and coin. I even risked visiting a known Imperaré marked shop. How else could I get the tools I needed? It wasn't a hard job for a professional, but Secundus trapped the sphinx. It had been enchanted to protect itself with a rare and expensive spell."

"And that's when the widow got ahold of you?" Silo asked.

"Yes. It was clear they were expecting something, as they had hired four mercenary guards. But it was a thief they were waiting for, not a murderer. I think Luciano tipped Secundus off somehow. Made him expect a robbery, not an assassination. I think my meeting with Luciano was plain bad luck. His idea to use me as a distraction must have been a last moment improvisation. It was only a cruel prank to him."

"Why?" Silo interjected. "Why does he hate you? What's your history back in Mist View?"

"It was really Arrius Ghostwalker, my mentor, that he hated. It went back years, and for reasons Arrius never discussed. You know Luciano? Then you know he's a petty man, eager to take offense and full of resentment. I don't think he cared if I walked away with the sphinx or died at the hands of that bitch, Aquila. As you said earlier, it's all a laugh to him."

Silo was silent for a moment. When he spoke again, Ulric thought he detected a slight softening of his tone. Was the truth working for once?

"The report I had said they beat and tortured you with hot irons half the night. Yet you escaped, despite the efforts of four reliable ex-soldiers. Mind telling how you managed that?"

"Very simple, Silo. Arrius Ghostwalker taught me: the best godsdamned thief to ever tread the Shadow Ways."

"Pfft! Don't listen to boy's lies." Luciano spat. "All Ghostwalker teach boy is to lie good."

Silo turned back to Luciano, "Speaking of lies, there were some important details left out of your little story. What was the item Secundus acquired? Who were they stolen from? Who was his client?"

"You expect everything? Over a bit of... rough play? No, no."

"You want me to bring in the professionals? I've got two retired soldiers from Macula's campaign against the Harathi. Ooh, the things they learned. I've seen them—"

"Boss! Boss!" A young man burst into the shop, interrupting Silo.

Silo angrily spun around. "What in the Nine Gates, Nepos?"

"Sorry, boss." Nepos took a moment to catch his breath. "The Imperaré is in council. You're expected."

"And what prompted this, not that I need to ask?"

"Whisper is they know we have Secundus' murderer," said Nepos.

Gwynedd stepped forward. "That was quick. But not unexpected."

Silo looked at his primus, his second-in-command. "Let's take a guess who called the Imperaré Concilium." They both looked back at Nepos. "What's the whisper?"

As Nepos spoke, Silo and Gwynedd said the name along with him: "Cornelius Brocchus."

Gwynedd spoke the name again and made it sound like a curse. "Brocchus!"

"Son of a bitch," was all Silo said.

Only Ulric noticed the faint smile creeping across Luciano's battered face.

Silo wasted no time and prepared to leave for the Concilium immediately. They blindfolded Ulric and Luciano with a couple of blood-soiled rags; then each had an old sack secured over their head. Ulric's sack smelled of nothing but fish.

Unseen hands lifted Ulric to his feet and led him out the back of Epicydes' shop. Even with the blindfold and sack, he could still detect shifts in light and shadow, feel the contrast of sun or shade, and hear the sounds of his captors and the din of the great city.

After a short trek through back alleys, Gwynedd dismissed the Harbor-Men with orders to keep anything they had seen or heard at Epicydes' shop "shadowed", which was street-speak for keeping their mouths shut. Silo, Gwynedd, and a few Portus Collegium men remained, although Ulric couldn't be sure exactly how many. They continued, following an erratic path until Ulric had lost all sense of direction. Still, there was a distinct drone to the distant crowds and the hint of a sea breeze, which meant they remained in the Portum Mare District.

Everyone stopped. Ulric heard a door open, and they moved from the shade of an alley into the cool dark of a quiet building. There was a brief exchange with someone already inside.

"We're going down." It was Gwynedd.

"Of course." It was an old, haggard voice Ulric hadn't heard before.

There was the jangling of keys and the sound of a heavy metal gate being hauled open. Then feet shuffling, everyone moving, and a pair of firm hands directed Ulric forward.

The hands spoke. "Down you go. The next step." It was Silo.

Ulric stepped into nothingness. For an instant, he feared Silo would throw him into a pit and be done with him. He let his right foot drop, and it hit solid stone. The unseen hands steadied him, and they began their descent beneath the city.

Ulric smelled lamp oil. He watched shifting patterns of light and shadow dance across his blindfold as he struggled to negotiate unseen steps. Everyone's footfalls and exertions were echoing off the close stone walls. The air grew dank and foul. The sound of running water drew nearer, and then the stairs ended. They marched Ulric along a path of slick stone. The stench of raw sewage left no doubt where he was: they were traveling through the Cloaca Maxima, the great sewer that emptied into the Nanpela River.

The fishy sack on Ulric's head only made the stink of the sewers worse. He was feeling ill. He was about to beg Neesis to make it end when he found himself directed upward onto a flight of stone steps. More proof of the Goddess' efficacy! They left the foul air behind, and stone steps became wooden steps. The cold echoes of stone tunnels gave way to the warm resonance of wooden walls. There was a faint but steady thrum in those walls, but from what, he could not guess.

He counted the switchbacks as they ascended. They stopped on the sixth floor, and someone opened a door. There was movement. Sandaled feet shuffled about the landing as others filed through the door, then a firm hand dragged him several steps away and pressed him against a wall.

"Listen, Ulric," Silo said quickly. "You came into my shop the other night and said if I helped you, you'd owe me. Right?"

"Yes. I did," Ulric reluctantly replied.

"So, you owe me?" Silo pressed.

Ulric hesitated. He had made the promise, but to a jovial fence, not an Imperaré prince.

"You owe me." Silo stated it as fact.

"Yes. I owe you."

"Damn right you do," Silo said, now satisfied. "If you want to walk out of here, you will do two things. One of these is you will keep your mouth shut during the Concilium. The only thing the Imperaré is interested in is power. The murder of Marius Secundus is a slight against our dignity and, therefore, a threat to our power. We will avenge it. But the motive behind his murder could hold the key to more knowledge, leverage, wealth, and therefore more power."

Silo paused, giving Ulric time to digest his words. "Do you understand?"

"Yes. Don't stand too tall when the sword stroke takes Luciano's head."

Silo chuckled. "Right. Luciano is the prize here. If you go running your mouth, you'll get yourself tangled up in his fate. Now, there's one other thing you must do to survive."

"What? All this talk of survival is very interesting!"

"You must pledge your loyalty to me here and now. Invoke Neesis Umbra, the goddess of all thieves, and take the Sacramentum!"

Ulric was glad for the sack over his head, so Silo couldn't see the angry yet resigned look on his face. It wasn't fear of provoking Silo's anger. He simply didn't want the man to think he considered him an unworthy master. He liked Silo, but service in the Imperaré was everything he had been trying to avoid since arriving in Trumric.

"Speak the Sacramentum, boy." Then, in a voice as cold as iron on a winter's battlefield, he said, "Or one word from me to my fellow Imperaré and its torture and death."

"Uh… is there a particular Imperaré form you prefer?" Ulric asked. "And for the love of Neesis, can I get this sack off my head?"

"The sack stays on for now: Imperaré rules. As for the oath, I'm sure whatever you learned in Mist View will do."

Ulric cleared his throat as if he was about to step on stage at the Polyminius theater. "Neesis! Look to the shadows! I call upon Neesis Umbra, the protector of all thieves, to witness this oath. I, Marcus Octavius Ulric, known as Darktalon by the gangs of the Dark Assembly, offer the use of my skills and the strength of my arms in the service of…" Ulric tilted his head and waited for Silo: a Sacramentum needed the true names of both parties. Silo spoke, and Ulric continued. "Horatius Silo, Imperaré Prince and praeses of the Portus Collegium. If I break this oath, may my luck run out, my penis wither, and madness take me."

"I, Horatius Silo, Imperaré Prince and praeses of the Portus Collegium, accept you into my service and extend to you my protection."

It was done. There was no way out after a sacred oath to Neesis Umbra. Only Silo could release him now.

Silo

Silo led Ulric into an anteroom, where hard words and threats of cold steel still echoed. The voices fell to an angry grumble as they entered, and someone hurried closer and spoke. Ulric could see nothing through the blindfold and sack, but he recognized Gwynedd, keeping his voice low. "The Concilium guards tried to get their hands on Porteles, but we told them to fuck off."

"Good and proper, I hope?" Silo sounded pleased with his second-in-command.

"Always, Chief. They had no right." He paused, then with a hint of disbelief, he added, "And a damned indignity they thought to try."

"I recognize a few of the guards," Silo said. "Looks like the Wine Sellers Collegium is providing some of the security, and that means Tullius."

"Of course, Brocchus' lickspittle!" Ulric noted a hint of genuine fear in the Northman's voice. "I don't like this. Maybe we should have brought more men?"

"No need, no need, Gwynedd," Silo replied in an unconcerned, almost mocking tone. "No one's gonna flash steel here, especially at a Concilium." More seriously, he said, "And showing up with too many men now would be a sign of weakness."

"You're right. Sorry, Chief. Orders?"

There was the sound of leather and jangling metal. "Hold on to my blades. Wait here and stay alert."

Silo walked away. Ulric heard a pair of heavy doors open, then close, and Silo was gone. He stood bound and hooded in a room with Gwynedd, and his men, surrounded by an unknown number of Imperaré guards even Silo didn't trust. And somewhere nearby, there was Luciano Porteles. He had said nothing since leaving the butcher's shop, but that was about to change. What if, despite Silo's assurances, the Concilium accepted Luciano's lies?

Ulric had hardly begun to worry when he heard the doors open again and Silo's voice calling, "Gwynedd! Numa! Bring the prisoners."

His unseen guard marched him forward across the anteroom. Hardwood floors gave way to marble tile, and behind him, the heavy doors shut with a deep thud. He knew he had entered a large chamber by the sound of their echoing footsteps. Suddenly, they stopped and forced him down onto his knees. His guard snatched away the fishy-smelling sack and removed the blindfold.

Ulric took in a deep breath that smelled of lamp oil and incense. Luciano knelt several paces to his right, and Silo, Gwynedd, and a broad-chested, olive-skinned man who must have been Numa stood nearby. They were at the center of a large chamber with tall walls and a ceiling supported by four columns. High, narrow, slit windows created pools of sunlight and shadow. On a dais before him, six men and women sat arranged in a semicircle. A seventh chair stood unoccupied. The walls were painted in cream, crimson, and gold, the columns black and ornate, and the chairs were the curule style, reserved by tradition and law for magistrates holding imperium.

Gods Above, Gods Below! I thought the Dark Assembly was pretentious. The wealth that must pass through the center of the Republic! I'll be richer than a Kosian priest! If I can get out of here alive.

Silo took his seat on the dais while Gwynedd and Numa remained behind Ulric and Luciano. Several other armed men stood in the shadows at the edges of the room. An old man seated in the center chair spoke first, with a weak and cracking voice. He looked ancient to Ulric's eyes, with a head of pure white hair and a deeply lined face.

"Are these the murderers of Quintus Marius Secundus?"

Ulric's instinct was to protest, but he remembered Silo's warning.

Silo looked at the old man and casually said, "No."

"No?" The old man sounded surprised.

"What do you mean by 'no'?" asked a heavyset man topped by a karakul hat, a peaked cone of dark lamb's wool. Ulric thought it looked silly on his round, pudgy face and uncomfortably hot. "We didn't summon you to the Concilium for you to"—he paused, his eyes searching the air for the best turn of phrase—"play games with us. Yes, don't play games with us, Silo."

"No one summoned me, Brocchus," Silo said as if explaining to a child. "A Concilium was called—clearly too soon—and I came."

A man next to Brocchus spoke up. Ulric guessed it was Tullius, Brocchus' toady. The man had disturbingly large eyes bulging from a flat face, punctuated by a long pointy nose. Greasy ringlets of hair the color of dirty straw grew from his head like an infection. "You try to hide things from your fellow princes, and then you dare lecture us?"

A spasm of anger seized Brocchus' round face. When he spoke, his voice kept rising, his face growing ever redder. "We called the Concilium because you were going to keep these murderers'… secrets… for yourself. The assassination of Marius Secundus is an affront to us all. We must strike back at the Dark Assembly! We should all share in this vengeance!"

Everyone raised their voices in support and looked at the old man. He spoke in the same tired, flat tones as before. "Yes, if there is to be vengeance, all the princes of the Imperaré will act as one." Everyone nodded in agreement. Then the old man looked pointedly at Silo.

"Am I to call a Concilium over every report of drunken brawlers on the docks?" Silo offered. "What would be the point of bringing my fellow princes nothing more than questions and confusion? Once I learned we had captured Luciano Porteles, I ordered everything shadowed to keep business running smoothly, which is our duty as the Imperaré and our only mandate from the Senate."

Ulric studied the faces of the assembled princes. Silo's rhetoric had persuaded everyone but Brocchus and Tullius. They said nothing, only stared at the old man at the center.

He gave a nearly imperceptible nod and then looked at Silo. He asked, "Now, if not the murderers, then who kneels before us?"

"Luciano Porteles, who we all know, is a Dark Assembly assassin and an untrustworthy jackal. I believe he, and he alone, murdered Marius Secundus. Who ordered it and why? I don't know yet."

"And the boy?" the old man asked.

"A former Dark Assembly thief named Ulric Darktalon. Claims to be the protégé of Arrius Ghostwalker, a man whose reputation some of you may know and a formal rival of Porteles. The boy was fool enough to have a go at Luciano. Praise Neesis Insania for his madness! If he hadn't got himself nearly killed this morning, Luciano would already be sailing back to Mist View."

Tullius leaned forward in his seat. "If it pleases my fellow princes, I'd like to hear from our prisoners. What says the Concilium?"

They took a quick vote, and the questions began.

Silo had told him to keep his mouth shut during the Concilium, but now Ulric had to speak. So he spoke carefully, with few words, and almost always the truth. He watched with hidden glee as Luciano had to decide which of his previous lies to keep, which to discard, and what new ones to create. He didn't let the assassin bait him and never responded to his lies directly. When needed, Silo's own questions gave Ulric the opportunity to defend himself.

After an hour or more of questioning, he believed the Imperaré was finally seeing through Luciano's lies. They had asked Ulric fewer questions as the interrogation wore on, which he thought was a good sign. The only uncertain moment came when he confessed to living rough near the River Market, and the man called Brocchus had given him an unexpected look of recognition.

"We've heard enough," the old man said. "Luciano is clearly Marius Secundus' assassin. We will discover why it was ordered and by whom."

"Good!" Silo said cheerfully. "Luciano's a tough one, but my boys can drag it out of him in a couple of days. Three at most." He made it sound like a trip to the market, not the brutal torture of a man.

"What?" Tullius interrupted. "Surely we will not reward Silo's earlier scheming with custody of the assassin?" His brow furrowed, which made his eyes look as if they would pop from their sockets.

"Oh, by the Infernal Twins!" Silo erupted. "I thought we were past this! Do we want to get the truth out of the Verdan bastard or what?"

"Of course, we want the truth. In wine lies the truth, so I value truth above all else," said Pontius Tullius, the praeses of the Wine Sellers Collegium. "I propose we give the assassin to the esteemed Cornelius Brocchus. He, too, has professionals in his employ. Shall we vote?"

Everyone turned to the old man, who nodded in agreement. They voted on Tullius' motion, which passed by a margin of four to three.

Cornelius Brocchus spoke, barely able to keep the triumph out of his voice. "Take him! Hold him below and make him uncomfortable."

Two armed guards emerged from the shadows; they were Brocchus' men. Numa, scowling, stepped aside. They seized Luciano and dragged him to his feet.

Luciano screamed, "You want Luciano talk! I talk! I warn Imperaré! It was too big for Dark Assembly! Too big for Imperaré!"

Once again, a sack was secured over his head, which did little to muffle his shouts. Brocchus' guards dragged him out of the chamber, leaving Ulric alone before the Concilium.

Ha! Looks like it will be torture and a creative execution after all! And sweet, beautiful Neesis! Did you hear Silo? He said if I hadn't gone after Luciano, they would have never captured him. I know I haven't personally sent him to your ample bosom, but I'm doing my part. Then Ulric remembered his prayer in Aquila's garden and the promises he had made. *Yes, yes, I still owe you a fine young lamb—fair enough.*

"And now for the fate of the boy," the old man said.

Those words demanded attention, ending Ulric's musings on the divine.

"His past transgressions of Imperaré law have been minor," Silo said to the Concilium. "The worst of which was performed under coercion. His skills are substantial." He looked at the old man. "I could use him. What says the Concilium?"

One of the Imperaré princes, a younger woman adorned in gold jewelry, said, "To challenge a man like Porteles at his age shows spirit. No mind at all, but plenty of spirit!"

"You think his crimes are minor because he hasn't told you the whole truth." It was Brocchus, and neither Silo nor Ulric looked surprised. "This Dark Assembly thief has been lurking about the River Market for untold months, running schemes, tax collecting, interfering in market operations, and harassing local gangs like the Gutter-Fish."

"Wait… what?" was all Silo got out. He did nothing to conceal his amusement.

"And all before he admittedly tried to steal a highly valuable item from an important Imperaré associate!" His wool hat shook with each angry word. "The boy is an unsanctioned thief, and we should, at the least, take a hand and exile him from the city!"

Hmm. I must admit the Harbor-Man who bound my hands knew his knots, but I could still be out of these ropes in a blink. Then it's ten guards remaining, twelve if Silo's men join in. Let's say I can get Numa's blade off of him before he knows what's happening. It's either out the way I came in, where I know there are even more guards or risk the unknown of that side door lurking in the shadows. Yep, I'm doomed.

"Wait, Brocchus." Silo raised a hand and gave his fellow princes a wide smile. "Did I hear you complain this boy was 'harassing' your Gutter-Fish?"

"What? I meant—"

"How many Gutter-Fish are there? Two, three dozen up and down the river? And young Ulric has been '*harassing*' them? Been bullying them, has he? Been taking their coin, bedding their women, things like that?"

A few Imperaré chuckled. The young prince laughed. "As I said, this Ulric has plenty of spirit!"

Brocchus was in a red-faced fit of rage and embarrassment. "Fine! I will admit 'harassing' was a poor choice of words! It does not change the fact that… that…" he struggled to find the right word.

"The fact is," Tullius interjected, "this Ulric has broken our laws, and we must not allow him to go unpunished." He looked at Brocchus as if seeking approval.

"Yes! He has insulted the dignity of the Transnanpela Collegium!" Brocchus stood, knocking his karakul hat off his bald head.

"No!" Silo stood and walked to stand beside Gwynedd. "My fellow Imperaré, I propose that any young man who can come to our city, without coin or ally, and launch such a terrifying campaign of harassment against Brocchus' fearsome Gutter-Fish is a man we must have on our side." Silo reached down and pulled Ulric to his feet. "That man is a man I want in my service! What says the Concilium?"

The Concilium spoke, and Ulric's freedom was won and lost on a vote of five to two.

THE DOMINATOR

Luciano awoke to a spicy, acrid aroma assaulting his nostrils. There was no sight but darkness and no sound but a constant popping as if dozens of tiny eggs were being cracked one after the other.

My hands and feet are bound, eyes covered. I'm gagged and tied to a chair. What the fuck is this?

He pulled against his bindings, but they only cut deeper into his naked skin. He could feel the cold floor under his bare feet; his boots had been removed, as had his tunic and pants.

Where the fuck am I?

He refocused his thoughts on what he could remember.

I was standing in front of the Imperaré Council. Along with… the boy.

The last thought dripped with disdain, like feral saliva.

The Council deliberated. Argued. Fought over our fate. Silo spoke up for the boy. And the man in the karakul hat, Brocchus, spoke for me. His men dragged me off; put me in a cell. That's all. Nothing after that. No, not nothing… blurs. Flashes of memories, but nothing to latch onto. What the fuck happened?

A door opened, then heavy, ponderous steps echoed across the room, followed by the lighter footfalls of two others. Luciano grew still and listened; the door was gently closed. A bitter scent swept past him, catching his breath.

Someone began untying his blindfold. The fingers reminded Luciano of an old woman: cold, soft, and slender. Midway through the knot, the fingers retreated.

A familiar voice in front of him reached out. "Now there, Porteles," said Cornelius Brocchus, "I'm assuming you will demonstrate the…" the voice paused, seeking the right words, "respect and decorum you Verdans are known for, once we remove your blindfold."

Luciano imagined pinning the Imperaré prince's wagging jaw to his skull with one swift thrust of Aguja.

"A nod will do, Porteles." Luciano tilted his head in response, taking in a healthy dose of the spicy odor as he did. "That will suffice."

The delicate fingers finished their task, and Luciano's eyes flashed open, then reflexively closed from the onslaught of light. A cold fingertip traced his earlobe and neck, which sent him recoiling in revulsion. He turned to see Pontius Tullius hovering behind him, smiling coyly. Luciano jerked forward, his chair scooting away with a piercing screech.

"That's enough of that, Tullius." The scrawny man took a step back, but his fingers lingered uncomfortably on Luciano's shoulder before eventually withdrawing.

The Imperaré prince sat at a small table, upon which rested an obscenely large bowl of pickled figs alongside an equally extravagant silver cup. He shoved an overly ripe fig into his mouth and eagerly leaned forward, staring at his captive prey all the while.

"Good afternoon, Porteles. It brings me… joy. Yes, it's a joy to see you again." Luciano's eyes spoke every syllable of hatred his tongue yearned to utter. "Such contempt toward your… savior. How ungrateful. And to think I expected so much better from a

Verdan, not to mention an esteemed member of the Dark Assembly. So disappointing, and so... confounding." Brocchus crammed another fig into his mouth, chewing as he talked. "Perhaps you don't fully understand the situation you have found yourself in, Porteles. The old man wanted you dead—right then and there—but I convinced him otherwise. The old man is short-sighted, but I know what... an asset you could become. What an asset you will be, once you're brought"—his eyes moved toward the fourth man in the room—"into line."

Luciano followed Brocchus' gaze to the far corner of the room. Standing in front of an inconsequential table stood a small man; his back turned to them. He was dressed in a style that spoke: "I am not of Trumric." He wore loose trousers that fell in elliptical folds to his ankles, where they were fastened around and under soft leather shoes. At his waist, a narrow bronze-colored belt accentuated a snug, hip-length coat. The color and cut of each item of clothing signaled utility over fashion. His brown-skinned head was devoid of hair, but many scars covered it in rune-like patterns. The man stoked the coals of a small incense burner, seemingly oblivious to anyone else in the room. Luciano heard the popping sounds of the burning seeds as the man gently wafted the delicate tendrils of smoke back and forth with a slender hand. The gray curls reached out to Luciano, seeping into his nostrils and invading his mouth. The taste was both sooty and sweet. All the while, a second invasion loomed: Luciano felt an unknown Presence lurking just outside the entrance to his mind. The Presence spoke in a soundless voice, echoing in Luciano's head.

Greetings, siyad, I've traveled a great distance to be with you.

The stranger's voice was dominating yet strangely comforting.

I came to your house seeking shelter, seeking knowledge. May I come in?

The Verdan suppressed an audible laugh.

May I come in, siyad?

"Don't know you. Don't know how you know me. Don't care."

I have traveled so very far, and I tire. May I come in, siyad? Just for a short time.

"Fuck off."

You will not turn away a weary traveler, will you?

Luciano's eyes burned holes in the back of the man's head.

I'll not overstay my welcome. You have my word. May I come in?

"I said—" The last two words stuck in the back of Luciano's throat.

The stranger stirred the coals once again.

May I come in?

Luciano swallowed his words of defiance as the stranger's words echoed in his mind, over and over, rebounding and growing louder and louder. "May I come in?" Such a simple request, such a harmless request. When the roaring echo overwhelmed every last thought, then, with a newfound sense of hospitality, the great assassin of the Dark Assembly opened his mind's door and, without further hesitation, willingly ushered the Presence inside the halls of his mind.

Thank you, siyad. Now, shall we begin?

"Begin?" Luciano asked out loud.

Please, save your energy, siyad. You will need it. No need to tax your voice. After all, you have invited me in, and I can hear your thoughts; thoughts are so much more efficient than words. Speaking will merely confound our communication and tire you, siyad. And you will need all your strength in the hours to come in our pursuit of the truth.

Luciano felt the Presence wandering unabated in the front of his mind. It made him uneasy, like the feeling of an uninvited guest who's made himself too comfortable in one's home.

Before we proceed, siyad, do you have any questions?

A myriad of questions raced in convoluted circles through Luciano's brain, making it difficult to latch onto any singular thought; they swirled and tangled in his head, merging into confusing combinations of syllables and words that came out in nonsensical gibberish when he uttered them. Only one recognizable word came out: "Who?"

The prince licked his lips. "I'll tell you this, Porteles: he's no mere dragon magi."

Shhh. Do not speak.

Luciano frantically tried to organize his thoughts; he was working at a frenetic pace, laying piles upon piles of questions at the threshold of his mind. All the while, he stared at the back of the man's skull, watching as he calmly stirred the incense. Luciano's head pounded as he snatched thoughts out of the pile and attempted to categorize them, prioritize them. He felt his brain explode, launching a cacophony of queries at the Presence.

Who are you? If not magi, then what? Why are you here? What do you want? Why won't you show me your face? What do you mean 'the truth'? Who are you?

The man continued to stir the incense without reaction. It was Brocchus who interrupted the silence. Before he spoke, he sucked his bottom lip under his top teeth. Was he savoring the taste of his last fig or the effect of his next words? Luciano suspected the latter. "He's from Bayjon. He's unlike anything you've ever known. They call his kind… 'Dominators.'"

Luciano bristled at the word. The magi of Verdith had heard rumors of these Bayjoni Dominators. Their reputation for extracting information was unrivaled, but their methods remained as much a mystery as the disappearance of the Eltarans.

The bald man, still coaxing the coals, extended the palm of his free hand passively toward Brocchus while reaching out to Luciano's mind once again.

These are not the questions you truly wish to ask, siyad. Dismiss them. Ask me the question of whose answer you truly seek

The Verdan hesitated.

There, that one, in the back, buried under all the others. Ask that one, and I will answer. Truthfully. I will never lie to you, siyad. Throughout this entire process, I will never lie to you

Luciano, dizzy and disoriented, fumbled through his thoughts, tossing aside one after the other until finally, he uncovered what he sought…

258

I know why you're here. You're here to torture me. Interrogate me. Extract some information that Brocchus deems valuable. So here is my question: what methods will you use in the pursuit of your task, Dominator?

The man stopped stirring the coals and placed the ebony-handled spoon neatly in its place amongst the other tools besides the brazier. He turned around slowly, revealing to Luciano for the first time his granite-like gaze, bereft of emotion or intent.

That, siyad, is entirely up to you.

Luciano's eyes moved to Brocchus, then Tullius, then back to the Dominator.

Can they hear us?

No.

What do you want?

To complete my task—as you have named it—and move on.

Luciano straightened in his chair as much as his restraints would allow.

A professional. I can respect that. I'm a professional myself. Complete the job and move on. When do we get started? This isn't my first bout with an interrogator.

In due time, siyad. But first, I must conduct a cursory search.

Of?

You have not concealed any treacherous phantasms for me, have you, siyad?

Phantasms? Luciano laughed out loud. *How? How could I conceal something from you?*

Then I am sure you will not object if I check for myself? As a professional courtesy.

Luciano's eyes flashed open. It felt as if the Dominator let loose a thousand serpents inside his head. They slithered in all directions, their long forked tongues flicking out, sniffing, seeking. It was a maddening sensation, and he was helpless to stop it. His neck tensed, and his eyes felt like they would pop from their sockets. It subsided as quickly as it had begun, and Luciano slumped in his chair, out of breath.

You've done well so far, siyad. Now we may explore further, together, in pursuit of the truth. I am about to ask you a series of simple questions. Are you ready to answer them?

I'm tied to a fucking chair. How much more ready can I be?

Luciano snuck a glance at Brocchus, then at the toad, Tullius. Each met his gaze with an eager smile. He stared at the Dominator, whose face held no expression and entertained the notion of not cooperating. But how, exactly?

Brocchus' impertinent voice once again broke the silence. "Get on with it! I've no time to waste. I need him—"

The Dominator's eyes never left Luciano. He only raised a quiet hand toward Brocchus, and the Imperaré prince was silenced.

Luciano bared his teeth at Brocchus with a mocking smile. After receiving the glare he sought, he gave the Dominator a nod.

What is your given name?

Luciano Porteles.

Where were you born?

Erriberako, Verdith.

What was the year of your birth?

During the 5th year of the reign of the High-Sorcerer-King, Cimera Fausto. The year 1043 AUC, as these Trumins say.

Who is your current employer?

Luciano paused. Brocchus knew this already. Why ask the question? No reason to lie when the truth is already known.

The Dark Assembly of Mist View.

You've done quite well so far, siyad. Tell me, why are you in Trumric?

Again, this was surely something that Brocchus and the Imperaré already knew. The Dark Assembly. The scroll. Secundus' treachery.

A scroll? Please, tell me more.

Luciano froze. How? The word had barely entered his thoughts! He tried to clear his mind of Secundus, of his mission, of the stolen scroll. He cleared his mind of everything.

That is disappointing, siyad. You were doing so well. This new tactic will accomplish nothing; you merely prolong the inevitable. We will find the truth.

Luciano closed his eyes and attempted to clear his mind. He concentrated on the still blackness behind his eyelids.

I see. Very well. We shall move on then, siyad.

The Dominator plunged past the gateways of Luciano's mind into the twisted halls of his hidden thoughts. He beckoned Luciano to follow.

One hallway spilled into the next, which spilled into another, and eventually, Luciano was led to a dark passage with seemingly no end. The Dominator commanded several doors to open within the passageway, which lined both sides for as far as he could see. Luciano could not convince himself that the doors had even been there before. Perhaps the Dominator had created them himself?

The Dominator extended his hand toward the first door. He fought the urge to move, but his curious nature won out. As he approached, his heart thudded in his chest. The door opened, revealing a large iron-banded barrel sitting at the center of a gravel-strewn courtyard, its lid laying nearby. The sweet odor of fresh milk and honey competed with the stench of half-rotten food scattered on a crude table, along with a sturdy hammer and a pile of rusty, finger-length nails.

The Dominator tugged at him once more, dragging him to another door. Inside, he saw an unkempt pasture dotted with several mounds of sod. In the center, a singular shovel impaled the dirt, and a coil of rope dangled off its handle. Alongside the shovel, a long river reed pierced the center of a ceramic bowl. Just out of arm's reach, a cat of nine tails hung from a wooden post.

Again the Dominator beckoned, and again he moved to another door. Beyond, there was a large, knee-high, rectangular stone platform. Iron manacles reached out from each corner of the slab, and a hood of dark linen lay in the center. Along both lengths of the stone table were stacked several semi-flat stones of various weights.

The Dominator led him from threshold to threshold. With each door, a sense of foreboding and discomfort grew until, after a dozen or more doorways, his dread became overwhelming. The unmistakable smells of rot and decay oozed from behind the final door. He was propelled forward once more. The door flew open, and the source of the stench became clear: a donkey's carcass lay splayed and exposed in the center of an open field, slowly roasting under a cruel sun. The animal's insides had been gutted, its empty, putrescent shell left to the whim of flies and maggots. A spool of leather cord and an abnormally large needle waited nearby.

Now, at the end of the hall, Luciano turned to face the strange presence he knew to be the Dominator. It floated at the far end of the passageway: mere wisps of shadow forming an amorphous cloak around an indistinct body. Luciano stared at it, looking for a crumb of familiarity but finding none.

So… which manner of interrogation is your preference, Dominator?

In an instant, the figure was upon him, looming over him, though Luciano could still discern neither face nor emotion.

Why do you assume we must choose, siyad?

Luciano swallowed his bravado like a rotten date. Then, one by one, the mysterious Bayjoni Dominator ushered Luciano into each room. There, he tortured Luciano until the Verdan succumbed to the pain and died. Afterward, the Dominator brought him back to life to start anew in the next room. After the first few rooms, Luciano willingly entered the next, wishing more than anything to succumb to the pain and agony of it all and truly die, but with each resurrection came newfound defiance. Luciano cursed this zeal and prayed for weakness. It did not come. Making matters worse, he found himself once again fighting his own stubbornness. It was this infernal stubbornness that prevented him from simply telling the Dominator everything he sought. This internal struggle—a battle that had become familiar to Luciano over the years—was now culminating in a truly masochistic and maddening experience. Finally, after more resurrections than Luciano could count, the Dominator led Luciano to the last room at the end of the hall.

Upon crossing the threshold, the sickening stench of rot hit him like a punch in the gut. He pressed the back of his hand over his mouth, barely staving off the urge to retch, and stared at an open field of wild grass sprawling beneath a blazing sun. Thirty paces in front of him lay the carcass of a donkey rotting at the center of a dark cloud of buzzing flies. Next to him stood the misty, inchoate form of the Dominator. Though he knew it was pointless, he glanced over his shoulder; as expected, the doorway had vanished. The faceless Dominator said nothing. He only pointed to the center of the field, coaxing Luciano forward.

With each step, the stink of rot and decay thickened, and the heat became unbearable. Every step became more hesitant until only the Dominator's will drove him forward. He faltered and slipped in a pool of congealed blood to land face down in a pile of viscera, scattering the thick cloud of flies with an angry buzz. He steadied himself and looked up into the donkey's rotting skull. The beast's head lay close by, resting on a mass of bloody, matted grass. Its lifeless tongue spilled out of its mouth and onto the ground. A trail of hungry, squirming maggots led into one eye socket and out the other.

Luciano staggered away from the carcass just in time to double over and vomit at his feet. Once the nauseating convulsions ceased, two pairs of unseen hands seized him. He struggled, thrashing wildly, but his strength was no match for his abductors. They bound his hands behind his back, then his feet to his hands.

He was lifted by the ropes until his body dangled in an awkward curl a foot above the ground and lowered inside the hide of the donkey. The stench overwhelmed him again, and a series of dry heaves wracked his body. A pair of strong hands held him down as the warm, sticky flesh of the animal was folded around him. Then Luciano was sewn into the rotting carcass, leaving only his head uncovered.

For several days, the donkey's body decomposed in the sun, slowly cooking Luciano in the process. He watched as flies danced around his face, occasionally darting in and out of his mouth. He felt the maggots crawling over his flesh and burrowing into his body. Vultures flew down and pecked at the animal's decaying flesh, staring at him as they tore away strips of sun-baked hide and rotting meat as if to warn him he was next.

After days of this, Luciano—lips too cracked and throat too parched to speak—reached out to the Dominator with his mind. He told him everything. Every fact he could muster about the Dark Assembly, Ghostwalker, Ulric Darktalon, and his mission. Everything.

He explained how the murder of three senatorial couriers returning from Arkanay began the hunt for an Eltaran scroll case that eventually led to Quintus Marius Secundus. The Dark Assembly had learned the case contained a map. Where the map led, Luciano did not know nor care. He only knew the Assembly was mad for it. There were rumors the Elts of the Dragon's Breath Mountains would pay a king's ransom to possess it. He wondered if he had returned to Mist View if the Assembly would have found the courage to challenge the Collegium. He'd never know. Now, given his fate, he thought the Eltaran map was cursed, and all who pursued it were doomed.

When he had finished, he felt a weight lift from his chest, and he gratefully took a large breath of the rancid air. He waited for a response from his torturer or the final death.

We are so close, siyad. I believe you are now ready for the truth.

The truth? I've told you everything. Everything! I've given you everything. I have nothing left to give! Release me from this misery. I have nothing left to bargain with. What more could I possibly tell you?

You do not understand, siyad. It is I who will reveal a great truth to you!

Obligation

Silo scowled but didn't say a word. The silence made Ulric uncomfortable. He held the dangling charms higher, ignoring the dull pain in his wounded shoulder, and repeated himself.

"How much?"

Silo leaned his long frame back against the counter of his shop and folded his arms. "Were you listening to me or shopping like some lovesick poet?"

"Of course," Ulric said with a trace of wounded pride. He took a deep breath and recited the duties and obligations he owed to the Porte Mare Collegium. "I must pay dues on the Kalends of each month. In addition to these dues, I owe the Imperaré seventeen percent of all tax collecting, back alley parley, shadow walk, and honest scheme jobs. Only you and Gwynedd can authorize knife or shroud work. The Imperaré restricts operations during religious festivals, except during the Orgy of Neesis. And do no work or start any trouble at a taberna called the Quadrivium."

Ulric had been learning the ways of the Imperaré since the Concilium had ended, and his first lesson had been trust and security. Silo had ordered Ulric's ropes cut, and Gwynedd obeyed. He had rubbed his chafed wrists and rolled the soreness out of his shoulders.

"What now?" he asked, eager to leave the Concilium chambers.

"Now," Silo said, "you leave the same way you arrived." He looked at Gwynedd, who held up the blindfold and fishy-smelling sack.

"God's Below!" Ulric cursed. "Is there not another sack about, at least?"

Silo looked at Ulric and, with a wry smile, said, "It's not that we don't trust you..."

"But we don't trust you!" Gwynedd said in his sharp northern accent.

Silo and his primus shared a laugh as they tied his blindfold and secured the sack. Ulric's complaints had changed nothing; he was once again being led around in the dark. When they returned to the anteroom, where the rest of Silo's men had gathered, the Imperaré prince retrieved his blades from Gwynedd and spoke to his men.

"I'll take the direct route. Numa, Postumus—with me!"

"Orders, Chief?" Gwynedd asked.

"You take the rest of the men and our eager recruit back to the beginning. From there, get him cleaned up and his wounds tended. And get him inked. Once it's done, bring him straight to the shop."

"Will do, Chief."

"And Gwynedd," the hard iron returned to his voice, "pass the whisper: I expect trouble from Brocchus. Look for Gutter-Fish, Sons of Mania, Shrine Alley Soldiers, and even Transnanpela Collegium men crossing into our territory. We catch any of those bastards starting trouble? The boys have my blessing to bleed them good."

What would an impending war between the Portus and the Transnanpela Collegiums mean for him? After all, the Polyminius Theater and Julia were in the Transnanpela District and dangerously close to Gutter-Fish territory. Would his association with the theater be a problem? He wanted to ask Gwynedd about it but feared Silo would forbid him from the theater, so he said nothing.

A short time later, Ulric found himself back in the sewers, and familiarity didn't make the stench any more bearable. To distract himself from his misery, he asked Gwynedd the one question that had been gnawing at him since the Concilium. Thus began the second lesson: never anger Gwynedd.

"Gwynedd? What happens to Luciano's stuff? That spatha he carried was Ghostwalker's. It should be mine, by right. What's going to happen to him?" Ulric's voice echoed off the dank stone walls of the Cloaca Maxima.

Gwynedd, his voice low, said, "Something painful, then fatal. Now keep quiet."

The reply only encouraged Ulric. "Executed? Any chance I could be there?"

"Quiet!"

"I need to see the bastard die!" The word 'die' echoed loudly through the tunnels.

Out of the darkness, a wall slammed into Ulric, and the world twisted and spun about. All he saw was a whirl of shadows racing across his blindfold, and then he heard Gwynedd's voice, suddenly very close.

"Listen, you little shit," he whispered, "unless you want to join all the big shits below, you'll stay quiet until we reach the streets." Gwynedd had him by the throat, leaning him over the sewage channel.

Ulric said nothing.

"Will you shut up?" Gwynedd asked.

Ulric gave an exaggerated nod underneath his hood, and the world was set upright once again.

"Listen, boy. We only travel under the city when we have to remain shadowed. It's filthy, it stinks, and... it's dangerous." With equal parts reverence and revulsion, he said, "There are things down here. Things cursed by the gods seeking darkness and things that have escaped the infernal realms seeking the light. Or so the Trumin priests tell me. We keep quiet until we're back on the streets."

Ulric didn't speak another word as they marched him through the sewers and back alleys all the way to the rear of Epicydes' shop. He stood there, his blindfold a band of dull orange in the bright sunlight, silently enjoying the smells of roasting duck and the pleasant warmth on his neck and shoulders. The sun must have been directly overhead; he guessed it was near the sixth hour since sunrise.

Gwynedd passed on Silo's warning about the Transnanpela Collegium, dismissed the men, then pulled the sack off Ulric's head and tossed the blindfold to the ground. He walked toward the canal bridge, summoning Ulric with a terse, "Follow me."

The streets were chaotic and teeming with people: shoppers, merchants, tradesmen, and mariners. And they all stepped out of Gwynedd's path. Most scurried with down-turned eyes. Others stepped aside with a dignified nod. Some called out as if greeting a friend. Gwynedd acknowledged few, ignored most. And Ulric walked the same path. After months of living rough among the poorest plebs and strays, he felt the pride of belonging and the thrill of being feared.

Sweet Neesis! It feels good to be walking the streets with dignity again. But that's the trap! They show respect because I walk in Gwynedd's shadow— The Imperaré's shadow. Ghostwalker walked alone! It's your legacy I carry, Arrius! Somehow I'll—

"You've been quiet too long. You're either bleeding out or planning something stupid."

Gwynedd's unexpected comments shook Ulric out of his thoughts. He looked at the man's fire-scarred face and tried to read his mood. Unfortunately, the burns left him capable of only two expressions: bored or cruel. "I've just been thinking," was his unexpectedly truthful reply.

"You better if you're working for Silo." They cut through another crowd. "I thought you'd be whining about your wounds the whole way?"

"I can deal with pain," he said, trying to sound eminently stoic.

"I might believe you. We heard from Secundus' widow she had you under fists and hot irons for half the night, but you gave her nothing." Did he hear a hint of grudging respect? "Why not give her Luciano's name?"

"Ghostwalker trained me to never share our secrets with outsiders. Besides, that harpy was mad for vengeance." Ulric paused and imagined a woman finding the body of her murdered husband. "Maybe I shouldn't blame her, but there was no guarantee she'd free me, no matter what was promised. I had to escape if I was to kill Luciano."

"You mean *'get killed by* Luciano?'"

"I had no choice by then. I had to face him," Ulric stated plainly.

Gwynedd nodded in silence, and Ulric knew he understood.

They were now deep in the Portus complex, like a city unto itself. The outer harbor was a vast basin carved from the coast, protected by two massive stone breakwaters. Where they met, an impressive lighthouse rose from an artificial island. A series of broad canals connected this harbor to a smaller inner harbor, a hexagonal basin with sides twelve hundred paces long, each stuffed with docks and shipyards. Granaries, warehouses, governmental offices, and, most prominently, the Temple of Ulorin, Trumric's powerful sea god, surrounded the inner harbor. The streets were bursting with all manner of men, wagons, carts, slaves, horses, and ox. Anything useful in the loading and unloading of ships was present. Anyone not loading or hauling was haggling or shouting orders. The only exceptions were the swarms of clerks that tallied in dutiful silence and the hard-eyed men who watched it all from the shadows. These men were Portus Collegium and wore the red scarves of the Imperaré, and each gave Gwynedd their respects as he passed.

As they passed the many columned porticoes of the Temple of Ulorin, Gwynedd turned to Ulric. "They tortured you with hot irons, but there's not a burn on you. How?"

"Didn't you hear me tell the Concilium about the healer?" Ulric responded as if it was a simple matter.

"The old stray? Who just happened to be a gifted healer?" Gwynedd shook his head, "No. It takes more than a salve and a prayer to heal such scars." His face turned cruel. "You're hiding something. The Concilium didn't spot it 'cause they were too busy weighing Luciano for the slaughter."

All the talk of burns and scars made it impossible for Ulric to ignore Gwynedd's own fire-ravaged face. He dared a few furtive glances as they walked, wondering what must have happened.

"A thrice-damned fire magus."

"What?"

"I know when people are looking," Gwynedd said without resentment. "You ever faced a magus?"

"Ha! Oh no!" Ulric leaped back as if an angry magus had appeared. "Ghostwalker did, several times. When I'd ask him about it, he'd say, 'Listen up, Darktalon! My final lesson will be on how to deal with magi and magic. Until then, run away from the bastards, or your end will be tragic.'"

"Good advice, although I'd add one thing."

"I'd like to hear it."

"Of all the magi, fear the fire magi most, for they become like Ukorus, the God of Earth and Fire: obsessive, secretive, and ill-tempered."

"What happened to your magus?" Ulric asked.

Gwynedd put his hand on the broad blade of the axe at his side. His fingers wistfully traced the curves of its interlocking etchings. "I pulled his guts out a good twenty paces before I let him die." He turned to Ulric and smiled. "Such a sweet noise he made."

Ulric was trying to decide if he should hazard a reply when Gwynedd abruptly stopped.

"Your burns. The truth!"

"I'm not hiding anything," Ulric lied. "I left out a detail or two, that's all." He had lied to the Concilium to protect Julia. He was certain the blessed medicine, or physic as she called it, had to have been worth a small fortune. Did she still have valuable friends at the temple? And what of her family? If they were well-connected, then the Imperaré wouldn't hesitate to exploit her. He had seen similar relationships leveraged and ruined by the Dark Assembly. Then there was the matter of the Gutter-Fish. Until he knew more, he wanted Julia to remain shadowed.

"What details?" Gwynedd advanced, his fingers still ominously roaming over the blade of his axe.

Ulric felt the sudden chill of impending danger. He couched his next lie in as much truth as possible. "It was the blessing of two goddesses: Neesis and Myrill! I was lucky the old man had hidden some medicine: a vial, a potion… a physic, he called it. He said Myrill had blessed it.”

“Something like that costs two hundred denarii or more! You’re lying.”

“Gods Below! I said all this at the Concilium! I gave my sacramentum to Silo. I owe you—”

A battering ram-like impact sent Ulric sprawling onto his back. For a moment he could see nothing but blinding sky, hear nothing but his ragged breath, feel nothing but a crushing pain in his chest.

“I’m a primus of the Portus Collegium, you little shit. You owe me respect.”

The sky slowly came into focus as Ulric caught his breath. He staggered to his feet and looked around. Gwynedd had led him onto a sparsely used street between two tall granary buildings, well away from prying eyes. Had a rough interrogation been his plan all along?

“I want the truth!” Silo’s primus closed in, his face a hellish mask of cruelty.

“To the Nine Gates with the truth! I’m tired of questions! When I talk, I’ll talk to Silo.”

“Fine. Talk to Silo. When I’m done with you.”

Gwynedd charged in, throwing a flurry of swift punches. Ulric stood his ground, ready to match the giant Northman’s anger with his own fury and frustration. It wasn’t Neesis inspired madness; it was plain stupidity, but he didn’t care. He just wanted to land one good hit on the man’s hideous face before the end.

The Northman's first punch smashed into his guard, nearly knocking him off his feet. It felt as if his arms were broken! Ulric abandoned any thought of blocking Gywnedd's blows. Instead, he did all he could to evade those hammer-like fists.

"You're a fast, slippery little shit, aren't you?"

Gwynedd surged forward, fists flying. Ulric fell back, ever elusive. Did he see frustration on Gwynedd's face? He couldn't be sure. The man's fire ravaged features masked all but a few emotions.

"Damn, you are fast," Gwynedd said. "But the Imperaré is full of fast little shits like you."

Somehow Ulric weaved into the hammer's path. The blow snapped his head back and sent him crashing against the granary wall.

Gwynedd chuckled. "What use is speed when I can make you move where I want?"

Gods Below! He was tired of losing fights. Rage and the rough stone wall biting into his back were the only things keeping him on his feet. Ulric rubbed the ache out of his jaw and tried to set his anger aside.

"That won't happen again, you bastard."

"Bastard? I'm Gwynedd, Son of Cenydd and Eilwen Flame-Eye of the Volceni. I know my lineage. Doubt you can say the same."

Ulric launched himself off the wall, feigning an uncontrollable fury. Gwynedd fell back to the center of the street, blocking each wild punch. Behind a mask of rage, Ulric calmly waited for Gwynedd to set him up for the next devastating blow.

Gwynedd's fist cut through empty air.

Ha! Is that surprise I see?

His unexpected move created an opening, and he threw everything he had into it. Lightning quick, he smashed his fists into the Northman's face, each impact sending a satisfying surge of pain from his knuckles to his elbows.

Gwynedd took a half step back. And laughed.

"Not bad. If you were a man with some weight behind you, I might have felt that."

"Sweet—" The hammer fell again and Ulric found himself on his ass blinking away stars of pain.

Gwynedd reached behind his back and produced a broad-bladed dagger. He tossed it to Ulric.

"What the hells?" Ulric caught the dagger and held it in a very nonthreatening manner. It had a long, leaf-shaped blade covered in intricate etchings.

Gwynedd drew his axe and held it in a tight two-handed grip. "Get up!"

Sweet Neesis! Does he want to kill me? Ulric stood and spread his hands wide in surrender. "Look, Gwynedd! First, I apologize for earlier. Second, I don't think Silo wants me dead. Third—"

اپسر را به ما بده یا بمیر

Ulric spun around at the sound of the unfamiliar voice to see six men approaching fast. Each wore sand and black-colored robes with a tight head wrap and veil-like masks. Broad-hilted triangular bladed swords hung from their belts.

A hard yank on Ulric's tunic pulled him back to Gwynedd's side. "The blade's for *them*, you turd-brained idiot."

The speaker repeated himself. He spoke Bayjoni. Ulric recognized the word 'boy', only because it was part of several crude insults. The man next to him stepped forward and spoke Trumin.

"Give us the boy. Or die."

"Whatever was promised, it isn't worth the coin. You're in deep Portus Collegium territory. All I need do is stamp my feet and men will come running." Gwynedd gleefully hefted his axe. "But what would be the fun of that?"

The Bayjoni drew their swords, and the sound filled the air with an ominous hiss. The lead man shouted, "The boy!"

"The next one who calls me 'boy' gets gutted."

The Bayjoni swordsmen uttered a piercing war cry and charged. Gwynedd gave a guttural cry of his own and rushed to meet them.

More noise, the better, I guess. With luck—and I'm always lucky— Harbor Men will arrive before we're cut to pieces. Ulric brandished his borrowed blade and screamed. He hoped it sounded more of an intimidating war cry than the disguised cry for help it really was.

Gwynedd crashed into the leader, and Gualdean axe met Bayjoni blade. A single stroke from the giant Northman broke the man's guard and bit deeply into the crook of his neck with a terrible thudding, cracking sound that made Ulric wince. With a triumphant cry, Gwynedd kicked the dying man into the oncoming Bayjoni, breaking their ranks.

The swordsmen ignored their fallen leader and split into two groups. Three Bayjoni surrounded Gwynedd, who disappeared behind a storm of sand and black-colored robes and flashing steel. The remaining two headed straight for Ulric.

He backpedaled and cast a quick glance down the narrow street: the path was clear. Should he run? Would the swordsmen follow? Would *all* the Bayjoni follow? Or would fleeing simply abandon Silo's primus to their enemies?

Ulric stood his ground and fell into a low guard stance, testing and stretching his tired and aching muscles. His earlier wounds threatened to tear open, sending a stab of pain through his thigh and shoulder. The time spent healing in Shadow Mind back at Epicydes' shop had been all too brief.

We just have to stay alive till help arrives.

One man attacked, swinging his blade in wild strokes that sent Ulric dodging and rolling. The other man stood back, watching silently from behind his veiled mask. Somehow that unsettled Ulric more than the Bayjoni's scything blade.

A horrible, gurgling scream erupted from within the circle of blades surrounding Gwynedd. *Sweet Neesis, no!* Had the Northman met his end? Ulric's feet turned to lead as a rising panic washed over him. He faltered and nearly fell under the swordsman's blade, only dodging at the last instant to turn a killing blow into a long, shallow cut down his back. To Ulric's great relief, a Bayjoni stumbled away from the ring of foes surrounding Gwynedd. His veil was gone and his face was a red ruin of meat and jawbone. He took two steps and fell onto the street. Gwynedd fought on.

Sweet Neesis! Now our odds are only two to one.

Ulric dodged another clumsy attack. He pointed to the man lying in the street and said, "Not your lucky day, is it?"

The swordsmen growled something incomprehensible in Bayjoni, and Ulric shot back with one of the many Bayjoni insults he knew, calling him either a lover of goats or a bucket of bull piss. He wasn't sure which.

"So, who sent you? Not that I can't guess."

The swordsman said something that didn't sound like an answer as the silent, watching Bayjoni tried to slip out of view. Ulric moved fast to keep him in sight, turning in time to see the man reach into his sleeve and fling a small, oddly shaped knife. It was just the sort of move he was expecting, and Ulric knocked it out of the air with a sweep of his dagger.

It wasn't a knife, but a dart the color of molten copper shaped to resemble a wasp. It rang with a tinny clang as it tumbled through the air, but instead of striking the ground, it sprouted insect wings and flew toward Ulric.

"God's Below! I hate magic!"

The two Bayjoni closed in and he guessed they would try to slow him down and hamper his movements until the dart struck. Whether it held poison or a narcotic, the wasp's sting meant death.

Now Ulric had to evade the swords of two Bayjoni and a furiously buzzing wasp-dart! He cleared his mind and let his instincts and Arrius' training guide him through the rain of blows and the endless buzzing, swooping attacks of the metal insect. A few moments later he stood, sweat soaked and near exhausted, trying to ignore the line of fire that was the wound on his back. All he could do was take some small measure of solace from the frustrated looks of the two swordsmen.

The wasp-dart circled, wings humming loudly, and plunged toward Ulric's neck. Without looking, he batted it away with a flick of Gwynedd's dagger and smiled; its incessant noise made it easy to track.

The smile was false bravado, of course. He was simply lucky that the Bayjoni wanted him alive. He grew more tired by the moment and Gwynedd was bloodied and hard pressed by two foes who did not need him alive. Ulric feared his luck was running out.

The two Bayjoni shared a brief, impatient sounding exchange, then hurled another dart. He leaped out of the way as it soared past, transparent wings unfolding from a shining body of black onyx. It looped in the air and flew toward his back as the copper wasp dove at his head. The cacophony of two angry wasp-darts made it impossible to track their movements by sound alone.

"Sweet Neesis!" *My luck has run out. What did Ghostwalker always say? "When Neesis Fortuna won't give you your due, it's Neesis Insania you must woo!"*

Ulric charged the two swordsmen, who, having only seen him avoid battle, seemed entirely startled by his sudden change in tactics. At the last moment, he dodged under their swords and dove between them, quickly rolling behind the man on his left. When he sprung to his feet, one wasp-dart had gone silent.

The swordsman turned and raised his blade. The wings of the copper dart puncturing his chest fluttered once and were still. He took one halting step and fell to the ground.

Ulric lunged for the man's fallen sword, but the remaining Bayjoni drove him back. He dodged a flurry of razor sharp steel while flashes of shining onyx danced at the borders of sight and the air reverberated with the buzzing of metal wings.

Ulric heard more than saw the wasp-dart change course and shoot toward him as if launched from a bow. The buzzing grew louder and louder, setting his teeth on edge. Instead of batting it away as he had done before, he snatched it out of the air. Beneath his grip the wasp's strange wings squirmed against hot metal.

The swordsman hesitated. Ulric knocked his blade aside and slammed his full weight into the man, hoping to stab him with dagger or dart. They hit the street hard, and everything became an exhausting blur of tangled limbs and flailing blows. A flash of pain, a snarled curse, and they staggered to their feet.

The Bayjoni yanked the onyx dart from his shoulder and cast it aside.

"Ha! Not so lucky," Ulric said.

The man mumbled something and pointed to Ulric's arm, where a trickle of blood ran from a small cut made by the wasp-dart's sting.

The Bayjoni lunged. Ulric tried to escape, but the street was suddenly uneven and treacherous. It felt as if he was moving through deep, churning water. He needed rest. He needed sleep. His dagger slipped from his numbed fingers. Thick hands seized him by the throat and slammed him to the ground, leaving him gasping for air. The man cackled and cursed as he squeezed, then his grip weakened and he collapsed atop Ulric, driving the last of the air from his lungs.

Nearby, Gwynedd fought on, though the sounds of battle were muted and hollow and the street had grown dim despite the midday sun. Gwynedd needed his help; he was sure of it. He tried to push the unconscious Bayjoni off of him, but the man's bulk was too much. *Nothing to be done but sleep,* he thought. The street darkened once again, but then a bellow from Gwynedd cleared his vision. One swordsman had somehow grabbed the Northman's axe and was trying to wrest the weapon from his grasp. The other man circled ever closer, looking to deliver a killing blow.

Neesis Fortuna! Where's the dagger? Ulric ran his free hand over the dirty cobblestones, desperate for a touch of metal. *Stay awake, you bastard.* The Bayjoni swordsman prepared to strike. *There! Stretch!* He grabbed Gwynedd's dagger and readied a most awkward throw given he was on his back, trapped under a sleeping Bayjoni. *Damn. Blade's poorly balanced for throwing.*

Ulric summoned the last of his strength and threw the dagger just as the swordsman was about to strike. Then he fell into a dream that began with a distant scream.

Ulric awoke to a sharp pain in his side. Then another. Someone was kicking him in the ribs.

"What the hells!"

"You're alive."

Gwynedd stood over him, looking bloodied and bored. The narrow street was swarming with Harbor Men and Imperaré who were disposing of the dead and, he guessed, preparing to interrogate the living. He noted one particular dead Bayjoni with Gwynedd's dagger still buried deep in his back.

Gwynedd acknowledged the dead man and said, "Nice throw." He extended an open hand toward Ulric and waited. Ulric took the offered hand and Gwynedd lifted him to his feet. The Northman retrieved his dagger and cleaned it with the dead man's robes. "Come on. The doctor's not far."

A short time later, Gwynedd stood in front of a large building with a colorful facade of pale Nyssan yellows and cool Ulorin blues. He motioned to Ulric and then pointed to the building's wide-open doors. "Time to get those wounds sorted out."

"Already?" Ulric called from the street. "But getting to know you has been such fun."

Gwynedd chuckled. "You're afraid of doctors?" He stopped laughing. "I don't care." He set his hand back on his axe. "Get in there."

Ulric raised his hands, palms forward. "Easy, easy, Gwynedd! I'm going, I'm going. It's not that I'm afraid of doctors; it's just the sort of healers we could afford back in Mist View didn't leave me with much confidence in the profession. Most were fools, cheats, and schemers; a bunch of nonsense-spouting grizzled old men."

Gwynedd laughed again. "You'll want to see this doctor."

Ulric stepped through the open doors and waited for his eyes to adjust. The gloom dissolved into a well-organized shop lined with shelves filled with various neatly labeled containers: pots, jars, urns, open boxes, and sealed chests. Rows of drying herbs and other strange plants hung from the ceiling, filling the cool air with a dozen competing fragrances. At the center of the room was a low padded table or a high thin bed. Ulric wasn't sure which. Nearby sat a sturdy wooden chair, several stools, and a long bench holding a variety of knives, levers, forceps, hooks, saws, and several tools whose purpose he did not want to know. When he stepped forward for a closer look, a dark-haired, olive-skinned Kreslan boy appeared in a doorway at the back of the room, interrupting his examination of the cruel-looking instruments.

In awkward Trumin, the boy said, "Bring doctor. Wait here."

The boy left, and Gwynedd entered the shop, closing the doors behind him. As Ulric waited, he looked over the shelves. Someone had written all the labels in Trumin and Kreslan, which he could read. The oldest temple dedicated to Neesis was in the Kreslan Isles, and he had learned their language as another way to please the Goddess.

He heard several people approaching and turned to see a tall Kreslan woman sweep into the room, trailed by a gaggle of young men and women. Thus began the third lesson of the day: the subject would be politics and diplomacy.

The woman had unfashionably short wheat-colored hair, a well-tanned and athletic body, and the face of a goddess. Stunned,

Ulric looked to Gwynedd, who leaned in and said under his breath, "All grizzled old cheats, are they?"

The woman addressed Gwynedd in a strong Kreslan accent. "What have you brought us?" To Ulric, she said, "Hello, I'm Leda, and these"—she waved a hand casually over her shoulder—"are my students."

"Μια τιμή για να σας συναντήσω, είμαι ο Ulric."

"Μιλάς Kreslan. Φανταστικός! This θα σας φανεί μια an odd ερώτηση, but είστε a prisoner?" Leda asked.

Ulric continued in Kreslan, "That is an odd question, but no, I'm no prisoner. I'm the Portus Collegium's newest and most eager recruit. Once I had no choice, I practically volunteered!" He gave a mischievous wink.

Leda laughed and replied in Kreslan. "Good. I warned Gwynedd I wasn't sewing anyone up to just have his brutes hack them open again."

Gwynedd had been listening to the exchange in increasing frustration. "Enough! Speak Trumin, or do not speak at all! The boy earned his wounds in a sword duel this morning. And a more recent ambush. Silo wants his wounds tended. Now do it, and do it in Trumin, and you'll be paid well, like before." Satisfied, he took one of the stools and sat by the door.

"And what about you?" Leda asked Gwynedd. "You don't look much better."

"I need nothing more than a salve and a few bandages. Set one of your students to the task."

Leda motioned Ulric to the center of the room, where he had a choice between the tall table and the sturdy chair; he sat in the chair. She sent one of her older students to tend to Gwynedd while the others gathered around and watched while she examined the wounds on Ulric's back, left shoulder, and right thigh. As she moved around the chair, peeling back clothing and washing away the blood and grime, her body would inevitably brush against his. A muscular thigh would rub against his knee, or a firm breast graze his shoulder, and he'd do his best not to react. It was made worse when he noticed she wore a short-sleeved, knee-length white tunic and little else.

Gwynedd was watching it all with a look of boredom, which Ulric interpreted as impish amusement. When Leda had finished cleaning the area around the wounds, she turned to Gwynedd and asked, "You said he was wounded this morning?"

"That's what everyone tells me," he said, sounding annoyed.

She turned back to Ulric, who looked away, pretending to examine the nearby surgical tools instead of the gaps in her tunic. "Is it true?" she asked.

"Huh? What?" He planned to play indifferent to her charms, but then a thought occurred to him: what if she had no idea the effect she had on men? Or what if she didn't care? "Oh, yes! This morning, sometime after the third hour, I think. The slice on my back I got on the walk over here. It must be how you drum up business."

Leda ran her hand along the slash on Ulric's thigh, which caused him to wince, but not in pain. "This cut appears to have been healing for a full day, maybe more. Did you visit a priest or another healer before you came here?"

"It's been a busy morning, filled with rooftop chases, duels, lucky escapes, secret meetings, and ill-timed ambushes. No time for doctors until now, but you're doing a wonderful job!" Ulric studied her hazel eyes and smiled.

"Only time or the gods can heal a wound this way. Or"—one of her students handed Leda a large ceramic vial and a fresh cloth—"do you happen to speak Bayjoni as well as Kreslan?" she asked with a knowing look.

"I know a few phrases, but none fit for the ears of such a beautiful lady."

"Ha! I'm no useless Trumin matron." Leda leaned in close to examine Ulric's shoulder and whispered in Kreslan, "If you know anything of the Bayjoni self-healing disciplines, return, and I'll help improve your Kreslan. Your accent is atrocious."

"That didn't sound like Trumin to me," Gwynedd warned.

Leda began cleaning Ulric's wounds with a solution that smelled strongly of vinegar. It stung sharply but not as much as her comment on his Kreslan. As she worked, she spoke loudly for Gwynedd's benefit. "I'm sure these cuts weren't cleaned properly. We need to wash out the dirt, the filth, and the Unseen."

"The Unseen?"

"Don't fill the boy's head with your Kreslan nonsense, woman," Gwynedd said.

Leda ignored him. "The 'Unseen' are tiny creatures our eyes cannot see. They breed in filth and swamps. Normally, they float through the air and enter the body through the nose and mouth. They can cause sickness and even death. They also enter through wounds, so cleanliness is especially important."

"What? There are tiny little monsters everywhere?" Ulric did not like the idea.

"Don't listen to her, Ulric," Gwynedd interjected. "It's a Kreslan scheme to drum up more business."

Leda began stitching up the puncture wound in Ulric's shoulder with quick, practiced movements. "You Trumin men don't like the idea because the Unseen aren't easily put to the sword. You can sail to the Kreslan Isles, take advantage of our troubles, steal our wealth, enslave our people, but somehow learn nothing!"

"Leda—"

"You Trumins would still shove unwashed wool in every wound if it wasn't for Kreslan doctors. You'd—"

Gwynedd leaped from his stool. "Leda!"

She finished the last stitch and broke it off with a painful yank. "What!"

"Yell at Silo if you want. These are not my people: I was born in the far north, beyond Cearalon."

"Yes, of course," Leda said apologetically. "But as a foreigner here, I thought you'd understand."

"What I understand is this: I love this city. I have a good life here." Gwynedd sat, leaned forward, and rested his elbows on his thighs. "What I don't understand is: if you don't like Trumric, then what are you doing here?"

Leda said nothing and turned back to Ulric. "You're Trumin? What do you think of the Republic?"

"I've been taught to avoid politics," Ulric said. "My views on the subject begin and end with my coin."

Leda's perfect mouth frowned, which made Ulric regret his flippant remark. "Very practical. You'll do well in the Imperaré."

Leda's students fussed over bandaging his wounds while she and Gwynedd haggled over payment. Afterward, Ulric walked around the room testing his new bandages, wondering where he'd be off to next. He still needed to receive the Portus Collegium XVII standard, and when he learned Leda would do the inking, he couldn't hide his surprise.

Leda set her hands sternly on her hips. "If I'm spending any more time with you, you must bathe first. You're a filthy mess, and you stink!"

Her students escorted Ulric to a small peristylium at the center of the building. They provided him with clean water and oils and left him in the garden to bathe alone. His pants and tunic, all cuts, burns, and bloodstains, were thrown away and replaced with a fresh loincloth, tunic, and a pair of old sandals. He noticed two of Leda's students, a young girl, and an older boy, were watching him from the far end of the garden, whispering and giggling. Ulric ignored them but kept glancing at the edge of the peristylium, curious if Leda took a similar interest. She did not.

When he finished, they directed him to a nearby room where colorful pictures and designs from across the Republic covered every wall. Ulric lowered his new tunic and laid back on a comfortable couch while Leda assembled the necessary inks and needles.

He pointed to the Low Street standard on his chest. "You know, Gwynedd, more ink only makes it harder to run an honest scheme amongst the wealthy."

"Pay a fabricator to mask them."

"You talk like magic is cheap!" Ulric rolled his eyes and asked, "Are there special Imperaré discounts?"

"We have our connections," Gwynedd boasted. "Now shut up and let Leda work."

Ulric had the collegium XVII placed above his left bicep. The numbers were slender and black, outlined in a nimbus of crimson fire written across a smaller black hexagon. He guessed the hexagon represented the inner harbor of the Portus complex. Leda's skill and speed with the needles amazed him, but it still took a little over two hours to complete the job. When she was done, he looked down at the fiery XVII, and in his mind, he saw the anagram VIXI, which meant "I have lived" in Trumin. The young man who had come to the capital with dreams of freedom was dead.

⚔

"And…" Silo prompted.

Silo's voice brought Ulric's thoughts back to the present, where he had been learning the fourth lesson: duties and obligations.

Ulric finally gave up and lowered the charms he had been trying to buy. "Publius Gabinius Licinus leads the College of Bakers, and there is a hidden ledger in his office that can prove he has been shorting the city of festival bread. Secure it, and the College of Bakers will suddenly become more cooperative." He grew quiet, then asked, "If that's all there is to the job?"

"Fearing another setup?" Silo asked with a smile.

Ulric gave a noncommittal shrug.

"Don't." Silo's smile vanished. "If I wanted rid of you, I'd kill you here and now."

"That's reassuring… I think."

"Just don't be so naïve to think you'll know the reasons behind every job."

Silo thought for a moment.

"Let me rephrase that for the apprentice of the famous Ghostwalker: don't be so arrogant as to think you deserve to know the reasons behind every job."

"All right, Silo, no more questions. I should have the ledger in two or three days at most." Ulric hesitated, then asked, "Uh, assuming I could get an advance on a resupply? I don't even own a set of lock picks anymore."

"Look at you, trying to scheme money out of me," Silo said with exaggerated pride. "You're already like all my other men." He let out a long sigh. "I'll see if I have anything secondhand lying about."

He had one of his assistants fetch a small chest from the back. The man dropped it on the counter with a loud thump.

"Let's see what we have here." He pulled back the lid.

"Sweet Neesis! The Goddess really loves me!"

Inside the chest was the equipment Aquila Secunda had stripped from him the previous night. He searched through the chest and found everything, including the enchanted quartz and even Titus' purse. The presence of a few remaining coins was a surprise, but what were a few sestertii to a woman like Aquilla Secunda?

"How did you get it all back?" Ulric asked.

"When the Imperaré visited Secundus' widow, she handed it over. She has no use for a thief's kit and hoped it might lead to her husband's killer."

Ulric eagerly collected his things. "Thank you, Silo! Neesis bless you!"

"Neesis' blessing upon us both, for no thief ever made it far without her luck. But luckiest are those that make their own odds, so I'll take a seventeen percent finder's fee out of your payment for the Ledger Job."

Silo watched as Ulric rolled his thieves' kit into his cloak. There was the hint of a smile on his thin lips, and Ulric thought he was about to say something, but he stopped himself when he saw the charms still in Ulric's hand.

"Now you have some coin, so don't even think about leaving with those until you've handed over at least two sestertii."

Ulric handed over the two bronze coins. "You're not leaving me with much."

"I'll pay you when you bring me that ledger."

"Then I better get on with it!" Ulric grabbed his kit and started toward the exit.

"Wait!" Ulric spun around with his arms wide and shot Silo an impatient look. "Where are you off to?"

"To scout the mighty stronghold of the bakers, of course."

"And afterward?"

Ulric hesitated, sensing a trap. Finally, he admitted, "I hadn't thought that far ahead."

"Do you ever?"

"Only when absolutely necessary!"

"Well, I always do, and I can't let you dishonor the Portus Collegium by living rough on the streets, so you'll have to take a room here. There's one on the northeast corner of the fourth floor that should do."

Ulric wanted to protest he had a very comfortable arrangement at a certain theater loft, but he knew its location near the River Market would be a problem. Unsure of what to say, he said nothing.

"Most people express some gratitude when pulled off the streets."

"Uh, thank you! Sorry… I was left speechless."

"Oh, yes, just like you," Silo said, raising one dubious eyebrow. "One last thing: After the Concilium and the Bayjoni mercenaries, it's clear Brocchus thinks you know things about the Dark Assembly's plans that even Luciano doesn't."

"Then Brocchus is an idiot. I've told you everything, Silo." *Well, everything but for Julia's part.*

"I believe you. Cornelius Brocchus does not. Things will get bloody between us and the Transnanpela Collegium. Until it quiets down, you need to stay out of the Transnanpela District. Especially the River Market. Understand?"

Stay out of the Transnanpela District? Sure, right after I make things right with Julia.

"Of course, Silo. I'm not stupid."

Ghostwalker

What more could I possibly tell you?

The truth, siyad. The truth. You may have forgotten the truth, but it still exists. We cannot murder memories like men. One cannot merely assassinate a notion. We can bury thoughts like bodies, yes, but never truly kill them. Buried for a time, but only to be resurrected eventually.

Tell me, siyad: what have you hidden beneath the soil of your reason? Show me. What memories have you buried? What thoughts have you forgotten, locked within the deepest mausoleum of your mind? Show me, siyad. Lead me to them.

Luciano and the Dominator wandered through the twisting corridors of his mind until they stood at the edge of a steep stairwell. Together, they descended into the shadows of his thoughts. Luciano led this now-familiar stranger to a black corner of his mind that even he had forgotten existed. A crypt stood there, caked in dust and cobwebs. A thousand chains wrapped themselves around its stone walls, and a thousand locks secured its iron doors.

Break the chains, open the locks, siyad. The truth awaits beyond.

Luciano did nothing. The Dominator waved a hand, and the chains and locks disintegrated.

Cast the doors open, siyad.

Luciano, convinced the Dominator could simply will anything to happen, complied.

Ah yes. I see now, siyad. I see. Let's rescue—you and I—this buried memory from the catacombs of your mind. We will revisit this precious memory together and make the past the present. You will discover—once and for all—the truth. Shall we?

Luciano felt the Dominator shove him forward. Thought and memory swirled through his thoughts like storm clouds, and when his mind cleared, he stood in Mist View, looking down on the streets of years past.

I've come to the Warrens hunting for someone, but not my usual sort of prey. I settle into the gloom shrouding the roof of a slaughterhouse and search the refuse-strewn yard below. The stench of rotten meat hits me despite the place having been abandoned long ago, and even a week's long cold drizzle can't wash the taste of death out of the air. The slate-gray sky is thick, close, smothering every sound except the dull patter of rain. It is—*no, was… what's happening?*—a perfect day for an ambush.

Close behind me, a roof tile grates and cracks ever so slightly. A rain-soaked wooden beam groans. Too damned close!

No! I'm not here. Only a memory. Isn't that so, Dominator? What sort of truth could I find here? These memories no longer have meaning. Are you listening, Dominator? Answer me, damn you!

Daggers are in my hands in an instant. A dark mound rises from the rotting roof beams above me, the shape swiftly dissolving into the form of a cloaked and hooded man.

"Any closer, Hound of Nyx, and I'd be pulling your tail." The voice is deep and resonant, the Kreslan words sharp and precise.

"Only you," I reply in Kreslan, "only you, Ghostwalker, could get so close." I relax and sheathe my blades. "Careful not to get too close. It would be a pity to kill my only friend in Mist View."

"A pity to be killed." Arrius glides silently over the roof and joins me at the edge. Under his hood, his brow furrows as he searches the yard below. "And what's so interesting?"

"First, why were you looking for me, eh?" I bare my teeth in a feral smile. "And don't say you just tripped over me in the Warrens."

"Would I lie to that face? Vicar Suetonius put me on the hunt. He likely has a new job for you."

"Good," I say, turning my attention to the shadows below. "I've grown bored lately."

"Hence your fascination with an empty lot?"

"Empty, eh?" I shake my head with disappointment. "Sloppy thinking like that gets a man killed."

Arrius looks again and sees the boy. "He's hidden himself well. Dark tunic. Mud covering his exposed limbs and face. Deep shadow on the threshold of the ruins. Not bad, given what he had to work with. The boy is clearly waiting to ambush someone. Looking for a parley? Or a bit of knife work?"

"His first shroud."

"Ah. They grow up so fast." It's a joke, but there's sadness in his voice. "If they grow up at all."

I'm wondering how a thief with such a hard reputation can be so sentimental when a hulking figure appears at the far end of one alley that spills into the slaughterhouse yard. He's walking hurriedly, whether to escape the rain or on some secret errand; I have no idea.

"The north alley: the boy's mark."

"And your interest?" Arrius asks.

"The Vicars have decreed that the best among us should pass on our skills," I say proudly. "Perhaps this boy…"

"The great Luciano Porteles, dreaded Hound of the Night Goddess, pass on his Verdan secrets to a Trumin orphan? Really?"

"Fuck off. Even a bastard like you has that Gualdean boy."

"His name's Johan, not that 'Gualdean boy'," he said, switching to Trumin just to annoy me. "Although I've taught him all I can, given his temperament. He's set on leaving for Conric in the spring. He wants to be closer to home. Join the Silver Shadows."

"Ungrateful little shit," I reply in Trumin. The words are heavy and sharp in my mouth, like gravel, but I must master the language of the Republic if I'm to impress the Vicars.

The mark enters the yard and slows a moment to probe the chill shadows. Despite his immense size, he's not quite a man yet, made plain by a patchy beard and awkward stride.

"That brute's Fabius," says Arrius. "Leader of the Low Street gang. Your boy better have dropped a coin at the shrine of Neesis."

"I know. Boy hunts worthy prey. Maybe boy stupid? Maybe end up dead? I've watched boy prepare ambush for many days. We watch now. We see if boy can kill."

Fabius tugs at a too-small cloak draped over a pair of massive shoulders and resumes his hurried pace, doing his best to avoid the worst of the mud and filthy water. With heavy footfalls, he splashes past what appears to be another empty threshold.

We watch the boy dart out of the shadows, knife slashing, then Fabius screams.

The Low Street leader turns, cutting the air with an old pugio, a broad-bladed infantry dagger. He takes an uncertain step as rivulets of blood wash down the back of his legs. Fabius shouts a challenge to an empty rain-soaked lot. We see the boy crouching in the water behind a short wooden fence, the remnants of an old sheep run.

"Bad move. Should made killing strike. Not cripple."

"I have to agree. A boy that young, that small, toying with the likes of Fabius?"

The boy stands, and recognition flashes in Fabius' eyes. They exchange a brief round of taunts and insults, then Fabius charges. He's nearly two heads taller than the boy, and he simply smashes through the rotting timbers when he reaches the fence. The boy leaps clear, and Fabius' legs suddenly sink into deep water, pitching him face-first into the muck. Then the boy springs back onto Fabius, gleefully slashing with his knife, then leaping away again. He runs to the center of the yard and starts hurling some creative insults.

I quietly chuckle. "Good Move. I make this boy into good killer."

"Sweet Neesis. The boy *is* toying with him."

Fabius staggers to his feet, his pugio lost somewhere in the murky water and unleashes a barrage of barely comprehensible threats. As he lumbers forward, several more youths enter the yard. They're mostly boys, a few girls, some as young as ten years, others nearly as old as Fabius. It's the Low Street gang, and they look even more wet and miserable than your typical denizens of the Warrens. They spread out along the edge of the yard and watch Fabius and the boy go at each other.

"No one's helping their glorious commander," Arrius observes.

"Fabius, he plays with boys and girls under his command. Oh, he plays Arrius. But he don't play nice."

The boy darts in, quick as death, strikes and is gone before the shambling Fabius can touch him. I can see every step sets his legs on fire thanks to the slashes on his hamstrings, and half a dozen other knife wounds are bleeding heavily. When Fabius musters the strength for a charge, the boy falls back and always finds a conveniently placed stone to fling at the gang leader with painful accuracy. Slowly the rest of the gang begins openly rooting for the boy. Ulric? Odd name. Gualdean sounding. The boy looks Trumin to me.

"So boy make big show of taking down Fabius. Why?" I ask. "Too young to lead himself."

"He certainly enjoys putting on a performance." Arrius pulls his hood back and gazes up into the gray. The cool drizzle strikes his face for a moment; then, he runs a hand through his reddish-brown hair. He turns to me, and a huge grin erupts across his face. "Not the performance, Luciano. The audience!"

"Us. We watch audition." I look down on the fight with growing pride. "This Ulric make good assassin."

"The Vicar's decree was no secret to anyone with ears to hear the whisper. The boy's clever. Ambitious. You'll have a promising student if he survives. If he doesn't stray too close."

And, of course, the boy does. Perhaps the cheers of the Low Street gang led to overconfidence, or he underestimated Fabius' endurance, or maybe he simply grew too tired. Whatever the cause, he rushes in, slipping under one wild, rage-filled swing to cut another long slash across Fabius' chest, but he turns back too soon, greedy for another strike. Fabius' mallet-like fist connects with a crack we hear clearly on the slaughterhouse roof. The boy tumbles through the air and hits the muddy ground, sliding a good two-body lengths through the muck.

"Damn you, Ghost! Why did you say it? You Trumins: always talk, talk, talk. You talk too much."

"Don't blame me. My words had no power." He pulls his hood over his head and sighs. "And I was really rooting for the boy."

Down below, the yard is quiet; there is no more cheering. The only sound is the constant rain and Fabius' curses and grunts as he fishes the boy's knife out of a shallow puddle where it fell. The boy lies unmoving in a deep furrow of mud.

Arrius leans over the edge. "Come on, get up."

Before I realize what I've done, there's a throwing knife in my hand. I could save the boy so easily, but interceding in such a life-and-death struggle is a great offense to Nyx, the Goddess Beyond

Night. Could I do penance enough to justify the deed? After all, spilling blood in her name is my profession.

The boy finally stirs. But what could he do, dazed and weaponless? Fabius tells everyone what he'll do with the knife. Nothing new or creative, but effective all the same.

"Through the Nine Gates with this." I see Arrius make a strange sign in the air. "Neesis Umbra! This boy, please protect, then I'll steal, as you direct!"

Fabius steps forward, towering over the boy who is now crouched in the mud, desperately searching the refuse for anything he can use as a weapon.

I ready my throwing knife.

The boy springs out of the muck, something dark and curved in his hand. He vaults over Fabius' knife, past his shoulders, and hooks the talon-like blade into his right eye. His momentum yanks the huge gang leader off his feet, and Fabius crashes into the mud. The boy stands back and holds up the bloody curved blade—a dark animal talon—and the Low Street gang cheers. Fabius, half-blinded and overwhelmed by pain and shock, was forgotten.

A subtle pressure nudged him forward, and once again, Luciano's thought and memory deformed to the Dominator's will.

I crash through the door of Bucco's taberna and plow through the crowd toward the back benches, where I find Arrius sitting among a group of young Assembly idiots like an orating Kreslan philosopher. They can see I'm on a rampage and scatter. Arrius raises a hand, and there's a drink waiting for me when I sit. I down the swill in one gulp and slam the cup on the table so hard it cracks. I take a deep breath full of sea salt from the harbor and the stench of drunken fools.

"Denied! Bastard Vicars denied me," I shout, not caring who hears.

"Sorry," Arrius says. I barely hear him over the drunken crowd. He motions, and a young slave girl brings more wine, then quickly retreats.

"Sorry? Just sorry?" I search his face for something hidden. "No stupid poem? No mouth on and on about Assembly politics?"

"What should I say?" Arrius leans both elbows on the table and takes a drink. He remains there, staring down into his cup for a long moment, then continues. "Should I say you're better off forgetting it, burying it? That they'll approve your next petition? You don't need the distraction? That the world has enough killers?"

"You can say they wrong!"

My cup shatters on the dingy stucco behind Arrius with a dull crack, the cheap wine just another stain on Bucco's walls. A hush falls over the nearby tables as eyes turn our way. Arrius, his expression flat and inscrutable, rises to leave.

"Perhaps it was your temperament?" he says.

I grab his wrist as he walks by and sound out the Trumin world slowly. *'Temperament?* Vicar Gratianus said so. Seemed wrong. Not Vicar's word. Your word!" I stand up, my anger rising with me.

"Arakru take us both!" he says, but his anger quickly fades into resignation. "Gods and Vicars have their own plans."

"Say you no speak against me, then I bury this." His silence gives me my answer. I give him mine. My fist sends him sprawling onto the warped planks of the floor.

The young idiots gather around, cheering and hooting like a day in the arena. The older assemblymen are quieter, more respectful; they know they stand before a funeral pyre. I pay them all little attention. My focus is on the Ghost.

He rolls to his feet, his eyes hard, his jaw set, his anger leashed. He gets in my face and holds up one finger. The crowd grows quiet as death when he says, "You get that one for free. I probably deserved it."

Beneath the anger and guilt on his face, I see the smug grin trying to break through. "You speak against me, then dare say how much I take or not take?"

Who in the Hells does this sneak-thief think he is, anyway? He may have two or three seasons on me here in Mist View, but he hasn't had to overcome what I have. He hasn't labored under the mark of an outsider. And now Arrius—this thief, this coward—has the nerve to slander me in front of the vicars?

"Luciano takes what he wants!"

I lash out, ready to take and break his finger. Astonishingly, I grasp at air and then wood as I hit the floor. I hear laughter somewhere in the crowd. Arrius is quick. Of course, he is; he's the Ghost. But I'm the damned Hound of Nyx!

I hear his voice above and behind me. "Bury it, Luciano. You don't want to do this. Not here."

I rise and face him. He's still hiding that godsdamned grin. I close in, fists at the ready. This time my eyes are wide open, looking for his dodge. I quickly jab, I feel a light touch on my shoulder, a pressure on my back, and somehow I'm on the floor again. More laughter.

"No, that… No monkey tricks!"

Arrius looks around at the growing audience. "Oh? You're setting rules now?" A few more chuckles.

I tell myself to ignore the crowd; the humiliation isn't real. But it feels so real. I'm fooled into thinking I have a choice, but it's only a memory.

I stand up and take a defensive posture, hoping he'll come at me. He doesn't. He just stands there.

"Tell me, why stop petition?" I ask. "Now boy will waste talents in filthy Warrens."

"No." Arrius slowly shakes his head, then quickly spits out the rest like a man ripping off a scab. "The vicars have decreed I'll train the boy in the Shadow Ways."

Fire rages in my chest. A war drum beats at my temples. The crowd responds with shouts of "Thief!" and "Take him!"

I bullrush him.

I soar over a table and smash a couple of old stools to splinters on my way down to the planks once more, my breath gone. The assemblymen's eyes are upon me, so I do my best to conceal the stun and pain. I rise, my arms behind me, propping myself up, and try to catch a breath. Arrius offers his hand to me. Nothing could make me angrier.

"Luciano," he says, his voice low, "when I appealed to Neesis Umbra to save the boy, the goddess answered. You saw it: the unlikely weapon, the prodigious leap! As payment, I had to steal as she commanded. And She demanded I take the boy. There was no choice. Forgive me, friend."

Bury it, you imbecile!

I grab his arm and pull hard. I bring his head down toward my knee, but it misses. He rolls on the ground and out of my grasp; he's up and back on his feet. Still winded, I struggle to stand.

The brawl, if one could even call it that, lasts a few more moments. I never land a blow. I end up on one knee, my arm pinned behind my back, Arrius behind me, twisting my wrist to the point of snapping. Tethers of pain streak up my arm into my shoulder. Just when I think my wrist will crack apart, he releases his grip. Arrius turns away and leaves without giving me another look. The crowd simply returns to their drinking.

I've buried this memory, Dominator; it's true. Why? What exactly happened that day? Arrius Ghostwalker betrayed me. Slandered me before the vicars and stole a student of great potential. Then he refused to fight like a real man, instead resorting to cowardly Kanchean tricks to humiliate me.

Or is that really what happened?

I could have walked away. I could have forgiven him, buried the matter. What choice does a man have when the gods command? What did my pride and my temper cost me all those years ago? So many years of wasted hate.

Maybe this is the truth you've been in search of, Dominator?

Another push, and memory and thought collide once again.

I slap her, knocking the smug smile from her perfectly red lips. She stumbles and drops onto the dining couch. My hand stings with cruel satisfaction.

Rhoswen rises to her feet and pointedly smooths out her green silk stola. She adjusts the jade serpent hairpin that's keeping her auburn locks piled fashionably high atop her head, then casually licks away a drop of crimson at the corner of her mouth and smiles. Her display is both maddening and seductive. "And I thought it would please you to learn I discovered where Marcellus keeps his mistress. He'll be vulnerable—"

I step forward, trying to contain my rage. I speak through gritted teeth, the Trumin words strained and difficult. "Not what you learn, but how... whore."

She reaches out and gently strokes my cheek with the back of her hand. "I am a whore, dear," she boasts. "Not yours, though. I've never asked you for money, have I?" She leans forward and kisses me; at first gently, then urgently. Finally, she bites down and tears a gash into my lower lip.

"Godsdamned bitch!" I throw her back onto the couch. She watches the blood trickle down my chin and laughs. A delicate tinkling sound, cold and sharp like broken glass. It cuts deeply. It always does. "You take Rhos. More than any weight of silver."

She expels an exasperated sigh. "Oh, Luciano, what jealous fantasy has that twisted Verdan mind of yours conjured now?"

"How you find Marcellus' woman?" I ask. "What was cost? What filthy things you do for him, eh?" I give her a savage grin, revealing bloodstained teeth: it's a warning.

Rhoswen leaves the couch and hurriedly walks to the veranda. I note the nervousness in her too-quick steps and eagerly follow. The night air is chilly. No… the air *was* chilly, just as I remembered. Autumn was ending, and icy rains had drenched the city. I look over the railing and down the cliffs of the Tiers District. Cold columns of fog spread throughout the streets of the lower warrens like an invading army.

Rhoswen turns and leans against the railing. "You make no sense, dear. We could speak Gualdean if that would be easier?"

"No, we speak Trumin. I must learn. Luciano always learning." I step closer. "I learn you seen with Arrius. Many times. Very recent."

"Oh, really, Luciano! How boring you've become." Her eyes admit it all. She raises a hand to strike me, but I grab her wrist and seize her by the throat. I squeeze, slowly pushing her back and down over the railing until she's suspended in the empty air above the cliff. I remember the look of surprise and terror in her eyes as her feet left the floor. Had she finally realized you can push a killer only so far?

I've done all this before! It can't be happening again. Yes… only a memory. The past has become the present, just as the Dominator warned. What truth do you hope to find here, eh? Answer me!

I feel the betrayal, humiliation, and rage I felt that night so many years ago. I can only see an arrogant, filthy whore who thought she could toy with the affections of an assassin.

"I warned you. I warned you, Rhos! Anyone. Anyone but him! What price? What did he demand? How did you… betray me?" I imagine her body in Arrius' arms. I imagine her body tumbling down the cliffside to shatter on the street below.

"I… Arrius… never touched me." She gasps. I loosen my grip on her throat but dip her lower over the railing. "Please… Luciano! He asked for silver—only silver! A very reasonable sum! Our profits from this Shroud will be immense. Enough to leave Mist View!"

I ease her up from the railing, just enough to keep her talking. "No, no, no, Ghostwalker never sells cheap," I tell her. "What demands? Exact?"

"Only five-hundred denarii."

"And…"

"He demanded we meet in public. That's all."

"Oh, that all?" I toss her back onto the veranda. She collides with a pedestal hard enough to knock it from its plinth, sending a statue of Mantius and Mania tumbling toward the floor. Rhoswen and the Infernal Twins, gods of death and madness, hit the marble floor together. Divine brother and sister fly apart, their incestuous embrace broken. It was an ill omen.

Forgive her, you fool!

"How you so stupid, Rhos? I told you stay away from Ghostwalker! Now everyone sees!" I scream the words and begin slowly advancing toward her. "The Assembly think you betray me! With Arrius!" I draw Aguja: so sharp, so beautiful, so faithful.

She groans and picks herself up from the floor. She moves into a crouch, her eyes on Aguja. "Curse your jealousy! I've fucked half the men in this city. You knew that long before our little partnership began."

I'm towering over her now. "Not Arrius. Never Arrius. You agreed. Have you forgotten? Aguja remind you!"

"No! Have you forgotten what we've accomplished— together? We've become wealthy. We've earned the respect of the Assembly. We've bathed this city in blood by the barrel! Now you want to destroy all that, destroy us, over… appearances? Your stupid pride? I swear to the Infernal Twins he never touched me."

I see the look of desperation in her eyes. No, only a memory… I think. I should have forgiven her! Is that the truth I'm supposed to discover? Are you watching Dominator? Does this amuse you? Say something!

"Aguja cut you, bleed you. Maybe Aguja forgive before you lose your value?" I step forward, and her eyes fill with hate.

"I told you I'd never submit to Aguja again! Don't do this, Luciano. Please."

"It's Arrius that does this. Not me." I reach for her, but she springs past me like a coiled serpent. I turn to follow, but my movements are amateurish and slow. She rolls to her feet, and her auburn curls unravel like writhing snakes. I struggle to take a step forward, but a sharp pain in my thigh stops me. I know its cause before I even look: Rhoswen's jade hairpin is stuck in my leg. She's dipped it in poison, of course. I feel my limbs turning to stone. I hit the floor.

I slowly count the tiles in the ceiling mosaic. Rhos comes into view and kneels to retrieve her hairpin. "I did warn you, Luciano." Her image becomes blurry as my eyes fill with water. Not tears, of course; I simply can't blink. She wipes away a drop rolling down the side of my face and pries Aguja from my hand. "How do you like my little concoction? I call it Medusa's Kiss. I'd tell you how it's made as one last professional courtesy, but you have little time left." She stands and stares down at me for a long moment. "Damn you."

I've always remembered triumph, cruelty, and hatred in those green eyes, but now I see the hurt, the sadness, the regret. I did this. Was that the truth I had forgotten? Is it? Are you still there, Dominator? Watching from the shadows of memory? Why won't you answer?

I watch the hurt, sadness, and regret retreat deep behind her eyes. She is Rhoswen again: infamous prostitute and Dark Assembly assassin.

"I suppose I must thank you, Luciano. Now that you're gone, there's enough coin to establish me in Arkanay—with style." She turns and walks away.

I've counted thirty-two mosaic tiles.

I blink.

I seize her from behind. She screams as I twist her wrist, trying to make her drop Aguja, but she stubbornly holds on. I press my forearm into her throat and nuzzle her ear. I can smell her sweet perfume and panic. "Two portions Suhtean sand viper. One portion of fat-tailed scorpion. Water and simple millet make thick paste. Cause paralysis, then dead." She asks me how. "I know long time. Made ready for this day. Small, small doses first, then more. Very... unpleasant."

There is still time. Forgive her, you fool. Release her. Let her flee the city. Let her go!

Somehow, she twists out of my grasp and nearly impales me on my precious Aguja. We struggle for control of the dagger. She knows she's gone too far. The night can only end in murder.

I knock Aguja from her hand, and it goes clattering across the veranda. She rakes her nails across my face, nearly blinding me. I shake my head, clearing my eyes of blood, and strike her hard. She staggers back and hits the railing. It gives. For an instant, she's balanced on the precipice, her arms flailing pathetically. I take one halting step forward and stop.

I watch.

Without a sound, she disappears over the edge.

I peer down the cliffside. The lower warrens are an expanse of misty black and dull torchlight. Rhoswen is gone. I curse the name Arrius Ghostwalker.

They found her body the next morning. It was a simple matter for the Assembly to ensure there were no consequences. Only there was. The whisper was on the streets. They said I had murdered her to avenge my cuckolding at the hands of Ghostwalker.

Yes, I've buried this memory. If I thought about Rhoswen at all, it was to curse Arrius, to blame him for her death. But...

I killed Rhoswen. My jealousy. My pride. My weakness.

Is this it, Dominator? Is this the truth you wanted to uncover?

Another jolt. Like an unexpected fall...

It's a crisp day. Just enough of a salty breeze blowing in from the bay to open your nostrils, widen your eyes, lift your wings. A perfect day for an ascension. As I walk down the street toward the Congressus Celatus, I feel empowered. When I see him approaching, my fists clench. As we near each other, my jaw does as well.

I spit words at him. "No time for you, Arrius." I bump his shoulder as I pass. "No time for your shit."

"You would be wise to hear me out, Luciano. I know the plans you're hatching."

I pause but don't turn around. I'm not about to give him the satisfaction. "You know nothing, I think, eh? Nothing." I resume walking.

"I know you plan to assassinate Governor Livius."

I stop.

"I know you plan to announce it to the Archon and the Assembly this afternoon. Don't do it. It's a foolish idea."

I turn and laugh in his face. "I think you jealous, eh, Arrius?"

"It's a stupid plan. More than stupid: dangerous. You'll have the Assembly playing right into their hands."

I'm not sure what he's getting at, but as much as I despise him, I convince myself that it can't hurt to listen for a moment; see where he's headed with this.

"The Senate won't let such an act go unpunished. If you do what you're planning—if you kill Livius—the Senate will seize the opportunity to move on the Assembly the way they've wanted to for years. We're no match for the legions."

I bite down on my lower lip and suck the air between my teeth as I glare at him. The smug look on his face boils my blood, though I can't help but laugh. "You jealous, Arrius. You know I do this, and the Archon take me in. Make me equis. Maybe even vicar, eh?

Vicar Luciano! Meantime, Arrius nothing. You jealous of me. You afraid."

He shakes his head like some disappointed father, which angers me even more.

"Don't say I didn't warn you, Luciano."

Seething, I march toward the Congressus Celatus, even more determined than before.

Don't do it… Listen to the Ghost. Just listen to the bastard, you damned fool.

I'm inside the Congressus Celatus now. The main hall. The Archon sits on his oak throne at the head of the table. All the vicars have taken their places. I must wait until after dinner before I'm allowed to speak. When that time finally arrives, I'm "given the center," meaning I'm allowed to stand in the center of the room and address the Assembly. I lay out my plan to assassinate the governor, Penna Patreus Livius, who has long been a thorn in the Dark Assembly's backside. I brag to the vicars about how I will use Aguja to end the weasel's life. I meet the Archon's gaze as I declare I will bring him Livius' ears as trophies. When I have finished, I bask in the adulation of the vicars like a triumphant gladiator. Even the Archon wears a rare smile of approval. When the toga-flapping and chants have subsided, I bow to the Archon, who gestures to an empty seat next to him.

I move to take my place at his side, but I am interrupted by the sound of a slow, deliberate clap within the shadowy columns at the side of the hall.

Arrius emerges from the darkness—still applauding—and two Assembly heavies rush to his side. He passively raises his hands and allows the men to seize him, never breaking eye contact with me. The two brutes, now all but lifting Arrius off his feet, look to the Archon. His eyes move from Arrius to me and then back to Arrius. He waves off the men with a single gesture.

"What is this intrusion, Ghostwalker?" a voice asks.

Other voices chime in, echoing the Archon's disapproval.

With a single raised hand, the Archon silences them and, with a similarly effortless wave, beckons Arrius to take the center. I glare at him as he approaches, and though protocol dictates I leave the center for him, I remain. The two of us now stand beside each other in the center of the Great Hall, surrounded by the vicars of the Dark Assembly.

Arrius speaks, and all my plans unravel.

Another shove from an unseen presence…

I'm in a lush office. It's the Archon's—Mallius was his name—the most respected and feared man within the Dark Assembly; we do no business without his knowledge and approval. The Archon, sitting in another of his throne-like chairs, hangs his head and takes in a slow, deliberate breath that screams condescension. "Begging, Porteles? Now begging? Pathetic." Mallius shakes his head in mock disgust. "I would never have thought Luciano Porteles—the great Verdan assassin—would debase himself like this. Pathetic. You realize that's what you are, Porteles? Worthless and pathetic."

I can't bring myself to meet his gaze, choosing instead to stare at the intricate tilework on the floor.

The Archon screams at me, prostrated as I am: "Say it. Say it!" Then, lowering his voice once again, he squeezes the next words through his teeth: "Say it, Porteles, and you may once again kiss the ring."

What? This is not how it happened. Something's wrong. This is not what happened that day! What's going on?

"Say it, you spineless worm!"

A mountain of self-doubt weighs on my chest.

"Say it. Say that you serve at the pleasure of the Archon!"

I look up and see the man sitting on his throne, sadistic glee contorting his face. The visage is overwhelming, and I turn my gaze downward once again.

"Say it! You are worthless, and you serve at the pleasure of the Archon!"

I glance up again, only to watch in confusion as the face of the Archon convulses into that of Arrius.

"Say it," the Ghost repeats. "Say it!"

When the visage spasms again, it's Brocchus sitting on the throne, screaming at me.

"Say it, you worm. Say it! Admit you are worthless. Tell me you serve at my pleasure."

I close my eyes, but to no avail. The images burn in my mind, as do the voices. A chorus of them screams: "Admit it. Admit the truth. You are worthless and always have been."

The boulder of self-doubt crushes the breath out of me. My head falls as I take in a labored breath. I try to rise; no strength. The visage flashes between the three men, disorienting me. Eventually, it is the image of Brocchus that remains. Atop his throne, he looms impossibly far above me.

"Say it! Admit what a worm you are and that you serve at the pleasure of Cornelius Brocchus. Affirm the truth, Luciano. Affirm it, and you may return to my good graces."

My arms and legs tremble, and my belly clings to the floor as I look at him. I exhale all self-worth and take in a deep breath of self-loathing.

"Affirm that you are worthless."

"Yes…"

"Affirm that you serve at the pleasure of Cornelius Brocchus."

"Yes!"

Now that you have discovered the truth, siyad—concluded and affirmed the truth— you are ready to receive your new edicts.

Luciano stared at the Dominator, and though he knew this Bayjoni man standing in front of him was as real as the chair he was tied to, his features seemed as indistinct as had those of the Dominator's presence in his mind.

These, siyad, are the edicts which will govern your decisions until your last breath:

You must always obey Brocchus.

You must never betray Brocchus.

You must never harm Brocchus nor allow harm to come to Brocchus.

Do you freely accept these edicts, siyad?

"Yes."

Look at him who has worth, siyad. Look at Brocchus.

He pivoted his head until he saw the Imperaré prince, who smiled lewdly at him.

Look to he who has worth and speak your affirmation to him.

"Yes."

The Dominator approached. He cupped Luciano's chin in one hand and tore his gaze away from his new master. A long spike of pallid yellow light erupted from the fingertips of his free hand, and the Dominator gently placed the blade of light at his temple. Luciano felt it prick his skin: sharp, cold, violating. It went no further.

The Dominator leaned in close to Luciano's ear and whispered a single word.

Miyudi.

At that utterance, with a single fingertip, the Dominator slowly pushed the yellow spike into Luciano's temple. As the spike neared the center of his brain, he screamed, and the once-great assassin succumbed to darkness.

A Cup of Truth

Ulric's new room was on the fourth floor of the same dilapidated insula that housed Silo's shop. The room was small and simply furnished but with a good view of the inner harbor and the clouds rolling in over the bay. His fellow tenants called the place Portus Towers, although the building had a distinct lack of towers of any kind. His nearest neighbors, fellow collegium members and their young families, eyed him warily. Did they resent Ulric for having a corner room all to himself? Whatever the cause, he needed a place to hide his belongings. There were no good hiding places inside, so he secured his stash beneath the small balcony overlooking the harbor. If he was to be robbed, at least it would be by a professional.

As it was well into the tenth hour of the day, leaving less than two hours till sundown, he left with the presumed intention of scouting the College of Bakers. Instead, he crossed into the Transnanpela District and raced toward the Polyminius Theater. He was late, but the sight of his bruises and bandages headed off what could have been a severe lecture from Leufroy. The rehearsals for their next play, a blood-drenched Kreslan tragedy for the Festival of Mantius, were long over, and the old theater owner climbed the stage and dramatically announced the choice of their next production was theirs to make. The actors groaned, resentful of the burden. Suggestions were made and quickly rejected. Discussions began and soon ended in arguments. With no agreement in sight, everyone drifted apart to different corners of the theater.

Ulric tried to get Julia's attention, but she walked past him to join Cordus and Ebbo in a debate over the merits of the Kreslan play *A Dragon Comes to Kos*. Ulric stood alone in the center of the orchestra, uncertain if he was feeling more foolish or angry. Leaning toward anger, he determined to find the beautiful Severa and flirt outrageously. He spun on his heels and headed for the theater's leading actress.

She stood before Leufroy, arms waving wildly, hands gesturing dramatically, blonde hair—and everything else— bouncing forcefully. She was reciting a list of complaints and demands, rendering the older man incapable of little more than nodding blankly. As if on cue, Piso blocked his path.

"Ah, young Ulric! Have you given any thought to my first lesson?" He moved to block Ulric's view of Severa, then asked, "Have you sharpened your voice?"

"Yes, I have!" Ulric said, his voice powerful, precise, and tinged with annoyance. Piso's sudden appearance had ended any chance of a flirtatious rendezvous, but it reminded him of his unique solution to his imprisonment in Aquila's icehouse. "I need to thank you, Piso! Your advice may have saved my life."

Piso adopted a dubious look. "I see that, like most actors, you have an inclination toward histrionic outbursts." Ulric pretended to know what that meant. "Let's put your voice to the test." He shoved one of the many scrolls he had been carrying into Ulric's hands and led him far away from Severa. "There are several voice exercises you must learn. To begin…"

For the next hour, Ulric studied with Piso, doing his best to remain attentive, but thoughts of Julia constantly distracted him, and he snuck furtive glances across the theater, hoping to catch her attention. He did once, but she quickly looked away. In embarrassment or displeasure, he wasn't sure.

Piso was once again stressing the importance of proper posture and breathing when Ulric glanced at the throne-like seats on the rim of the orchestra, where Julia had been chatting with Cordus and Ebbo. Only the two young actors remained. Ignoring Piso, he looked around in a panic.

Julia was gone.

Ulric bolted out of the theater and surveyed the busy street, frantically leaping into the air to get a better view above the swiftly flowing crowd. He spotted Julia's petite yet unmistakable contours vanishing around a far corner and dove into the street, racing against the current in pursuit of her bobbing green palla, which she had draped over her head and shoulders.

The narrow streets became ever more crowded, but Ulric moved through the throngs easily, closing in on the green silhouette. With a last burst of speed, he overtook her.

"Julia!" He slid to a stop in front of her, suddenly feeling terribly nervous.

"Ulric!"

Her lips betrayed a faint smile when she spoke his name. "I can't talk now." She tried to step past him. "I'm in a hurry." The jostling crowd prevented escape, and her always expressive eyes flashed with something more akin to mischief than frustration.

Ulric took a deep breath and began his long-rehearsed apology. "I'm sorry for some things I said this morning. I should have been more grateful." He searched her dark eyes for some sign of encouragement, but they remained set against him. "You were right. I was a fool to go after Luciano, and I'd be dead if not for your lucky kiss."

Julia let out a long sigh and relaxed. "I'm tempted to forgive you, but…" She tilted her head and looked away into the distance. Before she could speak Ulric produced, as if out of thin air, a small charm hanging from a silver chain. It was a disc of ash wood containing a carving of a fig tree topped by a crown. It was smooth, well-polished, and inlaid with highlights of silver that flashed in the setting sun.

Julia gasped, and her eyes widened. "Myrill's tree and crown!"

"It's for you. A token of my gratitude."

Julia, eyes still wide with surprise, reached up to take the charm, but she hesitated, her eyes narrowing. "Ulric, the man you spoke of this morning—did you kill him?"

Ulric had his answer prepared and stated confidently, "I did not! I swear to you and all the gods I did not kill Luciano Porteles. Others he offended brought him to justice, and I will not deny that it pleases me."

"Justice?"

Ulric's eyes hardened. "Julia, Luciano is a murderer, an assassin. He meant to have me killed, and, as you saw with your own eyes, he nearly succeeded. Any fate, however harsh, would have been divine retribution, but he lives, as far as I know."

Julia's expression softened as she considered his reply. Finally, she asked, "Am I the only one owed an apology?"

"Certainly not!" With an exaggerated motion, he pulled down his tunic to reveal an identical charm hanging around his neck. "I owe Myrill an apology, too. For having saved my life… and for having blessed you."

"You do say the most foolish things sometimes, but other times you know just the right thing to say." She took the chain and hung the symbol around her neck.

Julia stepped back and gazed into his pale blue eyes, studying them. "I'm still not certain which Ulric I can trust."

He lifted her into his arms and spun her about, kissing her deeply. "You can trust both of us!"

Julia leaned back and gave him a comically wary look. She slipped her hand inside the neck of his tunic and felt the bandages on his shoulder. "I hope this Luciano didn't wound you too badly."

"Not too bad, but it was about to get much worse until some, uh, new friends arrived."

"New friends?" she asked. "Like whoever bandaged your shoulder? They did well."

"Oh, one of her students."

"Her? Another healer? Should I be jealous?" she asked with exaggerated concern.

"A Kreslan doctor in the Portum Mare District. And no, I don't think you have anything to worry about." Ulric adopted a severe tone and said, "Unless... you've run out of magic potions."

Julia stuck out her tongue and made a disapproving face.

Ulric laughed. "You're so adorable when you do that. I just want to kiss you!" And he did. "I have a few coins left, so let's find something wonderful to eat, and you can tell me all about how you sorted out the Gutter-Fish. Then I'll tell you the truth. About everything."

"If you're ready?" Julia sounded like a magistrate pardoning the condemned.

"I want to. You see, I don't get to tell the truth very often. And tomorrow I'd be most grateful if you would come with me to Via Delubrarum. I need to offer prayers and show my gratitude to the Goddess."

"Yes. I would like that."

Ulric led Julia through the twilight streets, searching for a place where they could share a meal and the truth. The smell of sizzling meats and warm bread led them to a corner where two boys hung lamps above the wide-open doors of a busy popina. Calls for more wine and raucous laughter spilled invitingly into the street.

The locals called the place Capito's Corner, although the owner, Capito, never named it such; he simply called it "my place." And it was a rough place. Ulric had been there before; he had drunk too much wine and ended up brawling over a game of dice.

The place was as he remembered: a long narrow room, lamp lit and shadowed. Capito worked behind his well-worn counter at the threshold while three barmaids ferried food and drinks to the customers, and his young boys mostly got in the way more than helped. People ate, drank, and spoke crudely. Dice crackled in their cups before spilling onto the floor to inspire cheers or curses. Near the back, women writhed to the tune of an unseen flute: prostitutes vying for their next tryst. The place was filled with bargemen, dock workers, laborers, gamblers, and whores.

What would Julia think of such a place? The idea of moving on caused Ulric's stomach to grumble in protest. "Maybe we should walk on?" Ulric had to shout to be heard over the rowdy crowd. "You wouldn't like it here. I doubt you'd want to be seen in a place like this."

"Oh, it smells wonderful! And you promised me wonderful, remember?" She grabbed his hand and pulled him into Capito's Corner.

"It's Julia! Sweet Julia! Welcome back!" called Capito.

"Capito!" Julia waved and pulled Ulric inside.

The popina's owner thrust his plump face over the counter and motioned Julia to join him. She took Ulric by the arm, and they sat before the grinning Capito.

"Where have you been? And why aren't you with those delectable little peaches, Ide and Murena? They said you'd moved out! And who's your dark-haired young friend?"

Julia dropped her elbows on the counter and rested her face in her cupped hands. "Capito, so many questions are hard to answer with empty stomachs and dry lips."

Ulric glanced toward Julia and echoed, "Yes, *so many questions.*"

They ordered a plate of sausages, flatbread, a small bowl of olives, and a pitcher of passable wine. Julia introduced Ulric to Capito, who eyed him like a father sizing up his daughter's lackluster suitor. The news Julia had had a falling out with Ide and Murena disappointed Capito to no end. His stories of the girl's misadventures made it clear they had once been as inseparable as the Infernal Twins. Julia assured Capito there had been no hard feelings between them, not really. She simply couldn't share a room with them any longer.

When Capito asked why, Julia smiled and fluttered her eyes at the big man. "You don't get to know everything." Then she popped an olive into her mouth as if to say the conversation was over.

"Fine. I'll get the rest from Ide. She's working here tonight."

Ulric followed Julia's gaze to the rear of the popina where the women were dancing. Of course, Ide was one of the two girls she had shared a room with, the room with an arrangement of cheap rent for sex. For a moment Ulric's mind wandered, but he decided he didn't care about the past.

Capito refilled their pitcher and then they took what was left of their food deeper into the popina. They searched for a place to sit, struggling to navigate the rowdy crowd without spilling any wine. They set their eyes on a short couch near the back, between a group of men throwing dice and another group drunkenly ogling the writhing prostitutes.

As they approached, one woman began excitedly waving and calling Julia's name, nearly bursting from her pale golden stola. Julia smiled and waved back. Then she made a strange hand sign, and the woman gave her a nod and a wink from behind a cascade of mousy brunette curls.

"I bet I can guess," Ulric said. "Ide?"

"Oh, yes. She's a good friend, but sometimes I think she's crazy. You'd like her! And you should: you're in her debt."

"What? How?"

"If it wasn't for Ide, we would have never met."

"Now I have to hear this story."

They reached the couch and Julia reclined on it the best she could. She gave Ulric an inebriated smile. "You will, cause now it's time for the truth."

"Yes, now that we've drunk a little, it's a perfect time: In wine, there is truth, and wine is a gift from Neesis!" Ulric raised his cup to toast the Goddess, spilling a few drops on his tunic.

"But wine must first come from the grapevine, which is a gift from Myrill, the mother of all growing things, and her daughter Caris, who taught men the art of agriculture." Julia's smile announced Ulric had already lost the debate.

Each refilled their cup and shared their story of the previous night's tribulations. When they were done, they had drained the pitcher to the dregs.

"See? A wild plan is always the best!" Ulric said with drunken enthusiasm. "But I'm happy Myrill spared you the worst of Gemella's cruelty. She is merciful."

"I'm sorry Neesis couldn't shield you from Aquila's anger."

"Don't be. Neesis gave me something better than mercy. She gave me the luck I needed to turn an inescapable doom into a chance at life. *I* did the rest."

Julia tossed back the last of her wine and considered what he'd said. "Hmm. Fortune or mercy?"

"Nevermind that," he whispered, "you do know no one can learn your real name? We keep that shadowed," he warned. "People will try to take advantage of your family connections."

"Ulric, look at us." She motioned around the popina. "There are no more family connections. I'm no longer a Trumerii."

"Trust me, Julia, the fools on these streets will hear that name and think only of how much gold you're worth."

"Fools like our friends, the Gutter-Fish?" Julia used her eyes to point behind him.

Ulric leaned back on the couch and took a deep drink. He kept the cup at his mouth, covering as much of his face as possible, and glanced toward the front. Two men sat at a small table near the middle of the building; each bore the toothy pike tattoo of the Gutter-Fish. They stared back at Ulric. He was certain they were part of Titus' gang.

"It's time to go."

"Why? There shouldn't be any more trouble. Word should have come down from the temple by now?"

"But those men are part of Titus' gang, who have their own reasons to hate us, remember? And… uh, did I mention the part where my presence here could start a gang war?"

"No." Julia looked past Ulric, keeping her eyes on the men. "But I think you're right. Another has arrived, and they keep staring at us." She sat up and took a last drink from the near-empty pitcher. "I'll miss the wine, but it is a perfectly warm spring evening. We could take a walk on the docks?"

"An excellent idea. First, we have to get out of here. Let's go."

As they rose, the three Gutter-Fish abandoned their stools and started threading their way through the crowd.

Ulric flashed his remaining coins at the dancing women. "Ladies! Your beauty is comparable only to the goddess Nyssa. And your dancing! Well, it could make Mantius rise from the Underworld!"

Ide draped her long arms over Ulric's shoulders as she continued to dance suggestively in front of him. "My, my, Julia" she cooed. "Young, handsome, *and* polite. Admit it: I was right!"

Julia watched the Gutter-Fish draw closer. "Ide, we—"

"Polite *and* he has coin," said one of the other dancers. "It's extra if we're to please your woman too," she said in a suddenly business-like tone. Her eyes lingered over Julia. "Well, maybe not too much extra for a girl so dark and lovely."

"Wait…" Then realization blossomed on Julia's face. "What! Ide! Tell her… we're not here for that."

"Oh, Julia! Old trouble or new trouble?"

"A bit of both," Julia replied.

"I'm told I'm in your debt for bringing the two of us together, so all these coins are yours, but it's others who need your affections." Ulric motioned toward the front. "You'll know them by their fishy tattoos and glum faces. Do your best to convince them to stay while we slip out the back."

Ide took the coins. "Ah, I like this game. I know just the thing."

The other dancer asked, "Are you always so generous with your friends?"

Ulric grinned mischievously. "Who said they're friends?" He grabbed Julia's hand and hurried out the back.

They dashed from behind Capito's Corner, crossed the street, raced down an alley, and leaped onto River Market Street. Finally, they leaned against a wall and tried to catch their breath.

"All I ever do is run in this city!"

Julia looked around. "It worked! No more Gutter-Fish." She turned to Ulric, draped her arms over his shoulders, and gently swayed her hips. "But do you really think the Gutter-Fish could be so easily seduced?"

He pulled her close and leaned forward until his lips were barely brushing her own. "Why not? It's working on me. I'm nearly powerless… but…" He released her and stepped back. "No. They wouldn't give us up, even for such lovely dancers like Ide and her friends."

Julia narrowed her eyes and shook her head, tossing her dark curls into disarray. "Then you wasted a lot of coin," she said, sounding confused. "What was the point?"

"I needed to buy time for our escape. I bet the Gutter-Fish couldn't turn her away with any grace. And the musician and his friends no one was paying any attention to? Those were the dancer's pimp and his muscle. They were all likely brawling before we crossed the street."

"Oh. I guess that was clever." She seemed to imagine the chaos. "I hope Ide and the girls didn't get hurt."

The traffic on River Market Street was sparse. It was dark, and all the nearby shops and stalls had closed. Everyone was heading to the alluring glow of the Night Market: a large square filled with strays, thieves, street performers, odd shops, popinas, and brothels. It was the last place Ulric should go, but he told himself it stood between them and the safety of the theater.

He took Julia by the arm and headed toward the light. "Now that I know your real family name, it's only fair that I tell you about mine."

"You're not the unfortunate son of a Noldani veteran?"

"No. At least… I don't think so."

"Huh?"

"I was born in Mist View, a coastal city on the northern coast of the Noldani province. My mother was a whore, and I have no idea who my father was."

"Oh."

Ulric's voice was flat and cold, lacking the emotion of his earlier lies. "My mother abandoned me when I was very young. I don't know what became of her. It would have been death or slavery for me, but a Gualdean woman from a nearby brothel took me in: Tessa."

"Tessa!" Julia pulled Ulric closer as they walked. "I heard you call that name."

"Did I? When?"

"At dawn. You were so close to death. You were delirious."

"I remember now. I thought Tessa was welcoming me into the Underworld."

"She's dead? Oh, I'm so sorry, Ulric." She pressed her head into his shoulder.

In the same flat tones as before, he said, "Yes. Slaughtered by a Noldani patrician; slaughtered for the thrill of it."

"Myrill have mercy. So sorry."

"Enough!" He stopped walking and turned to her. "I'm the sorry one. Sorry that wine can make some men miserable bores." He took a deep breath of the night air and shook his head violently, as if he could shake out all the unpleasant memories of his childhood.

"You weren't boring me. Tonight's the time for truth, remember?"

"Right!" He smiled and skipped forward, his playful tone returning. "My family name? Tessa gave me the name Ulric. Then later, on the streets, I earned the name Darktalon from my gang. When I became Arrius Ghostwalker's apprentice, he had me added to the citizen rolls as Marcus Octavius Ulric."

"Ghostwalker? That was your mentor?"

"Yes. I said I didn't know my father, but that's not true. I had a father, and his name was Arrius Ghostwalker!" Ulric stopped at the edge of the market, outside the glow of a row of tall torches. "So, now we know the truth. You're the daughter of one of the oldest and noblest families in the Republic, and my mother was a whore and my father a thief."

"You forget, I've been disinherited," Julia reminded him. "I'm now a simple actress, and I have been told by no less of an authority than a former consul of Trumric we're no better than whores. So, who better for me than a dashing young thief?"

Ulric gave Julia a wide smile and ushered her forward with a flourish. "Then, on behalf of all the lowborn plebs, let me welcome you to the gutter. Our tour begins with the Night Market."

The merchants had planted their stalls with abandon, forming rows, twisted paths, and sudden dead ends. The square was like a chaotic garden of night-blooming flowers; each stall was exotic, alluring, and potentially dangerous. The narrow maze-like paths reverberated with the endless drone of hawkers, and the air was thick with the smells of lamp oil, incense, and exotic herbs.

They were a favorite target of vendors pushing Suhtean magic charms and supposed Eltaran aphrodisiacs, while others tried to lure them with strange and potent herbs and powders.

Then they rounded a corner and nearly ran into three bloody and battered yet familiar-looking Gutter-Fish.

Compulsion

"Is that defiance I see in your eyes, Porteles?" Cornelius Brocchus shifted his bulk over the table, an overly ornate bronze and marble piece that was out of place in the office of a Transnanpela fishery. His too-small chair creaked in protest.

"No, dominus." Luciano wanted to say no more, but something compelled him to speak. "It's hate."

Brocchus grabbed a honey-fried date from a platter before him and popped it into his mouth. Through smacking lips, he said, "It must be… what's the word? Excruciating?" An ugly smile crept across his face. "Yes, that's it. How excruciating." He relished the word as if it, too, had been dipped in honey. "How excruciating it must feel to have so much hatred stuffed inside you with no way to let it out."

Luciano stood before the Imperaré prince and silently seethed. Brocchus was right; the hatred inside him was screaming, snarling for release, and it was maddening. He wanted nothing more than to leap across the table and rend the blubbery flesh from Brocchus' face, but a yellow spike of pain murdered any thought of action.

Brocchus stood and moved to the front of the table, retrieving a plump date as he did so. "You must feel like this overstuffed date." He held up the delicacy stuffed with ground nuts and cheese and lightly rolled it between his thumb and forefinger. "Will your hate break free? Like so much stuffing?" He pressed harder on the date until cheese dribbled on the floor. "With the right pressure… Will you burst?"

"No, dominus." Luciano's hands and feet were shackled, but there was enough play in the chains to strangle—scorching yellow fire erupted in his head! He shuddered, and his left eye twitched. "I obey."

"On your knees!"

Luciano was on his knees before he realized there had never been a choice.

"Maybe you'll burst like this date?" He dropped it on the floor and slowly mashed it underfoot. "The Dominator's assurances are one thing, but I need to see proof of obedience." Brocchus tilted his foot back, displaying the remnants of the date smeared on the sole of his sandal. "Such a mess. Clean it."

Luciano looked up at Brocchus, momentarily confused. What could he do? They had shackled his hands behind his back. Then he knew, and his eyes filled with hate. So much hate he felt he could burst his shackles and murder the man who dared call himself his master. Then the yellow spikes of pain returned, piercing thought, rending action. A sickly yellow light filled his vision; the color of piss, the color of filth, the color of self-loathing. Luciano flattened himself on the floor and licked the bottom of Brocchus' sandal while staring at his new master with impotent hate.

"Yes! The Bayjoni was worth his price. You see, Porteles, I want the Dark Assembly's best assassin, not some… useless wretch; I can buy a dozen of those on any market day. If a

Dominator truly breaks someone, then they're only good for tormenting or fucking. No, I need your skills, so we had to let you keep your mind. And your hate."

Brocchus sat down behind the table, then strained forward on his creaking chair when he realized he could no longer see Luciano prostrate on the floor. "By the Gods, Porteles! Stand up!"

He stood, and Brocchus said nothing, considering him in uncharacteristic silence. Luciano glared, struggling to calm the anger raging inside him. He closed his eyes and focused on the steady drone rising from the work yards below. Anger couldn't help him now; he could do nothing. Not yet.

"Well, Porteles, there is… damn, what's the word? Uh, consolation? Yes, that's it! There is some consolation for what's left of your dignity. You see, my men won't know of our… peculiar relationship. If I'm to use you as intended, you'll have to work with them, even command them on occasion. You'll need their respect. Understood?"

"Understood, dominus."

"And no longer address me as dominus." He crammed two small dates into his mouth. "We're an informal bunch, us Imperaré." Luciano could barely make out the Trumin words over his chewing. "Cornelius Brocchus, or simply Brocchus, will do."

"Yes, Brocchus." Luciano imagined the portly crime boss choking on those dates, his eyes bulging, thick fingers clawing at his fat neck. Before he could enjoy the vision, a yellow flash of pain tore through his brain, and he saw himself rushing to Brocchus' aid.

Brocchus swallowed and shouted, "Evander!"

Three men entered the office bearing the hard looks and red cloth of the Imperaré. They were each armed with short swords, and one carried a long linen-wrapped bundle. Two men stayed by the door as the third, wearing expensive, colorful cloth and displaying excessive jewelry and scars, walked up to the table and sat the bundle down before Brocchus.

"My prince calls, and his primus answers!" said Evander. He leaned casually on the white marble table top and fished out one of the few remaining honey-fried dates. "What has our guest," referring to Luciano, "decided?"

"He's decided," said Brocchus, "that Trumric is indeed the center of the world, and he'll no longer waste his talents in the provinces. He has renounced all prior allegiances and joined our collegium." Nodding toward Luciano, he said, "Free him."

Luciano barely suppressed an outburst of hyena-like laughter at the irony of the command. *Ha! So the accursed Bayjoni left me with a sense of humor, too? Just as useless as all my hate.*

Evander retrieved a set of thick iron keys from beneath his tunic and removed the shackles. "Welcome to the Transnanpela Collegium, Porteles."

Luciano said nothing. He only glared at Brocchus and tried not to think about freedom.

Brocchus unfurled the linen bundle, revealing Luciano's clothes and belongings, including his Trumin spatha, in its scabbard of ebony wood and bronze, and his needle-like dagger, his precious Aguja. Brocchus picked up the spatha and drew it partially from its scabbard. The Eltaran etchings on the steel blade flared in the waning sunlight streaming in from the narrow office windows. "How unusual. The etchings… Verdan? Where magi and"—he searched the office ceiling for the word—"malefici rule? Is the blade enchanted, perhaps?"

"The etchings are actually Eltaran. A gift. From… a friend," said Luciano.

Brocchus slid the scabbard down upon the blade, making a loud clack. "Hmm. You're lucky to get this back, Porteles. Fortunately for you, the blade's too long for my tastes. Growing up on the banks of the Nanpela, I prefer my fists or a fileting knife."

He rolled up the bundle, pushed it to the edge of the desk, and motioned for Evander to step closer. "How goes preparations for our little foray into the inner harbor?"

"The men are gathering as we speak, O' prince. Antonius and that giant brute Petrus are leading the rabble. It leaves few men to keep order in the Night Market, but I'm not expecting any trouble."

"No, neither am I," Brocchus said, sounding very pleased with himself. "Silo's too cautious. He's turning into an old woman." He stuffed the last date into his mouth and savored the taste. "Still, double-check our preparations. I don't want a repeat of earlier today."

"The Bayjoni fighters had come highly recommended. If we had more time perhaps—"

"Don't bore me with excuses, Evander. Now get Porteles cleaned up, return his possessions." Speaking to the men by the door, he added, "All of them! I'll know if you don't."

Evander tucked the bundle under his arm and started for the exit. "And what do I do with him once he's cleaned up and geared up, O' prince?"

"Take him to the Night Market. Show him how we run things." To Luciano, he said, "Evander is my primus; obey him as you would me. And try not to look so miserable, Porteles. You'll like the Night Market. There's always something interesting happening there."

Luciano toured the Night Market with the ever-garrulous Evander. It was no wonder, he thought, that the man had risen to the rank of primus as he enjoyed the sound of his voice as much as his pompous prince. Luciano preferred silence and had always found small talk tedious, even in his native Verdan. In Trumin, it was intolerable. So he nodded, grunted, and harrumphed as Evander explained the ways of Trumric, the Imperaré, and the Transnanpela Collegium.

"Hold a moment, Porteles." Evander thrust out a hand heavy with several rings and stopped them in front of a stall selling foreign trinkets and charms. "We have business with this lizard-looking fellow."

A tall, gangly man with dark features and bulging eyes stood behind the stall, hawking his charms to every passerby. Luciano recognized the cut of his robes: he was a man from Thar, a kingdom of the far south bordering Verdith.

"Edur! Edur!" Evander said, his arms open wide. "Edur, most favored of all my friends, I'm so pleased I found you!"

"Evander?" The merchant looked around nervously, eyes bulging, then quickly composed himself. "What brings you to my humble shop? A Suhtean ward against evil? Bayjoni dream smoke? Perhaps an Eltaran charm?"

"How about the tribute you owe us?"

"Tribute? But… but the night's only begun. You don't collect till the eighth hour."

Evander slapped the man across the face, his rings drawing blood. His friendly demeanor was gone in a flash. "Are you telling me when I can collect and when I cannot collect? Is that what you're doing? Is that what I'm hearing?"

Edur clutched the side of his face and whimpered, "No. Never, Evander. Forgive me, please."

Bored with the intricacies of collecting tribute, Luciano spotted the Old Fluvius in the distance and forced his mind down the road along the Nanpela River into the harbor and out to the sea and freedom. Every imagined step away from the River Market brought greater and greater pain. As yellow light dulled his vision and the spike of pain split his head, he had to abandon even the fantasy of freedom.

"You dare treat me like some Gutter-Fish or Shrine Alley thug? We're talking about the last market's tribute. You were short!

You think we've forgotten!" Evander slapped the other side of his face, drawing another line of blood on his cheek.

"I'll have it! I'll have it!" Edur pleaded. "It looks to be a very good market night. When you return, I'll pay. All of it! I swear to all the gods!"

Evander shook his head. "When I return, I'll be collecting *this* market night's tribute. I'm here now for *last* market night's tribute."

"But… It's early. No coin."

Evander sighed and grabbed Edur by his thinning hair, and forced him to look at Luciano. "You see my silent, twitchy friend here? He's got a nasty reputation. He's a killer, a Verdan. Do you know what that means?"

Luciano bared his teeth in an ugly grin. "Oh, he does, Evander. He does. Tharian blood mother's milk to men of Verdith."

Evander secured Edur's tribute inside his tunic and continued his tour of the Night Market. "You're a Verdan of few words, Porteles, but those were well chosen."

"Hmph. My Trumin… never good."

"Look, after the Concilium, I can imagine the, eh, 'recruitment speech' might have gotten a bit rough—I don't need to know the details—so if…" Evander trailed off as he watched a pair of Shrine Alley Soldiers dash through the crowd, followed by a gang of Gutter-Fish. "Hold up; something's happening. We best find out what."

Evander grabbed one of the trailing Gutter-Fish. "What's going on?"

"They say he's here! In the Night Market! The one who insulted our prince. Can you believe it, Evander? The fool showed up alone. Mostly. Just him and some girl."

Darktalon! Hate and rage once again filled Luciano to the point of bursting, but now he could let it explode in violent action. He had a target for his wrath: the boy whose obsession with revenge had condemned him to a hellish slavery. And if killing Ulric Darktalon also pleased Cornelius Brocchus? Well, that couldn't be helped.

The Night Market

At the sight of the Gutter-Fish, Ulric and Julia ducked behind a row of stalls and plunged further into the dark maze of the Night Market, keeping a wary lookout as they sought a safe path back to the theater.

"We'll not get out on the Old Fluvius Road. Let's head north. Quick, but not too quick."

"No running?" Julia glanced back and saw no Gutter-Fish. Instead, there were men bearing the marks of Shrine Alley Soldiers and Sons of Mania: tattoos of bloodstained altars and lewdly smiling theater masks. They followed at a slow, deliberate pace, a savage anticipation in their eyes. "Are you sure we shouldn't be running?"

"No." Ulric stopped at a busy intersection filled with begging strays, acrobats, and dancers cavorting in the torchlight. He reached for his coins with thoughts of creating a well-timed distraction, then remembered he was broke. "If we ran now, it would be like running from a pack of wild dogs."

They tried to escape the Night Market, but Transnanpela gangs blocked every path. As Brocchus' men slowly tightened their net, Ulric realized what a stupid mistake he had made.

It's one thing to get myself killed, but I've put Julia in danger! What was I thinking? Oh, but I know. No one, not even Silo, could keep me from going wherever I pleased, even if it was the most sensible advice. And only Arrius Ghostwalker's protégé could spend a night carousing on his enemy's streets the very day I humiliated their boss, right? Please, Neesis and Myrill, I'll need both your wild luck and divine mercy to save Julia!

The constant drone of hawkers and hagglers deformed ever so subtly, and he knew something far worse than Brocchus' gangs had drawn near. He pulled Julia close and searched the maze-like paths.

"Do we run now?" She asked in a surprisingly calm voice.

"Not yet," He replied, quickening his pace. "Soon."

A man dressed in a bright yellow and red trimmed tunic and half-cloak marched through the street, scattering the crowd in his wake. Faint scars covered his bare muscular arms, and all manner of rings adorned his hands. The red sash hanging from his belt marked him as Imperaré; Ulric guessed he was a high-ranking collegium enforcer. He locked eyes with the man just as the enforcer motioned to someone behind him.

"Now we run."

Out of the darkness stepped Luciano Porteles, a length of Imperaré scarlet trailing from the black scabbard at his side.

Ulric faltered. His bowels twisted and ran cold. All of Brocchus' men hadn't frightened him. They were a cause of alarm or a call to action, but they brought none of the dread that Luciano did. The men of the Transnanpela Collegium were a challenge to be overcome, and they always had been with madness and bold action. But the Verdan assassin? He had faced him aboard the Neesis Insania and had been beaten. Luciano had nearly killed him.

"Ulric!" Julia tugged at his hand. "Are you all right?"

Luciano's hyena-like cackle echoed throughout the Night Market.

What did I say earlier to Julia? That I was a fool to go after Luciano. And I'd be dead… if not for a bit of luck! Trust the goddess. Praise Neesis!

"This way!" Ulric said and ran with Julia deeper into the maze of shops.

"Take him!" commanded the collegium enforcer. Brocchus' men, who had been lurking nearby, ran after them.

"No one kill boy but me!" Luciano joined the chase.

They weaved through the packed crowds with the gangs in close pursuit. Julia yelped as Ulric suddenly yanked her off the path into the narrow space created by two vendor stalls. They shimmied, then crawled until they emerged on the far side of another lane of shops, toppling a small display of pottery as they stood.

"Oh, no! I'm so sorry," Julia said, addressing the stern-looking potter. The woman stretched over her counter and glowered down at the broken shards. She grumbled and mumbled a quick calculation. "Six and a half sestertii! Or I call the collegium guards."

"No time for this. Let's go!"

"Sorry," Julia said as she ran after Ulric. "The collegium is already on the way!"

They hadn't gone far before a small gang of Gutter-Fish blocked their path. It was Titus and two of his men. Ulric and Julia skidded to a halt. "Oh, of course!" Ulric cried, looking skyward in exasperation. They fled back down the lane.

"Don't run, you whoreson coward!" Titus and his men gave chase.

As they ran past the potter, she eagerly cheered on the pursuing Gutter-Fish. "They're vandals! Thieves! They owe me coin!"

Ulric and Julia turned into another lane of stalls and slammed into a crowd haggling over Surokon rugs and fabrics, knocking several shoppers onto the hard paving stones. With all speed lost, Titus and his men would soon be upon them. There would be no choice but to fight, and he had only a dagger to match against three men. Why hadn't he come to the Transnanpela District better armed? He'd trade a host of awkward questions earlier at the theater for his gladius and knives right now!

Ulric reached beneath his tunic and pulled out his only dagger, an excellent length of Noldani steel nearly as long as his forearm. A gasp rippled through the already agitated crowd. He yanked one of the long torches down from its tall post and tossed it to Julia, who snatched it out of the air and held its length clumsily with both hands. It was nearly as long as she was tall.

"A torch? What am I supposed to do with this?"

"Uh, I don't know," Ulric said, sounding more panicked than he'd like. "Smash them over the head? Set them on fire!"

"Myrill have Mercy!"

"There'll be no mercy for Ulric," Titus said as he and two other men pushed through the crowd. "But I honor my vow, Julia. So run while you can."

"I'm going nowhere!" Julia said defiantly.

Ulric switched his dagger to his offhand and grabbed another long torch from its post, brandishing it at the Gutter-fish like a sword. "We just want out of here." Noting Titus' crude splint on the wrist he had broken in their earlier fight, he warned, "It won't even be a fair fight. Walk on."

"Gaius, find Evander. Tell him I have the bastard." Titus drew a well-worn gladius with his off-hand. "I'm as good, left or right-handed."

"Don't stand in my way. Not again." He pulled back the short sleeve of his tunic, revealing the fresh Portus Collegium tattoo. "I'm Imperaré now."

Ulric's boast of newfound Imperaré allegiance should have been a warning but he feared it was only a bluff. He had crossed into the Transnanpela District against Silo's orders, so how could he expect the Porte Mare Collegium to back him if things got bloody?

"Don't matter. Whisper is, the Prince wants you. And here you are, causing trouble in our market. You couldn't have made it easier for me."

Ulric stepped in front of Julia and flourished his torch with a loud whooshing sound and a trail of smoke. "Enough talk. Do your prince's will."

The crowd scattered to the edges of the narrow lane while Titus advanced cautiously, despite the advantage of his gladius. His remaining companion, a lean Kreslan youth armed only with a broad knife, circled nervously toward Ulric's dagger side flank. The crowd watched with nervous anticipation. They smelled blood in the night air.

Ulric could feel Luciano drawing closer with every moment wasted with Titus.

"Did you come to kill me? Or bore me?"

Titus sprang forward, and Ulric met him with a roar, swinging his torch in wide, flaming arcs. Titus fell back, unprepared for the sudden ferocity of Ulric's attack, clumsily blocking the firebrand as it swooped in from one side, then the other. The surrounding crowd burst into a cheer.

The Kreslan raised his knife and lunged at Ulric's back.

"Behind you!" Julia's torch crashed into the man's head with a loud crack and a shower of sparks and ash. The blow sent him sprawling onto the street, his knife clattering across the paving stones. He gave a cry of pain and humiliation as he pawed at the side of his head where hair singed and skin blistered.

"You bitch!" He climbed to his feet and threw himself at Julia, latching on to her torch. "Your turn to burn!"

Julia! Ulric became a whirlwind of fire and smoke, madly swinging his torch. Each blow descended from one side then the other, drawing Titus' guard ever wider as he shifted his gladius from right to left, left to right to block each attack. The irony that he was once again fighting Titus before a bloodthirsty crowd caused a grim smile to spread across his face.

"You did this, Titus. You never had the goddess' favor."

"I don't care—"

Titus jerked his sword far to the right, ready to block a descending torch that never came. Ulric leaped forward and plunged his dagger hilt deep into the base of Titus' neck. He pulled the blade free, and Titus fell face down onto the street, clutching his throat as blood poured through his fingers. The crowd cheered. Julia screamed.

Ulric turned, fearful Julia had been harmed, but she was watching Titus, her eyes wide and her jaw slack with horror. With her grip momentarily weakened, the Kreslan yanked the torch from her hands with unexpected ease, and it tumbled through the air to land among the stall of Surokon rugs.

The Kreslan youth grabbed for Julia, perhaps hoping to use her as a shield against Ulric's fury, but she twisted out of his grasp, her palla unraveling. Ulric dropped his torch and fell upon him, his dagger rising and falling several times before they hit the ground.

"Ulric! Stop!" Julia tried desperately to pull him away. "For Myrill's sake, stop!"

Ulric stood over the bloodied Kreslan. "You dare not touch her! Arakru take you! You Verdan bastard!"

"What?"

Ulric stared at the dying man as flames raced up a stand of Surokon rugs and enveloped the wooden stall, spreading panic throughout the crowd. The hue and cry of the approaching Imperaré grew louder.

Julia took his hand. "We have to go."

"Wait!" He slipped his bloody dagger beneath his tunic, snatched Titus's sword from the ground, and retrieved his torch. They fled from the dying Gutter-Fish, and no one dared to stop them. "Yes! Neesis has shown the way. It's a night for madness, blood... and fire!" He dashed toward an impromptu popina:

simply a row of stalls and wagons selling wine and other spirits from a collection of jars and amphora. Two men rushed out to meet him. One ran at the sight of Ulric's madness while he folded the other over with a vicious kick. He swept his torch the length of the bar, laughing as he smashed the clay containers, spilling and igniting the liquid within. "We'll burn our way out of the Night Market!" The counter erupted into flames, joining the larger fire Julia's torch had started among the Surokon rugs.

"Are you mad?"

He spread his hands wide and shot her a knowing glance, then tossed his torch into the crackling flames.

The sounds of panic rose around them as Ulric dragged Julia through the smoke and told her to keep her eyes open. "Neesis will guide us."

"Myrill, forgive us!"

The Night Market became a den of chaos. People stampeded through the narrow, maze-like paths pursued by billowing waves of smoke and an ever-advancing wall of heat. The swiftest vendors who had already packed up their stalls tried to roll their carts and wagons out of the square with predictably disastrous results. Familiar lanes vanished, new paths opened, and old paths became dead ends. Simple survival vied with greed and pride as merchants refused to abandon their goods or foolishly fought over the right of way.

Ulric looked for a clear path, but he only got lost in the confusion he had created.

The collegium enforcer appeared amidst the chaos, his expensive yellow tunic soiled with soot and ash. A shining gladius was in his hand, a large orb of amber embedded in its pommel aglow with reflected firelight. Ulric looked at his own nicked and dull blade and felt a pang of jealousy. The enforcer raised his sword, and a host of men burst out of the crowd.

Ulric and Julia ran a desperate race again, but this time they had the aid of wildfires, panicked hordes, and divine chaos. The madness of Neesis Insania fired him, the luck of Neesis Fortuna guided him, and the cloak of Neesis Umbra protected him. Trust the goddess, he told himself. She was why they had lost Brocchus' men. She was why an exit to the Night Market was finally in sight. She was why... Luciano Porteles stood in their way.

Neesis, you bitch!

Luciano loitered in the middle of the lane, the long blade of his spatha resting casually against his shoulder. The screaming mob streamed past, ignoring him in their haste to flee the burning market.

"I told you. We play again soon, boy."

"How?" Ulric pushed Julia behind him and thrust his gladius out on point. It was a useless gesture. He had yet to recover from their earlier duel, and even if he had, he was no match for the assassin.

"Is that?" Julia asked, peering over Ulric's shoulder.

"It is."

"So much hate." He felt her shudder.

"You should be in chains!" He knew it was a foolish thing to say the moment it left his lips.

"Stupid boy. Think Imperaré throw away skills like Luciano?" He flourished his sword, cutting the smokey air with a deadly hiss. "You think man like Brocchus not *keep* Luciano? You think Brocchus not *use* Luciano?" Rage contorted his features into a mask of wolfish anticipation.

"But you're Dark Assembly. You killed Imperaré! No justice for Marius Secundus?"

"Boy, so stupid. Justice? No justice in world! No justice in Imperaré! You learn wrong lessons from Ghostwalker. Thought you could run to capital and be like the Ghost? Thought you earned right to walk alone in the shadows?" Luciano released a short, cackling laugh. "Boy, so stupid, killing be a mercy."

Had he been a fool, expecting justice from the Imperaré? Was there ever any from the Assembly? No. He wanted to tread the shadow ways alone. Why? Because Arrius did? A thief whose legendary deeds spanned decades, deeds mostly done in the service of the Dark Assembly.

The assassin advanced as Brocchus' men stalked up the lane; it was now clear they had only been herding them toward Luciano. Ulric lowered his gladius in defeat and fled with Julia deeper into the Night Market.

Billowing clouds of stinging smoke swirled past as they were driven back toward the flames. He ignored Julia's questions and cries for reassurance while he silently prayed to the goddess. *O' glorious goddess! Forgive my harsh words earlier. It was a lucky meeting, but now I need a miraculous escape. Give me that, and I'll spread the tale far and wide! Every thief in the Republic will know the glory of Neesis Umbra!*

The sudden rumbling of wheels on stone interrupted Ulric's prayer as a great dark shape shot out from the smoky haze. It was a dappled gray stallion dragging a towering vendor's stall and cart, barely packed up and ready for transport. The cart careened behind the fire-maddened beast, smashing stalls and crushing anyone in its path.

Julia pushed Ulric aside and cupped her hand to call to the beast. "Fear not, beloved of Ulorin!"

"Julia! No!" He grabbed her arm, meaning to yank her to safety, but to his surprise, the horse calmed and slowed to a stop.

"We don't have time for this, woman! We need to—"

She ignored him, lowering the stallion's head and gently stroking the frightened animal's neck. "Let a true servant of Myrill help you." She unhitched the horse as Luciano and the gangs closed in.

Ulric suddenly recognized the stall from earlier that evening. Julia had bought dried yarrow and powdered sunblossom while he weighed an empty purse and eyed pouches of black wolf and shadow-dust. It was an apothecary's cart filled with herbs, powders, and elixirs: all manner of drugs to soothe, heal, and even kill.

"Are you not tired of running, boy?" Luciano marched onward. "Whole collegium know you coward, eh? Face me. Die for what you have done."

Brocchus's men taunted Ulric, naming him a coward for not meeting steel with steel. He tightened the grip on his sword and was about to respond when Julia whispered something in the stallion's ear. The horse bolted forward and reared, neighing madly, its hoofs flailing wildly. The beast battered Luciano to the ground and nearly trampled him as it charged through Brocchus's men and disappeared into the haze.

While Luciano recovered, Ulric snatched a large bag of powder bearing the Kreslan symbols $\mu\lambda$ stamped in blue ink. If he only had time to loot the stall properly! Where were the apothecary and his cadre of guards? Ulric cursed to leave such a fortune behind as he and Julia ran from the assassin and toward the advancing flames.

"What's in the bag that's so important?" Julia asked as they sped down a lane of abandoned stalls.

He showed her the blue stamp. "A surprise!"

The cries of the panicked crowds became a distant roar as they sped down a zigzagging lane of abandoned stalls and overturned carts with only the red glare of the burning market to light the way. They passed only a few stragglers now, merchants hauling what few goods they could salvage or desperate people as lost as they were. They pressed onward, their eyes watering from the thickening smoke and their skin prickling from the furnace-like heat, and still, Luciano and the gangs pursued them.

"This way! Look!"

Ulric looked back and watched Julia disappear into a side lane. He reeled about and followed her toward a small square.

"That's where I bought those herbs, remember?"

"Yeah," Ulric said, looking ahead where several bloody bodies lay before a chain of shops built against a row of river dock warehouses. "Looks like a dead end. One that's about to burn to the ground!"

Luciano surged forward with one last burst of speed, closely followed by the swiftest of Brocchus' men. "Trapped now, boy! Turn and fight me!"

Ulric spun around and, gripping the now open μλ stamped pouch at its bottom, he cast his arm in a wide arc, scattering a cloud of blue powder into the air. The hot wind rushing toward the wildfires at the center of the market swept the mist of blue lotus powder straight into Luciano and his men.

The assassin immediately screwed his eyes shut, covered his mouth with his free hand, and dropped to one knee, but it was too late. He had already inhaled the narcotic powder. The men behind him ran headlong into the mist. Some fell as they ran, skidding and tumbling along the paving stones. Others slowed, lumbered to a stop, and tottered comically before falling to the ground in a fitful sleep.

"Praise Neesis!"

"Yes! Praise the goddess. You said She would guide us, and I think I see a way out."

"Good! But first, I have a vow to fulfill."

Ulric adjusted his grip on his well-worn gladius and charged. Luciano groggily rose to his feet and spat something at him in Trumin so slurred he had no idea what it was. The assassin retreated, his movements uncharacteristically clumsy and slow. Ulric released his pent-up fury in a relentless rain of steel. Swords flashed and sang, their blades drenched red in the light of an all-consuming fire.

"Brought low by a blue lotus mist, you Verdan bastard! Perfect!"

Ulric drove his gladius past Luciano's sluggish defense and thrust the sword into his gut, where the dull blade caught in his leather jerkin, averting a killing strike. Luciano didn't scream; he only clutched his bloody wound and staggered away.

Behind Ulric, Julia cried out, warning him more of Brocchus' men were coming. She pleaded for him to run, but he couldn't leave his vow to Neesis unfulfilled. He fell upon the assassin once more, but the sudden pain of his wound must have shocked Luciano out of his narcotic swoon.

"Almost!" he said in clear Trumin. "You would have made a good assassin, Darktalon."

Gladius and spatha clashed again, but Ulric still held the advantage while Luciano strove against the blue lotus and bled and weakened with each passing moment. Ulric could literally smell blood in the air.

He saw an opening and prepared the killing strike.

Luciano stumbled back and swept his sword up in what would have been a clumsy block, but the Eltaran etchings on the blade erupted with white light as his spatha cleaved smoothly through the well-worn gladius! Ulric's blade clattered noisily to the ground, leaving him holding little more than a hilt and a brief span of steel ending in a line of molten metal.

Ulric stood dumbstruck, staring at the end of his blade where the metal still glowed like a dying ember. Luciano lurched forward, swinging his spatha wildly, but he easily ducked under the strike. Ulric backpedaled furiously and threw the remains of his gladius at the assassin. Luciano tried to knock the missile out of the air, but the hilt soared past his spatha to strike him in the chest with a resounding thump. He jerked to a stop, swayed, then shook his head as if trying to cast off the lethargy of the blue lotus powder.

"What could you have become, boy," he said, his Trumin speech becoming clearer, "if I was not robbed? Remember"—the assassin paused to straighten his stance and adjust his grip on his spatha—"you chose this."

More of Brocchus's men eagerly ran into the square to join Luciano.

Ulric was about to respond when Julia stepped forward and grabbed his arm. To Luciano, she said, "Arakru take you! You wicked man!" To Ulric, she said, "Enough pointless swordplay. Let's go!"

An Offering of Blood

Ulric and Julia ran to the far end of the square, where several shops stood against the back of a row of river dock warehouses. The apothecary's stall had come from here, and Ulric recognized some bodies sprawled in the square as the merchant's guards. Someone must have seen the fires and chaos he had created as an opportunity. No, not *someone*. Fellow thieves. Thieves who created more chaos. And corpses. Did Julia see the same thing?

She led him toward the empty space where the apothecary's stall once stood, a wide gap between shops that now revealed a narrow alley between two towering stone buildings.

"Oh, this is perfect! Into the alley!"

"I've had little luck with alleys lately, but I'll take it!"

Julia leaped over a tangle of wild vines growing in the gap between the two warehouses and ran inside. The gangs closed in, and Ulric followed.

"Thank Neesis! I think this leads to the docks." He raced ahead, then looked back and shouted, "Don't stop! Now's the time to keep running!"

Julia stood several paces inside the alley, casually facing the street. She ran a sandaled foot across the loose dirt of the alley floor ."This place *is* perfect!"

Ulric saw a dark, narrow alley like any other. Wild vines and shrubs had taken root in the bare earth. Some refuse showed signs of a recent Stray encampment. There was nothing remarkable or useful at all. "A perfect place to die if we don't hurry!" Ulric took a few steps forward and motioned for Julia to follow. She remained steadfast.

"I thought you were tired of running?" Julia punctuated her question with an outstretched hand. "Give me your dagger."

He pulled the dagger from under his tunic, then hesitated. "Even if you're about to reveal you're secretly a ferocious knife-fighter, there's too many of them. It's madness."

She thrust out her hand again. "But Neesis adores madness, doesn't she?"

Realizing Julia had outmaneuvered him, he gave her the dagger.

"Praise Nyssa's wild sister! But don't worry: we're not fighting. That would be stupidity, not madness." Julia grasped the dagger and held it up to the heavens. She began reciting a prayer. "Nurturing Caris, Myrill's wise and dutiful daughter, I pray, I entreat, I ask your indulgence, to this place I ask that You come; come then to favor me and mine. If You make this to happen, that we know and are given a sign of Your acceptance, I vow to You offerings and to well serve in Your devotion."

A couple of Shrine Alley Soldiers charged into the alley and skidded to a halt. Two people patiently awaiting their fate in the middle of a dark alley must have looked like a trap. One man called out, "We got him! In the alley!"

Julia knelt and jerked the sleeve of her tunic back from her left arm. "I pray to you in good faith and make this offering of blood." She made a swift cut across the back of her wrist and let the blood drip onto the ground.

More gang members, Gutter-Fish and Sons of Mania, joined the Shrine Alley Soldiers. They muttered among themselves, no doubt wondering why the thief and the beautiful young woman weren't running. What could they be planning in the darkness?

Julia held out the dagger. "It will be more powerful if you also make an offering."

"More power, the better!" He took the dagger and cut his arm, adding his own blood to hers.

She scooped up the bloody soil and rose to her feet. Julia stepped forward and stood erect, defiant. She cupped the handful of soil up to her mouth and began chanting, "Caris, assist us. Mother Myrill, delight us. Caris, come to our aid."

Luciano arrived with the collegium enforcer in tow. They pushed the gangs aside and made their way through the tangle of vines, shrubs, and refuse to the head of the mob.

"Caris, assist us. Mother Myrill, delight us. Caris, come to our aid."

Brocchus' men drew their knives and daggers. Harsh steel flashed in the dim light of the burning Night Market.

"Caris, assist us. Mother Myrill, delight us. Caris, come to our aid."

Ulric overheard the enforcer say, "Remember, you fish-brained idiots: Brocchus wants this Ulric alive."

Luciano's head snapped toward the enforcer. "What!"

"Worry not, Porteles. Of course Darktalon will die. But not before our prince has his pleasure."

"The boy—" A spasm of pain suddenly cut off his rage-filled words. Luciano said nothing more. He simply clutched the bleeding wound in his stomach and glared at Ulric.

"Oh, have you been trying to kill him"—the enforcer pointed at Ulric—"this whole time? That's got to be terribly embarrassing." With even greater condescension, he added, "You should thank Neesis you failed."

"What of his whore?" asked the Sons of Mania leader.

"I no longer have any order concerning the girl," said the enforcer. "But we know what to do with whores." He laughed, and everyone joined in, but for Luciano.

"Caris, assist us. Mother Myrill, delight us. Caris, come to our aid."

Over a dozen men had entered the alley, moving cautiously at first but quickening their pace once it was clear there was no hidden danger. They only saw a foolish thief and his unfortunate woman desperately praying for help that wouldn't come.

"Toss the dagger aside and give us no more trouble! Do that, and your woman walks out of here alive," said the enforcer.

"Ha! Hobble out, maybe, after we're done with her," said the Mania leader.

"Or…," Ulric said, "you could all fuck yourselves on the way to the Nine Gates?"

"Gods Below! You are stupid as—"

"Caris, assist us. Mother Myrill, delight us. Caris, come to our aid!" Julia flung the bloody soil into the alley.

For a beautiful instant, the narrow space filled with morning sunlight and the smell of freshly turned earth. Then the sound of distant rain showers swept through the alley, and Ulric felt the peace of fertile fields and well-tended gardens.

When the strange ecstasy had passed, the sparse vines and shrubs had grown and multiplied, bursting to life with an excess of divine vitality. The plants now filled the end of the alley with their roots, branches, and vines; each a grasping, tangling, choking thing in the service of the Goddess's will. Luciano, the enforcer, and Brocchus' men were trapped: they struggled to escape, to move, to even breathe.

"Praise Caris!"

Ulric leaped into the air and laughed. He grabbed Julia by the shoulders. "Praise Caris, indeed!" He gave her a quick kiss. "Maybe we should move to the country? Try farming?"

"We'd probably end up like your fictional parents: farm sold off to pay our debts." She slapped her hands together to knock away the remaining dirt and looked heavenward. "Please forgive us, Caris, but we're both city-born Trumins."

Ulric suddenly realized the city was darker and quieter than before. The sky was no longer lit by the red glare of wildfires, nor was the air filled with the crack and roar of the burning market. Looking past the tangled mass of greenery, what little he could see of the Night Market glistened wetly in the faint moonlight. He looked back to Julia, amazement plain on his face.

"When sudden rains quench night's flames," she whispered as if that was explanation enough. Looking in awe at the tangle of men and plants, she said, "We should go."

"And what of them?" Ulric asked. The choking foliage muted their cries. Whether they were curses or pleas for help, he couldn't tell. "Will they suffocate and die in there?"

"That will depend solely on Myrill and Caris' mercy." Her voice rose to a shout directed at the trapped men. "It will depend on how much the goddesses enjoy taunts of rape!" At her words, the plants writhed and constricted, causing a sudden outburst of muffled screams.

"Hold on. Give me a moment," Ulric said, his voice hard.

He approached the leafy mass, dagger in hand, and searched for the enforcer. The man was at the edge; his body lifted and twisted at an uncomfortable angle. He could only glare as Ulric reached through the writhing greenery in search of his purse. Infuriated by the indignity, he chewed through the thick vine covering his mouth and did his best to spit the remains at Ulric. He was so out of breath that the pulp fell far short of its mark.

"Do you know who I am? I'm the Transnanpela Collegium primus! You're dead! You... you've..." he labored to catch his breath, "allied yourself... with a temple?" The waited-for reply never came. "Did Silo... arrange this somehow? Is this... part of a bigger scheme? Is that it?"

"Save your breath, friend. Silo's already several moves ahead in this game." Ulric was bluffing, hoping to plant a seed that could grow into something that could salvage the disastrous evening.

"Tonight was about showing everyone that the Portus Collegium doesn't give a fig if Brocchus throws a tantrum at the Concilium. We just wanted a friendly drink, but your lot had to make a move, and it cost you. Silo says: 'Think about that next time.'" With a grunt, Ulric pulled his hand back to reveal a heavy purse. "At least Brocchus is paying you well, I see."

"You little shit! When I get out of this, you're dead."

Ulric ignored the threat and turned to where Luciano had vanished within the writhing mass. He hacked and sawed at the branches and vines until he uncovered the Verdan assassin. Luciano thrashed and cursed at the clinging vines, but they only twisted tighter with his every movement. He stilled and watched Ulric clear the greenery away through half-lidded eyes, his hate palpable in the darkness. Once Ulric exposed his head and shoulders, he stepped back and wiped the dagger clean on his tunic.

"Boy, have one last trick, eh? Good trick. But not his trick, I think."

Ulric raised his dagger and readied the killing strike, but he could find little of his earlier anger. He had never killed anyone before the fight with Titus, but that had come easily enough in the heat of the battle. He hated Luciano like no other and had vowed to Neesis he would murder the assassin. So why the hesitation?

"I promised Neesis Fortuna I'd send you to her ample bosom."

Was it because Luciano had been right about him? His grand dreams of life in the capital had been those of a naïve child. Arrius Ghostwalker's independence had come at an extraordinarily high price. Freedom like that wasn't a treasure to be stolen or schemed. It could only be earned. Luciano was right. He had been a fool.

"Do it, boy!" Luciano screamed as if forcing his words past some terrible pain. "You do Luciano a service. Do it, Darktalon!"

Was he simply ashamed to kill a helpless opponent? But he had already fought the assassin face-to-face, and it had been a trifecta of pride, stupidity, and naïvete worthy of legend. The dagger plunged toward Luciano's neck.

"Ulric! No!" Julia yanked his wrist aside, and the dagger cut into the greenery.

"What in the Nine Gates, woman?"

"Mercy, Ulric. No more killing."

"This is Luciano Porteles. An assassin. You know what he's done. What he deserves."

"Myrill's Mercy saved us." She cupped her hands around his and gently lowered the dagger. "Share Her mercy, Ulric."

"No listen to stupid girl, Darktalon," Luciano said. "Women weep and talk nonsense."

"I made a vow to Neesis!"

"Yet Myrill and Caris put this man at our mercy. *I* delivered him helpless before you. Please, don't make me complicit in his murder."

"Don't listen, Darktalon. A man acts. A man kills. Do it!"

"Ulric, please."

"Damn you!"

Ulric tore his hands free and raised the dagger, stabbing again and again.

The Noldani blade was an excellent tool for murder but poor at pruning. With some effort, he freed Luciano's sword arm and pried Ghostwalker's spatha from his grasp. He held it up in the dim light of the alley, and the etchings on the blade glowed with an inner light.

"I claim Ghostwalker's sword!" proclaimed Ulric. "And one day, I'll earn the right to claim his legacy." He pressed his dagger into Luciano's hand and stepped back. "Praise Myrill!" he said bitterly. "Now you can free yourself."

Luciano Porteles burst into a peal of hyena-like laughter that sent a chill down Ulric's spine. He backed away, grabbed Julia, and fled down the alleyway. He had expected more threats, insults, or taunts, but not this. The assassin's laughter echoed after him, filled with a disturbing mixture of hatred, despair, and absurdity.

Fortune & Mercy

Ulric led Julia out of the alley and onto a street running parallel to the Nanpela River. They took a moment to enjoy the smoke-free air, but before they could catch their breath, they saw three Gutter-Fish running straight at them.

"God's Above, Below, and Beyond! More? How?" Julia threw up her arms, knocking her green palla off her shoulders.

"I bet they were sent the long way around as soon as we ducked in the alley. There can't be many left, right?" He looked over the warrens of quays and piers that made up the river docks. "Come on! We'll hide on the river."

They crossed the street and snuck onto the docks, but losing their pursuers was more difficult than he had imagined. Julia had to remind him they were Gutter-Fish, after all; the docks were their territory. A series of wrong turns led them to the end of a neglected pier, leaving them no place left to run. In desperation, they crept into a small skiff, and Ulric quietly untied its mooring. He pushed off from the pier, and the Nanpela's strong current seized the craft. Without a sound, the river carried them to safety.

They peeked over the skiff's edge and watched the docks shrink away. The voices of the Gutter-Fish became distant and hollow. No boat followed. Ulric threw himself back onto a thick pile of netting and gazed at the stars beyond a break in the clouds. "Ha! We've escaped and made fools of Brocchus' men. With a little help from Neesis and Myrill, of course."

"So, you're no longer upset? You now see mercy was the right path?"

"Oh, no. Luciano will prove us very wrong when he murders us both in our sleep." Ulric laced his fingers behind his head and made himself more comfortable. "But until then, I will live in the moment as a faithful follower of Neesis should."

"Myrill *and* Neesis will watch over us. So, now we have two temples to visit tomorrow." Julia rolled over to rest against the skiff's frame and center thwart, setting the boat rocking. She threw out her arms and grasped the hull so hard the wood creaked. "I don't think I like boats much!"

"Then I better row to shore. Let's find the oars." He felt along the bottom boards and against the frames. "Uh… help me find the oars. You know, long wooden paddle things."

"There are no oars?" She lurched forward, then froze when the boat began rocking again.

"Don't worry, silly; you won't swamp the boat just by moving about."

"I'm worried we have no oars! Myrill, have mercy! How far will the river take us? To the bay? Out to sea? Have I told you I can't swim?"

"You mentioned it." Ulric kept searching the small skiff as if oars would magically appear. "God's Above! God's Below! What sort of fisherman doesn't keep oars in his boat?" Instead, he found a large wineskin at the stern. "What's this?" He pulled the stopper, sniffed, and took a cautious sip. "Wine!" He took a drink.

"Excellent wine!" He passed the wineskin to Julia. "Here, I think you need this more than I do."

"Ha! Ha!" Julia mocked. She tipped up the wineskin, took several long gulps, and then returned Ulric's stare. "What? I didn't say you were wrong."

Ulric laughed. "No oars, but wine and a beautiful woman: love, luck, and madness. See, *I am* Neesis blessed!"

Julia stopped mid-drink. "Yes! That's what I was thinking of earlier. We've lost our families, but now we're both blessed by the gods. You by Neesis, and me, Myrill. We're the children of Fortune and Mercy."

Ulric leaned back and made himself comfortable on the netting. "Hmm, I'm not sure."

She finished her drink and lay next to him. "Think about it. One morning I see a handsome stranger, and he looks to be just what I need, and for some reason, I can't get him out of my thoughts. Then there you are at the theater! And even though you turned out to be nothing but trouble, you were there to save me. And I was in the right spot to save you."

"I'll always be grateful. And I can't deny that such a coincidence didn't have the hand of the Goddess behind it."

"See. You can't tell me you survived the last few days without the blessings of both Neesis and Myrill. I think the Goddesses have brought us together for a reason."

"Hmm. Maybe." Thoughts of too much divine guidance always made Ulric feel like a slave; Neesis' fickle luck suited him better. "Growing up in Mist View, we always heard, 'Neesis helps those who help themselves'. We thought it meant 'helping themselves to other people's property', but Arrius tried to explain it was about the balance between fate and free will. I never really understood it."

"I have faith in Myrill's will," Julia said with finality.

"I'm sure She doesn't want you swept out to sea. I see a bridge ahead." He rose and gathered the mooring line. "I have an idea."

If not for the lamps burning along the length of the bridge, the structure would have appeared as nothing more than a great black wall sunk into the water. Ulric hastily tied a loop at the end of the line and crouched at the ready, rope in hand. As they passed under one of the broad arches, he cast the line at an abutment. It caught on a protruding stone near the base.

"Now hold on!"

The line went taut, arrested the bow, and the boat swung forward until it came to rest under the bridge.

"Thank Myrill! We've finally stopped moving." She took another drink from the wineskin and tossed it to Ulric. "Now what?"

"Let me think." He took a thirsty drink of wine. "We have plenty of rope, and that gives me an idea. Wait..." He looked over the stone walls of the arch and the bridge above. "This is the Polyminia bridge! Sweet Neesis!" Ulric descended into mad laughter.

"What is it?" Julia asked. Then realization struck her. "Oh, the bridge!"

"Yes! Not long ago, I was under this very bridge, miserable and dying. My only thought was to get back to you. That kept me moving forward. And now I'm here in a boat sharing this excellent wine with you after the best evening I've had since… since I can remember!"

"It was a wonderful evening… until the swords and the fire." Julia settled next to him on the netting. "It has to be the Goddesses at work."

"Hmm… that's it. You could ask Ulorin for help. Surely he could send one of his river naiads to tow us in?"

She looked at Ulric as if he had suggested they should drink the river and walk to shore. "Oh, no! He won't send the river spirits. Myrill and the sea god are not on good terms. Haven't you heard?"

"I guess not. What's the whisper?"

She leaned closer and lowered her voice. "Have you heard of the famous adventurer Prince Cyrus?"

"The crazy sea raider who boasts he's the son of Ulorin?"

"Yes. And he is; the product of a union between Ulorin and a Laconian princess, but never mind that. In the month of Nyssius, Cyrus and his crew came ashore on the wild coasts south of Gualdé. The forests grow near the sea there. A small party of Myrill's dryads strayed too close, and Cyrus and his men ravished them."

"Ravished?"

"You know… *took* them."

"They stole their leaves and berries or something?"

"Oh, stop making fun! You know what I mean."

Ulric slipped his fingers into Julia's black curls and leaned forward, nuzzling her ear. She smelled of perfumed oil, wine, and sweet sweat. "Did no one teach these dryads not to trust strange pirates?"

Julia pulled back, brushing her lips softly against his. Ulric felt the tip of her tongue briefly trace his bottom lip and quickly retreat before he could pursue. "Myrill was furious. But Ulorin claims the dryads seduced Cyrus and his men, intending to imprison them."

"Prisoners of love? How terrible."

"Word around the temple was that the dryads had wanted them."

"Those naughty nymphs!" He could barely catch his breath before plunging back for another kiss. This time he pursued her tongue back into her perfect mouth, only to retreat and begin the chase again. Each kiss set his skin tingling and made his stomach feel strangely queasy and light. His kisses moved to her cheek, her earlobe, and along her delicate neck.

"Very naughty," she mumbled. Julia gasped and sighed and tightened her grip on his tunic.

Her caramel skin was salty-sweet from their earlier exertions, and Ulric thought he would never tire of the taste of her. He let his hand slide down from her shoulder, then hesitated. She reached up and dragged his hand over her breast. Her body was all divine curves and a heavy roundness under his fingers.

"Oh, Ulric… the dryads wanted it." She pushed her hands under his tunic and began tracing the muscles along his broad back. She nibbled at his ear and whispered, "Do you want me?"

"When I first saw you in the theater. Our first night in the loft. Every moment since!"

Julia pushed Ulric over onto the bed of netting. She straddled him, forcing her long tunic to slide up her body, revealing slender brown legs glistening with sweat. The boat rocked back and forth, but she didn't notice. The heat and pressure emanating from between her thighs were creating a need, an urgency, a madness he could barely contain. His body was so hard that he ached.

"I want you. I want you to see me. Earlier, you spoke as if you could see in the dark." She tossed aside her palla, which long ago had become a thing of tangled greenery, and pushed the straps of her tunic off each shoulder one by one, and the tunic fell to her waist. "Can you see me?"

"I can." Ulric reached up and gently ran the tips of his fingers along the sides of her torso and across her dark nipples. "You're absolutely beautiful. I said you were goddess sent, remember?"

She smiled at the memory. "I guess I shouldn't have laughed when you said that. Now, take off your tunic. I can't see as well as you, but…"

Ulric pulled his tunic off with surprising speed.

"I'll just have to see what I can find in the dark." She slowly ran her hands over Ulric's chest, lingering at his nipples and playing with the sparse hairs at the center of his torso. "Very nice! So broad and powerful. Is it all the sword fighting?"

"Now you're making fun of me." Ulric grasped her hips and began slowly pushing against her. She said nothing for a long moment, just murmured and rocked gently back and forth.

Julia leaned closer. "Oh, I'd never be so naughty." Her hands descended across his stomach. "So smooth. Little ridges; muscles. Must be all the acrobatics." Her hand continued their journey. "Oh, wait! There's something else. Mmm, something wonderful."

He gasped and tried to endure as much as he could, but the madness of Neesis overwhelmed him. He seized Julia in his arms and took her, ravished her, loved her. There was a strange intensity to their lovemaking, a desperate longing.

It wasn't the first time for either of them, but Ulric didn't care about Julia's past. He had been with several girls before, and growing up in a brothel had quickly cured him of any shyness about sex. Unfortunately, the girls he grew up with in Mist View were all prostitutes or gang members, often a distinction without a difference. Both, by necessity, grew hard and cynical. They learned to use sex as a tool and a weapon. Such women had provided plenty of sex but twice as much heartbreak and betrayal.

It was different with Julia. He could detect no guile, just need, longing, love. Had the goddesses brought them together, as Julia said? When the final moment came, and he flooded his body into hers, he gave silent thanks to Neesis Amoris, Goddess of Lust. Love wasn't Her domain—that belonged to her bright sister Nyssa, Goddess of Love, Beauty, and Music—but She was close enough.

They fell asleep entwined among the netting, awakening a few hours later when a grizzled old fisherman rowed next to them and curtly inquired what in the Nine Gates they were doing under the bridge. After getting a closer look at Julia, the old man smiled and towed them to shore. Ulric had a difficult time coming up with a story that made any sense. When he mentioned they had lost their oars, the man winked and said, "No Oars? That's a new trick."

It was nearly dawn when they slipped into the theater loft.

"I love watching the sunrise, but"—she paused and let herself fall onto her makeshift bed—"I may have drunk too much wine last night." She stared at the ceiling and gently massaged her temples.

Ulric considered his dry mouth and the dull throbbing in his own skull. "The priests of Neesis know a brew that can cure any hangover."

With an imperious voice, Julia said, "Then fetch me some, slave! Or what use are you?"

He knelt over her, letting his tangle of black hair mix with her dark curls, and gently kissed her. "Oh, but you do know how to use me."

She wrapped her arms around him and pulled him closer. "Oh yes, so many wonderful uses. I guess I'll have to keep you after all."

"And I'm yours! But now—" He leaped to his feet, making his head throb harder. "Ugh, shouldn't have done that. But now I have to scout the College of Bakers, which I should have been doing last night. I'm afraid I might be in a bit of trouble."

"Are you ever not?" Julia asked with a smile.

"No."

Despite his hangover, Ulric raced across the city with boundless, joyful energy. Against all odds, he was alive. Julia had not only forgiven him, she loved him, two outcomes so unlikely he knew the Goddess had done her part. Was it as Julia said? Had Neesis and Myrill brought them together? Neesis was also Neesis Amoris, a goddess of love, sort of.

And she was also a goddess of luck! With Neesis' help, he had survived two duels with Luciano, although the cost had been high. He had come to Trumric to escape the Dark Assembly, only to exchange them for the Imperaré. It was a fate he had been fighting against for months, but it could have been worse. The Imperaré hadn't exiled or punished him. Nor had they pressed him into a street gang or the lower ranks of one of the criminal collegiums. Instead, he was working directly for Horatius Silo, a powerful man who controlled the entire Portum Mare District. The arrangement was peculiar, which worried him, but despite his suspicions, he couldn't help liking the Imperaré prince.

Before I can impress Silo with the theft of the legendary ledger, I have a goddess to please. Actually, two goddesses! I'll let Julia take the lead with Myrill, but I promised Neesis the sacrifice of a fine lamb. Ooh, very expensive!

Hmm, I mentioned doves, if I remember correctly. Could I satisfy you with that? Oh, wait! I remember I promised to send Luciano to your lovely bosom, and he still lives. Yes… yes, sorry, it's a fine young lamb for you, Neesis!

The thought of a vow unfulfilled to a goddess worried him.

I haven't forgotten my promise, Neesis. I may yet kill Luciano. I'll likely not have a choice. I wonder how he spent the rest of his night. Ha! Not in the arms of the most beautiful woman in the republic! Did he conquer the daughter of a consul of Trumric? Did he humiliate his enemies? Well, Julia did most of the humiliating, but still…

Ulric stopped mid-stride as the dull pain in his head suddenly scraped the inside of his skull. He stumbled out of the street and slouched against a wall.

Julia's torched. And I did it.

After the confrontation with Brocchus' men, there was no hiding Julia from the Imperaré. After lying to Silo to protect her, his foolishness had exposed her.

Slaves of the Imperarē

Silo sat quietly at his desk while Gwynedd raged. The Northman's burn-scarred face looked cruel.

"... were the orders not to stay in our territory and watch for Brocchus' men? But this idiot"—he thrust a finger at Ulric, who stood silently before Silo's desk—"goes peacocking into the River Market and pokes Brocchus in the eye!"

He caught his breath and looked at Silo. The Imperaré prince sat silently behind his desk, idly unfurling a map. His expression revealed nothing. Gwynedd resumed shouting.

"Now there's a whisper on the streets that we've employed a magus or, worse, have a rogue priest as an ally! You know the trouble we'll get if that reaches temple ears! It's the girl, of course! He paraded her around the Night Market like a damn fool!"

He looked back at Silo, who appeared lost in thought, saying nothing.

There was a long pause, then Gwynedd exploded. "He has to be punished! Such stupidity! We must make an example!"

Silo straightened and leaned back in his chair. "What of last night's skirmishes?"

"Huh?" Gwynedd tried not to sound annoyed. "Reports of Brocchus' men massing west of the inner harbor. A few minor brawls along our border."

"And then?"

"They returned to the Transnanpela District once word of the market fires spread. What does that have to do with—"

Silo cut him off with a raised hand. "And today?" he asked.

"Nothing. It's quiet. So far."

"Good! Then my scheme worked."

"What!?" Confusion made Gwynedd's face more frightening. "What scheme?

Ulric stood motionless, doing his best not to betray his own surprise. *Yes, what scheme? Was I part of a scheme?*

"I sent the boy into the Night Market. Brocchus thought he had our measure; I wanted to show him we're not so predictable. Now the fat bastard realizes he doesn't know the lay of the land at all. He doesn't like surprises. He'll stand down, reassess."

Sweet Neesis! He's echoing my own lies. It sounds much more reasonable when he says it. Maybe this is all going to work out? I am a lucky whoreson, after all. Thanks to the Goddess, of course!

"Hmm." Gwynedd's face settled back to bored. "Why wasn't I told?"

Silo smiled like a man with a secret. "Inspiration struck at the last moment. You were already dealing with matters back at the harbor. I ordered the boy to keep it all in deep shadow."

Ulric played along. "Sorry, Gwynedd. I couldn't say anything."

A short grunt was his only reply.

Silo stood and moved to the front of his desk. "Now that we've cleared that up, continue keeping an eye on our borders. My orders concerning Brocchus' men stand: bleed them good and proper if they start any trouble. Dismissed."

"Right, chief." Gwynedd gave Ulric a sidelong look, then headed for the door.

Ulric hesitated, then followed, barely hiding his relief.

"Not you, Ulric. We need to discuss a few details about our little scheme. "

He stopped mid-stride and turned to face Silo. Of course, it wouldn't be that easy.

Silo waited for Gwynedd's footsteps to recede down the hall, staring silently at Ulric as the Northman's heavy steps faded away. Ulric stared back while his bowels tied themselves into new and unpleasant configurations.

"You're a devious little shit, aren't you, boy?" Silo's voice was calm, casual; this only made Ulric's stomach twist further. "After claiming you at the Concilium, how could I let anyone know you're already causing me such trouble? I'd look the fool in front of the Imperaré and the entire city." There was a pause, and Ulric knew it was an opportunity to say something stupid, so he kept his mouth shut. "I can't punish you, not openly, at least. I must pretend your actions in the Night Market were part of my own scheme. Was that *your* scheme?"

"Silo, I only—"

"Shut it. I don't want to hear your horseshit. I'm giving you too much credit imagining there's some grand strategy behind your recklessness. Just tell me: why go into Brocchus' territory against my orders?"

"Uh… I needed to gather some things from the theater," Ulric stammered, "and… I had made a promise to this girl and—"

Silo charged forward, stopping so close Ulric felt his hot breath as he screamed, "A promise to a girl! Are there not brothels enough in the Portum Mare District?"

There was nothing he could say, so he waited for the inevitable blow in silence.

Silo broke into peals of laughter and returned to his desk. He dropped into his chair and cheerfully said, "Oh, you young fool, I've just thought of a punishment for you. It's a job: long, boring, and worse, there's little money in it. You'll begin after you bring me Licinus' ledger, which I expect before the Festival of Mantius."

"Yes, of course, Silo. I'll have it no later than tomorrow night."

Silo nodded and began pouring over the map on his desk. Ulric exhaled and hastened toward the exit. The office had begun to feel like a prison, one he desperately needed to escape.

"Oh, I almost forgot."

Ulric had just grabbed the bronze door handle. He held on tight and waited.

"After last night, your woman isn't safe in the Transnanpela District. Better you bring her here, hey?"

Ulric didn't look back; he only stared at the door. "Right. That's best. I hadn't thought…"

"Right, you hadn't thought. I want *Persius* Julia here tonight. No later."

Ulric's bowels coiled and turned to ice. He hadn't mentioned Julia's name to anyone. He pulled the door open with a jolt.

"Oh, and Ulric, what do we say when our friends are pulled off the streets and given a proper home?"

"We say thank you, Silo." Without turning, Ulric said, "Thank you."

People were sneaking behind the Polyminius again, seeking the old stone pine that grew close to the rear of the theater house. Julia easily heard their heavy footfalls and too-loud voices. She raced for the loft's singular window, eager to catch them in the act, but crashed into a collection of prop weapons and painted clouds. With a cry of "Arakru, take this clutter!" she fell to the floor in a clatter and thud of canvas and wood.

By the time she untangled herself and stumbled to the window, the street was empty, filled only with the deep shadows of the day's end. No one lurked beneath the tree, but what looked like fresh oat cakes had been added to the offerings already piled high against the trunk of the old stone pine.

"Myrill thanks you!" Julia shouted into the empty street, hoping whoever left the cakes was still in earshot. "But you should really leave an offering at the temple. Or Her shrine on the Via Delubrarum!"

Since the previous evening, when a miraculous downpour had saved the Transnanpela District from the fires ravaging the Night Market, Julia's supporters had recalled her words—"when sudden rains quench night's flames"—and proclaimed her a true messenger of Myrill's will. Now they honored her with a new shrine, but it was terribly embarrassing. She and Ulric had started the Night Market fire, after all.

What will Pompilius Gemella say when she hears about this? And what of a Myrillian shrine so close to the theater? All theaters are consecrated to Nyssa; if she grows jealous, I'll trip across the stage and choke on my lines. And if Leufroy sees it! How could I explain it? No, this won't do.

Julia grabbed a basket and plunged down the stairs, determined to gather the offerings and take them to Myrill's shrine on the morrow. She burst out of the theater house and ran straight into Leufroy.

"Ah, Julia!" The old man righted himself and straightened his tunic. "You nearly knocked me across the orchestra."

"What are you doing here?" Then she sheepishly added, "I mean, sorry."

"Well, as you may recall, I own the theater."

"Oh, of course. You're probably wondering what I'm doing here. Wondering what I was doing in the loft. Why am I holding a basket? Why am I in such a rush? Why am I still talking?"

Leufroy laughed. "Julia, I play the part as it suits me, but I'm no fool. I know you've… ah… taken residence in the theater loft. It's the least I can do, considering the patronage of your father."

"What? You know my father?"

"Yes. He insisted I keep an eye on you. Forgive me. I know I shouldn't have said anything, but my silence has felt like ingratitude. Without your father's generosity, our upcoming renovations wouldn't be possible."

Julia turned away to hide the sudden swell of tears in her eyes. "Forgive me!"

"No, I'm the one who's sorry." Leufroy reached out a hand to comfort her, but she bolted for the exit. "Julia, wait!"

She ran headlong into the dark passage leading to the street, heedless of Leufroy's calls, and threw herself at the gate. The wrought iron flew open with a crash, but not onto the Via Lucretius.

Instead of shadowed streets, Julia ran through lush gardens bathed in scintillating sunlight. Her momentum propelled her to the edge of an impossible mountainside, where a balustrade of marble and gold saved her. She gripped the railing and tried to catch her breath. The air was pure and invigorating in a way she could never have imagined, and she had walked among the trees of the Silva Aurea. Above her, the sun hung low in a sky of perfect azure, and below, a sea of thick white mist covered the world. It stretched in undulating waves for miles, sometimes gathering in towering hills of billowing… clouds.

Julia laughed out loud, tears of joy streaming down her face as she realized she was seeing the tops of clouds! She wondered how few mortals had seen such a sight.

This place can only be… But how am I here? Unless… Oh, no.

"Fear not, Trumera Julia Minor. You are very much alive."

Julia hesitated, unsure if a mortal should dare gaze upon a goddess. Finally, she turned and saw a woman that much resembled the statue in the temple of Myrill, but there was also something else, something barely hidden, something blazing beneath the beautiful mask. Something *other.* Julia fell to her knees and looked away; she had to, lest the power of the *other* destroyed her.

"O Mother Myrill! Queen of all the gods! How may I serve you?"

Like a scorching sun momentarily obscured by clouds, the *other* was hidden. **"Arise and look upon me."**

Julia did as she was commanded. She gazed upon Myrill's beauty and was content.

Behind the Goddess, the mountain rose to a slender peak lost in a roiling mass of dark clouds. Suddenly, thunderbolts lit up the sky, and the very air shook.

Myrill looked to the mountaintop and said, **"A moment, for pity's sake."** Then Myrill turned back to Julia. **"Alakur grows impatient. You must return."**

"Why am I here? Why choose me?"

"You have always been here. You are an ikon of Myrill."

"But…"

"You still doubt, worried past sins cast a shadow upon your spirit. Fear not. I have no need for my temple's notions of rigid perfection. As long as you carry my message of love and mercy in your heart my strength is yours."

"Gemella? Damia? Everyone is forgiven?"

Myrill took her by the hand and smiled. Julia was never happier.

"Yes. Together we turned Pompilius Gemella from a bitter and lonely path. The temple, and the Trumin people, will be the greater for it."

"Must I go?" Julia asked, tears of joy and regret streaming down her face.

"Yes, but this time has been my mercy, Julia. A perfect moment, which will be, when you leave, only a memory. But this memory will give you strength for what's to come."

"I don't understand."

Another rain of thunderbolts struck the mountainside.

"Listen and obey. They will not chase us from this world as they have others. I have need of my wayward daughter's shadow cloak. Stay close to the thief. He will lead us into cold Eltaran stone. And once there, he will kill you with a dagger thrust to the heart. But fret not, for you will do the same to him."

Luciano stood alone on the heaving deck of a Mist View bound ship and watched the city of Trumric slowly burn in the glare of the westering sun. He was finally returning home. Gripping the rail and closing his eyes, he concentrated on the sharp snap of the canvas sails and the scent of the salt breeze and let himself imagine he was returning to freedom.

Pain! The yellow spike was sharp, quick, and agonizing. His knees went weak, and he doubled over so fast that his chest slammed into the rail hard enough to bruise his ribs. He hung there a moment, fighting down the urge to retch. With grim humor, he thought it must have looked simply like a bout of seasickness to the crew.

Luciano composed himself and headed toward the bow of the ship. There he could gather his thoughts and face the truth: there was no freedom, no escape, only the mission.

After the debacle in the Night Market, he had anticipated more humiliating torture from an angry Brocchus, and while the Imperaré prince had been red-faced and almost speechless in his fury, it surprised him when the greater part of his ire fell on Evander. Instead of further discipline, Brocchus charged Luciano with the Concilium's mission of revenge.

The Imperaré princes had demanded retribution for the slight against their dignity that was the murder of Quintus Marius Secundus. His assassination had broken long-honored agreements, and now blood demanded blood. Luciano had listened to Brocchus' carefully crafted orders and knew he would have no choice but to return to Mist View and murder Vicar Lepidus and Vicar Gratianus. It would be easy, of course: they were expecting his report on the Eltaran map.

Nearly two decades! Two decades of labor! Of blood! All that time proving myself a man of trust, a man of excellence. Lost. Two decades of smiling at fools and killing at their behest! Wasted. Was it for nothing?

And after betraying the Dark Assembly, I will have no choice but to return to the Imperaré, return to that fat bastard Cornelius Brocchus, and continue my humiliating servitude. Now I'm little better than a slave, an assassin forced to avenge my own actions. Absurd.

Luciano mounted the bow as the sun set behind him, and the ship sailed into the open sea. He stood there, unmoving, among the roar of the waves, ignoring the cool sea spray striking his face and dampening his clothes, obsessing over the absurdity of his fate. Luciano Porteles, the Hound of Nyx, greeted the oncoming night with a howl of hyena-like laughter.

Ulric returned to the Transnanpela District and made his way back to the Polyminius Theater, one hand proudly resting on the smoky quartz pommel of his spatha, all the while far more worried about Silo than either Broccus, Luciano, or any Gutter-Fish. The Imperaré prince knew Julia's name. How? Was she in danger? Did he know her true name and family? Or had he only heard the name Persius Julia? Could he shield her from the Imperaré?

Up ahead, an old stray sat against a wall, head down, hands held out over his knees. The man had an unkempt gray beard, wispy hair, and a tattered blue cloak covering his boney shoulders. Ulric quickened his pace, then stopped before the old beggar. He took the silver chain from around his neck and placed the ash wood and silver charm into the man's trembling hands.

"Here, for your kindness. A token of Myrill's blessing."

The old man looked at the expensive charm with surprise. "Thank you. Thank you, citizen!" When he looked up at Ulric, his eyes widened. "You! You're alive! I feared the worst for you, young man, but gods be praised, you're alive."

"I am! Praise be to Myrill and Neesis. May their mercy and fortune find you."

Ulric walked on, taking from his pocket another silver chain and placing it around his neck. Two small wooden cubes inlaid with silver dots dangled from the chain—the Tesserae, the sacred symbol of Neesis, goddess of Luck, Lust, and Madness. As he lowered his arms, he paused to rub his wounded shoulder. Underneath his tunic, the fresh Portus Collegium XVII tattoo still itched, a constant reminder of his new status.

For he knew there was one inescapable truth: Marcus Octavius Ulric was a thief and an Imperaré slave.

Acknowledgments

First and foremost, thank you to our spouses, who at different times have been our harshest critics and our most enthusiastic cheerleaders. We appreciate the fact that neither of them kicked us out on the street for pursuing this crazy notion of writing a fantasy novel.

Derrick Cummings, whose feedback regarding character development and inter-character relationships was invaluable in the early drafting stages of this book.

Michael Hanna, who helped with the Latin phrasing and grammar within the text and on the maps. Apparently, we were not as versed in Latin semantics as we thought we were, and he was happy to set us straight. Any Latin guffaws result from our own stubbornness to stick with something, much to Michael's dismay.

Melissa Nash and BMR Williams, each of whom was able to bring their incredible cartography skills to bear; Melissa, on the city of Trumric, and BMR, on the larger world. It's quite humbling to see one's setting brought to life through such detailed maps. They are truly talented professionals.

About the Authors

Dennis is a 6th grade English teacher. He has dabbled in writing his whole life, but *Fortune's Shadow, Mercy's Light* is his first novel. Dennis has previously written a children's book series titled "Azarah and Baldur." He lives in Texas where he is happily married and has three grown children.

Riley has created scores of characters and hundreds of scenarios as a roleplaying game enthusiast. *Fortune's Shadow, Mercy's Light* is his first foray into novel writing. Riley is happily married and lives in Texas with their cats, Cleopawtra and Clawdius.

Dennis and Riley have been friends since 1979. Their shared interests over the decades include comic books, cats, video games, roleplaying games, world history, and the literary works of Howard and Lovecraft. They watched *Return of the Jedi* together at the theater in 1983. They stood in line together at the mall for the release of the original Playstation in 1994. Notably, Riley has been the game master in an ongoing tabletop roleplaying campaign in which Dennis and their other friends have played since the early 1980's. The setting of that TTRPG was the inspiration for the backdrop of this book series.

FORTUNE'S
BLADE
MERCY'S
CLOAK

Herald of the Conflagration

A wall of cool, fragrant air greeted Ulric as he stepped inside the Quadrivium. Despite the thick crowd and summer heat, the taberna was kept comfortable thanks to the expensive enchantments of a freelance ice magus. He took a deep breath, enjoying the enticing smells of cooking herbs, scented oils, and good wine.

Rows of Eltaran lamps hung from the high ceiling and mounds of candles glowed at the center of every table, filling the interior with a warm, golden light. People drank resolutely, laughed loudly, threw dice carelessly, and argued… cautiously. He didn't spot his Mark, the awkward youth who had sputtered the name Flaccus, but he noted the grim stare he received from the taberna's owner.

Gwynned had told him the history of the taberna. Decades previously, the crime lords of the city had seen the advantage of providing a place where the wealthy and powerful could solicit their services without fear, and they had decided the Quadrivium was as good a place as any. At first, this meant secretive visits by republic agents, collegium clerks, and the trusted slaves of wealthy patricians. When the Imperaré began using the taberna as a meeting place to settle disputes among the criminal gangs and collegia, the building became something of a local landmark. As the Quadrivium's reputation grew, the boldest among the wealthy disguised themselves for a personal visit. After a time, the thrill of safely consorting with plebeians, thieves, and murderers had become fashionable.

The forbidding look from the proprietor was a reminder that while Ulric was in the Quadrivium, there would be no tax collecting, no back-alley parley, no honest schemes, and Myrill have mercy on anyone caught performing knife or shroud work.

If I had wanted so many damned rules, I'd have conned my way into a temple! But in this scheme, honesty is key. So, I'm not really breaking any rules, am I?

Ulric left the chaos of the main floor and climbed the stairs to the second tier. The area was a broad gallery projecting from the rear and side walls of the taberna, overlooking the ground floor. A small bar at the back kept simple foods and the most common wines close at hand. Whether hunched over close-packed tables or sequestered in shadowy alcoves, furtive men and women conducted their business in hasty whispers. The whole of the upper floor was filled with a low, steady drone: the sound of serious deal making.

Ulric joined a small crowd moving toward the bar. He immediately spotted the back of Flaccus' head; he couldn't miss the disheveled hair and those ridiculous ears. Flaccus sat at a table across from a much older woman draped in the unmistakable gold and blue robes of the Collegium Draconis Aurei.

All right, no need to piss myself. No surprise, this scheme leads straight into the jaws of a dragon magus. I have a role to play, and if I stick to the script, I'll recruit a merry band of players. Unless? What if she knows the spells that can unmask any lie? It'd be over quick… and end badly. Maybe bloody? But only a few know the trick, or so I've been told. And they guard the secret jealously 'cause of all the coin it brings. So, it's another throw of the dice, and for once, the odds are in my favor. Besides, I didn't lift the Eltaran map to have Neesis watch me slink away at the first sign of trouble.

As Ulric wove his way through the gallery, he couldn't help but take a closer look at the magus as he passed. She must have been beautiful once, but time had turned her once pale skin pallid, streaked her dark hair with gray, and sullied once bright eyes with lines of ambition. All to be expected after a long life at the collegium. What really did her beauty a disservice, he thought, were the dueling expressions of exasperation and rage battling across her face.

Ha! I see the missing map has come up. This should be a good bit of fun.

Ulric walked past their table without fear, confident Flaccus had never seen him. He loitered in the shadows near the bar and listened.

"Proceed without the scroll? How do you propose we do that, hmm?" The magus' voice was surprisingly loud. Unlike the others in the gallery, she seemed to think nothing of secrecy.

Flaccus sank into his chair. "I... I... I don't know." The magus' only response was a burning stare. "You've seen the map. Maybe you remember enough. Maybe... we can find it without the map?"

The woman erupted in a short, angry laugh. "You half-wit! You jar-eared clunk! Even if we found it, how could we attain it without the cipher?"

So that's what all the strange writing and weird diagrams are? Some sort of cipher? I'd never have sorted that out!

"Did you pay any attention during the planning of our little expedition, hmm?"

"I… of course I did."

"Do not interrupt me; that was a purely rhetorical question, you slack-headed moron!" Exasperation struck again. "Why the administration has punished me with such a discipulus I know not. Perhaps a rival has placed you for the sole purpose of ruining my career. Is that it, hmm?" She sighed loudly, then continued. "I'd return you to the rank of precator and be rid of you, but the collegium doesn't want your family to suffer anymore embarrassment."

Flaccus had sunk into his chair and nearly disappeared under the table, but he sat upright at the mention of his family. "My father has nothing to do with this." He balled his fists and slammed them down onto the table. "Besides, I wouldn't have been carrying the map if you hadn't forgotten it!"

That's the spirit Rat-Face! Give it back to the old bitch. I talked back plenty to Ghostwalker. Still have the scars to prove it!

"And I wouldn't have been attacked and robbed if you'd keep your dealings in the respectable parts of the city! Instead, we sit here surrounded by thieves, drunks, and whores. What business could an honorable Trumin woman have at the Quadrivium… hmm?" He emphasized the last part as he thrust his sharp chin forward.

Ha, ha, ha! Blood drawn! Nicely struck, Rat-Face.

Rage vanquished all competing emotions and consumed the magus like wildfire. Whatever courage Flaccus had possessed turned to ash in mere proximity to her fury.

Sweet Neesis!

She struggled to spit out every word. "You would impugn the honor of a dragon magus? Mock your betters? Imply I'm a whore?"

Flaccus recoiled into his chair. "I didn't call…"

"I didn't say you did! I said you implied it, you ill-born imbecile!" Her shouting attracted the attention of the closest tables. "I've been too soft on you. That's now clear."

"Forgive me, Magus, please! I was wrong to speak so disrespectfully."

"Yes, I've been soft for far too long. What you need is a return to discipline. Maybe then you'll develop the character needed to advance." The magus thrust her right hand forward. She contorted her fingers strangely, something between a claw and an accusation. A single word was whispered.

Ulric heard it; just barely. He could never recall the precise sound of the word, but it hurt to hear it. Although he wasn't the spell's target, a searing wave of heat passed through his body.

For Flaccus, the pain must have been incessant and debilitating.

His body jolted upright and his legs kicked out spasmodically, pushing his chair away from the table with a loud screech. His skin reddened and sweat ran down his face. A shuddering moan escaped his lips as he forced his trembling hands to grasp the edge of the table. There was a short, high-pitched scream, then he fell over the table and sobbed.

The macabre display caught the attention of the entire gallery. "Not… here! Please! I'm sorry!" Flaccus was clearly struggling to speak past the pain. "Not… in front… of… everyone."

"Oh, but why ever not?" The magus asked in a mockingly sweet voice. "You'd insult me in front of them, would you not? And, as you said, they're only 'thieves, drunks and whores', so why care what they think?"

This elicited a round of jeers and laughter from the rough crowd. Ulric didn't think it was possible for Flaccus to look any more miserable, but he did.

It's not my fault. Not my fault he doesn't know when to shut up! No, not my fault. But Myrill's Mercy, I've seen enough of collegium discipline. Damn them both!

Ulric emerged from the shadows and headed straight for their table. Without a word, he sat down in an empty chair and slammed the missing scroll case onto the table with a loud thwack. He looked Flaccus in the eyes and said, "This belongs to you."

The magus snatched up the case, releasing Flaccus from his torment. His body relaxed, and he slumped exhausted into his chair. He stared down at the table and wiped the tears from his face with trembling hands. He asked, in a weak, cracking voice, "Who are you? And how did you find the map?"

The magus, who had been doing her best to authenticate the contents of the case without sharing them with the gallery, peaked over the weathered parchment. "Two surprisingly intelligent and essential questions. Let's hear his lies first. Then we'll reason the truth."

"Who am I? I'm Ulric Darktalon: professional thief, part-time actor, and full-time liar. Except for tonight. Tonight, I am that rare species of Trumin—an honest man." There were looks of confusion from one side of the table and skepticism from the other. "Who do I have the pleasure of speaking with?"

"I'm Gnaeus Pinarius Flaccus, a discipulus of the Collegium Draconis Aurei."

Ulric nodded and turned to the magus, who had secured the map and hidden the case somewhere within her expensive robes. She said nothing for an uncomfortably long time. Ulric thought she stared at him like an augur might examine a particularly portentous set of entrails. He wondered what she saw. A young man not much older than Flaccus with an athletic body, pale skin, and night-black hair. Did she think he was handsome? Could he charm or flatter her? What did she make of his expensive tunic, fine leather belt, and well-made shoes? And what of the silver and bronze rings and arm bracelets he adorned himself with? What did she think of the silver chain supporting two small wooden cubes inlaid with silver? What did a priestess of Eltarus, God of Magic and Mischief, think of a follower of Neesis Fortuna, Goddess of Luck?

"I am Magus Vipsania Tertia of the Collegium Draconis Aurei, priestess of Eltarus—May His Lamp Shine Eternal—and Herald of the Conflagration. Now, for the second question."

The Conflagration? Ulric felt the searing agony of Aquila's hot irons; recalled the smell of his own burning flesh. He saw Gwynedd's scars; again, heard his warning.

"Fear the fire magi most, for they become like Ukorus, the God of Earth and Fire: obsessive, secretive, and ill-tempered." I hear you, Gwynedd. But Neesis is my goddess, and She demands madness and bold action.

"How did I find the map? That's not the right question at all—because I stole it!"

DENNIS RILEY

FORTUNE'S
SHADOW
MERCY'S
LIGHT

FROM THE SECRET SCROLLS
OF THE IMPERARE